P9-EDR-703

THE JUPITER CRISIS

Also by William Harrington

Which the Justice, Which the Thief
The Power
Yoshar the Soldier (*One Over One*)
The Search for Elisabeth Brandt
Trial

THE JUPITER CRISIS

by

William Harrington

DAVID McKAY COMPANY, INC.

New York

THE JUPITER CRISIS

LIBRARY OF CONGRESS CATALOG CARD NUMBER: 79-165086

MANUFACTURED IN THE UNITED STATES OF AMERICA

AUTHOR'S NOTE

The Jupiter Crisis is a work of fiction. I made up all these people and events, out of my imagination, and therefore any resemblance between them and any real, specific persons or events is coincidental. Also, there are only so many proper names in this world, and if any character in this book bears the name of any real person, that was not intended, and I sincerely hope it does not cause any embarrassment for anyone.

THE JUPITER CRISIS

HONOLULU

The message came shortly after President Bradley had sat down at the table at the New Year's Eve dinner. An Air Force major approached very discreetly and put the special envelope down on the white linen cloth, beside the President's hand. The President, without withdrawing his attention even for an instant from the man who was talking to him, recognized the special envelope and covered it with his hand to conceal the printing on it. It said URGENT TOP SECRET FOR PRESIDENT ONLY.

For a minute he sat with the envelope under his hand, his fingers rubbing it tensely, his eyes flitting down to it every few seconds, while courtesy required him to smile and nod and seem to listen to the soft-spoken, politely giggling small man at his left—Japanese Premier Susumu Hatoyama. Then when the Premier paused to reach for his cigarette, the man at the other side of President Bradley touched his arm, required his attention, and began to talk. That was President Jesus Fernandos of the Philippines. He had been conspicuously anxious to have President Bradley's attention, and now he leaned toward him and spoke earnestly. Premier Hatoyama frowned and cocked his head and listened.

The Air Force major stood quietly to one side, from where the President could summon him with a nod, and waited. He had delivered the message so discreetly that he had not caught the attention of more than two or three people in the room, and he had not interrupted the gaiety of the dinner. The Secretary of State, sitting at a nearby table with the Foreign Minister of Malaysia, had not noticed him. He and the Foreign Minister were watching the raised stage in the center of the room where six grass-skirted girls swayed in a modest, sinuous Hula. The musicians in white duck pants and bright shirts, strolling around the room, came between the President and the major, so for a moment they could not see each other, and for the first time the major moved a little forcefully, into another position where the President could summon him instantly. The Chairman of the Senate Foreign Relations Committee, Senator Vester, stirred the fruit punch in his hollowed-out pineapple, glanced across the major, and did not recognize him. But at a table a little farther back, Lattimer Young, Special Assistant to the President, sat rigid and quiet, with narrowed eyes, watching the President's fingers move on the envelope while he waited for a chance to open it.

A reporter for the Honolulu *Advertiser,* sitting above the dinner on a balcony, where some press tables had been provided, had also noticed the major. He saw him deliver the envelope, and he too watched to see the President open it. His speculations about what it might be, had interrupted his work. He had been sketching out an article for the morning paper. It was the first time President Bradley had visited Hawaii, and it was the first time this reporter had seen him in person. He had written—:

"It has been said of President Warren Bradley that he has no charisma, which is no doubt true. It has also been said, and let us hope it is true, that his election and re-election without charisma has probably banished that overworked word from the American political vocabulary. If he doesn't have charisma, he has something more important. He has presence.

"Like everyone else, he does not look the way he looks on television. He is thicker, stockier, more broad-shouldered, and more muscular-looking than he appears on the tube. His solid, topheavy bald head, cold and humorless eyes, big strong jaw, and direct, intense manner combine to give him an air of grim, stubborn power. He inspires confidence in many Americans. You might not be taken by him at first sight, but he does look—as someone has said—like a good man to have on your side in a fight."

The *Advertiser* man watched President Fernandos, still leaning toward President Bradley and engaging the attention of Premier Hatoyama as well with something he was saying with great seriousness. The reporter wondered only for another short moment what the conversation was. Then he looked again to his notes. He'd had a long day, and it wasn't over. The two presidents and the Premier had arrived in Honolulu only this morning. They had made a motorcade through the city. Each of them had addressed the closing session of the Western Pacific Trade Conference. After this dinner they would attend a party the Japanese were giving. That would be private, with no media representatives allowed in. But Air Force One was scheduled to fly at midnight, or a little after. President Bradley was flying back to California to be in Pasadena for the Rose Bowl Game tomorrow afternoon, and the reporter would have to go out to the airfield and see him leave.

President Bradley was anxious to open his envelope, and President Fernandos knew it. President Fernandos would be asked much later just what he had talked about so seriously that evening while the President of the United States held in his hand unopened the message announcing the Jupiter crisis. President Fernandos would remember vividly, and would tell.

In the first place, he had judged this would be his only

chance really to talk to President Bradley. They were all travelling on tight schedules. He had been told that President Bradley customarily drank two double martinis before dinner—which he had definitely done this evening, as had become obvious to President Fernandos as soon as he sat down beside him. He had been told that President Bradley would likely have another drink or two after dinner, and then he would be tightly surrounded by his aides, who would see to it that the conversation was kept light.

In the second place, President Fernandos wanted to say what he had to say while Premier Hatoyama was there to hear it.

In the third place, he thought what he had to say was important.

President Fernandos wanted a clarification of something President Bradley had said in his short speech to the closing session of the conference that afternoon. What he had said had seemed inconsistent with the secret agreement which had been reached between the Secretary of State and the foreign ministers.

The public sessions of the Western Pacific Trade Conference had been paralleled by secret sessions in which negotiations were conducted on the real primary purpose of the conference. Japan and the other nations had asked of the United States a relaxation of United States opposition to their trade with Communist China. They had asked the United States to permit them to act as intermediaries between the United States and China, looking to full diplomatic relations within a few months. They had asked the United States to cooperate in attaining what they called the normalization of diplomatic and commercial relations between China and the rest of the world. The Secretary of State, on behalf of the United States, had agreed to each of these points. Now, an ambiguous comment dropped into his speech by President Bradley—fortuitously, President Fernandos hoped—seemed to contradict what the Secretary of State had agreed to.

President Bradley obviously wanted to open his envelope. But President Fernandos felt he had to have clarification.

President Bradley shrugged. "My Secretary of State speaks for me," he said. "He was in daily contact with me all during the conference. Whatever he agreed to, I agree to. I did not intend to suggest anything to the contrary this afternoon."

Prsident Fernandos smiled broadly, relieved and happy. Premier Hatoyama giggled and nodded with satisfaction. President Bradley at last opened his envelope.

He scowled over the message:

TOP SECRET
PRIORITY URGENT
ATTENTION PRESIDENT ONLY

MESSAGE
CONCLUSION NOW INESCAPABLE THAT SOVIET UNION HAS INTERFERED WITH ORBIT OF JUPITER TWELVE. BESIDES LOSS OF ALL TELEMETRY, WE ARE ALSO UNABLE TO MAKE RADAR CONTACT. SOVIET VEHICLES ARE NO LONGER IN JUPITER ORBIT. EVIDENCE SUGGESTS SOVIET VEHICLES ATTACKED AND DESTROYED JUPITER AND HAVE NOW LANDED IN SIBERIA RECOVERY RANGE.
END MESSAGE

President Bradley folded the paper slowly and reinserted it in the envelope. Still scowling deeply, with hardened eyes that seemed not to see but to peer back into his thoughts, he turned first toward Premier Hatoyama and then toward President Fernandos. He already had their full attention. They had watched curiously while he read his message.

"I am sorry, gentlemen," he said to them. "I am very sorry. But I have to fly back to Washington—immediately."

ANDREWS AIR FORCE BASE

For the great majority of Americans, the Jupiter crisis began on New Year's Day, in the morning, when they switched on their television sets to see the Rose Bowl Parade, and instead of a happy parade in the warm California sunlight, they saw the sudden, ominous return of Air Force One to the snow-swept runways of Andrews Air Force Base.

The air of crisis was heightened sharply by the fact that no announcement had been made as to why the President had left Honolulu so abruptly, cancelled his Pasadena holiday, and flown directly back to Washington. The very fact that he did was ominous enough, and the television reporters could add that all morning the Cabinet and National Security Council had been arriving at the White House. No one could get near enough to any of them to ask for a statement, and the White House press office was saying nothing. So the television cameras were focused on the dark skies over Andrews, watching for Air Force One, and that was what Americans saw when they turned on their sets.

Air Force One appeared suddenly out of the heavy gray overcast. One second there was nothing in the cold, dull sky. The next second the brilliant, blue-white lights under its wings gleamed in the gray, and the huge aircraft, imposing and majestic, drifted smoothly and silently downward, toward the runway. For a long time it seemed to hang in the air, unmoving except for its measured, ponderous descent. Only at the last moment, just before it touched down, was it clear that it was gliding forward, and only then could it be heard, as a rush of wind. Its wheels touched the concrete with an abrupt, protesting shriek, making a wisp of smoke which the wind took immediately. A second later the great machine roared, as its jets were reversed to slow it on the runway.

The President's helicopter was waiting on the ramp. Its

red lights blinked bright, and one of its rotors turned slowly, driven perhaps by the gusty wind that drove a light, hard snow across the field. The ramp was guarded by two open jeeps of Air Force men, sitting hunched and bundled, clutching their stubby automatic rifles in gloved hands. As Air Force One made its turn and started back toward them, they climbed out of the jeeps and stood at attention near the helicopter.

No greeting party waited for the President. The television cameras were behind the fence, and so were all the reporters. When Air Force One stopped, the stairs were quickly rolled up, and half a dozen Secret Service men rushed out the forward door and down. They stationed themselves along the short distance between the airplane and the helicopter. One of them nervously slid his foot back and forth on the concrete, to see if the slight accumulation of snow was slippery.

The President came out, followed by the Secretary of State and by Lattimer Young. Only the President had a coat. The other two were still wearing the tuxedos they had worn at the dinner. The President crossed the ramp to the helicopter without a glance toward the television cameras. The Secret Service men followed him to the helicopter, and two of them got in with him. In a moment the helicopter was moving. In another moment it lifted off.

Lattimer Young would remember the helicopter flight because it was then that he had his first chance to read the messages the President had received on Air Force One during the return from Honolulu. All night he had worked hard, making minutes of the President's telephone calls, taking calls while the President rested, reviewing emergency and alerting procedures, seeing that the President had coffee and food and a change of clothes. Young had a strong sense of history, and he had made some notes for himself of what he saw and heard all night. He'd seen the messages come in, had seen them pulled off the machine and handed to the President, and he knew what they said but had not had a chance to read them one by one. Now they were in his briefcase, and in the helicopter he took them out and read them. They made an ominous series.

TOP SECRET
PRIORITY URGENT
ATTENTION PRESIDENT ONLY

MESSAGE
JODRELL BANK CONFIRMS IT LOST JUPITER AT SAME TIME WE DID. IT ALSO CONFIRMS SOVIET VEHICLES WHICH SHADOWED JUPITER MADE SOFT LANDING ON SOVIET RECOVERY RANGE SHORTLY AFTER LOSS OF JUPITER.
END MESSAGE

TOP SECRET
PRIORITY URGENT
ATTENTION PRESIDENT ONLY

MESSAGE
CONFIRM STAGE ONE ALERT ORDERED.
END MESSAGE

TOP SECRET
PRIORITY URGENT
ATTENTION PRESIDENT ONLY

MESSAGE
INABILITY TO TRACK ANY JUPITER DEBRIS SUGGESTS POSSIBILITY SOVIETS MAY HAVE CAPTURED IT, NOT DESTROYED IT. THAT JUPITER WAS SHADOWED BY LARGE SOVIET VEHICLES FOR SEVERAL HOURS IMMEDIATELY PRIOR TO ITS DISAPPEARANCE, PLUS FACT SOVIET VEHICLES THEN SHORTLY LANDED, ALSO SUGGEST THIS POSSIBILITY, WHICH NASA REGARDS AS TECHNICALLY FEASIBLE.

ARE NOW INQUIRING OF NASA AND OTHERS IF SOVIETS MIGHT POSSESS ABILITY TO DECIPHER TELEMETRY JUPITER WAS STILL CARRYING AND HAD NOT YET TRANSMITTED AT TIME OF LOSS.
END MESSAGE

TOP SECRET
PRIORITY URGENT
ATTENTION PRESIDENT ONLY

MESSAGE
NATIONAL SECURITY COUNCIL RECOMMENDS UPGRADING OF ALERT TO STAGE TWO.
END MESSAGE

TOP SECRET
PRIORITY URGENT
ATTENTION PRESIDENT ONLY

MESSAGE
CONFIRM STAGE TWO ALERT ORDERED.
END MESSAGE

TOP SECRET
PRIORITY URGENT
ATTENTION PRESIDENT ONLY

MESSAGE
IT IS JUDGMENT OF NASA THAT SOVIETS LIKELY POSSESS ABILITY TO DECIPHER TELEMETRY JUPITER WAS CARRYING AT TIME OF ITS POSSIBLE CAPTURE. IT MUST BE REGARDED AS POSSIBLE THEREFORE THAT SOVIETS MAY BE ABLE TO CONSTRUCT THE PHOTOGRAPHS TAKEN BY JUPITER DURING ITS ORBIT IMMEDIATELY PRIOR TO LOSS. ITS RECONNAISSANCE MISSION DURING LAST ORBIT WAS TO PHOTOGRAPH CERTAIN

GROUND-TO-AIR MISSILE SITES IN SOVIET UNION, ALSO LENA RIVER POWER STATION, ALSO SUSPECTED CHINESE SILO CONSTRUCTION IN MANCHURIA.

END MESSAGE

CLASSIFIED DIPLOMATIC
PRIORITY ONE
ATTENTION PRES, SECY STATE

MESSAGE

HOT LINE FROM MOSCOW AS FOLLOWS. 001 MOSCOW CONFIRMS THAT IT HAS CAPTURED JUPITER TWELVE. 002 MOSCOW STATES THAT SAME COMPLETES ALL ACTION NOW CONTEMPLATED, IS NOT PRELIMINARY TO FURTHER ACTION. 003 MOSCOW NOTES OUR STATE OF ALERT, AFFIRMS IT HAS NOT ALERTED ITS OWN FORCES. 004 MOSCOW STATES IT IS INSTRUCTING ITS AMBASSADOR TO CALL EARLIEST AND COMMUNICATE FULLY.

END MESSAGE

TOP SECRET
PRIORITY URGENT
ATTENTION PRESIDENT ONLY

MESSAGE

NOW RECOMMEND UPGRADING ALERT TO STAGE THREE.

END MESSAGE

NEW YORK

The Soviet Union called a special emergency session of the United Nations Security Council, and Soviet Foreign Minister Yevgeny Bychevsky flew to New York to address that session, on the evening of January 2. The meeting was televised, giving Americans another vivid look at the developing crisis.

By that evening, the President knew that most of what he had feared that night when he was flying back from Honolulu, had happened. The Russians had in fact captured Jupiter Twelve, the United States' most sophisticated reconnaissance satellite.

The highly refined television cameras in Jupiter Twelve were capable of taking pictures of such excellent quality that—with augmentation by special computer programs on the ground—the face of a man could be recognized in a picture taken from two hundred miles in space. (This, of course, required ideal conditions, with everything working optimally.) The Jupiter was maneuverable. It could fly over any point on earth. Its television cameras took pictures and recorded them electronically on magnetic discs. Later, when it passed over a United States receiving station, it would transmit the pictures and erase the discs to make them ready for the pictures it took on its next orbit. The Russians captured Jupiter while it was still carrying pictures on the discs. They simply overtook it in space, sent cosmonauts on board it to disable its navigational rockets and cut off its power, and then encapsulated it in the heat shield on the nose of the largest Russian vehicle.

Even knowing the Jupiter was captured with pictures still being carried inside it, the President had entertained some hope that the Russians would not possess the sophisticated computer programs it would require to decipher the electronic impulses on the discs and make pictures of them. That hope was lost when Foreign Minister Bychevsky announced he was going to display the photographs from the Jupiter to the United Nations Security Council. A final hope was that the Russians did not have the computer techniques necessary to clarify and augment the pictures, the way our technicians did in a major computer complex located underground in Hughes County, Oklahoma. But *Pravda* published two pictures from the Jupiter in its edition of January 2. In one of them you could see a man standing on the ground. The picture was so clear you could tell he was wearing a military fur cap and a military greatcoat with shoulder boards. It was from *Pravda,* ironically, that Americans learned just how good their Jupiter had been.

Foreign Minister Yevgeny Bychevsky was a little prune of a man, all pinched and wrinkled and pursed and solemn. He was one of the new generation of Soviet *apparatchiki*—full of expertise and caution. He spoke English, and that night he spoke it to the Security Council, so Americans watching television heard his icy words in his own accents.

He spoke formally, to the president of the Security Council, with cold white lips barely moving to form his words, and he said: "I point out, Mr. President, that the Soviet Union, in a long series of diplomatic notes, has repeatedly protested United States violations of its sovereignty and territorial integrity, through the illegal incursions of the Jupiter spy satellite. The Jupiter is an elaborate and costly system of space espionage, in violation of basic principles of international law and in violation of treaty commitments solemnly entered into by the United States. It was because the United States coldly ignored the just and reasonable protests of the Soviet Union, and indeed of other peace-loving nations, that the Soviet Union was compelled finally to act in its own defense."

Bychevsky was a thin, gray little man, dressed that night in a pin-striped gray double-breasted suit. So far as Americans were concerned, his English was doubly accented. It was Oxford English to begin with, and besides that he spoke it with a heavy Russian accent. He read most of his statement, and his eyes rarely rose from the papers on the desk before him. He spoke with cold, unemotional, accusing precision. When his aides began to display on an easel the enlargements of the photographs taken from the Jupiter, he referred to them without looking up at them—being entirely confident that his aides would display the right pictures and change them on cue.

The orbit in which the maneuverable Jupiter had been travelling just prior to its capture had carried it in a long arc across European Russia, south and east over Irkutsk and Lake Baikal, then on across Manchuria and the Sea of Japan and the northern reaches of Honshu, and finally out over the Pacific Ocean, where it was overtaken and captured by the Soviet space vehicles. All along this orbit it had been taking pictures. One by one Bychevsky's aides displayed them to the Security Council, as he described them. The first group of pictures displayed were of a Soviet ground-to-air missile station somewhere in European Russia. The second group were of a Russian hydroelectric power station and its associated industrial complex, on the Lena River. The third group of pictures—and the ones which ultimately were to have the greatest impact—had been taken over Manchuria and showed the site where the Red Chinese were apparently building deep launch silos for long-range rockets.

The American ambassador at the United Nations was Alexander Eagleton, a plump, red-faced Texas newspaper publisher, a Republican who had long been a faithful supporter of President Warren Bradley. For some reason, the Administration had not warned him fully of what the Russian was going to show the Council, and he did not conceal his surprise and distress from the television cameras.

When all the photographs had been displayed, Bychevsky looked up at last and told his aides to revert to the group showing the ground-to-air missile site, which he claimed was in European Russia and hundreds of kilometers from any of the international frontiers of the Soviet Union. He characterized the installation as purely defensive—necessarily so, because its rockets did not have sufficient range to reach as far as the Soviet frontiers, much less beyond them. The ground-to-air missiles were emplaced, he said, only to protect Soviet industry from possible attack by hostile aircraft intruding hundreds of kilometers within the boundaries of the Soviet Union.

"And I am prepared to yield the floor," Bychevsky said with chilling scorn, "if at this time Mr. Eagleton cares to offer any explanation as to why the United States finds it necessary to fly its elaborate and costly spy equipment over the national territory of the Soviet Union and take these devilishly clever pictures of wholly defensive weapons. I yield the floor, Mr. President, if Mr. Eagleton is ready to explain."

He stopped. He glanced coldly at Ambassador Eagleton. And he clasped his hands across his script and waited, looking down at his desk.

Eagleton was not ready. He looked at Bychevsky for a moment, then at the president of the Council. His face was red, and his brows turned downward in a perplexed frown. "Let Mr. Bychevsky continue his statement, Mr. President," he said. "I'll make mine in good time."

Bychevsky smiled. He did not look up, and his smile was almost imperceptible, but he did smile, slyly, genuinely amused for an instant. "I had thought now would be a good time," he said dryly.

WASHINGTON

When the vote was taken, early the next afternoon, the Security Council rejected, 9 to 6, the Soviet resolution condemning the United States for using the Jupiter as a means of engaging in unlawful espionage against other nations. Immediately the ranking Republican on the Senate Foreign Relations Committee, Senator Frederick Crankshaw, told some reporters he encountered in the White House when he was on his way to a meeting with the President that the UN vote was a victory for the United States and probably the end of the Jupiter crisis. His statement was widely reported in the late afternoon editions of some newspapers and on the evening television news broadcasts. President Bradley saw it, and that evening later, in the Oval Office, he shocked Lattimer Young by furiously denouncing Senator Crankshaw as stupid, to his face and in the presence of some of the members of the Ad Hoc Committee which had been formed to deal with the crisis.

The President, behind his desk, was smoking a cigarette. His elbow was on a stack of files heaped on his desktop, and his great bald head was leaned into his hand. "It's not over at all," he said, with anger and tension. "They've challenged our right to fly our satellites in space as we see fit; and it doesn't make any difference what the goddam United Nations does, that's a challenge and a threat that we can't leave unanswered. We've got to *do* something. There's the crisis—: When we respond to their challenge, then how do they respond to our response? That's when the going gets tough. Then's when it gets dangerous. The confrontation hasn't happened yet. But it has to come."

Lattimer Young had heard the President say very much the same words more than once before—and as early in the crisis as the night when they were flying back on Air Force One. He was not surprised by what the President said, but he was a little surprised and more than a little troubled by the President's vehemence. With his sense of history always alert, Lattimer Young had been watching President Bradley manage the first real crisis of his presidency. In general he had admired him. The President had assembled a special group, which they were now calling the Ad Hoc Committee, consisting of men best able to contend with the mixture of political and scientific issues raised by the crisis, and discussions in the Committee had been generally reasoned and calm. That evening it seemed that the President himself might be the first to be overwhelmed by the tension.

Senator Crankshaw had slowly risen from his chair. He was a tall, white-haired old man. He had served in the Senate with Warren Bradley for many years. "You may be President of the United States, Brad," he said softly, "but if you think you can sit behind that desk and call me stupid, then maybe I'll join the ranks of those many thoughtful Americans who hold it was a great mistake to put you there." He started toward the door.

"I'm sorry, Fred," the President said quickly, with as much and as quick sincerity as there had been anger a moment before. "Sit down, Fred, please. I'm sorry."

The Senator hesitated for a moment, then sat down.

The President ground out his cigarette and began to rub his forehead and his eyes with the heel of his hand. "In half an hour the Committee is meeting again," he said. "I'll tell you something in confidence, Fred. This is absolutely not for publication."

(Lattimer Young smiled inwardly. The President was functioning again. He was using an old political trick of his—gaining or regaining a man's confidence and friendship by trusting him with what you made him think was a secret.)

He went on to tell Senator Crankshaw that the Ad Hoc Committee was sharply divided in its counsel (which was true) into a faction which wanted to take stern measures against the Russians and a faction which counselled waiting and caution. Blair Bruce, Deputy Under Secretary of State led the faction which professed to see something very peculiar and illogical in the Soviet capture of the Jupiter and advised the President to let some time pass, during which careful diplomatic probing might discover hidden motives for what the Russians had done—such as an effort to distract the attention of the world from something more important but less dramatic that they were doing somewhere. He was supported in this position by General David Kerr, Chairman of the Joint Chiefs of Staff, who said the military really had no appropriate way to react to the capture of a satellite in space, and by the Director of NASA, Dr. Donald Jones, who was a quiet advocate because he was unaccustomed to sitting in such high councils but who was an effective spokesman nevertheless. Gerald Durand, Special Assistant to the President on National Security Affairs, a young Republican from Michigan who was very close to the President, argued for quick retaliation. He suggested the United States destroy the orbiting space station the Soviet Union was in the process of building. Durand alone, with his special position and his fierce, combative style of argument, was enough to hold up his end of the dispute; but he had support from the Secretary of State and the Secretary of Defense, both of whom argued that the very least the United States could do was launch another Jupiter and dare the Russians to touch it.

The President frowned at Lattimer Young. He wanted something, but Young could not guess what.

"You'll really have to forgive me, Fred, if I get upset with some of the statements being made by members of Congress," the President said wearily and quietly. "Look. Eight senators, the last time I counted, have made public statements calling the capture of the Jupiter an act of war."

"Many newspapers are saying the same," said the Senator.

"Do they know what they're saying?" the President asked. "Do they really know what they're saying?"

The Senator shrugged.

General Kerr, who had been sitting quietly on one of the couches near the fireplace, having a sandwich and listening and keeping out of the conversation, intruded into the moment of introspective silence and said, "Well, we have to do something, don't we, Mr. President? If we just take it and don't do anything, it's a defeat. I don't know what we can do, but we have to do something."

The President glanced at the general with an expression of surprise and scorn, as if he could not believe anyone could be prosaic enough to inject such a truism into a conversation. He softened in a moment, though, and began to nod. "Yes," he said. "The pressure to do something is irresistible."

The President was an hour late for the meeting of the Ad Hoc Committee. Just when he was about to leave his office for the meeting, he received word from the State Department that Soviet Ambassador Konstantin Dobrodomov had requested an appointment to deliver a note from his government. Lattimer Young and the Secretary of State were with him when he received Ambassador Dobrodomov, and when they finally left the Oval Office to meet with the Ad Hoc Committee, the President was angry again and yet laughing. Dobrodomov had solemnly delivered his government's offer to return the captured Jupiter, saying it was after all the property of the United States.

The meeting of the Ad Hoc Committee lasted until midnight that night of January 3. At the end the President announced to the Committee his decision as to the United States response to what the Russians had done, and he gave the orders to set the response in motion. The United States would launch another, identical, reconnaissance satellite—Jupiter Fourteen. He deferred a public announcement of this decision until the evening of January 6, to give NASA more time to prepare the launch.

TOKYO

Premier Susumu Hatoyama kept a diary. Every night, without failing once during all the months he served as Japanese Premier, he sat propped up in his bed and, with a ball-point pen, he recorded on notebook paper—in Japanese characters, of course—a detailed account, not only of what had happened that day but of his intimate thoughts and incisive impressions. When he died, his notebooks were immediately published—to which he certainly never would have consented.

He had written, for example, of the night when President Bradley received the message announcing the Jupiter crisis, that the President had seemed to him to have taken too much to drink. He added that it had made the President more cordial and almost likeable. He also wrote that a certain United States Senator, whose name had not impressed itself on him, had been left behind when Air Force One made its abrupt early departure, had gotten utterly sodden at the party the Japanese had given later that evening, and had finished the night in bed with a Honolulu call girl—in the hotel room of an aide travelling with the Premier. The diary was frank and complete and meant to be private.

Premier Hatoyama's thoughts when he heard President Bradley announce the launch of Jupiter Fourteen were also recorded in the diary.

It was on the evening of January 6 in Washington, at seven p.m. That was nine a.m. January 7 in Tokyo. Premier Hatoyama had the text of the President's speech before him. It had been delivered by the United States Ambassador an hour before the President was scheduled to talk. But Premier Hatoyama and some of his staff listened to the speech on the Voice of America and followed the printed text. The Premier recorded the scene in his diary that night: the bright, sunlit morning, the troubled members of his staff sitting around him, each with his own copy of the text, following the words with fingers that moved across the page as the occasionally garbled voice of the President of the United States came in on the shortwave.

"Many Americans have urged me to take stern, decisive action, in the nature of retaliation for the gross misconduct of the Soviet government. It would be easy to do so. Any nation which keeps satellites in space is vulnerable. The

United States could readily capture or destroy any Russian space vehicle now in orbit. The United States could, for example, destroy the huge orbiting space station the Soviet Union is now building—which we see in our skies every clear night. Such a course of action has been specifically urged on me as President."

Premier Hatoyama knew that President Bradley was not regarded as an effective public speaker. He was called wooden and forced. He usually spoke on television with his chin jutted slightly forward and his eyes fixed unmoving on the camera, with an intense, sober sincerity that seemed too forced to be real. This speech sounded honest. The Premier wished he could see him—on the television, the way the Americans were doing—as well as hear him. He wondered if it would give him a different impression from what he received from hearing and reading the words.

He and his aides had scanned the text. They knew they were already disappointed in it, in a sense. It made no reference to the aspect of the Jupiter crisis which was most significant to Japan. The events since New Year's Eve in Honolulu had already precipitated a political crisis in Japan, which was threatening the government of Premier Hatoyama.

Soviet Foreign Minister Bychevsky had displayed before the United Nations Security Council a group of photographs identified as pictures of a vast construction site in Manchuria, where the Chinese were apparently building a complex of launch silos. The Japanese had urgently requested and had received from Moscow a set of copies of those pictures. The launch silos, being located where they were, could have only one target for the deadly, atom-armed missiles they would contain. That target was Japan. The Hatoyama government was confronted with evidence of this threat to the very life of the Japanese nation at the very time when the government was openly seeking, in fact sponsoring, the normalization of commercial and diplomatic relations between China and several other nations—and was secretly acting as mediator between China and the United States. Radio Peking had been screaming for days that the photographs were fakes, the result of a plot between the American imperialists and the Russian revisionists to prepare for armed aggression against China. But the publication of the photographs had caused violent street riots in Japanese cities and a shrill debate in the Diet. The Hatoyama government despaired of its survival.

President Bradley knew this, of course, but he didn't mention it in his speech. Probably it was not appropriate to the thrust of his message.

Premier Hatoyama had placed the text of the speech in a patch of sunlight which lay shining on the table where he sat and listened, and he thought of how dark it must be in Washington and New York on this winter evening.

"It would be easy to take destructive measures," the President went on to say, his voice sounding ever more unnaturally thin and high as the shortwave transmission deteriorated. "After much counsel and careful thought, however, we have determined it more likely to be effective if we confine our response to the Soviet aggression to a constructive measure. Accordingly, I have directed the National Aeronautics and Space Administration to launch another reconnaissance satellite, identical to the captured Jupiter Twelve. This launch will take place within a few days.

"The new satellite, Jupiter Fourteen, will circle the earth in such orbits and will make such photographs as the government of the United States, in its sole discretion, shall think proper."

The words came across strong, even on the shortwave, and Premier Hatoyama again wished he could see the President's face, to see if it hardened or softened the challenge.

"The United States asserts the right to conduct photographic and other surveillance from space of any point on the earth, just as the Soviet Union has long done—though never with equipment as ingenious and sophisticated as the satellites of the Jupiter series. It is no violation of international law or of the sovereign rights of any nation, and the United States regards such surveillance as vital to its national security.

"I have this evening, only a few minutes ago, advised the government of the Soviet Union, through Ambassador Dobrodomov, of our intention to launch Jupiter Fourteen. I have advised the Soviet government also that should the Soviet Union interfere in any way with the flight of Jupiter Fourteen, such interference will require a response by the United States involving the application of destructive force against such Soviet space vehicles as we shall, in such event, choose."

So there it was. The President had spoken the hard challenge that was printed on the paper the American Ambassador had delivered. He had chosen a direct confrontation with the Kremlin. When the Jupiter Fourteen was in fact launched, the peace of the world would be in immediate peril. Premier Hatoyama had hoped for some word of conciliation that might ease the tension, not tighten it. He was afraid his government could not survive any deepening of the crisis.

The Premier wrote finally that night, that unless something happened in the two or three days before the next Jupiter was launched, something conciliatory from one side or the other, to avoid the threatening confrontation, his tenure as Premier was at an end. He had not come to office on a program of seeking a *rapprochement* between Red China and the other nations of the Pacific. He was no admirer of Chinese Communism. But it was his honest analysis of the facts of international life that stability and prosperity for all the Western Pacific depended on bringing China fully into the community of nations. Now, with the Chinese apparently aiming a dozen atomic warheads dead at Japan and with a major clash developing between the United States and the Soviet Union, with all the fear and tension that would involve, he was caught in a political trap. He wrote that unless something happened to save him, his premiership and all his hopes for a new era of friendship in Asia and the Pacific would come to an end.

Premier Hatoyama was right. His government fell the day after Jupiter Fourteen was launched. His successor repudiated the secret agreements that had been reached at Honolulu.

WASHINGTON

In the Ad Hoc Committee there was a sense that the President had been leaning to some more forceful action than simply putting up another Jupiter—which Gerald Durand said would only become another target—and there was a sense that the restraining influence had been Under Secretary of State Blair Bruce. For a while then—for a few days, really—Bruce was deferred to by insiders as a sort of man of the hour. As a career diplomat, former ambassador to Moscow who spoke Russian and was personally acquainted with most of the Soviet leaders, his judgments did carry a special weight when the United States was designing a response to a Soviet challenge and then was waiting to see how the Soviets would respond to that response.

Bruce was too astute to take his momentary ascension seriously. He knew perfectly well how fleeting it would be. But he was glad his presence was demanded at the White House and in the Oval Office all during the Jupiter crisis. He had spent his whole life preparing to be effective in a situation like this, and he was happy to have a chance to be so. He was glad also to be where he could see everything developing.

The President, as soon as Jupiter Fourteen was launched, was faced with a national reaction he had hardly expected. Literally, the United States of America stopped and held its breath. Bruce was with the President in the Oval Office when the President called the commissioner of professional football and asked him not to allow the postponement of the championship game, scheduled for that Sunday. It was too late. The postponement had already been announced. The game was not played. Neither were the college basketball games scheduled for that weekend. In fact, some universities closed, and their students went home. Miami Beach hotels were deserted. People went home. Some cities reported heavy food-buying—hoarding. Businesses closed. The whole nation was rigid with dread and sat at home with all radio and television sets switched on, so as not to miss any bulletin.

The President was appalled by the nation's reaction. But there was nothing he could do about it. The Ad Hoc Committee discussed the possibility of his going on television with a message of encouragement or reassurance, but it was decided it wouldn't do any good. All anyone could do was watch the new Jupiter and wait to see what, if anything, the Russians would do about it.

Blair Bruce was with the President in the White House Situation Room at three in the morning on January 11—five days after the launch of Jupiter Fourteen—when NASA, and later Jodrell Bank, reported the Soviet launch of three huge vehicles, any of them capable of attacking Jupiter Fourteen. It was the only time Bruce ever saw the President come down from his private quarters dressed in anything but coat and tie. He came into the Situation Room in a pair of slacks, with a sweater hastily pulled over his head, and wearing a pair of bedroom slippers. They sat there four hours, staring at the board where the position of the Jupiter and the positions of each of the Soviet vehicles were shown by moving lights, while the reports from NASA and Jodrell Bank and Denver came in quick succession over the teletype and rattled out on yellow paper that poured off the machine and down to the floor.

Lattimer Young edged Blair Bruce aside that night and asked him quietly for an opinion. "What'll they do? You know them. What'll they do?" Young, who was not timid and no fool, was really afraid, and Bruce was surprised. He had not yet thought of the crisis in terms of personal fear. He looked around the room and frowned over what he saw in the rest of the men there. That night, briefly, he admired President Bradley. The President, sitting in his green sweater, smoking a cigarette and holding a paper cup of coffee in his other hand, was the calmest man there.

"What do you think?" Young asked again.

Bruce was a slight, bald-headed pipe smoker. He put down his pipe. "I'll stick my neck out," he said. "They won't do anything. They have nothing to gain by taking a shot at Jupiter Fourteen."

"Except the same thing they had to gain by capturing Jupiter Twelve," said Young. "What did they have to gain by that?"

"That," said Blair Bruce, "remains to be seen."

He was proved right about the first part of what he had said. The Soviets did nothing about Jupiter Fourteen. The three large vehicles which caused the United States to go on alert that night, all flew directly to the space station the Soviet Union was building, and they attached themselves there. Days went by and nothing more happened. The Jupiter flew, sending home a stream of photographs, and the Russians did no more than grumble.

On January 20, when Jupiter Fourteen had been in orbit two weeks, Warren Bradley was inaugurated for his second term as President of the United States. It was his hour of triumph, the high point of his presidency. The Jupiter was still up there. He had faced the Russians, and they had backed down. He had dared them to touch his new Jupiter, and they had not dared.

Blair Bruce watched the inauguration on a television set in his temporary office in the White House. (He moved out, back to his office in the State Department in a few days. The Ad Hoc Committee was disbanded.) He was troubled by the President's inaugural address, which stated the President's assessment of the Jupiter crisis.

"Once more we have faced a challenge," said the President, speaking into the cold wind which blew across the platform on the steps of the Capitol. "Once more we have faced a threat. Once more, my fellow Americans, we have proved that strength and firmness will prevail always against the menace of aggression.

"Once more it has been proved to us that the aggressive schemes of Marxism-Leninism have not been put aside by the Communist world. Once more we have been tested, to see if our resolution remains firm. Now they know it is firm. But they will test again. And when they do, we will be ready."

Bruce frowned over some of the President's lines. The President revived phrases that had been out of use for twenty years. (Once he even referred to "Godless Communism.") It was apparent that he was happy, even exultant, with the outcome of the Jupiter crisis. He had stood up to the Communists, chin to chin, and made them back down. That was his assessment of the crisis, and likely it was the one the nation would accept.

It was the one everyone who was talking accepted. Members of the Congress, Republicans especially, talked this way. The President, only this morning, before he left for his inaugural, had reviewed in the Oval Office a stack of editorials and columns from dozens of newspapers, all congratulating him on his leadership in the crisis. There was, for the moment, hardly a dissenting voice.

Blair Bruce knew of one. He had in his desk a Greenwich Village newspaper called *The Spark,* a one-time radical tabloid that had grown large and now had nationwide circulation and a degree of respectability while still remaining acerb and iconoclastic and lively. Bruce liked to read it, though he knew he would get a scowl from almost anyone in the White House who might see a copy of it in his possession. In yesterday's issue—the day before inauguration—*The Spark* had published a column by one of its young men. Blair Bruce had read it several times, amazed at how closely it reflected his own assessment of the Jupiter crisis.

Part of the column said:

> Something is wrong with the national triumph being celebrated with the apparent end of the Jupiter crisis. It is impossible right now to put a finger on it, at least from here, but something has happened other than what we are celebrating, and we will be forced, ultimately, to some very somber second thoughts.
>
> Why did the Russians capture the Jupiter? What had they to gain by such an illogical and dangerous adventure? Nothing that we can see. They had to know that no President of the United States, Warren Bradley or any other, could allow their challenge to remain unanswered. They had to know we would launch another Jupiter. Besides, what difference was there between Jupiter Twelve and all the rest of the fleet of snoopers and sensors we have in orbit all over the world? We have spy satellites, and so do they. Why did they choose this one for capture? And again, what did they think they could gain by capturing it?
>
> The men who govern Russia are cautious, unimaginative bureaucrats. They do not en-

> gage in dramatic adventures. They analyze what they do, and they act out of considered motives. In the current Washington mood of euphoric self-congratulation, it is assumed that the Soviet leaders simply made a gross mistake, tried to push the United States around and did not get away with it. This is a facile, hawkish, simplistic assessment, and we venture the judgment that it is wrong.
>
> Somewhere we are overlooking something important. It is entirely out of character for the Kremlin leadership to precipitate a noisy crisis and then lie down and play dead when the United States throws back the challenge. The Jupiter crisis has come and gone too illogically and too fast. We have missed the point somewhere. The Russians did what they did and have accepted an apparent humiliation for some good reason, and we had better start looking hard for their reason.

Blair Bruce made a mental note once more of the name of the young man who had written the column. Gilbert Hubbard. Maybe he would call Hubbard and talk to him. Because he was sure Hubbard was right. He wondered if anyone else would start looking for the Russians' reasons, as Hubbard suggested. Judging the mood of the nation that January 20, judging particularly the silence of potential dissenters, he was afraid no one would. But he agreed emphatically with what Hubbard had written. Something was wrong. The Jupiter crisis could not be what it seemed. Something definitely was wrong.

THE ERICH TRAVER AFFAIR

PAN AM FLIGHT 002: NEW YORK TO LONDON

There was no horizon. The dark sky faded imperceptibly into the dark sea somewhere out there, maybe fifty, maybe a hundred miles away—he was not sure how far, when you were five or six miles high. The Atlantic was cold. It had to be, in January. And because it blended into the sky with no horizon, it seemed all the more vast and gray. A while ago he had thought he saw some vague white shapes to the north—maybe icebergs. He was looking for the sun. It would appear early when you were flying toward it at this speed and this altitude. It would lighten the sky with blue, out ahead, over the wing. Then it would come up brilliant and fill the plane with dawn light, and everyone would waken, and he would not feel so impatient with himself for having been unable to sleep.

He was wide awake, sitting half upright with his head lying against a pillow he had tucked into the corner between the window and his seat back. He pushed down with his elbows on the arms of his seat and changed his posture. You could sleep, or you could sit straight up wide awake. There was *no way* to be comfortable in between.

The woman in the next seat glanced at him. He was aware of her. He knew she was awake too. Until only a little while ago she had played cards with the man in the aisle seat, probably her husband, and they had talked and laughed.

Now the man was asleep with his mouth open, and she sat with her head back and her eyes open. When he was sure she was not looking at him, he turned his head slightly and took a look at her. He had tried not to be conspicuous in glancing at her from time to time. He had no particular interest in her. But there is an unavoidable sharing of awareness between two people who are awake when everyone around them is asleep. He and this woman had not spoken a word to each other, and they had been careful that their eyes should not meet, but he knew she was awake, and she knew he was.

She was a small woman, well put together and well dressed, maybe thirty-five years old, maybe a little older. She was wearing a dress of some sort of brocaded fabric woven with metallic threads, which glinted in the dim light. It was stylish and, so far as he could tell, expensive. The skirt was short, and he could judge her legs with no uncertainty: they were sleek and long for a woman of her height, and from the way she held them, in a posture both ladylike and yet assuring a good display, he judged she knew they were interesting. He had noticed she had two martinis before dinner and two brandies with her coffee after. She smoked, but not heavily—just two or three cigarettes in the hours they had been on the plane.

Only because he had been looking for a diversion for his thoughts, he had done some speculating about her. Seeing her posture, her dress, her mannerisms, and hearing her talk and laugh until her husband went to sleep, he decided she was never self-contained but was on a little stage she made of life, always playing a role, and always acutely conscious of the people around her. She was probably especially aware of men and their judgments of her. And that thought made him smile. For if she could have known the sum of his judgment of her, she would not have been pleased, probably. It was an innocent judgment. It wasn't erotic. It was not cynical. He was simply thinking that she looked and acted something like his mother.

She was only about ten years older than he was, or maybe a little more, so he was not thinking of her as a motherly type, which likely she would not have taken as a compliment. But his mother was not motherly either. His mother was diminutive and solidly built, like this woman. In fact, she had a good figure—that was the only honest way to say it. She was always stylish and poised. She always had her martinis before dinner and her brandy after, with his father. She talked well, played bridge for master's points, and for a long time held the women's golf championship for their country club. She was pretty well satisfied with what the world saw of her, and of course she wanted her son to look good and talk well, to play hard and drink like a gentleman.

The Pan Am hostess, pushing her cart along the aisle, was offering coffee or another drink to anyone who was still awake. He decided he might as well have a brandy and coffee. The woman beside him took a Drambuie. And the serving, the passing across and all that, forced them to say a polite word or two. It literally forced them to. Then, being awake and erect, with drinks before them, while the others around them were all asleep, they could hardly avoid saying another polite word or two.

She spoke first, being ready with something that suited the moment, while he was not and was trying to think of what to say. "Is this your first trip to London?" she asked.

"No," he answered. "I was there a few days once. My father and mother took me on one of those fourteen countries in fourteen days trips when I graduated from college. We were in London two and a half days."

She did not smile at his confession, as he had thought she might. She didn't react at all. She just went on to say what she wanted to say. "We live there. He's with IBM," she said, nodding at her sleeping husband. "We were home for Christmas. Home's Indianapolis. We overstayed our leave three weeks because of the crisis. We figured, you know, if there was going to be war, better to be home in Indianapolis than in London. Though really, I suppose, if there were going to be atomic war, one place would be pretty much as bad as the other."

He nodded. "I postponed my trip too. I'm on my way to Amsterdam, after London. I'd planned to go three weeks ago, but I had to put it off because of the Jupiter crisis."

"Well," said the woman. "All I can say is, thank God Warren Bradley is President of the United States. Don't you agree?"

He most emphatically did not. But he nodded anyway. There was no point in becoming involved in a political argument.

She had talked with him this long while making an obviously conscious point of glancing at him only and not staring. Now she sipped her Drambuie and looked directly at him across the rim of her glass. "Are you, uh . . . ? Pardon me for prying. . . ."

"I write for a newspaper," he said, trying to smile in a way that would show her he forgave her prying and was willing to tell her. "I'm on my way to Europe to interview some people."

"Oh," she said, and her interest increased perceptibly, so much in fact that unconsciously she drew herself up a little more erect in her seat. "What newspaper?"

"*The Spark.*"

A little frown, a blank, a subdued fluster of embarrassment. "*The Spark?*"

"New York."

The frown deepened.

"Greenwich Village," he added.

Her eyes showed through her practiced imperturbability

and betrayed her. They hardened, or sharpened, or something. Anyway, they failed to cover the dynamics of a mental shift, the movement of a certain burden of ideas—including, he suspected, some settled prejudices—coming up from somewhere to the forefront of her consciousness. The frown vanished, and her eyebrows rose. She nodded. "*Avant garde?* Left wing?" she asked. She asked courteously enough, without challenge, but they really were not questions.

He was amused, and he did not try to hide it. Her judgment was facile, and it was now complete, based on three facts—: One, he said his paper was published in the Village. Two, he was young, only twenty-five, and he didn't look a day older. Three, he wore a thick but neatly trimmed blond mustache, and his hair in back fell down across the collar of his brown wool turtleneck and onto the collar of his olive green corduroy, double-breasted belted jacket.

Avant garde? Left wing? she had asked. "No," he said with a smile. "Not necessarily."

She couldn't argue. She had never seen the paper. "Is it a weekly paper?" she asked.

"No, daily. Six days a week. National circulation."

"Really? Well, do you write political news? I mean, about international events and things like that?"

"I covered the United Nations sessions during the Jupiter crisis—except when I went down to Washington to cover Senator Jordan's speech."

"Then what do you think of the crisis?" she asked. "I mean, is it really over? Have the Russians really backed down?"

He shrugged and turned a thumb toward the window and the dark sky. "Jupiter Fourteen was still up there when we left New York," he said. "They haven't done anything about it yet."

"Then they won't?"

"I don't know. I really can't guess. The whole thing defies understanding."

"How do you mean, defies understanding?" she asked. "We thought it was pretty clear. The Russians pulled a stupid trick, they found out we were ready to stand up to them, so they backed down. Wasn't that it?"

"There are two things the Russians are not," he said. "One is stupid, and the other is cowardly. So in my opinion, either we haven't heard the last of the Jupiter crisis yet, or there was never really a crisis to begin with."

"Well, I think it all goes to show," she said, "that the Russians understand force and respect courage. That's what I mean about President Bradley. He isn't handsome, and he has a cold personality. But he's tough, and they know it."

"Could be," he said. He really didn't want to argue.

She sipped from her glass. "That's what my husband thinks," she said. "And that's what I think. We were lucky to have a man like Warren Bradley in the White House. We're lucky he was re-elected. Did you go to Washington and cover the inauguration?"

It was best not to tell her than on inauguration day *The Spark* had run on its front page the same picture it had run on Bradley's first inauguration day—a full page photograph of the inauguration of Warren G. Harding. "No," he said. "I saw it on TV."

She nodded. "So did we." She paused for a moment. "If you don't mind my asking," she said then, "who are you going to Europe to see? If it's none of my business, just say so."

"No problem. No secret. In London I'm going to see Erich Traver. Then I'm going over to Amsterdam to see his daughter."

She inclined her head and frowned. Then her thin, finely plucked and painted dark eyebrows rose, and her blue eyes came up at him. She smiled skeptically. "*Erich Traver?* My God, is he still alive? And living in London, you say?"

"Yes, he's sixty years old."

"Sixty!" She shook her head. "Well, I suppose he would be

at that. How long ago was he sent to jail? How long did he stay there?"

"He went into the federal reformatory in 1953, and he was there three years. Then he was on parole two years, and in 1958, when he was released from parole, he took his wife and daughter and left the country. They've lived in London ever since."

"I guess I do remember when they let him go," she said. "It didn't seem like he was in very long. Three years. Is that all?"

"His family thought it was pretty long."

She understood she had been reproached, and she was quick to defend herself. *"For what he did?"* she asked.

"He was convicted of perjury."

"He was guilty of treason," she said.

"He was never even accused of that."

"Well, he was a Communist."

"He denied that."

"But he was," she said. "They proved that. That's how he was convicted of perjury, for denying it under oath."

"Before the House Un-American Activities Committee."

"Yes," she said. "Anyway, why do you want to interview him, after all these years?"

"Well, last fall I wrote a series of articles on the Traver case. . . ."

"For *The Spark*?"

"Yes . . . ."

"I don't see *The Spark*," she interrupted again. "Do you write for anything else?"

"No, but some of my articles have been quoted in other papers, and in some magazines too, occasionally."

"Really? Like what magazines?"

"My Traver series was mentioned in *Time*. It was quoted in several newspapers. *The Times, The Washington Post*. . . ."

"What's your name?"

"Gilbert Hubbard."

She repeated the name under her breath, nodding and lifting her eyebrows again. "I'm sorry," she said with a short, embarrassed laugh. "I can't say I've heard the name or read anything of yours. But anyway, why Erich Traver, after all these years?"

Hubbard considered for a moment before he answered. The conversation was already a good deal less casual than he wanted it. He had begun to doubt he could find an idea he and this woman shared. But she has asked a question, and he didn't see any way to avoid answering it. "Well," he said. "You know there are some people who still don't think Erich Traver was ever guilty."

"Are you one of those people? I mean, one of those people who think he wasn't guilty?"

"Not necessarily. I don't know if he was or not."

She thought for a moment. "He had a trial, didn't he? A fair trial?"

"Some people don't think so."

"You?"

Hubbard filled himself with breath. "No. Frankly, I don't think he did. He may have been guilty, but I don't think he had a fair trial."

"That's interesting," she said, as if she had never heard the idea before, and it occurred to him as something of a surprise that maybe she hadn't. Then she shrugged and dismissed Erich Traver. "Nothing much anyone could do about it anyway," she said. "Not any more. Not after all these years. Is there?"

"No," he said. "Nothing much."

She drained her glass. "Can I sit this on your tray for a few minutes? I have to climb over Sleeping Beauty here and go to the bippy."

To get across her husband's legs she had to straddle and struggle, and her tight skirt climbed and climbed, exposing all of her legs and finally even her panties. When she stood in the aisle, hurriedly and irritably tugging it down and smoothing and straightening herself, she gave Hubbard a fierce indignant glare that told him he should have looked down into his brandy, or turned toward the window, or closed his eyes, or done something, anything, except stare where he had stared. He looked away quickly then, as she stalked off toward the rear of the plane. But then it was too late. He had offended her.

He snatched up his brandy and finished it off at a gulp, shaking his head, angry with himself. It had been the kind of stupid clumsiness he managed far too often. He had not been particularly interested in the woman's legs, not enough to leer at her. But he hadn't had a quick enough social instinct to look away. He had no aptitude for relations with women. He was uneasy with them and miserably awkward.

This is what it was, precisely this, now underscored, which had been on his mind and had been keeping him awake earlier. He had left a girl at Kennedy Airport, and he had been thinking of how clumsy he had been with her.

Her name was Leslie Perruchot, and he was troubled by a vivid image of the way she had looked when he left her at the gate in the Pan Am terminal—a tiny, sad gamine in a great, floppy red hat, a long gray coat, faded and tattered blue jeans, and open sandals that exposed pale bare feet. She had stood there looking wistful and abandoned, watching him hurry through the tunnel to the plane, holding up her arm and waving weakly. A moment before, just as he was called and was about to break away from her and rush out through the tunnel, she had thrown her arms around his neck and startled him with a passionate, sorrowful kiss. He'd been startled because they had never kissed before.

He was not sure why she had kissed him, and he'd had no time to find out. He'd had no time even to respond to her. He remembered what he'd done: he had stiffened with surprise. It must have been like kissing a wooden man, and that was what she'd have to remember until he came home. He'd had to abandon her and leave whatever there was between them suspended until he returned from this trip. If only he had managed to say a word to her. . . . Maybe he should send her a wire from London, or maybe even telephone. He'd looked forward to this trip, and a week had seemed too little time. Now a week seemed too long.

"You goyish prick!" she called him when he mimicked the way she said Long Island—"Lawn Guyland." She called him Gib most of the time but Gibby when she was feeling playful. She called him and her together The Tubercular Twins, because he was small and thin and she was smaller. (She called her own breasts the same thing, grinning broadly and pressing her white cotton T-shirts in against them.)

He had never seen her in a skirt. She seemed to have a supply of variously faded blue jeans, plus one or two pairs of khaki chinos, grotesquely overlarge for her, that she rolled up at the bottoms and cinched in at the waist with a big old leather belt. She wore men's white T-shirts, and he had become accustomed to the sight of her pointed little nipples showing as two small bumps in the thin knit fabric. In winter she left her shoes at the door of his apartment and went barefoot inside. In summer she came in from the street barefoot, with the soles of her feet black with grime, and sometimes she would go sit on the edge of his bathtub and wash her feet. She was nineteen years old. She thought she was not pretty. She had heavy, unplucked eyebrows and slightly protruding teeth, with a litle gap in the middle between two incisors. Her eyes were big and dark, and her long brown hair hung around her shoulders, straight and glossy and beautiful. She was prettier than she thought she was.

People thought she lived with him. But she didn't. She only cooked for him. They had an eminently practical arrangement, her idea. She was devoted to a new experimental theater she and her friends were trying to open. She lived a few doors down the street from him, in a large and shabby flat with two other girls who were also working on the theater. The theater was a full-time project. To support herself, Leslie worked as a waitress two nights a week and modelled as often as she could for Village artists and art classes. But the money she made from that was hardly sufficient to pay her share of the rent, so she had proposed to Gib that he buy the groceries for the two of them and she would come to his apartment and cook their meals. It would be good for both of them. And that was the arrangement they had had for about six months. She came in the morning and woke him for breakfast, and in the evening she cooked dinner and afterwards washed the dishes. Each night after the dishes were done, she hurried away. She did not live with him.

He'd had erotic thoughts about her. He had speculated. But she had not invited an approach. She was too cynically, happily independent. And he was not strongly motivated. He had never touched her.

One evening a week ago he had come home late in the afternoon as usual. Leslie was there, in the kitchen, and he could see her from the living room. She was barefoot as always and was wearing her droopy chinos with a ragged T-shirt tucked into them. He went into the bedroom to change and was wearing his own chinos and T-shirt when he came into the kitchen to talk to her and see what she was cooking.

She was crying. She was sobbing softly under her breath, and the tears had run all the way down to her mouth.

"Leslie?" he said, startled. She lowered her head, so he could not see her eyes behind her hair. "Leslie?" he whispered, and moved by an anxiety to comfort her he slipped his hand up under the hair and timidly caressed the back of her neck. (He hadn't thought of it then, but sitting now on the airplane, remembering, he realized it was the first time he had ever put his fingers on her bare skin.)

She turned and sagged into his arms. "Gib," she sobbed, and she began to cry hard, in a moment hysterically.

He led her into the living room, put her down on the couch, and sat beside her. She put her head to his shoulder and wept, hard and long.

He had never seen anyone cry like that, no adult anyway. And he didn't know what to do. She had her head down against his shoulder, and he had his arms loosely over her back. But he sat bewildered and stiff. He wanted to comfort her, but he didn't know how. He didn't know if he should tighten his arms around her and hold her to him. He didn't know if he should bend down and kiss her neck, as he had an impulse to do. He didn't know if he should try to talk to her, or what to say. He didn't know if he should just leave her alone. He didn't know what she needed, or wanted, or would accept from him. So he just sat there with her, feeling inadequate and miserable, condemning himself.

Finally, when she was exhausted and silent, he did at least run his hand down the back of her head, pet her. And when he thought she could talk, he asked her what was the matter.

She shook her head. "Gib," was all she managed to whisper.

"Leslie," he said. "Leslie, what is it? What's wrong?"

She pulled in a long breath. "My theater," she whispered. "It's closed. For good. The man who was putting in the money decided to quit."

"Well, maybe that's not the end of it," he suggested. "Maybe you can find another backer."

"That's what I kept running around telling everybody. But they all just threw up their hands. All the flats and props we made are piled up in the alley. They tore up some of the costumes. The son of a bitch is going to Florida. He's going to put his money in a miniature golf course or something. He gave up the lease on the building, and it's already been turned over to a goddam church. They're going to have a goddamned evangelical mission in the building where our theater was going to be."

She began to cry again, and again he was unable to comfort her. He wanted to take her into his arms and hold her like a puppy, and whisper in her ear, and even cry with her maybe. But he didn't know, maybe she cried in movies. Maybe if he did too much, she would laugh at him later and tell him he made a bigger thing of the loss of her theater than she did. How much did it take to make her emotional? How big a tragedy was it?

She told him later, in the kitchen when she had gone back to her cooking and he was at the table watching her and listening. She spoke quietly, barely above a whisper. "I don't have any training for the theater, no talent. The only reason they took some of us on was because we were willing to work hard for nothing. My family thinks I'm nuts. I never told you this, but every week they come in from Long Island to try to talk me into coming home. What am I going to say when they come this week?"

"Exactly what did it mean to you, Leslie?" he asked.

"The same thing it means to you to write for *The Spark* when you could make a lot more money somewhere else. The same thing it meant to you to go out and work in the presidential campaign last fall."

He nodded. "I understand."

"It was my chance to say something, at least to contribute

to saying something. Now we've all been shut up. Nobody's going to hear what we wanted to say. Everybody's screaming all over the place, and we wanted a way to say what we wanted to say."

"You'll find another way, Leslie."

She shook her head. "I don't know how."

Sitting awake and restless on the airplane, he'd been thinking of all this before he interrupted his thoughts to talk for those few minutes with the woman from Indianapolis. He'd been wondering why he had not known how to comfort Leslie when she cried and put her head on his shoulder.

He had an idea why. Maybe it was because among the people in his home there was contempt for people who were what they called too emotional. He had never seen anyone in his family cry. Only once had he ever seen his father or his mother display an uncontrolled emotion—and that was at a high school football game when his father had stood up and utterly screamed his elation over a long touchdown run. And Gib remembered being embarrassed by that. In his family, among all the people he had grown up with in fact, what they called self-control was a prized and practiced virtue. Emotionalism was a trait that characterized . . . well, inferior people. Maybe he had grown up a contained, closed personality. Maybe women saw that in him, and maybe that was why they didn't easily take to him.

Like the woman from Indianapolis, who now returned. He was careful to stare out the window into the darkness as she spraddled her husband's legs and twisted into her seat. He grinned to himself because the reflection on the glass showed him more of her than he'd glimpsed before; but as soon as he could turn toward her he made his face sober and said, "I'm sorry I . . ." She interrupted. " 'S all right." She leaned her head back and closed her eyes. As he had expected, she did not want to talk any more.

He was glad for the moment of distraction, which had broken into thoughts that had become too heavy and pessimistic. He settled his attention for a moment on the smooth, nylon-sheathed legs he was not supposed to look at, and then on the empty face, now relaxed and content and confident that all was right with the world so long as Warren Bradley was President of the United States. Gib lightened his pessimism by telling himself that if he had to have deficiencies, he was glad he had his and not hers.

He might possibly, just possibly, get an hour or two of sleep yet.

LONDON

It was not easy, as it turned out, to arrange an appointment with Erich Traver. In one of her letters from Amsterdam, Melanie Traver had suggested he not write her father that he was coming but simply call him when he arrived in London. That way, she suggested, her father would not have time to find excuses for not seeing him. Traver found them anyway, and on the Friday evening when finally Gib took a cab to Bloomsbury to keep a seven o'clock appointment with Traver, he had been in London four days—a day longer than he had intended to stay there.

Three days was what he had been in London the summer when his parents brought him on the tour, and now he had spent four days. It was not much, but it was enough to make him know that London was his favorite city in all the world. In spite of the dull cold atmosphere of a London winter and the general air of shabby disrepair he saw everywhere, the city quickly took a certain hold on a visitor, particularly a civilized visitor, which was what Gilbert Hubbard considered himself to be. He had already resolved to return as soon as he could and stay as long as he could.

But he had a Saturday morning flight to Amsterdam, and this was Friday evening.

The cab driver let him out on a short street just off Tottenham Court Road, before a brick house that looked to have been built in the 1920's. There were handsome homes in Bloomsbury, but Erich Traver didn't seem to live in one of them. There were two flats in this house, and one of the doorbell buttons had the name Traver pencilled under it.

The door of the Bloomsbury house was painted black. The bricks were dull black with soot. The woman who opened the door was dressed in black, and she had sharp, unfriendly black eyes and black hair severely fastened behind and pulled tight along the sides of her head. When she opened the door she said nothing. She just stood there and looked at him.

"Mr. Traver, please," he said.

"I am Mrs. Traver," she said in a voice that yielded not a note of concession or welcome. He knew who she was: Jocelyn Adams Traver. He had seen pictures of her when he was researching his articles. He remembered especially the pictures taken when her husband was in prison: of her leading her daughter to school, of her shopping in a market, of her sweeping off her doorstoop. She had been a handsome, haughty, angry woman.

"I'm Gilbert Hubbard from the States. I called Tuesday and made an appointment to see Mr. Traver at seven this evening."

She softened a little. "Yes. The writer. Come in."

He followed her into her home, into the living room where Erich Traver was sitting under a lamp and behind a newspaper. She glanced around at him as he followed her, and caught him being a little too obvious in his appraisal of her home.

It was a curious room—to him. It was furnished in a style

he had seen before, not in his own grandparents' homes because they were too well off and their homes were too grand to be compared to this, but in the homes of grandparents of some of his friends. The room was rather dark, he thought. Three bridge lamps were burning, with low-wattage bulbs inside paper shades. The rug was predominantly dark red, but dark blue and green and brown were prominent too, in a pattern that suggested abstract urns of abstract flowers. The buff wall paper had a formless pattern in darker shades of buff: swirls and curls that looked like something curdled. The upholstery on the couch and chairs was maroon plush. Some coals glowed in the grate. He thought the place was oppressively warm and guessed that the coals supplemented central heating.

"Mr. Traver," the woman said, and she pointed at her husband. "Mr. Hubbard," she said, raising her voice a little to indicate she meant to interrupt Traver's reverie behind his newspaper.

With manifest reluctance Traver put down the paper. He thrust up his right hand to be shaken, and with his left he made a faint gesture toward his cane—his obviously customary and practiced apology for never rising. "Mr. Hubbard," he said. He glanced at the clock on the mantel.

It was nothing to meet Erich Traver. Gib had already decided, after the annoyance and delay he'd endured in making this appointment, that he would not be impressed: and he wasn't. The man was a martyr to many people, a hero and a legend actually to a few, but nothing about him contradicted Gib's prejudgment. He looked like a retired librarian. No, worse, he looked like a petty bank clerk who had embezzled and was living beyond extradition in Brazil—and hadn't had the imagination or the courage to have stolen enough to let him live in comfort. He was gray and balding and slight and weak.

Mrs. Traver pointed to a straight chair, and Gib sat there, near to Traver.

"I appreciate your time," Gib said. It wasn't what he had in his mind, but he said it anyway.

"We read your articles," said Mrs. Traver. "We still have friends in the States, and they send us anything that's printed about us."

"Are you planning to write something more about us?" Traver asked.

"Not necessarily," Gib said. "I might."

"You didn't come to England just to see us?" Traver asked. His tone suggested he wanted to be assured Gib hadn't come just to see him.

"I'm on my way to Amsterdam to see Melanie."

Both of them were startled by that, but it was Mrs. Traver who got in the first word—"Why?"

"She read the articles too," Gib said. "Since then she's written me several letters asking me to come. She says she has important new information about . . . well, about the things that happened."

Traver shook his head. "Unfortunate. . . ." he murmured very quietly. He wore thick, gold-rimmed spectacles which magnified and distorted his eyes, and sometimes he seemed to be hiding behind those spectacles.

Mrs. Traver started to say something. "Our daughter, Mr. Hubbard . . ." she got out before Traver interrupted.

"It's a strange time for a journalist to leave the States and come to England, I should think," Traver said. "A strange time to be following a will-o'-the-wisp about the Erich Traver case, I should think, too. With Jupiter Fourteen in orbit and the Russians threatening . . . They might decide to capture that one also. Any time. Don't you think?"

Gib nodded. "Any time this year or next," he said. "It just adds another dimension of danger to life in the world. We can't suspend everything and just sit around waiting to be blown up."

"You can imagine what *I* think of the Jupiter crisis," said Traver sharply. "What do *you* think?"

"Erich," said Mrs. Traver gently. "This is not what Mr. Hubbard came all the way here to talk about."

"Well," said Traver in a conceding, explanatory tone. "I keep reading that Warren Bradley is a hero in the United States now. That's a little hard to take. You can imagine, Mr. Hubbard."

"It's a little hard for me to take too," Gib said.

Mrs. Traver had risen from her chair and had come around behind her husband, so she was facing Gib. She smiled weakly. "I pray for Bradley's assassination," she said. "With all the good men who've been murdered in the States in the past few years, why couldn't it have happened to Bradley? Would you like some tea?"

She left the room, with Traver watching her intently, thoughtfully, as she went. And Traver said, "She had a bitter time of it. Worse than I had, I think."

Gib nodded and tried to change the subject. "What are you doing these days?" he asked. "Writing anything?"

Traver smiled. He lowered his eyes and nodded. "I'm going to put out a little volume of poems," he said. "It's not easy to get poetry published, you know."

"I know."

"I can always get a little money for some kind of article, something critical of the United States, or for something about the old case, the hearings, the trial, or something like that. But my biography of Christina Rossetti had only a very modest sale."

"It was favorably reviewed," Gib said.

"Yes. But it sold only two thousand copies here, and two or three thousand in the States. The book I wrote about my case was uniformly condemned, even by people with a predilection toward me, but it sold fifty thousand in the States. Stupid. Just stupid."

"Well, you're an historical figure," Gib suggested.

Traver put his hand idly, habitually, on the crook of his cane, which rested between his leg and the arm of his over-stuffed chair. "An historical villain," he said. His long, slender fingers slowly closed around the polished wood of the cane; and Gib, noticing, remembered reading that Traver had walked with a cane since 1942, the year he was drafted and was bounced out of a speeding truck on infantry training maneuvers in Oklahoma. The photographs taken when the marshals led him into the federal reformatory in 1953 showed him clutching the cane grimly with two handcuffed hands.

"Temporarily, I suppose," Gib said in response to the comment that he was a villain. "But maybe not in the long run."

"I won't live to see it otherwise. I suppose that's what you've come here for, to get a start at writing something more about me, reopening all the old stuff."

"Not unless I learn something really new," Gib said.

Traver sat silent for a moment, looking downward, covering the pause in the conversation by using both hands to straighten his spectacles. "I won't help you," he said finally.

"Erich . . ." She was in the door, Mrs. Traver, looking in from the hallway.

"No, I won't," Traver said emphatically. "No. I've gone through it all once, twice, three times. It's enough. I'm sick to death of it all. I've been hounded, even here, by reporters, writers, curiosity-seekers. I'm sixty years old, Mr. Hubbard. I have ten or fifteen more years to live, with luck. I have other things to do. Write. Think. I have no time for the old fights. Most of the people who cared are dead now anyway."

"Warren Bradley isn't!" said Mrs. Traver from the doorway. "He's President of the United States. The son of a bitch!"

"Joceyln . . ."

"You can forgive him," she said. "I won't. Never."

"I don't forgive him," Traver said. "I hate him too." He stopped and shook his head. "But what can you do? Where he's gotten, he's invulnerable."

"Well, you don't discourage someone who wants to look into the case again and maybe learn the truth," said Mrs. Traver. "That's what Mr. Hubbard wants to do, I gather. If he finds evidence of the truth and publishes it in the States . . . Well, *I'll* help you, Mr. Hubbard. Any way I can."

Gib had turned around in his chair, to see Mrs. Traver still standing at the door of the room, ready perhaps to go back to the kitchen if she heard the kettle. He remembered that she was as old as Traver, but she did not look it. In her late fifties, she still had everything that had made her a handsome woman, and if she wasn't now, it was not because of her age but because of the severity she affected in everything about herself—expression, makeup, hair style, clothes, posture, words, and voice. He remembered that in the pictures taken while Traver was in prison, she had always scowled at the photographer if she saw him, and in an incident that made news, she threw a snowball at one of them. She had taken her children and gone to live in Philadelphia, with her father, while her husband was in prison. Her family was well-off, in the importing business as he recalled, and she had married Traver, a modest little Yale graduate from Boston in 1937. In one of the articles Gib had read while researching for his series, it was said that the Philadelphia Adamses had never regarded Traver as a proper match for their debutante daughter. She had married him just the same, maybe defiantly. She was more the black sheep than he was, the article said.

Gib was anxious to lead the conversation into the channel he had planned for it. "I've had eight letters from Melanie," he said. "Do you have any idea what new information she's talking about?"

Mrs. Traver disappeared out of the doorway—probably having heard her teapot whistling at last—and Traver said, "Melanie doesn't know anything. I'm sure of that."

"Well, she writes a persuasive letter," Gib said. He had one of them—her last one—in his pocket, but he had decided not to show it to Traver. It was written on blue-gray airmail paper, and the forceful strokes of her ball-point pen had scored the paper until it was limp. But if her handwriting suggested a mannish woman, it suggested wrong, he knew—for he had seen pictures of her too, and she was a pretty, dark-haired girl, a year or two older than he was and conspicuously female.

"I suppose she does," Traver said. "She believes strongly in whatever at the moment she has chosen to believe."

"It wasn't only me she persuaded. She convinced my editors. My newspaper can't afford to send reporters overseas very often. I'm only the third writer ever sent to Europe by *The Spark.*"

"That's a good paper you write for, incidentally," Traver said. "Iconoclastic. That's what I like."

"Thank you," Gib said. "We work hard at it. But getting back to Melanie, she says her new information doesn't just rehash the old controversies. She says what she has to tell is of historic significance."

Traver shook his head. "You can't believe that," he said, and once more his eyes disappeared behind the reflections in his lenses, making it impossible for Gib to see if anything in his expression rounded off the sharp edge of his comment. "If you do believe it, you and your editors, you've been *had,* Mr. Hubbard."

Gib smiled, both from embarrassment and to invite from Traver a returning smile that might suggest he didn't mean what he said quite as flatly as he had said it.

"I'm sorry," Traver went on, "but you aren't the first newspaper reporter she's tried to peddle this tale to."

"Well, what *is* the tale?" Gib asked.

Traver smiled broadly—a superior, forbidding smile. "Really, I haven't the faintest idea," he said.

"Then maybe it isn't the same thing she's tried to tell other writers."

Traver shrugged. "An educated guess."

"Well, she writes an interesting letter," Gib said weakly. "She's witty, literate."

"She's an interesting girl," Traver said. "You're in for quite an experience. How much do you really know about her?"

"Not much, I suppose—except what I read when I was doing research for my articles."

"Tell me what you do know," Traver demanded.

Gib looked for Mrs. Traver in the doorway, hoping for some rescue, but he didn't see her. "Melanie is . . . what?—twenty-seven?" he said.

"Twenty-six."

"Twenty-six. She came with you to England in 1958, so she was reared and educated here. The last three or four years she travelled with a theater company. She had a baby last summer. Aside from the fact that she writes persuasive letters, I guess that's about all I know."

Traver nodded. "The baby is illegitimate. So is the theater company. She didn't use her own name, so the newspapers didn't identify her and didn't make much of it, but she was arrested for indecent performances in half the cities of Europe. I hate to attach bad names to my own daughter, so I won't call her a whore—though before she left England I think she was even that for a while. But I do have to call her an exhibitionist. I would be willing to make you a wager, Mr. Hubbard, that within a day after you meet her she'll manage somehow to get her clothes off and let you see her naked. But don't get excited about it. If you didn't see it, you'd be one of the few men in Europe to miss the sight."

Mrs. Traver had returned at last, carrying a tray with her teapot and cups. "He exaggerates," she said quietly.

Traver sighed. "I'm only trying to make him understand about Melanie," he said. "She's brought him over here with her promise to give him information. If he believes everything she says and publishes it in his paper, he's apt not only to make a fool of himself but fools of us as well."

She passed the teacups to Gib and to Traver. "You do have to understand, Mr. Hubbard," she said, "that Melanie is to be confronted with a degree of skepticism. Informed skepticism, not just a prejudice against her. She went through hell, you know. She was only a little girl, and like most little girls she worshipped her daddy. When he was taken away . . . well, you never saw a child cry like that. For days. She was old enough to know where he'd gone and why. She became sick, physically sick, and had to be put under sedation. I don't think she ever recovered. Her personality . . . Well, it's one of the reasons I pray for the assassination of Warren Bradley. It's one of the reasons."

Traver was stirring sugar into his tea. "She won't come home," he complained. He spoke quietly but with a jaw that hardly moved. His teeth were clenched, and he let his words out singly, with low, dull resentment. "She has an eight-month-old bastard child and has named it Erich Traver. But we've never seen it. She has no adequate home for it. She chooses to live on some kind of abandoned scow that floats in a garbage-filled canal in Amsterdam. The child's father doesn't live with them. She lives in squalor, and I should imagine she's in danger of having the child taken from her at any time."

Mrs. Traver interjected what she wanted to say. "The point with Melanie is to be independent. It always was."

"I never called it that," Traver grumbled.

"You never called lots of things by their right names."

And from then on, Gib was not part of the conversation.

AMSTERDAM

Melanie Traver was nursing a baby when Gib met her. The child's round little blue eyes widened with alarm when it saw him, and she began to pet it reassuringly. She looked up and smiled. The infant, interrupted only for a moment, gave all its attention once more to her heavy, milk-swollen breast, clutching with both hands, sucking noisily, and, as it stopped to swallow, gurgling its contentment.

Gib had stopped in his tracks, not sure if he should back out and wait until she was finished, or sit down as she had invited him to do. For a few seconds she was distracted from him, as she took a cloth and wiped the slobbers off her breast, and in those seconds while she was not looking at him, he stiffened to compose himself, settled his face into a bland, polite expression, and sat down where she had indicated, on a chair near her.

"Carole will make some tea," Melanie said. "Or would you rather have some *jenever*, or maybe some beer?"

"Tea," he said. "Tea will be just fine."

He spoke toward the other girl, Carole, the one who had come to the door and let him into the cabin of the boat. She had been standing aside, as though suspended, obviously waiting for directions from Melanie. Another child was crawling about on the floor, talking to itself and pushing a stuffed toy.

"Why don't you hang up your coat on one of the pegs there," Melanie said. "Make yourself comfortable. We're planning on your being here a long time."

He had come in from London on a flight that arrived at noon, had checked in at the Doelen, and after a late lunch and a bath he had asked the porter for directions. The boat, which he had found after a little walk along the Amstel River quay, was typically Dutch—squat and stubby, with a black-painted rusting hull lying low in the icy gray water. He had hurried across the short plank and knocked on the door of the white cabin that occupied almost the whole length of the boat. Carole had opened the door, and even before he went inside and saw Melanie nursing the baby on a couch at one end of the cabin, Gib had seen that Erich Traver's talk of squalor aboard a scow in a garbage-filled canal had been wrong. Melanie Traver had a modest, cozy little home on this hulk moored along the Amstel quay.

Melanie began to pat the baby on the bottom while Gib was hanging up his coat and his bright green muffler. The baby was still sucking furiously. "My but we're hungry," Melanie said, and looking up at Gib she added, "Her name is Ginny."

"Ginny?"

Melanie grinned and tipped her head to one side, looking at his bewildered face with amusement. "Well, you didn't think this tiny little thing was Erich, did you?" She laughed. "That's my Erich on the floor. Ginny is Carole's baby. Carole dried up. Ginny needed milk. Erich was old enough for the cup, so we turned the dairy over to Ginny. Okay?"

Gib smiled and nodded. "Sure," he said. "Okay."

"You'd think we only fed her once a day," Melanie said, smiling down at the infant. "Did you ever see a little girl so hungry?"

He shook his head. "I'm afraid I never saw . . . at all," he said.

Melanie laughed. "Some show for you then."

"Oh, I'm sorry," he said hastily. Another clumsiness. He tugged at his mustache and shook his head.

She still laughed, but there was something reserved.

She was a pretty girl, as he had expected. Her face was soft and young, without the slightest trace of the hardness that might have been there if anything they said about her was true. Her features were gently youthful, without a single irregularity to mar them. Her eyes were as dark as her mother's, and in them he saw—without having to use his imagination to create it—a pronounced, inward-looking solemnity, calm and wise. He guessed that no matter how much she smiled or laughed, those eyes would always save something of sadness and wisdom, maybe even of cynicism, that would burden her gaiety and keep it bridled.

Her mouth was very soft, with the lower lip thick and smooth and moist. It was a sensual mouth. Her hair, also dark, a very dark brown, was parted in the exact middle of her head and was so long it hung almost to her waist. She had pushed it away from the breast where the baby was sucking, but strands of soft, black-brown hair lay over the other nipple. She was dressed in a short white skirt and a man's violet-colored shirt, tail out and sleeves rolled back to her elbows.

"Did you see my parents in London?" she asked.

"Yes. They seemed well."

That brought a smile, an amused acknowledgment of his dutiful gesture in telling her her parents were well. "And my brother. Did you talk to him when you were writing your articles?"

"No. I've never met him."

"You know about him? He didn't leave the States when we did, in '58. He enlisted in the United States Army so he wouldn't have to go with us. He seems to be the only Traver who can live in the States."

"Apparently so," Gib said, but he knew she didn't hear him because she was looking down now at the baby. It had stopped nursing and was only slobbering over her breast.

"Carole, come take your baby, will you?" she said.

Carole brought a cloth moistened with warm water, and as soon as she took Ginny in her arms, Melanie began to wash off her breast. "I'm not sure whether something's wrong with the States or wrong with us," she said. "A good deal of both, I imagine."

"Some of us are trying to change the States," he said.

"That's a big job," she said. She began to button her shirt. "We'll put the babies to bed now. Then we can have our tea, and talk."

Carole took the satisfied little Ginny out of the room first, and Melanie went to gather Erich up from the floor. Erich wanted a breast too as soon as she picked him up, and when she wouldn't let him have it, he began to wail. He was still wailing when she took him into the other room of the cabin, the bedroom.

Left alone, Gib looked more closely at the cabin. One of his impressions was that it was surprisingly warm for a rusty old boat riding low in such cold waters. But the floor of the cabin was well below the level of the deck outside, so that the lower part of the cabin sat down inside the hull of the boat and was insulated from the wind and snow. Besides, the cabin was solidly built, with heavy wood beams arching overhead. It was littered with books and magazines in three languages. The furniture was obviously catch-as-catch-can, the adequate but nondescript couch, chairs and table the girls—or someone else who had furnished the boat—had gathered in with thought for their use and not for their looks.

Carole's baby had been ready to sleep, so she came back first. She made the tea, brought it to the table in the center of the room, and asked Gib to pull up a chair.

Carole was a blonde with a drawn, sad face, a tiny and unmusical voice, and a tense, timid manner. She was wearing a pink wool dress with a very short skirt that showed thin legs with skin that looked as if she had been walking bare-legged in the frigid Amsterdam wind. She poured the tea while he wondered what he could say to her, and she looked as if she would be happier if he could not think of anything. Fortunately, Melanie returned.

"I thought you'd be an older man," Melanie said.

"I am," he said.

She laughed, and after her laugh a faint, soft smile remained on her face. Her chin was a little high and her head turned a little away from him, so that she regarded him with her dark eyes coming toward him out of the corners, with gentle curiosity. Her expression was easy and calm, but he could tell she was intent on him, studying him, judging him.

He was self-conscious and, as he always was, ungenerous in his self-critical assessment of his own face and personality. He wondered what she thought of his small, unathletic frame and his thin pale face with blue eyes and mustache. He was apprehensive of what she might think, and he wondered if she could tell he was.

At last she lowered her eyes, looked down into her tea, and asked quietly, "How long can you stay with us?"

"Until Monday. I'm flying back to New York on KLM Monday afternoon."

"I'm sorry you went to London first," she said. Her eyes came up and met his directly. "My father told you I'm a whore, didn't he?"

She could say something like that in a quiet voice and with an unmoved face, but he could not hear it without shifting on his chair and blushing. He lied. "No," he said. "He didn't say that."

"It doesn't bother me," she said, "as much as some other things he probably told you." Her hands were clasped around the teacup on the table before her, and the last of her smile faded. "You knew a great deal about my father before you met him," she said. "I don't suppose you know much about me."

He grinned and shrugged. She was too direct.

"The point is," she said seriously, "that the whole purpose of your coming here, the reason for my wanting you to come and begging you to come, is all involved in your believing what Carole and I have to tell you. We don't have any evidence to show you. You just have to believe what we tell you."

"Well, that's a judgment I can't make in advance," he said.

"I hope you haven't," she said. "Because I'm sure my father told you not to believe a word I say."

Gib nodded. He might as well admit it. "Yes," he said, "he did say that."

Melanie lowered her eyes for a moment. He was conscious of the movement of her eyes. He was conscious—in fact, uncomfortably conscious—of how she held her eyes fixed directly on his most of the time while they talked. "He told you I'm a liar and a whore and God knows what else," she said, with a sigh, lifting her eyebrows and wrinkling her forehead. "And my mother probably confirmed it all and added that I'm mentally unbalanced."

"Oh, it wasn't as bad as all that," he said quickly. "Besides, I don't care what they said. I'll make my own judgments."

"Some of the newspapers in the States found out that I have a baby and am not married," she said.

"That doesn't make a liar of you," he said.

She persisted. "And I suppose my father told you," she said, "that I've been arrested for indecent performances on stage."

"You know, I really don't give a damn, Melanie," he said.

He was not sure, but he thought he saw an instant's flare of anger before she covered it adroitly with a forced grin that only gradually settled into a genuinely amused smile.

"Okay?" he asked.

She nodded slowly, thoughtfully. "Well, I'll tell you something I doubt my father told you. I don't think he knows. Do you know who Carole is?"

Gib shook his head.

"Her last name is Levine," Melanie said. "She's Esther Levine's daughter. Do you remember the name Esther Levine?"

Alerted more by Melanie's face and voice than by any significance the name had for him, he thought hard for a moment, trying to remember, certain that it was important to remember. "Esther Levine . . ." he said. ". . . one of the witnesses. One of the Communist witnesses."

Melanie nodded.

"Let's see," he said. ". . . she testified that she was a member of a Communist Party cell in Washington and that your father was an active member too."

"Exactly," Melanie said. "One of the chief witnesses. She made my father out a complete liar in his testimony that he'd never been a Communist."

"I remember," Gib said.

Melanie smiled and nodded, satisfaction evident on her face. "I can guess at something else my father told you," she said. "He told you I don't know anything about his case. Well, he doesn't know I live here with Carole Levine and nurse her baby."

Carole gathered the teacups and took them to the sink to be rinsed, working so abruptly and purposefully that he suspected the conversation had reached a point where she wanted to separate herself from it. He was distracted by her. At the sink she was rinsing the cups under a noisy, gushing stream of water. He glanced down and saw that she had kicked off her shoes under the table and was standing at the sink barefoot. She distracted him again by momentarily reminding him of Leslie.

"Carole and I have known each other for a long time,"

Melanie said. "Since 1958. When my parents and I reached London in 1958, the Levines met us at the airport."

"The *Levines* met you? Well, to start with, what were they doing in London?"

Melanie glanced at Carole. Carole's back was to them, as if she was not listening. "Mrs. Levine testified that both she and her husband, Carole's father, were members of the Communist Party," Melanie said. "That was at my father's trial in 1953. That was in the McCarthy era, you remember, and they figured they might be prosecuted next. They figured there might soon be a roundup of all Communists in the United States, herding them behind barbed wire in camps. That wasn't so fantastic, for them to think that. The United States government seriously considered it, you know. So the Levines decided to get out while the getting was good. They went to Canada and then to London. When my family arrived, the Levines had already been living in London almost five years."

"It must have been a dramatic confrontation at the airport," Gib suggested wryly. "Your father, newly released from prison, where he'd been sent on the basis of Esther Levine's testimony, and . . ."

"No," said Melanie. "They'd exchanged letters. I don't know what those letters said, but they'd made some kind of peace. My father and mother expected to be met by the Levines, and the Levines took us to stay in their flat until we found a place of our own and my father found a job."

"So you've all been cozy friends ever since," he said.

Melanie shook her head. "No. The circumstances were really too much of a burden for any friendship."

Carole turned at the sink. "That's not the reason," she said. "The reason is that no one could be a friend long to my mother. She's a nut, a fanatic, a bitch."

Melanie grinned. "Well, Cookie, *you* said it. . . ."

"They've gone back to the States, my father and mother,"

Carole said. "My mother's a big deal in the John Birch Society now."

"Birch Society, for God's sake. . . ." Gib said.

Carole tossed down the towel with which she had been drying the cups, and she stepped toward the table. "My mother is a pathological extremist," she said. "So long as she can be a fanatic in the company of other fanatics, she doesn't care what the fanaticism is about. The Birchers love her. She's their Exhibit A, the Communist who found Jesus, saw the light, and redeemed her soul. She goes around the country for them, making speeches about it."

Gib grinned at Melanie. "I can imagine," he said, "what your father thinks of that."

"*My* father doesn't like it any better," Carole said. "But he's a weakling and can't do anything about it."

Melanie spoke somberly. "Our parents are a despicable lot of people, all four of them," she said. "When Carole's father and mother decided to go back to the States, Carole didn't want to go. They threatened to force her. She was so young, they could probably have done it, so she came to me, and I helped her hide from them. There was a hell of a row, but in the end they left London without her. They abandoned her. She moved in with me then, in the room I had in Soho, and we've been together pretty much ever since."

"They don't even know where I am," Carole said. "I haven't used my name for years. I'd just as soon you didn't use it either, unless you absolutely have to."

Gib nodded his assurance to her, but only momentarily, for he was distracted by a thought that had been growing for the past minute or so. "If all this is what you think of your father," he asked Melanie, "why are you so dedicated to clearing his name?"

She sighed and shook her head. "I don't give a damn for his name. Or for him either—though I must say, he's probably what he is because of what happened to him. My mother is what she is because of what was done to us, and I suppose I am, too. Lord knows what we'd be if it hadn't happened. But you know what they did to us. All my family went through bloody hell so Warren Bradley could be elected United States Senator from Michigan. The whole Traver prosecution was a vicious scheme of lies contrived to make a few people a tremendous political profit, and if Erich Traver and his wife and children were hurt in the process, well that was just too bad. What I want is revenge. It's as simple as that. But I won't have to lie to get it. The truth will give it to us."

He nodded soberly and hoped she did not see any sign of the skepticism she had turned on in him with her tense, unembarrassed little speech. Maybe she did see some sign, for she drummed her fingers on the table between them and stared at them, showing self-consciousness. "You like honesty?" she asked, almost under her breath.

He glanced up at Carole, who stood rigid, staring down at Melanie with troubled sympathy all across her face.

"I gather," he said, "that the new information on the Traver case is something Carole learned from her mother. . . ."

"And my father," Carole said, nodding.

". . . and her father," he said. "And it has something to do with the testimony Esther Levine gave at the trial. Right?"

Melanie stopped her nervous drumming and looked up at him, but she looked suddenly unenthusiastic about going on with the discussion. She only nodded.

"Do you want to tell me now?" he asked, but he asked in a voice that suggested he was entirely willing to wait until she felt like telling him.

She looked at him for a moment, silent and so thoughtful

that her eyes seemed dead. She sighed. "I'd really rather not tell you yet. Are you in a hurry?"

He smiled. "I'm not leaving until Monday."

"Promise?" she asked.

"Sure. Why?"

"I was afraid you wouldn't come to Amsterdam. Now I'm afraid you'll leave. I mean, I'm afraid you'll make a quick judgment of what we tell you, and leave."

"I won't do that."

She relaxed and seemed assured. "It's getting dark," she said. "We should have some *jenever* and our dinner."

Carole circled the cabin, pulling the chains in the lamps, and the fading cold gray light in the cabin was brightened and warmed by the yellowish light of the bulbs. While Carole was busy making dinner, Gib and Melanie sat on the couch in the end of the cabin, while Gib drank *jenever*, the volatile, redolent, faintly oily Dutch gin, and listened to her talk about the theater troupe with which she had toured Europe. Then they had dinner, and it turned out that Carole was an inspired cook. They lingered at the table, and both girls talked about the theater. While they had their coffee, Melanie nursed the infant again, and Carole spooned baby food into Erich. With the children back in bed, Melanie returned with Gib to the couch, and Carole made more coffee.

"It doesn't take long to tell you what we know," Melanie said when Gib suggested they talk about the story he had come to Europe to hear. "What we have to tell you is short and simple, but it changes the whole complexion of the Traver case."

"Short, simple facts change history," he said.

"These do," she said.

Carole nodded emphatically. She was sitting tense on a nearby chair, clutching her bare knees between her hands.

"We lived in Washington," Melanie said. "My father was from Boston, you know, and they'd lived in Philadelphia until he was drafted in 1942. When he was injured in infantry training and was discharged, he took a job with the War Department and moved the family to Washington. I was born there. The Levines lived there too. Franklin Levine, Carole's father, worked at the State Department. You know all this?"

Gib nodded. "Yes, all of it."

"Okay," she said quickly. "Let me tell you something you didn't know." She pulled her lower lip between her teeth and paused and lifted her chin. "My father *was* a Communist. He joined the Party in 1937. When he testified at those hearings of the House Un-American Activities Committee that he'd never been a Communist, he was lying through his teeth."

Gib's mouth had come open, and he pressed a fist against it. "Then his conviction for perjury was . . ."

She nodded. "Proper, within the lights of American law. If a man can be summoned before some kind of inquisition and compelled to divulge his political beliefs and associations, then he was guilty as charged. He lied. He still lies about it. He was a faithful Communist for fifteen years. His judgment was as bad about that as it is about everything else."

"How long have you known?"

Melanie shook her head. "I suspected it for a long time—since I was a teen-ager, I guess. But now I know. And I know what you're thinking. You're wondering what's left to worry about if he was guilty all the time. Right?"

"The question occurred to me," Gib said dryly.

"Well, what we have to tell you about the Traver prosecutions is a lot more important than the question of whether Erich Traver was guilty or not," she said. "That's only a small side issue. Erich Traver himself was only a small side issue in what was going on."

"Wait a minute," Gib said. "What about the first trial? Was he guilty of that charge too?"

"I don't know. I suspect maybe he was. All I can say is, thank God for the jurors who held out. If he'd been convicted at that trial, he'd be in prison yet, and where would I be?"

"All right," said Gib. "Tell me the rest of it."

"Tell him, Cookie," Melanie said to Carole.

Carole stared down at her knees, with her fingers tightly curled around them. "I used to ask my father and mother why my mother testified against Melanie's father," she said quietly. "I asked about it when I was pretty young and naive, because it bothered me that Melanie's father had gone to prison because of my mother's testimony."

"There were other witnesses," Gib said.

"I know. But it seemed to me that if Mr. Traver was my mother's friend and Party comrade, it was a terrible betrayal to testify against him. When I'd ask why she did it, she'd just say she had been subpoenaed and had to do it. And then I asked why she hadn't refused. And she said she'd have been sent to jail for contempt. And I asked if it would have been for as long as Mr. Traver had to go to prison."

"And then what did she say?" he asked. She had seemed to be running down, and he thought it wise to encourage her.

Carole looked up from her knees. "My mother got very annoyed with me over it," she said. "I began to think she'd been a coward and worse, and she could see that was what I thought. So finally she told me why she testified. She said the Party itself, the leaders of her cell, ordered her to do it. They ordered her and other members of the cell to testify against Mr. Traver, and they wrote out the testimony in advance and rehearsed it together, so there wouldn't be any inconsistencies."

"Tell about your father," Melanie said.

Carole moved her lips and tongue as if her mouth were dry, and she picked up her coffee cup and sipped from it. "My father was a member of the same Communist cell. He was ordered to testify too, but he refused. He said he would not betray Mr. Traver, who was his friend and comrade in the Communist movement. The day my mother and father told me all this, they got into a bitter quarrel over which one had been a coward and which one had done right."

And that was all Carole had to say. She sighed heavily, leaned back in her chair, and began a nervous, arrhythmic slapping of her thighs, with both hands. Gib glanced at Melanie. Her eyes were intent on his face, watching for his reaction.

"Well . . . *why?*" he asked, with a hard frown. "Why would the Communist Party order its members to testify against Erich Traver?"

"That's the point, isn't it?" Melanie said immediately, nodding vigorously, excitedly. "That's just the point. You remember the official line, the story that everyone told and nobody questioned: that the members of the cell were tracked down by hound-dog investigators for the Un-American Activities Committee and the Justice Department, all goaded into action by Warren Bradley. The story was that they were found out, given subpoenas, and compelled to testify. That's what Warren Bradley took credit for." High with indignation, she shook her head and her fist. "*But it was all a lie!* The Communist Party itself provided the testimony that convicted my father. They provided the witnesses and rehearsed them in perjured testimony. They betrayed my father and scuttled him. They . . ." Melanie broke off and swallowed noisily, her face softening with defeat.

Gib was moved, but he could think of no better way to be sympathetic than to show more interest in what she wanted to tell him. So he asked, "Does your father know all this?"

"No," Melanie said softly. She swallowed and blinked. "The Levines never told him. They never talked about it at all with him. It was just too awkward. Carole and I never mentioned the subject with each other. It wasn't until Carole and I were both pregnant and came here to live together, that she told me what her mother had said and her father confirmed. So my father doesn't know, and I'm not going to tell him."

"No wonder he doesn't want the case reopened," Gib said.

"You know enough of the history to understand," Melanie said. "The historic injustice in my father's case was not that he was convicted. He was guilty. It's not even that he was singled out to be harassed and hounded and destroyed and his family literally tortured. All of that was bad enough. But what really was bad is that some kind of unholy alliance existed between someone in the government and someone in the Communist Party. Someone who made a big, pious thing about his crusade against Communism was in fact working with the Communists all the time."

"You have someone in mind," Gib said.

She looked up. "Sure. Who do you suppose? Who else could it be? Warren Bradley."

GREENWICH VILLAGE

Leslie was not at the airport. That was a disappointment. By the time he reached his apartment in the Village, it was time for her to be there cooking dinner. She was not there. He found a note, saying she had a new job and could not come to the apartment until she got off. She got off at seven.

Gib sat wearily on his couch, facing the littered expanse of the big round oak table which had been lowered to make him an immense coffee table, looking for evidence that Leslie had spent some time there during the week he was gone, and finding none. She had been there. The coffee cups they had left on the table had been taken away. But she had not opened the mail. She had not broken the wrappers on his magazines. He had dumped his suitcase in the bedroom and had noticed that she had not slept in his bed. The apartment, which had satisfied him well enough for a long time, suddenly was gloomy and lonely.

When he awoke in Amsterdam that morning, a bright, cold sunlight had been glistening on the windswept, choppy waters of the Amstel. When he left Schiphol Airport the plane had lifted off into crisp blue air and swung out over an ocean gleaming in the yellow light of the sun. But then all the way across the Atlantic the clouds below the plane had thickened, and the plane had landed at Kennedy in heavy mid-afternoon darkness. He'd come into the city on the bus and taken a cab down from the terminal to the Village, and the driver had complained all the way about having to drive into the Village.

The apartment was deadly silent. The cold darkness outside the windows was so threatening that even with all the lights on the rooms seemed dark. And suddenly, after a week of excitement in which a world of things had happened and filled him full of vivid impressions, he was sitting on his old couch in his old room, alone, and the impressions were fading, everything he had seen and heard was tucked quietly away in memory with all the rest that was there, and in a very large sense it was already as if he had never gone at all.

He was not hungry, even though it was approaching mealtime. He was not sleepy, even though he had not slept on the plane and in fact had slept but little the night before. He rummaged around in the kitchen, put on some coffee. He looked at his mail. He took a bath and shaved and put on clean clothes. He watched the news on television and waited for Leslie.

He was interested in one item in the news. The State Department was denying that the Western Pacific Trade Conference, which had been in session in Honolulu when it was interrupted by the Jupiter crisis, had been a cover for talks meant to lead to diplomatic relations with Communist China. The President had commented that what he had said in his second inaugural address remained the basis of United States policy for the moment—: that because the Jupiter crisis had demonstrated once more how much the Communist powers were committed to world aggression, this was no time to initiate basic changes in United States foreign relations; it was time to be strong and alert.

Leslie came about a quarter past seven. He had turned off the television by then and was trying to read. But as the time approached when she was due, his reading had become superficial, thinned by thoughts and images of her. He mused on the kiss at the airport and the impression he must have left on her when he rushed aboard the plane, and he wondered if she would kiss him when she came. He thought of how she had looked: the red hat and the gray coat, the jeans and the sandals. . . .

She used her key to let herself in. She was wearing the long gray coat and the floppy red hat, but . . . She tossed off the hat and coat, and underneath she was wearing an ugly light green dress with a row of white buttons down the front, dull stockings and square white shoes with thick rubber soles—the uniform of a waitress in some cheap restaurant.

He had hurried to the door as soon as he heard her key, and after she had tossed her coat and hat in the direction of his table, he put his arms around her. He wanted to kiss her before she could kiss him. And she let him. She put her arms around him and accepted his kiss with her eyes closed. Then she wrinkled her nose, and with her eyes still tightly closed, she drew a long audible breath through that turned-up quivering nose, as if he smelled good.

"Have a good trip, Gibby?" she asked, still standing with her arms around him.

He nodded. "Sure. But what are you doing? What's this deal?" he asked, looking down at her uniform.

She dropped her arms from around him. "Well," she said. "I've either got to make a living or move back out to Lawn Guyland. I'm afraid I can't cook for you any more. Breakfast I can, but not dinner any more, unless you want to wait at late as this."

"Leslie . . ." He wanted to kiss her again, but she had started toward the kitchen, glancing back over her shoulder and asking him brightly if he was hungry.

"No, I'm not hungry," he said. He followed her.

"Well, I am."

He sat at the table in the kitchen and watched her make their dinner, depressed by her stiff, pale-green dress. It had shiny spots on it from too much starch and too hot an iron. It didn't fit her. It was too long. But he talked with her. He tried to be cheerful because he supposed she was sad.

She asked him, after a while, about the Travers. "How about it, Gib? Was what she had to tell you worth all the trouble?"

Gib had his fist against his chin, under his nose, and he blew his breath through it. "It could be," he said. "It could turn out to be a very big deal."

"What is it?"

"I'll tell you," he said. "But you understand it's a secret, Les. I don't know what to do with it. I have to talk to some people about it. But anyway, what she told me is that the Communist Party of the United States contrived her father's conviction in 1953. The prosecution witnesses, some of them, were supplied by a Party cell in Washington. They were rehearsed in perjury. And someone in the government almost certainly had to know that."

"Who? Did she say?"

He smiled. "Well, of course she thinks it was Warren Bradley. He was the one who made political capital out of the Traver case."

Leslie, standing at the sink rinsing some lettuce, stopped what she was doing and turned to Gib and grinned. "She really wants to have Bradley's head, doesn't she? Was she telling the truth, do you think?"

He nodded. "I think so. But of course it doesn't at all follow that Bradley himself was the one who played games with the Communists. It could have happened without his knowing anything about it."

"How are you going to find out if he was or not?"

"That's the problem. She wanted me to stay in Europe, or at least come back. She says there are anti-Bolshevik Russian organizations that have all kinds of information about Communist operations in all parts of the world. She wanted me to go to Munich with her, to meet some Ukrainians she came in contact with during her travels. She thinks they might know something about it. She assumes that everything the Communist Party of the United States did in 1953 was done on specific orders from Moscow. I think she's being naive about that. I'd rather check out some people here. There was an attorney for the House Un-American Activities Committee who was the principal witness against Traver in the first trial. He was Bradley's right-hand man in those days. He's retired now. I want to talk to him. I want to talk to Senator Jordan too."

Leslie had turned to her lettuce again. "Suppose," she said, "that you can prove that Bradley did know what was going on in 1953. What would happen?"

"I don't know. It seems like old-time stuff now, but Bradley made his career by selling himself as a fervent patriot and anti-Communist. If you could really prove, as a matter of solid fact and not just opinion, that he accepted Communist help in rigging false testimony to convict Erich Traver, it would discredit him rather thoroughly, I would think. It might shut his pious mouth pretty firmly."

"And Erich Traver would come home in a blaze of glory," Leslie said.

"No. Because it will also come out that Traver was really a Communist all along. He was a member of the cell, just like the witnesses said."

"Then the witnesses didn't lie, Gib," she protested.

"No, they didn't—not on the major point: that he was a member of the Party. But they lied about things they testified he did and said, the details of their testimony that gave it impact."

"Maybe it's not so big a deal," she suggested.

Gib sighed and nodded. "You're right. That alone probably isn't, in spite of what Melanie thinks. But there is a much bigger issue in the Traver case than that. If what Melanie says is true, if the Party did supply the testimony to convict her father, then somebody in the Justice Department, or somebody on the staff of the Un-American Activities Committee, or maybe even Warren Bradley himself, made a deal with the Communists to rig the Traver perjury trial. Now, it's easy enough to see why Bradley might have done it, if he was that dishonest. And it's easy to see why someone prosecuting the case might have done it—simply to win the conviction. *But what's impossible to understand is why the Communist Party would have done it.* Why would they scuttle Traver? Why would they expose and destroy an active Party cell to do it? That's what interests me, and the answer to that is what I'd like to find out."

Leslie grinned at him. "You have some idea why they did it, don't you? You have a theory."

"There could be a thousand reasons. It's easy enough to think they just wanted to destroy Traver, because of something he'd done—a matter of Party discipline maybe. But why go to such elaborate trouble? Why destroy an active cell? The Levines were members of that cell, and Levine worked at the State Department, in a rather sensitive position. Levine's effectiveness was lost to the Party because his wife testified against Traver and admitted that both she and her husband were Communists. The Levines fled the country. No, I think it has to be something more than that. Maybe the Communists were protecting something more important. That's an interesting thought, don't you think?"

Leslie shook her head. "It was a long time ago, Gib. Before I was born. Does anybody really care any more?"

Gib paused for a moment, frowning introspectively. "Maybe that's what we're going to find out," he said. "But suppose we did prove, really prove, that the President of the United States, back when he was a congressman, lied and schemed and rigged perjured testimony in a trial, to promote his own reputation and his political career. It would be a big story, wouldn't it? It might change the history of the United States, as Melanie says."

Leslie looked hard at him for a moment, before she turned her back to him and went on with her work. "You'll get burned in the process," she said.

Over their dinner he told her about London, about the plays he had seen and the walks he had taken through the city, the days and nights he had waited for his appointment with Erich Traver, and he told her about Amsterdam and the boat where Melanie lived. After they finished eating, he asked her to let the dishes sit for a while. He wanted to take their coffee into the living room.

He sat beside her on the couch, wtih his arm around her. He told her he had thought a lot about her while he was gone. He kissed her.

"My family is really hounding me to come home," she said. His hand was on the back of her neck, petting her there, and she lifted her shoulders and twisted her neck. She liked it. Still, she was casual about liking it. "Did I ever tell you my father is eighty years old? My mother is fifty-nine. They want their baby to come home, and they sent two of my sisters down here to pressure me."

"You aren't going, are you?"

"I don't know. I can go back to school if I do. They won't pay tuition for me if I live down here."

"Is your theater group really dead?" he asked.

"And buried," she said. "What about Melanie Traver . . . ?"

"I said you'd like to be part of a company like theirs. She said come on over. Maybe you could join. I warn you, though, they all seem to go naked on the stage. Was anybody going to do that in your group?"

She shrugged. "That's old stuff," she said. "I wouldn't care, but it's old stuff. That's for people that are hung up on it."

He laughed and hugged her closer to him. Her face was not toward him, as if she were making a point of presenting him only a cheek to kiss, and he put his hand on her chin and turned her head so he could kiss her on the mouth. She let him kiss her. She closed her eyes and moved her lips under his, but when they separated she looked away again.

"Would you take a job at *The Spark* if I can get you one?" he asked. "I don't like this . . ." he said, nodding toward her green uniform.

"Doing what?" she asked. "What could I do for *The Spark*?"

"Well. . . . Can you type?"

She shook her head.

"We can find something. I know you can do better than . . . wait on tables."

He opened one button of her dress and slipped his hand inside. He found her breast, small and solid, and the pointed little nipple quickly hardened and swelled between his fingers. She looked curiously into his face, and he kissed her.

"You having fun?" she asked quietly. It was not an accusing question, not sarcastic—just blandly curious.

He sat silent for a long moment, stopped with his mouth open and without an answer. Finally he looked away from her and said, "I'm sorry if *you're* not. I thought maybe you would."

She grabbed his wrist as he started to pull his hand out of her dress. She held it and pushed his hand back toward her breast. "It's all right," she said. "I kind of like it. But you sure are changed. Melanie Traver must have made you terribly horny. Did you sleep with her?"

Leslie regarded him with playful eyes, with her head tipped, with her lips apart in an amused smile, showing her teeth with the tiny gap in the middle. Her glossy brown hair framed her face and neck and lay against the jarring green of her uniform. He wanted to pull the dress down off her shoulders and let her hair lie on her skin. He wanted to take the dress off. He wanted to take her to bed.

"Well, did you?" she asked again. "Did you sleep with her?"

He sighed and closed his eyes. He nodded.

"Congratulations. I thought you probably would, from the sound of those letters she wrote you."

He pulled his hand out of her dress so he could put both arms around her. "I wish it had been with you, Leslie," he said gently.

She pulled her head back and stared into his eyes in mock surprise. "Hey, are you Gib Hubbard?" she asked. "Are you the one that lives in this apartment, that went to Europe a week ago? What happened to you over there? What'd she do to you?"

"Les . . ."

"C'mon! You're *different!* What happened to you over there?"

Only this morning, only two hours before he was to leave for Schiphol Airport, the bright sun shining on the rough cold Amstel waters, had been broken into diffused glimmering reflections that had come in through the riverside windows of the boat and filled the bedroom with a dramatic light, bright and yet soft. The cabin was white. The walls and ceiling were white, freshly painted and shiny, the sheets on the big brass bed were white, and the blankets on the two cribs at the foot of the bed were white. Colors glowed in that white room, in that light. The yellow brass curlicues of the antique bed gleamed. The soft pink of Melanie's skin, smooth and translucent, had glowed too.

Melanie had wakened Gib unintentionally, with a gentle motion of the bed. She was rocking the baby in her arms as she held her to nurse. Melanie was nude, and so was the baby. She hummed to her as she rocked and let her suck and gurgle, and Melanie's whole body swayed from the hips.

Melanie soon knew Gib was awake, though he had tried not to stir and alert her, and she glanced back over her shoulder and smiled at him.

He had not been surprised when, at the end of his first evening with Melanie, she had suggested with quiet ingenuous candor that he stay and sleep with her. She said she'd rather expected he'd want to. He did want to, and he had rather expected she would let him. He thought he'd interpreted the hints in her letters right. Then what her father said had heightened his piquant expectation. And, when he found her the quintessential female he had anticipated, before the evening was over he was not so much hoping she would suggest he sleep with her as he was afraid she might not. She could not guess how much it meant to him, how much more undoubtedly than it meant to her.

He understood she had a motive. She wanted his confidence. She wanted him to believe what she and Carole had told him and to accept her interpretation of its meaning. She would make herself much more difficult to disbelieve or deny—or, as she put it, *they would be much better friends, much more quickly, wouldn't they?*

She was very right about that. The first night, when they were lying contentedly in each other's arms after their first intercourse, when he was so full of intense thoughts and savoring such feelings that he could hardly give words enough attention to understand anything she said, she said something about sensitivity training, about people learning confidence in each other by touching and by confession. At that moment he did not understand what she said, but before their two nights were over he recalled and agreed, because by then they had become such friends that she had told him startling things about herself, things he could not believe she would tell anyone but a well-loved friend, and he had responded by confessing to her something he had long resolved never to admit to anyone.

"Gib?" she had whispered to him, late in the quiet darkness of their second night, when he had been sure she was asleep and he had been allowing his own consciousness to wander and slip. She pushed the sheet down off their shoulders and put her arm over him, and she rolled against him. Her body was a little moist, and the warm darkness smelled of baby oil and powder and faintly of Melanie's sweat. "What did my father and mother say about little Erich?" she asked.

Her face was so close to his that he could feel the fluttering breath of her whisper. He kissed her on the mouth, and he said, "They want to see him. That's about all they said. They want to see their grandchild."

They whispered because the two babies slept in cribs at either side of the foot of the bed. Melanie was silent for a moment, and then she whispered, "I can't go home with him, Gib. They might even try to take him away from me."

He touched her cheek. It was too dark to see tears there, but he suspected he would feel them, and he did. He put his arm across her and petted her along the smooth skin of her hips and bottom, knowing—as he had not known with Leslie only a week before—that she wanted his touch and would take comfort from it.

"I don't want them coming here to see me, either," she said. "They'll start a fuss about Ron."

"Ron?"

Melanie drew a deep breath. "Uhm-hmmm," she murmured as she let the breath out. "I guess I haven't mentioned Ron. He's little Erich's father."

"I wasn't going to ask."

She moved her face up to his, and she turned her head back and forth, rubbing her moist lips across his mouth, nibbling on him. Then she tossed some of her long hair across his cheek and neck—which, he had learned, was a special affectionate gesture of hers. "I wasn't going to tell you," she whispered.

"You don't have to."

"Oh, but I'm going to tell you," she said. "I think you should know. I love you, and I want you to know."

He was not startled by her saying she loved him. He knew what she meant: that he was *one* of the people she loved. That was the way she used the word.

"The way Ron and I made Erich . . ." she said. "Well, it would settle everything between me and my parents forever, if they knew."

"You really don't have to tell me," Gib said.

"I'm not ashamed of it," she said, putting a little low voice under her whisper, for emphasis. "I don't live by the old rules."

"Nobody does," he said.

"Don't you kid yourself," she said, with an ironic chuckle.

"All right then," he said. "Tell me about it."

She laughed quietly. He could barely hear it, but he could feel all of it, in her chest and in her belly, which were firm against his. Then her body softened as the laugh ended. She took the breath she needed to say something emphatic. "I'm proud of my theater company," she said.

"I think you have reason to be," he said.

"We did our own plays mostly," she went on. "Some were adaptations. Carole was in a very modern *Lysistrata,* did it in the nude and didn't have a line to speak; she's no actress." Melanie stopped to laugh. "But I was in a play that Ron wrote himself. He wrote it and played the male lead. I played the female lead. It was called *Coupling*. Even our most vicious critics admitted it's a powerful, persuasive piece of drama. It's a great play. Ron is a great playwright and had a great future."

She had stopped, and Gib could not see her face distinctly enough in the darkness to know why. "*Had?*" he asked.

"Yes, had," she whispered. "Maybe he still has a future, but right now he's back in England, driving a lorry. What happened is that he and I conceived the baby. We couldn't be sure exactly when it happened, but it almost had to be on stage, Gib, in full view of three or four hundred gawking Germans."

She waited for him to say something, but he waited for her to go on.

"It was an accident," she said. "We'd been doing it on stage for more than seven months. It was part of the play, an essential part. Even when we were arrested for doing it, nobody charged we only did it for kicks, or to shock, or just to attract a big audience and make more money. The play is about love, both spiritual and physical, and what we did was essential to its meaning. I wish you would see it, or at least read it, so you'd know what I mean. Anyway, I'd been taking the pill for a long time, and I had to stop taking it. It was making me sick. Probably Ron should have gotten another girl for my part then. But he didn't. I got myself a diaphragm. And pretty soon I was pregnant. I don't know whether the damned thing slipped, or I didn't get it in right, or what. Anyway, we must have made little Erich on stage, because Ron used a rubber off stage."

Her low whisper had become deeply solemn, and as she finished, Gib reached for her cheek to feel for tears. He did not feel any, so he asked, "What happened to Ron then? His future in the theater?"

She sighed noisily. "He went home to Coventry, to drive a lorry and make some money. He has a wife and two children there, to support. And he sends me all the money he can. I hate to take it. I don't want him driving a lorry. I want him to go back and do what he has such a talent for. But I do need the money right now. The producer for our company owns this boat and has let Carole and me live here free. My mother sends me a little money from time to time. But most of our support, little Erich's and mine, comes from Ron, until I can get out and get back to work."

"Do you love Ron?" Gib asked.

"He's one of the people I love."

The first few times he heard her use the word love in her special way, he had thought it was an affectation. But shortly he had realized she was sincere and probably used the word better than he did. Anyway, she used it often. She loved both the babies. She loved Carole. She loved her parents in spite of everything. She loved him, Gib. And however casual she had seemed when she asked him to sleep with her, it had not been casual when they were alone together in the darkened bedroom. Even when they were undressed and in each other's arms in bed, still she had quiet things to say to him, and only gradually and naturally had they begun to kiss and fondle. He believed—with consciousness that he might be deceiving himself—that if he had not been gentle and almost deferential with her, she would not have let him into her bed a second night. Maybe he was a fool to think so. He knew that was possible, but he didn't think he was, and he didn't care.

"What do you think of me, Gib?" she had asked in a small voice.

He kissed her. "You are one of the people *I* love, Melanie," he said.

"You know all there is to know about me," she whispered. "I'll always be naked in your eyes."

He smiled in the darkness. He knew she could not see that, so he stroked her leg affectionately. "You're no more naked than I am," he laughed, and in an instant he regretted it, knowing his shallow joke was not at all responsive to her mood and thought.

"Oh yes I am," she said emphatically.

"Well . . ." he said. He was thinking again of what her father called her: an exhibitionist who wanted to be naked before everyone.

She kissed him. Her thought was entirely different. "Tell me something about *you,*" she whispered.

It was then that he told her what he had not meant to tell. Thinking about it on the flight back across the Atlantic, he had been unable to recover the inspiration of the night or to re-create the impulse that had made him talk. He could recall that suddenly he'd wanted to tell her and that after he'd told her he was glad, lifted into a sort of euphoria about it. He couldn't recapture any of that now. He did not regret having told her, but he could not understand how he had so abruptly abandoned his long resolution to keep his secret.

"Melanie, I want you to know . . ." he had said, whispering with thin breath, impelled by excited determination. He stopped for a moment to reinforce his sudden decision. "I want you to know that you're the first girl I . . . I ever was a success with. I mean, I'd never really, fully . . . enjoyed a woman before last night. I guess you'd have to say I was a virgin."

A moment later his hands were behind her head, entangled in her hair, pressing her tight to him so he could kiss her all over her face. He loved her for what she said to him. Having fully expected someday some girl would laugh at him if he ever told what he had just told Melanie, he had caught himself up in rigid apprehension to hear what she'd say, knowing Melanie would not laugh, but apprehensive just the same and alert for any nuance he could detect in whatever she said. Her whisper was soft and solemn, and she said to him, totally ingenuously, with candor and sincerity he could not doubt—"Gib, I wouldn't have known if you hadn't told me."

He kissed her mouth and nose and eyes, her throat and shoulders and breasts, even her nipples. (Last night when he'd kissed those, she had made him taste her milk, had insisted only half playfully and had made him feel he had to do it, even though he emphatically did not want to, and he had almost gagged on the warm, sweet sticky stuff.) He hurried on, to kiss her belly and thighs, and she was aroused and invited him to cover her again. He caught himself up. He had not really meant to try again. He had thought he was depleted. But she wanted him and told him she did, so he worked hard and accomplished it. When he slipped off her hips and dropped heavily on his side of the bed, he was exhausted and his high emotions had been damped.

Spread wide on her back and apparently too comfortable

to move, Melanie groped for his hand, found it and squeezed it, and asked him in a low whisper—"Gib, didn't you ever have a girl, like when you were in school, that you might have . . . ?"

"No."

She squeezed his hand tighter. "I don't understand that."

"Sure you do."

"No, Gib."

"Well, it isn't a very interesting subject."

She pulled his hand up to her face and kissed it. She licked his palm. "Tell me," she whispered.

He might have refused. But she'd told *him* things. He sighed so loudly that she started and lifted her head to listen for a baby stirring in one of the cribs. "A girl . . ." he said. "Well, you know how it is when you're sixteen or seventeen. When I was that age I had some of the most miserable days of my life out at the country club pool. We lived in a country club subdivision, and summer afternoons you went to the pool. That's what you did, *you went to the pool.* I . . ."

"Couldn't you swim, Gib?"

"I could swim like a goddam fish," he said grimly. "Except that I couldn't see where I was going without my contact lenses, and I couldn't wear them in the water. But I was five-foot-seven and weighed a hundred and twenty-four—which is about what I am now, hadn't you noticed? When I was seventeen I looked like I was twelve. I wore boxer trunks, and I looked like you could pull the pucker string and pinch me in two at the waist. The other guys—most of the other guys—were sleek and muscular and tanned. They'd have on these tight little trunks made of some kind of shiny elastic, and down in the crotches they'd be showing great big heavy bulges that . . ."

"Gib," Melanie whispered. She rolled on her side to kiss him.

He took her kiss, but he kept on talking. "Girls," he said. "The girls at the pool. Golden blondes, sixteen and seventeen, with a litle baby fat on them yet and spilling out of their bikinis in all directions—so beautiful they'd give God an erection, so beautiful you could cry for wanting to touch one of them. And little Gib, sitting on the hot concrete and dangling his feet in the water, would pretend he was indifferent to them, pretend he didn't see them, because he didn't have a chance with one of them."

"Gib, for God's sake, did you think you were inadequate?"

"How the hell was I supposed to find out?"

He didn't think he could tell Leslie all that he'd told Melanie. Leslie was no virgin. (She had made some kind of scornful joke once about her cherry, as she called it, and her high school boy friend—and Gib remembered.) He could never tell Leslie, as he had told Melanie later on, that he had known how to put himself in her because he had read about how to do it, in books. He could not explain to Leslie, now, that all day, all the way across the Atlantic, he had built a hope, admittedly naive and boyish, that she would let him show her how he had suddenly learned, not just to caress and comfort her when she needed him, as he had failed to do only a week ago, but more, to love her better than he had loved Melanie. Leslie was the girl who would laugh at him.

She was laughing now, chuckling quietly while she held his hand against her breast and grinned at him with a cocked chin. He unbuttoned her dress, pulled it open, and slipped it back over her shoulders, exposing both little breasts and hard, wrinkled little nipples. Her skin was dark, not pink like Melanie's.

She looked down at herself. "Big deal," she said.

He tried to pull the dress on down, but she bent her elbows so the sleeves held it.

"Les . . ."

"What's next, lover?" she asked. Her eyes came up to his. "Do you expect me to go to bed with you?"

"Why not, Les?" he asked quietly.

"Just like that? Just like that, Gib?"

"I love you, Leslie."

She tossed her head scornfully. "Bullshit," she said.

CANTON, GEORGIA

"I have *read* some of your articles," Benjamin Slusser said to Gib shortly after they met and sat down in Slusser's law office with drinks he served from a refrigerated bar behind his desk. "I found them *interestin'.*"

"Thank you," Gib said.

"I do not sub*scribe* to your *paper,*" Slusser said. "In all frankness, I do not subscribe to its editorial point of *view.* But some folks sent me clippin's of your articles about th' old *Traver* matter, and I read them with some interest."

Gib was fascinated by Slusser's deliberate, carefully inflected, expressive way of speaking. The man took the time to select his words carefully, to place his emphasis thoughtfully, and to inject minor pauses meaningfully. He spoke with an accent of course, but it was a controlled accent, an accent he had fully analyzed and used consciously.

"I cannot accept your *judgment* of th' Traver *case,*" Slusser went on. "But that's all *right.* That's one reason I'm glad to *talk* to *you.* It has been my experience with newspaper *people* that the more facts you give 'em, the closer they'll come to acceptin', *ultimately,* somethin' closer to your own point of *view.*"

"I try to keep my mind open," Gib said, smiling. "I'm willing to be convinced."

"I couldn't ask for more than that," Slusser said.

For Gib, the problem in meeting Benjamin Slusser was to avoid the facile judgment, the quick categorization. A lawyer in a town like Canton, Georgia, who drawled with a Cherokee County accent, offered you a bourbon and water in his office before noon, and settled down comfortably in his shirtsleeves with his drink and pipe and began to philosophize about winning a journalist to his viewpoint by supplying him with the facts, was altogether too easy to dismiss as a whisky-sloshing cornpone boob—particularly if you were Gilbert Hubbard.

"I do gather, from your articles," Slusser said, "that you don't *believe* Traver was ever guilty, was ever a Communist."

"I'm sorry I give that impression," Gib said.

"Well, maybe I misread you," Slusser said quietly. "But there has been much *said* and *written* to the effect that we *did* the man a gross *injustice.* I want to tell you, my conscience is *clear,* on the *Traver* matter."

"I was in London two weeks ago and spoke to Traver for about an hour," Gib said.

"Were you really? Did he mention me? I suppose he hates me pretty thoroughly."

"No. Who he hates is Warren Bradley."

Slusser nodded and smiled faintly. "Figures," he said.

He took Gib across the street to lunch in what apparently was the only restaurant in town. They sat at a table adjoining the wide plate glass window in the front of the restaurant, and Gib had an hour's view of the town in the rain, while they talked and ate their lunch. This table in the window was apparently where Slusser had his lunch every day. Men going by in pickup trucks honked their horns and waved at him. Two or three pedestrians in an hour, all tapped the glass and grinned.

On the wall of Slusser's office, Gib had noticed, hung an autographed picture of Warren Bradley, taken twenty years ago when Bradley was fat and sleek and had all his hair. Gib remarked on it now in the restaurant, as Slusser lit his pipe with a big wooden kitchen match and broke the match in two before dropping in into the glass ashtray. "Do you ever see him, now that he's President?" Gib asked.

Pursing his lips and sucking on the pipe to start it, Slusser shook his head. "Not often," he said. "I see him *occasionally,* at political meetin's or social functions. 'Course I'm not a Republican."

"Do you go back to Washington often?"

Slusser shook his head again. "No. I'm sort of *out of style,* as you might say, in *Washin'ton.* People up there figger I'm down here whuppin' Niggers and choppin' cotton," he added. He smiled broadly, as if he were not quite sure Gib would understand it was a joke.

"There are some in Washington yet who glory in just that," Gib said, unable to resist the sarcasm.

"Well . . ." Slusser began cautiously, and then apparently he decided to forgo whatever response had first come to his mind. "There's no *call* for me to go back to Washin'ton," he said. "Hasn't been for a long time. You bein' a student of th' Traver *matter,* you know what it did for my *reputation.* That is, in *Washin'ton.* Traver has had a lot of sympathy from some people, but he's not th' *only* one that come out on the short end of the stick."

Slusser paused to invite a comment, but Gib's head was too full of thought for him to be alert. He was trying to put impressions together into some kind of judgment. When Slusser left his desk and rolled down his shirtsleeves to come across the street for lunch, he had put on the jacket of a silk suit, and Gib—who had something of an eye for such things—recognized the suit as having been expertly cut and shaped for Slusser's portly frame by a tailor who knew his business. The accent was disarming. It was meant to be. The eyes in that ruddy, sixty-year-old, fleshy face were bright and active.

"What I *mean* is," Slusser said, "that when the jury was

hung in the first Traver trial, it was *apparent* that some of those jurors simply did not *believe* what *I* testified to."

"About Konstantinov, you mean."

Slusser nodded. "I followed Traver to New York, *just* as I testified. He went to the New York Public *Library,* and he sat down at a table across from Konstantinov. He slid some kind of little package across the table to the Russian, and the Russian picked it up and stuck it in his coat pocket. When Traver swore he never *saw* Konstantinov, didn't *know* 'im, he was lyin' through his teeth. Traver was not just a Communist. He was somethin' *worse.*"

"Why wasn't there another witness to the meeting?" Gib asked.

"Well, that's where I made a *mistake,*" Slusser said. "There *should've* been. That was my mistake. I was just a *young* fellow come up from *Georgia* and workin' for the Un-American Activities Committee, and I suppose I got a little excited, huntin' *Communists* and all." Slusser finished by showing Gib a sly little smile.

Gib smiled back, and both of them laughed.

Their lunches were fried steaks, smothered under thick brown gravy. On each plate there was a dollop of mashed potatoes as big as two fists, with a crater punched in the center with a spoon and filled with more gravy. To the side of each plate there was a bowl of lima beans in butter. Slusser ate all of his, hungrily.

Gib had no need to ask many questions. Slusser seemed glad to talk. But he never quite reached the point in which Gib was most interested, and finally Gib tried giving him a little lead. "I had an interesting conversation not long ago with a daughter of Esther Levine," Gib said.

Slusser was pouring sugar into his coffee—without measuring it in his spoon—and he went on pouring until he was finished and then stirred slowly until he was satisfied the sugar was all dissolved, before he said anything. "Esther

Levine," he said finally. "Tough little woman. Tough, scrawny, *fierce* little woman."

"Her daughter thinks she may have lied."

Slusser shook his head. "No. Other witnesses corroborated everything she said."

"Other members of the cell," Gib suggested.

"Yes. Other members of the Communist *cell* that Traver was a member of."

"That was the key to the whole perjury case, wasn't it?" Gib said. "I mean, finding that cell and getting its members to testify, that was the whole key."

"Yes, I s'pose *so*."

"In all I've read about the case," Gib said, phrasing his question carefully and yet trying to conceal his caution, "I don't think I ever read how you did it. How did you find the cell, and how did you get a fanatic like Esther Levine to agree to testify?"

If Slusser understood this was the question Gib had come to Georgia to ask, he didn't show it. He lowered his eyes modestly and said smoothly, "I take some credit for that." He glanced out the window. "We had informers that helped us. The FBI was workin' on the matter too. But I think I can *say*, with all due modesty, that it was the work *we*—I mean, we the lawyers for the House Un-American Activities Committee—did, that broke the *case*. We were the ones that found the cell and got the members to talk."

"How did you manage that?" Gib asked. "Esther Levine's daughter calls her a pathological extremist. I'd have supposed a fanatic like that would simply refuse to testify."

"She did refuse. All of them refused. What we did was, we subpoenaed them. We issued subpoenas through the Un-American Activities *Committee*. We subpoenaed 'em in, one by one, all the members of that cell. We didn't haul 'em before a public session of the Committee. We just got 'em in the *office*, where we could talk to them in *private* and explain the facts of *life* to them. Some of 'em were pretty scared. Some must have figured that what was happenin' to Erich *Traver* could happen to *them*. Anyway, some agreed to testify against Traver."

"Esther Levine did," Gib said. "But Franklin Levine didn't. Why was that?"

Slusser's face opened in an amused, reminiscent smile. "Franklin Levine," he said, "was a crusty old fellow. He said we could subpoena him all we wanted, and he'd just take the Fifth *Amendment*. So we let him go. His wife was willin' to testify, and that was enough from one family."

"She must have been pretty frightened."

"I figure *so*," Slusser agreed. "I always figured that she and her husband were mixed up with Konstantinov, just like Traver was. I figure that was what she was afraid of: that we had that on her and might prosecute her like we did Traver."

WASHINGTON

"No," said Steve Novatny. "No subpoenas. As soon as I got your call from Atlanta, I sent two boys over to the House to use the Senator's name and get a quick look at the records of the Un-American Activities Committee. It was a long, hard, dusty job, but the boys came back and said they were sure about it: no subpoenas were ever issued by the Committee for Franklin or Esther Levine."

"Well," said Gib grimly. "Slusser lied to me."

"Hard words, ol' buddy," said Novatny. "Come on here. Gimme that wet coat. Sit down and be sociable. You're sure you had your dinner? What do you drink? Scotch? Have you met Pamela? Pamela Pitt, meet Gilbert Hubbard. Talk to him while I fix him a drink."

Pamela Pitt, a poised and smooth young blonde, dressed in blue, was sitting on Novatny's couch, staring at Gib with cool, unembarrassed curiosity. She had a drink in one hand, a cigarette in the other. "I've visited Georgia," she said. "Utterly ghastly place." She had an English accent.

"Pam's with the British Embassy," Novatny called from the kitchen. "Tell her how much you love London." Clattering at his work in the kitchen, he went on talking, either to himself or under the impression they could understand him in the living room. He'd had too much to drink, and he was mixing himself some more.

"You were in Georgia two days?" Pamela Pitt asked Gib, conversationally.

"A day and a half, actually. I flew down there yesterday morning and back this afternoon. If my plane had been on time, I would have been to Steve's office this afternoon and wouldn't have had to spoil your evening."

She showed him a faint, shallowly polite smile, one that told him she hadn't any patience with his apologetic manner. "You're not spoiling anything at all," she said with emphasis. "Steve has been talking about you, and I've been interested in meeting you. So you spent a day with Benjamin Slusser, did you?"

"Half a day," Gib said, wondering how much Novatny had told her.

"I think the absence of those subpoenas is intriguing," she said. Apparently Novatny had told her everything. "If that makes Benjamin Slusser a liar, things begin to fit together for you, don't they?"

Gib nodded. "They begin to, yes."

Uneasy, wishing Novatny would return from the kitchen, Gib went to the window and looked out at the rain. From this window of Novatny's apartment in Harbour Square, he could see the lighted dome of the Capitol a mile or so away.

"Your Erich Traver was something of a public figure in England for a time," said Pamela Pitt. "I'd judge he's lapsed into obscurity now. Mousy little man, as I recall."

Gib nodded, and anxious to turn the conversation away from the Traver matter until Novatny came back, he said, "Handsome apartment Steve has, don't you think?"

She stared at him for a moment, obviously conscious that he wanted to change the conversation. She let him do it. She glanced around the room. "It was done by a decorator," she said without approval or enthusiasm.

Gib smiled. Yes, the apartment had been done by a decorator. You could see that. And somehow it said divorce. It was the home of a man who'd lost a home and had a new one put together for him, suddenly and impersonally.

Novatny returned at last, bringing Gib's drink, and Gib could tell from the color that Novatny had put in much Scotch and little soda.

"Look, we can have some dinner delivered," Novatny said.

"No, I ate on the plane," Gib said, which was a lie. "Besides, I can't stay long."

Novatny settled down heavily beside Pamela Pitt and put his arm across the back of the couch behind her. He did not touch her, but his posture suggested a long-standing casual intimacy. He was a big, handsome man, with self-confidence so total it was the source of his generosity.

"Staying in Washington tonight?" Novatny asked.

"No," Gib said. "I have a flight on to New York tonight. I left my bag in a locker in the airport. I want to be in New York tomorrow. I have things to do."

Novatny grinned, and it made Gib wonder if he had sounded self-important. "You move around," Novatny said. "One day in Washington, you see the Senator. One day in Georgia, you see Slusser. Did you move that fast through London and Amsterdam?"

"No. I took it a little easier in Europe."

Novatny stared thoughtfully down into his glass. He had a communicative face. He was an Eastern European of some kind of course, and his hair and complexion were dark. But he had pale blue eyes. His face was muscular and square, with a heavy jaw and a cleft chin. "So anyway, you talked to Slusser," he said.

Gib tasted his drink, which was too strong, as he had suspected. "Yes. Slusser was an easy enough fellow to get along with. When I called him the other day, he even told me what flight to take to Atlanta so I could rent a car and drive up to Canton by lunchtime. He was perfectly willing to talk to me."

"And to lie to you, you figure."

"Well, I suppose you could say he has a bad memory," Gib said cautiously. "But it fits with what Carole Levine told Melanie. Put Carole's story together with Slusser's lie or bad memory, and it makes a suggestive combination."

"Yeah, it looks like there's something to it," Novatny admitted. The liquor slurred Novatny's words faintly, but his logic seemed undiminished and his thought seemed intense. "If Slusser lied to you about how he got Esther Levine to testify, then maybe what Carole Levine says is true."

"It's just enough to keep me going," Gib said. "It's just enough to keep the investigation alive."

Pamela Pitt crushed her cigarette in an ashtray and looked up intently into Gib's face as she blew away the last of her smoke. "It's difficult for me," she said, "to think of Slusser telling such a *transparent* lie. He must have known you could check the records."

"I can think of two answers to that," Gib said. "One is that he was faced with a choice between lying or refusing to answer, so he lied and trusted I would not check the records. The other possibility is that he did not take me too seriously."

Novatny chuckled. "I got a feelin'," he said with a cocked chin, looking Gib up and down, "that he didn't take li'l Gib too seriously—and therein he made a big mistake."

Pamela Pitt had emptied her glass, and she rose and went to the kitchen. Gib watched her walk to the kitchen door, appraising her legs and hips so conspicuously that Novatny grinned. Gib checked himself and asked soberly, "Have you told the Senator?"

Novatny covered his mouth with his hand. He shook his head. "You don't have to report to Alan Jordan with everything you find out."

"I suppose not," Gib said. "But I also suppose it's to my advantage to have his help."

Novatny dropped his hand and lifted his sagging shoulders. "Do you trust him?" he asked.

Conscious that his retreat into thought was likely obvious, Gib took up his drink and sipped whisky. "Shouldn't I?" was all he could think of to say at the moment.

Novatny nodded, and his faint smile returned. "Sure. If you know what you're doing."

"That, uh . . . That implies that in your judgment I don't."

"That's what I'm trying to find out," Novatny said in a strong voice. He stopped for a moment and blew a breath, which puffed out his cheeks. "Alan Jordan is interested in you. He's interested in what you're doing. Not just a little bit, either. He's very interested. But you got to remember," Novatny said, emphasizing with a pointed finger, "he's not interested for *your* motives. He's interested for his own reasons."

"Which are?"

"I'm going to tell you something," Novatny said, ignoring Gib's question. "You probably detest Warren Bradley. To you he's a crude political hack, the apotheosis of the ward heeler, a living demonstration of democracy in action, showing how high a man can get without ability or principle. And Alan Jordan? Ah, the Senator is a handsome, articulate liberal, the idealist in politics. Right? Well, just remember this, Gib: Your friend Alan Jordan is a political creature, just like Warren Bradley. The similarities between them are deeper than the differences. The Senator hates the President. I mean, he personally hates him. And the President hates back. This is a long-standing personal antagonism. The Senator always has his eye out for a knife he can stick in Bradley. Right now he suspects you may have a good sharp one."

Gib kept his glass up and kept taking small swallows of the strong, dominating Scotch—because there was no way to answer talk like this, no way. The best you could do when you were getting hard advice like this was keep quiet and nod.

"Warren Bradley is President, Gib, and Alan Jordan wants to be. Someday, if he doesn't stub his toe, he probably will be," Novatny went on. "And for a man to be President or realistically want to be, he has to be a son of a bitch, a real son of a bitch. Any man who'll make the sacrifices you have to make to get to be President of the United States has to be a hard-nosed, hard-driving son of a bitch. And behind his public smile, that's what Alan Jordan is."

Given a chance to interject a word, Gib nodded and said quietly, "I can't help but think he has the right instincts—for the future of this country, I mean."

"If I didn't think so, I wouldn't be working for him," Novatny said emphatically. "But I'm telling you to be realistic. I don't know exactly what your motives are in wanting to dig up somethin' stinkin' in the old Traver case, but you had better understand what the Senator's motives are."

Gib nodded, and again he lowered his eyes from Novatny's affirmative, thrust-forward face.

He had thought of himself as a realist, about politics in general and about Senator Jordan in particular, though he did admire him and had worked on his pre-convention campaign when it had seemed the Senator might win the Democratic nomination. He had met the Senator three times and had come away from each meeting telling himself he was realist enough not to be cynical about the sun-lamp tan, the dramatic comb and cut of the prematurely white hair, the flawless tailoring, the die-cut smile, the quick, hearty laugh, the stance, the pose, or any of it. Gib acknowledged the necessities of politics, even when they were enough to embarrass him a little. The man was running for President, as Novatny said.

But Gib had been a bit surprised when they met in the Senator's office two days ago. The Senator off stage was a little more jowelly, a little better-fed, a little looser and slacker than what you expected. And, what was more, he was not the tightly-wound, forcefully outcoming personality he was when you saw him speaking or met him for a moment at a public meeting. He was distracted, inattentive, shallow —in the office. There was a phrase for what he was: *spread too thin*. You saw in a moment how his time and attention were elaborately rationed, and rationed thin. You knew he was a busy man and could not give you much time, but even in the little time he had for you, while you were talking, you could sense his mind racing ahead of you, looking for the point where he could interrupt and say, Okay, what can I do for you? Gib came away from the meeting with more encouragement and help than he had expected, but with a disquieting sense that the Senator had not really listened to him and had agreed with him too easily.

Novatny was sitting there watching Gib think—and probably congratulating himself on inspiring him to do it. "What's next?" he asked.

"I'm going back to New York and try to see Esther Levine. She's been out of town on a speaking tour for the John Birch Society, but she's supposed to be back tomorrow."

"You're a newspaper fella," Novatny said. "When you gonna write somethin' about all this?"

"Not until I have to," Gib said. "But *The Spark* isn't going to keep me on the payroll forever."

Novatny's chin rose, and he frowned speculatively. "The Senator told me to give you all the help you ask for, within reason. I don't think he meant money."

"I'm not asking for any money."

"Could be you might get some later. If you run dry, don't give up the story without coming around and asking here."

"I hope I won't need it."

Novatny nodded. "You sure you have to be back in New York in the morning?"

Not to see Esther Levine, he didn't. She would not be back in New York until Monday. He was hurrying home to be with Leslie.

He caught a cab finally, but the wind-driven rain beat so hard on the windshield that it overcame the wipers; and the driver, a taciturn black man, crept through the streets at only a few miles per hour, sitting bolt upright with his nose almost to the glass and straining to see. Gib in the back hunched moodily in his damp coat and glanced back and forth between the streets and his watch, glumly wondering if he would make the plane on time, or if the plane would take off anywhere near on schedule. Leslie would be waiting.

By now she would be at his apartment. He'd asked her to be there when he came home, even though it would be very late, and she had said she'd wait for him, no matter how late. She would be there by now. She worked until seven. Then some evenings—he was not sure if this was one of them—on her way to the shabby rooms she still shared with the girls from her defunct theater group, she stopped at the flat occupied by a charcoal and pastel artist and spent two or three hours posing for him. For two dollars an hour she had posed as a gypsy girl, a Dutch girl, a Hula girl, or whatever he wanted, in costumes he borrowed all around the Village, and he taped the sketches to the windows of his flat and sold them to tourists. Sometimes it was nine or ten before she was free.

Gib did not like the way Leslie was making her living. He didn't like to see her hustling dishes in a steak house, in a uniform he thought was degrading. But Leslie didn't care. She did not mind being a waitress for a while, and with the few extra dollars she made posing for the sketches, she made enough to be independent of her family. That was what was important to her. She'd find something better to do with her life, she said, and the few dollars a week she made from her jobs gave her the time and freedom to think about it. She was in no hurry. It was too important to hurry.

(Gib had met her father, who had come to the steak house one day to talk to Leslie about coming home and going to college. He was a great, patriarchcal, eighty-year-old man, brittle with age but still carrying his broad shoulders, long arms, and huge hands the way he had carried them when they were young and strong. He spoke with archaic courtly manners and with assured authority.)

Since Gib's return from Europe, he had spent a lot of time with Leslie. She did not cook for him as she had done before, but she came to the apartment almost every evening. They acted like lovers. Having spent months together before without ever touching each other, now they touched and kissed so often that if much time went by without an affectionate touch, one of them would be alerted and would begin to search the other's face, as if wondering if something were wrong.

Even so, an uneasy, self-conscious restraint existed as a barrier between them. Since the night when he tried to tell her he loved her but did it so clumsily he won only her skeptical derision, this barrier had been raised; and he had never yet been able to explain that he meant the word love in the sense he had learned from Melanie. He'd kept the explanation rehearsed and ready, but the right moment to offer it had not come. Part of the trouble was that they found new difficulty in expressing themselves to each other. They had an old habit of bantering cynicism. It was a hard habit to break, and he suspected she too had things she wanted to say and was blocked from saying them.

"I got to tell you something, really gotta tell you something," she had said to him one night, breaking into a chuckle she had tried to restrain. She had tossed her T-shirt on the table a few minutes before, to bare her breasts and let him pet them; and while he petted her, she had watched him with critical curiosity. She could not keep her words contained, so she began to chuckle, and she said, "When I first started coming here to cook for you, I had the impression you were a fag."

Gib had looked up at her face. A small smile had crossed his face, and a frown had followed very closely. "You're not the first one to make that mistake," he had said.

"Well. What was I supposed to think? You never made a move at me. You didn't have any other girl, and you didn't want me. I *am* female, as you've now discovered."

"It's something someone could assume, I suppose," he had said. "I didn't have a girl. . . ."

"You do now," she had said, and remembering it in the taxi in the Washington rain, he wished she had stopped there. But she couldn't. The old habit was too strong, and she had grinned then, glanced down at her small bare breasts, and said, "Not much of a girl, but a girl anyway—enough to save your reputation."

She had twisted away from him then and gone to sit on his old round low table, just out of his reach. She had sat there, hunched forward, with her hands clasped between her legs, looking back at him with a solemnity that he imagined was more than a little regretful, as if she knew she'd killed another good moment with just a few words too many.

He remembered how she'd sat there on that table. She

sat that way often, in the same posture, usually watching him read or write, often with a mischievous grin. It was another image he carried of her, a part of his increased consciousness of her and increased appreciation. Leslie thought she was not pretty, and she didn't try to be. But she was anyway. The artist she modelled for—if the man could be dignified with the name of artist—said she had a strong, interesting face. He was right. It was a natural face, unspoiled by fashion. She wore no makeup. Her unplucked eyebrows were thick, and they accented her deep brown eyes. Her nose was small, but it arched a little and did not turn up at the end—a Jewish nose, she said. Her teeth pushed her lips forward, so that when she talked her mouth was always expressively in motion, with her lips curling around her words. The structure lines of her face were clean and strong, unobscured by flesh. The sketch artist was right: it was a good face.

"You really want in my pants, don't you?" she'd said to him the night before he flew to Washington.

His eyes and mouth had hardened and then just as quickly softened again, and he sighed and nodded. "Okay, I do. Sure. Why not?"

"Why not? Why *yes?* Why should we?"

"Maybe because we mean a lot to each other," he had said. "How would that do for a reason?"

Leslie had smiled, and unless he was excessively optimistic, it was the most ingenuous, unguarded smile he'd seen from her since he came home from Amsterdam. Then she had sobered. "You going to tell me you love me again?"

"Yes. Because I *do,* Leslie. Maybe it isn't a great, flaming romance, but I do think a lot of you. That's what I was trying to tell you before. That's what I *meant* when I said I loved you."

She had frowned hard at him. "Oh? Well. Okay. I feel

something like that about you too, Gib. Something like that. Something kind of nice."

So tonight, if this damned rain let him reach the airport on time and if the plane took off at any hour reasonably close to schedule and if nothing else happened to foul him up, he was going home to sleep with Leslie. That was why she was waiting in his apartment.

"Okay," she had said. "If that's the way things are with us, then the game's over. There's no game to play any more. It wasn't much of a game anyway, to tell you the truth. I was guarding first base and wouldn't let you near it, but there've been lots of home runs. I'm no virgin."

"Neither am I."

"Tomorrow night, Gib," she said intently, gripping his arm.

"My God, Les! Tomorrow I'm flying to Washington."

"Then when you get back. Saturday night. I promise."

GREENWICH VILLAGE

On the Wednesday morning ten days following his return from Washington and Georgia, Gib was an hour and a half later than usual in coming in to *The Spark* office. His parents had driven down from Albany on Sunday. They had stayed in a hotel uptown and did not leave for Albany again until Wednesday morning. He had gone up to have breakfast with them before they left, and that was why he was late reaching the office.

On Sunday evening they had given him his first occasion to see Leslie in a skirt—other than the pale green uniform he detested. They had suggested rather firmly that he bring her to dinner. (He had mentioned her name perhaps once too often to them, and now whenever they called they asked about her.) So, when he went to her flat to get her to take her uptown, he saw her in a yellow dress—one with a full skirt almost to her knees, a yellow lace bodice, short sleeves, a belt at the waist. She had done nothing to her hair but brush it, but it framed her face, lying a little closer to one eye than it did to the other and hiding part of her cheek. She wore no makeup, but she had a tiny gold chain around her neck, and something hung down inside her bodice. He was proud of her, and he told her so. She spoke quietly with his parents, keeping a little smile they took for polite but which told him she was not saying anything she thought. They were very favorably impressed with her and told him so later. The evening was much easier than anyone expected.

But it was about ten-thirty when he reached *The Spark* Building—what they now called *The Spark* Building, a four-story red brick that had contained a block of eight apartments in years past. Even on this frigid morning there were loungers on the front steps, a couple of young men and a girl bundled in heavy coats and scarfs and wrapped in heavy blankets. Gib slipped around them and went inside.

Just inside the door he stopped to unwind the bright green muffler from around his neck and to unbutton his overcoat. This took a moment, and while he stood there he felt the familiar rumble of the press running in the cellar. That old press had once printed *The Spark*. It now printed only a little Village weekly called *The Clapper*. *The Spark* had built too much circulation to be printed in the cellar here, and now it was printed and distributed from a hard-driven modern printing plant uptown.

Gib started up the stairway where *The Spark* displayed its past glories. Famous editions from the paper's stormy ten-year history were mounted behind sheets of glass on the wall. (Gib's favorite was the edition printed on the day when the United States launched the first team of astronauts toward the moon. The paper had long protested that the space program was using money desperately needed for more urgent human needs, and on that day it published a composite photograph it had prepared for the occasion. The picture was of an Uncle Sam, lying on his back, with his head turned toward the camera to show a moronic grin. With one hand he pointed proudly toward his crotch, where a Saturn rocket rose out of his pants like a huge, erect, black and white phallus.)

On the second floor of the building all the walls had years ago been painted a drab butterscotch color which Gib complained made him sick. He made his office in a corner of what had been the dining room of one of the second-floor apartments, and he had turned the walls of his corner into a cluttered bulletin board and a gallery of posters and prints he had picked up in Village shops—including recently a charcoal sketch of Leslie dressed as an apache dancer.

His desk was an old white-enamel kitchen table, and during the night someone had sat there to eat a snack. Before Gib took off his coat he swept an empty milk carton and a sandwich wrapper off the table and into the long-sealed-off little gas-grate fireplace in the corner. It was his trash receptacle. He took off his overcoat and tossed it on top of a stack of cardboard boxes that contained his files. He sat down in a shiny aluminum and vinyl swivel chair.

He had duties other than investigating the Traver case, and when he left the day before he had been working on one of a series of articles he was writing on the disappearance of heroes from American popular culture. (He had dismissed the astronauts as "brave and competent, but uniformly bland, well-scrubbed, and inarticulate.") He was reading what he had written the day before, when Frank Kennedy, editor-in-chief of *The Spark*, came in to see him.

"Anything good?" Kennedy asked. He sat on the edge of the table.

"Heroes," said Gib, without much enthusiasm.

Balanced casually with one leg on the table and the other foot on the floor, Kennedy pinched some of his rich, coal-black beard between a thumb and finger; and his soft, gray, introspective eyes seemed to study his wrinkled khaki pants, as if he were absorbed with interest in them, while his lips remained parted, moving almost imperceptibly as he prepared what he wanted to say. He was one of the founders of *The Spark*, and he owned it, with his partners, but he was self-effacing and quiet.

"You look so casual and unconcerned," he said to Gib, "that I have to assume no one has shown you the Blair McKinney column this morning."

Gib shook his head. "I just got here. My family was in town and . . ."

Kennedy, looking around, had spotted a girl, and he called to her. "Rita, will you bring the Blair McKinney clipping off my desk?" Looking again to Gib, he asked, "How many people do you suppose know the details of what you've been doing about the Traver business?"

"Do you think McKinney knows too much?" Gib asked.

"It's not just that you have a little unfriendly publicity this morning," Kennedy said. "The way the column reads, I can't help thinking that whoever wrote it knows more than he could learn without a fink."

Frowning tightly, Gib considered for a moment. "Since the column comes out of Washington," he said, "the first person who comes to mind is Steve Novatny. He knows all the details. He's called me twice since I was in Washington. I don't know how much he's told Senator Jordan. I don't know how much he's told his girl friend Pamela Pitt either, but I'm afraid he tells her everything." And Gib stopped abruptly, deciding not to mention what had just occurred to him: that he himself had told everything to Leslie.

"You'll have to read the column before you can make any judgment," said Kennedy.

"Blair McKinney," Gib said speculatively. "Syndicated in how many papers? Fifty-five?"

Kennedy shrugged. "Something like that. Did Novatny call you here or at home?"

The girl had returned with the clipping, and as Gib took it he said, "He called me once here, once at home. Why?"

"Read the clipping. Your part is about two-thirds of the way down."

Gib scanned the clipping until he came to his name.

> "The Spark," radical Greenwich Village newspaper, and Senator Alan Jordan, defeated Democrat vice-presidential candidate, have apparently formed an alliance for the latest attempt to re-open the old Erich Traver espionage and perjury case. Gilbert Hubbard, a shaggy-haired and be-mustachioed cub reporter for the far-left paper, has been in and out of Washington lately, confabbing with Senator Jordan and his staff assistant Steve Novatny. The Senator has already assigned staff members to dig up records for Hubbard and has offered him more help if he needs it.

When Gib's eyes rose from the clipping after reading the paragraph twice, Kennedy reached for it and read it again himself; and while he was reading he said, "It doesn't say much. Yet it says a good deal. It says enough to tell you that McKinney has some information he shouldn't have."

"He could have guessed at most of it," Gib said.

"At some of it, not most of it," Kennedy said.

"Well, it's hard to believe Novatny would have told him anything," Gib said. "And I can't really believe Novatny is stupid enough to be involved with a girl who would tell a political columnist what she heard from him, either."

Kennedy, probably wearying of balancing on the edge of Gib's table, slipped off and stood against the wall beside the fireplace. "You're not known in Washington," he said. "No one just happened to notice that you were in and out of

Jordan's office. Either someone was specifically watching for you, or someone was told about you—more likely the latter."

"I suppose Slusser could have called McKinney. Or Esther Levine, even," Gib suggested.

"Possibly. But neither of them knew you had been to see Senator Jordan."

"No. Neither one knew that."

"What you were doing was no secret," Kennedy said. "But now it's notorious. That makes the job more difficult."

"Yes," Gib said. "I don't think Esther Levine would have seen me last week if she had read anything like this first."

Kennedy frowned suddenly and rubbed his bearded chin. "Did you say Novatny called you at home?"

"He called me once here at the office, once at home."

"Gib, are you sure your telephone is clean?"

"For God's sake, Frank!"

"Don't be naive," Kennedy said quickly. "We've found bugs in this building eight times. We've found them twice in my apartment. There's a company called Bug Killers, Incorporated, that I have on contract to check this building at least once a month. They check my apartment, too. Let me send them around to yours."

Gib agreed to let Bug Killers, Incorporated search his apartment. He was reluctant, but he agreed.

Then he and Kennedy discussed the prospects for publishing any account of the Traver investigation. Out of Gib's trip to Europe and his interviews in Washington, Georgia, and New York, *The Spark* had gotten only an article describing his visit with Erich Traver—a where-is-he-now essay, telling how Traver now lived and looked and what he was doing. So far, Gib had written nothing about Melanie Traver or Benjamin Slusser or Carole or Esther Levine. Kennedy was anxious to have something, but he agreed, toward the end of the discussion, that in spite of the McKinney paragraph this morning, it would be unwise to publish anything more about Traver for the time being. Kennedy was convinced that Carole Levine had told the truth. He saw how the lies and evasions of Benjamin Slusser and Esther Levine strengthened the girl's story. But still, he conceded to Gib, the information was not what they called hard enough to publish. It still only offered Carole's word against the word of too many others.

Kennedy did not ask Gib where he went from there, or if the investigation had now run into a corner. He didn't have to.

When he left the office it was already dark, in the dead of February. There was no snow, and the cold streets were black. He was in a mood to match the gloom of the streets through which he walked. The Traver business was now in the open—he had had calls about it all day—but it still didn't amount to anything. He might wind up looking like a fool. Half his hero articles had been published, and now, having read them all over again this afternoon, he was dissatisfied with them. They sounded juvenile to him. The expected vacancy in the subscription department still had not materialized, so Leslie was still at the restaurant. She was waiting tables right now, and he had to go there and eat and wait for her. She could not type, so if she did come to work for *The Spark*, it would be as an errand girl, and he wasn't sure he liked that. He could not keep putting off a letter he had to write to Melanie, telling her he saw no prospect now for his return to Amsterdam. She was weaning Ginny and was full of plans for him, but he saw no way to get back to her. In fact, right now he could not think of a single thing that was going right.

His routine was to stop at the apartment and look at his mail before he went to the restaurant. When he was at his door, taking out his key, a man came into the hallway from the street and came up to him.

"Are you Gilbert Hubbard?"

He looked up at the man. He saw a black and gray tweed overcoat which could have had two hundred fifty pounds of man in it. A black hat. A thick face, with a pink, shiny complexion, as if the man had been standing in the cold outside for a long time. Gib saw a hand coming toward him, showing him a black leather case, open to display a badge. Police.

"Are you Gilbert Hubbard?" the man asked again, a little louder, a little impatient.

Gib nodded. "Yes." He was chilled, rigid.

"I have here a warrant," the man said. He took a paper out of his coat and handed it over. "I'm Sergeant McAllister."

"Am I under arrest?"

"It's a search warrant."

Gib looked dully at the paper. He unfolded it, but as he looked at it he did not read it. The street door opened, and more men came in—two men in uniform and two more detectives.

"You going to let us in?" Sergeant McAllister asked.

Gib still had the key in his hand. He opened the door.

From that point they took over. McAllister pushed in ahead of him and began to switch on lights. Another detective went in, and the uniformed men came up behind Gib. They did not push him inside, but he had no choice but to go in.

"Would you sit down, please, Mr. Hubbard? I'd like to talk to you."

This was not McAllister talking. McAllister had already disappeared inside the bedroom. This man was not quite so big. He was a dark-haired man with a thin face. He wore his hat at a jaunty angle. He sat down on the couch and looked up expectantly at Gib, waiting for him to sit down too. Gib sat.

"Mr. Hubbard, I am Lieutenant Schuster. Our warrant

authorizes us to search your premises and your person. Will you cooperate with us?"

Thinking about it later, Gib decided what had been wrong with the man's speech: something that had impressed him at the time without his being able to name it. The man had been reciting a formula, words prepared in advance, which did not come naturally to him.

While Lieutenant Schuster asked for cooperation, the rest of them were searching the apartment, without cooperation. Gib still had the warrant in his hand. He stared at it.

"Will you cooperate, Mr. Hubbard?"

The insistent voice came out of a perfectly ordinary face. It had nothing ominous about it. If it was a little too solemn, that was only because the man was doing a job and was holding himself in the rigid posture he supposed the job required.

"Mr. Hubbard?"

"What are you looking for?"

"Narcotics. Marijuana. It says on your warrant."

Maybe he should have been relieved. They were not going to find any marijuana. They had come at the wrong time. Twice since he came back from Europe he and Leslie had shared a couple of joints, that she brought from somewhere. And one night a couple of months before, he'd had a party and had gotten very worried about the pot that was smoked. Everyone in the building must have smelled it. But they were not going to find any now. And thinking back, after it was over, he realized it was not what they might find that had made him afraid; it had been that they were going to search at all. No, not even that they were *going* to search. That they *could* search.

"You won't find any," he had said to the detective.

"I hope not, Mr. Hubbard," the man had said, and he had seemed sincere about it.

"I want to make a phone call."

"After we've searched you, Mr. Hubbard. Are you going to cooperate? Will you stand up and take off your overcoat?"

He stood up and took off his overcoat and muffler. McAllister, the one with the thick pink face, was there to receive them from him and to hand them to one of the uniformed men, who began to go through the pockets and to feel the lining.

"Now, Mr. Hubbard, turn your pockets out and put the contents on the table."

His hands trembled. They could tell how afraid he was.

"If you'll pull off your sweater now . . ."

The search of the apartment had stopped. They were standing around watching. If they were really looking for marijuana—and he never for a moment really thought they were—he wondered if they would search Leslie's flat too. If they did, they might find something.

"And your pants, Mr. Hubbard. Only for a minute or two."

He opened his pants and let them down. He kicked off his shoes so he could step out of the pants. All of them were watching.

"I'm sorry about this, Mr. Hubbard, but some of you fellows have learned to hide your stuff where an ordinary search doesn't get it. Now, if you'll just put your hands up behind your head, we'll be done in a minute."

McAllister handed the pants to the man who had searched the overcoat. Gib swore later—to himself only; he didn't tell anyone they had stripped him—that McAllister hid a smirk from the lieutenant as he viewed the thin white legs, the narrow hips and shoulders, and maybe the pained, frightened face as Gib clasped his hands behind his head as he had been told and stood there in his undershirt and briefs and socks.

Maybe the lieutenant did see it, because he said, "All right, McAllister."

McAllister stepped behind Gib. He seized Gib's undershirt and pulled it up under his armpits. Then he pulled it down again. He stuck his thumbs in the waistband of the briefs and pulled them down to Gib's knees. Only for a moment. Then he hauled them roughly back up again.

"All right, Mr. Hubbard, if you'll sit down now, over there, on that chair, and take off your socks, we'll have a look at those, and then you can have your clothes back."

He sat on that chair for most of an hour and watched them search his apartment. They went through the drawers in his bedroom and through the clothes in his closet. They took the bed apart and made it again. They went through all the drawers and cabinets in the kitchen. They turned his couch and chairs upside down to examine the structure and upholstery and springs. They took every book out of his shelves. They took the back off his television set and probed around inside. They dismantled his telephone. They pulled up the carpet. They looked inside the toilet tank. They took the globes off light fixtures. They unscrewed the gratings off the heating ducts and ran their arms back into the ducts, getting dusty sleeves for their pains. They took the plates off light switches. They tried to pry up floor boards.

When he got his clothes on and could think a little, Gib asked again to make his phone call. They let him call Frank Kennedy. But not until they were finished and left did they allow Kennedy and the lawyer he brought, and Leslie, inside the apartment.

Kennedy, when finally he got in, was angry and talkative. He was sure the search had been a threat to Gib and to *The Spark,* warning them to drop the Traver investigation. He admitted the New York police may have acted in good faith, on a warrant obtained after a tip from an informer they had no reason to suspect—maybe even a federal narcotics agent. In fact, the third detective, the one who never identified himself to Gib, might well have been a federal man. He might have been there on direct orders from someone in

Washington who anticipated being severely damaged by what Gib was learning about the Traver case. It could be proof that the investigation was coming close to something. Couldn't the lawyer file some kind of lawsuit to compel the police to identify their informant and each man who took part in the raid? Was a suit for damages possible? What should they do?

When Kennedy ran down, the lawyer only shook his head and smiled. If they took his advice, they'd forget it. The law does not offer a remedy for every injustice, he said.

Kennedy was subdued after that, and maybe a little embarrassed. He suggested that Gib write a full account of what had happened, and with a small, self-effacing smile he said the account had better be limited to the facts, without the kind of speculations he had himself just been making.

Gib hoped that by morning Kennedy would have given up that idea too. For himself, he wanted to be left alone, or at least left with Leslie. He was so upset he was sick.

When all of them were gone and he was alone with Leslie, Gib sat hunched on his couch and trembled. He sweated and shook—from rage and receding fear, from impotence and shame. Leslie, confused and anxious to show him sympathy, tried to get him to eat, and when she saw he couldn't, she knelt before him and held his hands and cried. She was still wearing her uniform, including the starched green cap, and he put his head down against hers, and he cried too.

He was shaken with impotent fury—not just toward the police for what they had done to him, but with himself for the shameful, paralyzing fear that had made him dull and dumb before them, a humble, obedient participant in his own humiliation. He'd learned something: that what you knew of your rights and what you knew of the limitations of police authority were not nearly as vivid a knowledge as what you knew of things they could do to you before your rights did you any good. They exerted force with smooth trained confidence, and in the face of that he was a coward. They had done what they wanted, and there was nothing he could do about it. What was maybe worse, they had come with a warrant and had, apparently, a right to do what they did. He could shake with rage, but it was all over, and there was nothing he could do about it.

The next afternoon Kennedy sent him home to let Bug Killers, Incorporated in to search the apartment. They brought a load of electronic equipment and set up a sweep of his rooms, while he sat disconsolate on the same chair where he had sat the night before. They had to keep quiet while the search went on. If there were a bug, it was better for it not to pick up a conversation that would tell the listeners that Bug Killers were at work.

The two men from Bug Killers were much like the policemen. They were courteous. They were skilled and thorough. They made their work a crisp, silent drama. It was another piece of role-playing, of a kind with which Gib was in a mood to be impatient.

And they had bad news for him. When they turned the couch over, they found a small lucite box taped up inside the springs. The tall, thin, blond young man with rosebud lips, the one who headed the team, showed it to Gib. He put his fingers to his lips to silence a question Gib was about to ask. The thing was still alive and functioning. He carefully pried the box open with a screwdriver and killed it by lifting out the battery.

"What I'd suggest, Mr. Hubbard," he said, "is that you keep the thing. Put it back inside the couch. Let whoever is listening hear all your ordinary conversation, and kill it when you want to talk about something confidential. The chance to feed through some false information may come along. You can foul 'em up good."

They found another one inside the telephone. It was another little lucite box full of tiny, brightly colored components, a pretty thing in its way. Probably made specifically to fit inside the standard telephone instrument, it was tucked under the dial, where there was just enough space for it to fit—almost as if the telephone company had accommodated possible buggers by leaving just enough room for the bug.

"It doesn't touch the wires, you see," the man explained to Gib. "It picks up both ends of the conversation by induction and transmits on an FM frequency to a receiver somewhere not far away, probably in another apartment in this building or in one somewhere on this block. It scrambles it, so if someone picks it up by chance, it won't sound like anything. The receiver is probably attached to a recorder, and the recorder only runs when a voice is coming through. The one out of the couch is the same, except that it has a little microphone in it. Someone is real interested in you, Mr. Hubbard. These two babies are worth about seven hundred dollars apiece. The receivers are worth as much. There's maybe three thousand dollars worth of equipment listening to you."

Gib lost track of what the man was saying, struck by a thought that angered him. "The police were in this apartment with a search warrant last night," he said. "They were inside the phone and up under the couch."

"You think they planted 'em?"

"Well?"

The young man shook his head. "Not likely. It's possible, of course. They've been known to use search warrants as their excuse to get in a place so they can plant bugs, particularly unauthorized bugs, the ones they plant without the proper court order. But this isn't the kind of equipment the police use, not in my experience anyway."

"Well, if they didn't plant them, at least they couldn't have missed seeing them," Gib said grimly.

"I see what you've got in mind. Unless these are put in by

court order, they're illegal. 'Course, when you find them, you have no way of knowing who planted them. Like, we don't know who planted this pair. So, I suppose, when the police find bugs, they just leave them where they are. Maybe other cops planted them. Maybe FBI. How do they know?"

When the men from Bug Killers were gone, Gib took the ingenious, expensive little transmitters to the kitchen. He put their batteries in and activated them. Then he laid them on the counter by the sink, took a hammer from the drawer, and pounded them until there was nothing left but wires and crumbs of plastic.

NEW YORK

"Is it Mr. Hubbard?"

The tall but stooped, broad-shouldered but wasted old man had appeared almost instantly from somewhere back in the darkness of the bar. He had to have been very alert and quick to come out of one of the booths and approach Gib as soon as he saw him push through the curtains of the entrance and stand questioningly just inside.

Gib nodded, and the old man extended his hand and said, "Mr. Hubbard, I am Franklin Levine."

Carole's father. Esther Levine's husband. He had called the office that morning.

Still holding the hand he had seized to shake, Franklin Levine turned Gib and led him back toward his booth, leading him so fast that Gib hardly had time to survey the place before he was guided inside the booth and his view was restricted.

The bar was on Seventh Avenue. He had paid a cover charge to get in. But the music was quiet, and there seemed to be no entertainment.

"I know I am inconveniencing you," the old man said. He

took up a cigarette which he had left burning on the edge of the ashtray. There were four or five butts there. Perhaps he had been waiting a while.

"No, it's all right," Gib said.

Levine nodded. "After reading of your experience with the electronic surveillance of your apartment," he said, "I find myself very enlightened. I searched my own apartment thoroughly on Tuesday, as soon as I read what you wrote."

"You are confident of *this* place, I take it, Mr. Levine," Gib said.

The old man, reading Gib's ironic tone correctly, smiled fleetingly, pursed his long white lips to subdue the smile, and nodded. On the telephone he had insisted that they meet here. He had said they had to go somewhere that would not be bugged and where they could not be expected. It looked suspiciously to Gib as if Levine were not entirely unexpected in this particular bar.

"You know my daughter, Mr. Hubbard," said Levine. He had before him on the table an empty shot glass and a half empty glass of water. His eyes fell, and he closed a long, thin hand around the shot glass.

Gib had anticipated this question all day but had not decided how to answer it. "I told Mrs. Levine I didn't," he said.

Levine's eyes rose. "Mrs. Levine did not tell *you* the truth, either," he said.

"I detected that."

Holding his lips pursed again, the old man shook his head slowly. "She is not insane, Mr. Hubbard," he said quietly.

Before Gib could say anything more, Levine turned away from him and leaned out of the booth to look for a waitress. He frowned impatiently. "I wonder . . ." he said and did not finish the sentence.

The voice was old and thin and yet rasping and harsh. The face was old too—long, and angular with a long, slanted jaw, reminiscent of Woodrow Wilson. The mouth was wide, and the teeth showed big and prominent. Small, round spectacles with pink plastic rims sat on a thin, pointed nose. The skin was pallid, and it looked naked, as though the face very much needed the covering of a beard. The hair was not yet gray, and it was long and fine and unruly. It stood high over the head and leaned to one side, likely the direction in which he had pulled off his hat. The suit was black, the shirt white and frayed at the collar, and the little black bow tie hung loose at an angle. If he did look like Woodrow Wilson, it was like the aged and tired Wilson.

"I know," said Levine when his attention returned to Gib, "that I have done you no courtesy, calling you all this way uptown in the middle of the evening, to a bar where . . . where you can't get a drink." Distracted with impatience, he leaned out of the booth again.

It would have done Gib no good to say it was all right, that he had nothing else to do that evening anyway. Levine was not listening. But it *was* all right. Gib would have come any evening to talk to Franklin Levine, but this evening he was glad to have something to occupy him. Leslie had a day off and had gone home to Long Island.

Satisfied at last apparently that a waitress had noticed him, Levine drew himself back into the middle of the booth and seemed to relax. "Mrs. Levine was rude to you, I imagine, and you formed a very ill impression of her," he said blandly, without embarrassment.

"I suppose I did," Gib said. He could see no reason to lie about it, or to be apologetic.

"She is not insane," Levine said again.

"No, I didn't think she was."

She was a fat, furious little woman, with her hair dyed an unnatural dull black. She wore bright red lipstick and a makeup that colored her face a deep tan. She had said she testified against Erich Traver to affirm her love for America. She also said she had sought out Benjamin Slusser and volunteered to testify. Since Slusser had said he ferreted her out only after a difficult investigation and threatened her with drastic consequences if she did not testify, one of them had to be lying.

"She disliked you intensely," Levine said in the same bland tone.

The waitress came. Her head was shaved. Gib had heard there were two or three of these bars now on Seventh Avenue, where the girls had to shave their heads to work. Levine looked up and welcomed the girl with a broad, friendly smile, as if he had not been impatient at all. He leaned toward her and said something quiet, which Gib could not hear, and she laughed. She seemed to know him, which heightened Gib's amused suspicion that he came here often. If he did, it said something about him. You paid a cover charge to get in here, for no entertainment, only to be served by a waitress with a shaved head.

After the girl had taken their orders and left, Levine faced Gib with a small new smile. Maybe it was embarrassment at last, or maybe Gib read it wrong. "Anyway," Levine said, "I suppose your interview with my wife was not fruitful for your investigation."

"I learned all I expected to learn from her," Gib said.

"Which was that she would lie to you," said Levine. "She lied to you because she saw no reason to tell you the truth."

"Did you call me up here to tell me the truth, Mr. Levine?" Gib asked.

Levine considered for a moment, conspicuously thoughtful. "Yes," he said. "The truth. Yes." His face and posture formed the picture of a weary old man, but the eyes, narrowed in thought, penetrating, and wholly under control, bespoke a keen intelligence still functioning. He began to nod. "The first part of the truth that you will want is to know *why*. Why will I talk to you? Why might I confess things to you that I have not confessed to others?" He stopped speaking, but still he nodded.

Gib, rubbing his mustache with one finger, held his eyes on Levine's face. "I do wonder why, of course," he said.

The lined old face firmed with determination, and Levine frowned hard. "You cannot understand, I am sure, Mr. Hubbard, what it means to be seventy years old and to be alone in this world. Friendless. I am married, but I have no wife. I am a father, but I have no daughter. I have a few acquaintances, Mr. Hubbard, but I have no friends." He stopped. His face remained hard, and he did not seem to be asking for sympathy. "If the storm breaks, I will be alone. A man alone is very vulnerable. My wife is not vulnerable. Her wild people will rally to her, no matter what. But I will be alone in the storm."

"What storm are you expecting, Mr. Levine?" Gib asked. He was not reluctant to press the old man a little.

"If you go on doing what you are doing, Mr. Hubbard, a storm will break. You may be sure of that."

"Are you asking me to stop?"

"Oh, no. No. I judge you, Mr. Hubbard, as much of a fanatic in your own way as any of the rest of them are in theirs. You won't stop."

"What kind of storm will it be?"

Levine shrugged: a gesture of tolerance for the question. "Who can tell? Who is a prophet? But it will be a great storm, one that will hurt many people."

Dissatisfied with that answer, Gib started to object, but the waitress came with their drinks and interrupted both his thought and the objection he was about to make.

He had to be patient while Levine, as before, tried to make banter with the girl. She smiled at him, but her eyes settled for an instant in Gib's and—unless his imagination was too active—appealed to him not to stare at her shaved head as everyone else did, because he was young like her and his stare would touch her self-consciousness in a way that all the gaping of men like Levine did not.

Levine sipped his whiskey and began to talk again. "You understand, Mr. Hubbard, I am sure, that in seeking out my wife and asking her why she testified against Erich, you have asked the key question. If you pursue this line, the Traver case may have to be reopened. That is the storm that will break over us."

Gib watched the old man purse his lips and suck raw whiskey off the top of his shot glass, savor it in his mouth, swallow it, and finally sip water to cool his throat.

"The Traver case will be reopened," Gib said. "That's the idea. That's what I'm working for, to get the answers to the unanswered questions."

Levine's long white lips tightened into little furrows, and he studied Gib's face for a moment before he went on. Then he said, "The people who are threatened will defend themselves. They will fight back. You can't expect them to let you do this thing unhindered."

"Who will fight back?"

"Many people," Levine said. "People who are threatened. Not just the people you think, but other people."

Gib shrugged. "They are fighting already," he said.

"To prove they were right, they will reopen the Traver case," Levine said ominously, looking over the tops of his glasses, a new and apparently emphatic gesture for him. "They will make new prosecutions. It will be . . ."

Alerted, Gib interrupted the old man. "New prosecutions, you think," he said. "Who? Who could be prosecuted now?"

"*I*, perhaps," the old man said. He was grim but did not seem afraid.

"And you are not asking me to stop?"

Levine smiled ironically and shook his head. "Would you stop?" he asked. "Could *I* convince you to stop? No, I don't ask you to stop, because I know you won't."

During a moment of silence then, a moment of separation between them because Levine took off his glasses and rubbed his eyes, Gib tried to think what the old man was driving at. He was convinced by now that Levine had a logical mind and his talk was driving toward a point, but Gib could not anticipate what that point was.

Putting his spectacles back on his nose, Levine sighed and suddenly his spirit seemed to slump in weary resignation. "No," he said. "You will go on. *It* will go on. To the end."

With an idea at last, Gib said, "Well then, I suppose what you want me to do is subdue your part in the story, to protect you. Is that what you want?"

"We are all old now," Levine said. He had heard the question only as an interruption and was going on with what he wanted to say. "Erich and I and nearly all of us that were in the old fight, on both sides. The future belongs to you. It belongs, not just to the young, but to the young like you, who know where the world has to go and have run out ahead and taken up positions where it must come. You are like the true Leninists of 1917. You are in place, you know where you are and what you are doing, and you are just waiting for the world to stop struggling and drop into your hands, as you know it must. And that, Mr. Hubbard, is why I wanted to talk to you. You are going to summon up a great storm. An old man alone will be vulnerable when it happens. I want to have friends on the side I am sure is going to win."

So there it was. There was logic. Gib nodded thoughtfully, and the old man, with a certain sense of drama, punctuated his statement by taking up his shot glass and tossing off the rest of his whiskey.

"My wife," Levine said with a voice made breathless by the whiskey fumes in his mouth and throat, "is not insane, as I have said. But she is a fool. She has chosen the wrong side."

Gib was ready to press a little more. "You chose the wrong side yourself, when you became a Communist," he said.

Levine nodded. "Who could have guessed it?" he asked bitterly.

"You say you could be prosecuted," Gib said. "Why? What kind of prosecution?"

Levine began to roll his empty shot glass between two hands. "The story," he said. "I'll tell you the story now. All right?"

"All right."

The old man sighed. "We really were Communists, members of the Party. Esther and I, Erich and Jocelyn."

"*Mrs.* Traver too?" Gib asked. "I knew the rest of you were, but . . ."

Levine nodded emphatically. "Jocelyn too. That's something even Melanie did not know, hey?" The old man gave Gib a sly smile. "Oh, yes, Jocelyn was a Communist. She was never an active member of the Party, but she was a member."

"I didn't know they allowed inactive members," Gib said.

"The Travers were difficult people to discipline. They did not like to be told that some things were required of them, or that rules were to be obeyed. Even for a cause, they would not accept discipline. It must have been very difficult for Erich to serve his term in prison."

"Are you still a Communist?" Gib asked.

Levine shrugged. "Philosophically perhaps. There is no room in the Party for the likes of me any more."

"So you were a Communist," Gib said. "You are not going to be prosecuted for that now."

"No, not for that."

"For what, then?"

Levine glanced furtively around him, melodramatically. He folded his arms on the table and leaned forward, so he could talk to Gib in a lower voice. "Erich," he said, "was prosecuted first for espionage, as you remember. It was only when the jury could not agree on a verdict in that trial that the government gave up and prosecuted him for perjury. Well. That first jury could properly have convicted him for passing secrets from the Department of the Army to agents of the Soviet Union, because that is what he did. And I helped him."

When the old man stopped, Gib let him have a moment and then asked him, "How did you help him? What did he do, precisely?"

Levine glanced around again. "He worked for the War Department all during the war, and after the war, when it became the Department of the Army, he was still there, making a permanent career of the civil service. He had access to information, some of it classified. So far as I know, he never took orders from the Party to get out specific information. He just watched what came across his desk, and when he judged it worth passing along to Soviet agents, he passed it along. There were information drops in Washington, at various places, where he could leave paper or spools of film and be sure it would be picked up by the right people. It was hazardous to some degree, so sometimes I received the material from him and carried it to the drop. So did my wife."

"What about the charge against him at the first trial, that he met a Soviet agent in New York and passed something to him there?"

"Konstantinov," said Levine. "I don't know about that. I suppose likely Erich did just what he was charged with doing."

"But the government didn't have enough evidence of it," Gib said.

"I have my theory about that," Levine said. He leaned back, allowed himself to smile for a moment, and his talk turned less conspiratorial. "That man Slusser," he said, "spoiled the government's case against Erich. That's my theory. He wanted all the glory of catching a spy. When he or his Un-American Activities investigators found out about Erich, instead of calling in the FBI, they tried to run down Erich alone. Maybe some of the politicians on the Un-American Activities knew of it and wanted some glory too. Anyway, Slusser followed Erich alone, to New York, and saw him pass his material to the Soviet agent. But Slusser was the only witness, and the jury did not believe him. After it was over and it was evident what a mess he had made of the matter, his Un-American Activities politicians protected him and let him retire quietly to Georgia, to keep the whole matter quiet. Slusser was a bad lawyer and no investigator. He was a political manipulator, a puller of strings. His clumsiness saved Erich from a *very* long term in prison. Erich would be a convict yet, probably, except for that."

Gib's eyes had begun to water from the heavy tobacco smoke in the bar, and his contact lenses began to drift and bother him. It made him nervous, and he pinched his mustache and rolled the hair between his thumb and finger. "It's the second trial I'm most interested in," he said. "Why did the Communist Party order you to testify against Erich Traver?"

"I never knew," Levine said. "It may have been Erich's penalty for his stupidity in allowing himself to be followed to New York by an oaf like Slusser and so causing the loss of Konstantinov, a valuable agent who then had to flee. But I really never knew."

"How did the orders come to you?"

"Ahh," said Levine. "That's the rest of the story. But if you will forgive me, Mr. Hubbard, first I am afraid I must visit the men's room. If our waitress should come, would you be good enough to order me another?"

The old man slid out of the booth, and as he stood he

glanced furtively around the bar with the pose and all the subtlety of a burlesque comic. Gib smiled, but only for a moment. He himself, he had to acknowledge, had been hardly less conspicuous about his suspicion that he was being watched. In the Village, on his block, someone had harbored the radio equipment which received and recorded the transmissions from the bugs in his apartment. Whoever it was probably knew him by sight, and whoever it was probably still occupied the premises where the equipment had been. Whoever it was probably watched him.

He thought he knew why the police raided his apartment. He'd tried to be rational about it, and he had decided that the police had acted in good faith—as good as could be anyway when acting under a law that let them enter a home and rummage through everything in it to search for a fraction of an ounce of marijuana. They had simply received a tip. The tip had come from whoever bugged the apartment. Whoever that was had overheard him and Leslie sharing a joint or two of pot and had tipped the police—maybe through connections in the police department and maybe not; it wouldn't make any difference. Whoever it was had seen a chance to put an abrupt period to the Traver investigation by having him, Gib, jailed for possession of marijuana. He might not have been in jail long, but his credibility would have been seriously damaged. Whoever it was, was playing for blood.

That was what Steve Novatny said, that someone was playing for blood, and he was quoting Senator Jordan. Frank Kennedy agreed, and he was aroused to fight. He had released Gib from doing much of anything else for the paper as long as the Traver investigation continued.

"Need a refill?"

The bald girl was standing at his elbow, and when he looked up he saw on her face a wan, gently amused smile—amused perhaps because she had hurried to the booth while

Levine was back in the men's room. She was Puerto Rican probably, from the look of her, a dark, chubby little girl.

"Scotch and soda," Gib said. "What does my friend drink?"

"Old Granddad," she said.

Gib leaned back a little so he could look directly up into her face. "Would you mind telling me something?" he asked.

She tipped her head and, in some kind of gesture he could not interpret—whether of self-consciousness or not—she ran the tips of her fingers along the smooth bare side of her head. "What?" she asked, in a faint, apprehensive voice; and he understood she thought she was about to get the usual question: how did she like having her head shaved, was it cold, or something like that.

"Does my friend come in here often?" he asked her.

She smiled and looked relieved. "Sometimes," she said.

"Do you know his name?"

"No."

"Does he come alone?"

She nodded. "Never saw him with anyone before."

"Thanks," he said. He pushed a couple of dollars under her hand, which was resting on the table.

She looked down at the money. "Thank *you,*" she said.

He looked at his watch after the girl was gone. Maybe Leslie was on the bus by now, on her way back from Long Island. He was anxious to see her, after she'd spent a day with her family.

One of the most sickening things about having had the bugs in his apartment was to remember that whoever had the tapes could play them and laugh over the little private things that he and Leslie said to each other—like their talk about his wanting to get in her pants, an expression which amused her and in which she persisted. He'd spent a lot of thought reconstructing conversations he now knew someone had taped.

Whoever listened to the bugs had overheard his telephone

conversations with Steve Novatny in Washington, when he had given Novatny a report for the Senator. That was the trouble. They'd overheard those conversations and all his talk with Leslie for . . . for how long? A week? Two? Depending on how long the bugs had been in place, the people who installed them could know as much about his investigation as he did himself, for he had told Novatny and Leslie everything.

Levine slid into the booth again. "Did our waitress come?" he asked. "What were you asking me when I left?"

"She came. I was asking how you got your orders to testify against Erich Traver."

"How do you know we were ordered?" Levine asked. "I know who told you. My daughter. I was thinking about it back there. That's how you know."

Gib set his face in what he hoped was an expression of firm determination. "I will not betray your trust, Mr. Levine," he said. "Please don't ask me to betray anyone else's."

The little confidence and challenge that had been on the old face slipped away. "If you see her," he said, "please be so kind as to tell her I love her and will give anything to see her again. Perhaps you could bring a message back from her. Her mother does not need to know."

Gib nodded. "If I see her. . . ."

"Thank you," Levine whispered. Then he found voice. "We received orders as you suggested," he said. "We were ordered to testify against Erich. We were told what to say. We were told we were being sacrificed, our cell was being sacrificed, to the greater good of the Party. My wife did as she was told. She was a fanatically loyal Communist. I refused. Because Erich was my friend. Yes, and because I was afraid that my own criminal guilt would come out somehow during the trial, and I would go to prison. I was subjected to the firmest pressure. When I persisted in my refusal, I was expelled from the Party. It was then that my wife became contemptuous of me."

"Who gave these orders?" Gib asked. "Who pressured you to obey?"

Levine sighed noisily. "We got our orders directly from a Soviet agent. I have no idea what his name really was—his Russian name. But he called himself John Steppel. He was in Washington for several years, and he made our lives hell all the time he was there. John Steppel. He showed up for the first time shortly after the war, and he was still in Washington when my wife and I fled the country. He was an agent of the NKVD."

"Was he with the Russian embassy?" Gib asked.

"Oh, no. Steppel was never identified as a Russian. He had a complete American identity. Spoke English faultlessly. He worked as a photo finisher. He rarely came to cell meetings, but when he did, everyone deferred to him. He was accepted as an American and spoken to as if he were the man he was assumed to be; but everyone understood he was of the NKVD and brought orders directly from Moscow. He appeared at a cell meeting and gave us orders directly and personally, to testify against Erich Traver. When I refused, he was furious. Some of the comrades were very worried about me. They said Steppel had authority to have me murdered."

"You have no idea where this Steppel is now? Or what became of him?"

"No. We went to England after the Traver trial was over, as you know. I never saw or heard of Steppel again."

Levine's voice trailed off as he spoke these last words. His attention had turned to another bald waitress—this one a tall girl with thick black brows and heavy makeup on her eyes—who was standing at the bar opposite the booth.

Gib smiled tolerantly at the old man—lecherous old man was the phrase that accompanied his amused thought.

Levine was smart, and he had once been brave, maybe still was. Probably it would be a mistake to believe a word he said. Obviously he had his own strong motives, and maybe they were what he said they were. Anyway, he had given Gib a new piece of hard information, something that could be checked—the name John Steppel.

"The story is not finished, Mr. Hubbard," Levine said, rubbing his chin with the back of his hand and watching the girl move away. "I have something more to tell you."

"I was hoping you might."

"Yes. This may be the most important information I have for you. When you spoke with my wife and asked her how she came to testify against Erich, when you persisted in that question and upset her with it, I knew you were the man who might be able to make something important out of this final bit of information I have."

Gib nodded and waited for Levine to go on.

"My wife and I were alienated when she accepted her orders to testify and I refused. I was immediately excluded from her confidence. Neither she nor anyone else would tell me what was going on during the weeks before the trial opened. I was afraid my own arrest might be imminent. I was not sure Steppel had not given orders for my liquidation. So, I began to spy and eavesdrop, trying to find out what was happening. My wife talked on the telephone a great deal. She would close the door to our study, where the telephone was, and exclude me from the conversations. She was so contemptuous of me, thought me so cowardly, that she simply assumed I would not go into our bedroom, pick up the other telephone, and listen. But I did. Most of the voices on the line were of people I knew. Once I heard Steppel talking to her. But there was one voice that was new to me. It was a man's voice, and the man had a very peculiar voice and accent. It was the kind of voice you would not forget. He discussed her testimony with her, examined her on it, assured himself that she knew how to answer every question. I heard them three or four times, always talking about the same thing, the testimony. I became quite familiar with that soft, accented voice and with the man's strange modes of expression. When I heard the voice later, in the courtroom during the Traver trial, I knew it was the same man, beyond any question. It was the Un-American Activities Committee lawyer, Benjamin Slusser."

PARIS

When Melanie saw him sitting on the bench she began to walk faster, and now, less than a hundred feet away, she had begun to run, and he had stood up to meet her. Brightly dressed in green and white, with her hair wild in the wind and her breasts bouncing as she ran, Melanie began to laugh as she ran into his arms.

"I'm hungry," she said. "I'm famished. I'm starving."

She was still laughing, and he was laughing. She kissed him on each cheek, and then she drew back her head and stared at him with a wide-eyed comic grin. She was exuberant. She had been, ever since he returned to her on the boat in Amsterdam. For the first time in . . . oh, years, she said, she was neither heavy in pregnancy nor heavy-breasted with milk, and she was caught in a euphoria of new freedom.

"Hungry," he said, shaking his head. "When aren't you?"

She would have eaten willingly nothing more than a sandwich and some of the ice cream they sold to children in a small pavilion in the Tuileries Garden, but he wanted lunch, so they went to a restaurant on the Rue de Rivoli.

"Was the morning wasted?" Gib asked.

Melanie was reading the menu. First she shrugged, but then she shook her head and said, "Not wasted."

"Are they going to see us?"

"Somebody will see us."

"I'm not patient," he said.

She looked up from the menu and grinned. "I know you're not. But unless you're running out of money, what have you got to be impatient about? You're in Paris. It's almost spring. You're sleeping with a good-looking girl. It's been a good week.'"

He knew of Melanie—he knew it well now—that her personality was a study in Hegelian dialectic. Each of her moods contained its own contradiction, an antithesis subtly visible and ready to grow. Within her crisp gaiety now, she was inwardly thoughtful. Under her bright cynical words was a soft appeal for him to agree—it had been a good week.

He put his hand on hers and squeezed it. But he said, "I could be an agent of the NKVD, the way they act."

She nodded. "You could be," she said. "Men have come to kill them in cleverer disguises than this."

"Seriously," he said.

"Seriously," she affirmed.

In New York they had held a meeting: Gib Hubbard, Steve Novatny, Frank Kennedy. They had before them Gib's latest letter from Melanie. Novatny had checked the name John Steppel—the name Franklin Levine had given Gib, the name of the Russian agent who had ordered the Levines to testify against Erich Traver. Steppel was listed in the Washington telephone directory for the years 1947 through 1953. He was listed in a city directory as a photo finisher employed by a large camera store. This much confirmed what Levine had said. Melanie's letter urged Gib to return to Europe to contact certain organizations of anti-Soviet Russians. These people, she said, kept close watch over Soviet intelligence operations in the West. Some of them had penetrated the Soviet agencies. She had met minor members of these organizations during her travels, and she was convinced they knew more than anyone else about the machinations of Communist parties in Western Europe and in America. They, if anyone, could throw some light on the mystery of the Traver prosecution.

Was it possible that any of these anti-Communist Russians could identify John Steppel? That was what Steve Novatny wanted to know, and he thought it was worth a trip to Europe to find out.

Gib had done some reading. He had been surprised to learn how large and active—and how effective—these anti-Soviet organizations were. The old White Russian cause was still alive, but most anti-Soviet Russians were now divorced from that. The cause of Ukrainian nationalism was alive and and a powerful anti-Soviet force. But most important, the cause of Russian nationalism and the ideal of parliamentary democracy was vigorously alive, nurtured by tight groups of determined men. These groups sent agents into Russia itself. They worked to confound Soviet espionage in the West. They penetrated Soviet intelligence agencies and were in turn penetrated themselves. For decades they had waged bitter war, marked not infrequently by murder. They killed and were killed. They were not of Melanie's imagination. They were real.

"It's a budget problem. I'll be altogether frank with you," Kennedy had said. "He'll have to stay over there a couple of weeks, maybe a month. *The Spark* . . ." Kennedy had shrugged.

Novatny was drinking. Sometimes it was hard to tell how serious he was, because when he was drinking his conversation acquired a tone of unreality. "Money," he said. "*We'll* pay it. Hell with it. Don't worry about it."

"That's a problem, isn't it?" Kennedy had asked. "If the Senator subsidizes the investigation, where does the independence of it go? The integrity? It's a matter of . . ."

"Shit, Frank. What do you want? Want us to arrange for somebody to buy some ad space? Get the money to you backwards? Would that make you feel better?"

Gib, in the spirit of the evening, had drunk a little too much too. He grinned. "Bismarck," he said, "maintained a regular fund that he used to corrupt newspapers. Called it the reptile fund."

"Nobody's corrupting anybody," Novatny said tersely.

Gib grinned again. "Because we're incorruptible."

"It gives you no control over the investigation or over what we choose to publish," Kennedy said.

"Agreed," Novatny said. "Agreed. What th' hell."

"I have another idea, too," Kennedy said. "I have an idea Traver himself has held back a lot of information. The time may have come for Gib to confront him with the new facts he's learned. Maybe Traver, knocked off his little pedestal of martyred innocence, will come through with the truth."

"Okay," said Kennedy. "It's worth the trip."

Gib had flown to Amsterdam equipped with the name of the organization he thought he should contact first—the National Alliance of Russian Patriots, which had its headquarters in Paris. That was not whom Melanie wanted to see. She wanted to talk first to the Ukrainians in Munich, because she was more confident of her contacts with them. (A Ukrainian couple, who she was sure were members of the Organization of Ukrainian Nationalist Revolutionaries, had travelled for a while with her theater group.) But Gib had read that the National Alliance, in Paris, had a permanent secretariat and kept records. Since no one had heard of John Steppel since 1953, an organization that kept files would be more likely to know of him.

Melanie thought she had a possible contact with the Alliance, through students she had known in Paris. But she soon learned how transient student friendships can be. It was almost two years since she had performed in Paris, and by now the students she had known were dispersed all over Europe. This was how she and Gib had spent their week: haunting the student quarter, searching. Finally she located someone who knew someone who knew someone who. . . . This morning she had at last had coffee with a young woman who acknowledged that she might be able to make a contact with someone who might be able to make a contact . . . and so forth.

Melanie had chosen their hotel. They had a small white room filled with a huge mahogany bed and an immense mahogany wardrobe. They had a toilet in a closet but had to wander down the hall to take a bath. Two tall glass doors opened on a tiny balcony, just big enough for the two of them to go out in the cold blue morning air and stretch and judge the day and watch the people beginning to move in the narrow, shop-lined street below. Melanie liked this hotel. She had stayed here when she was performing with Ron in his play, in a makeshift theater in the Rue de Faubourg.

Gib was no longer excited by seeing Melanie naked or by sleeping in the same bed with her. The excitement had been replaced by a pleasant domestic sort of intimacy—undressing in front of her as casually as she did in front of him, waking in the night to feel the unaccustomed warmth of her body and her skin touching his, knowing that whenever he felt the need of her she was there and willing, discovering that she had those feelings as strongly as he did, maybe more. Leslie had asked him if he would make love with Melanie on this trip. He had not promised he wouldn't.

She did not like to go out for breakfast. She liked to laze in bed as long as they could every morning, and she brought food so they could eat in bed. The room was littered with it. She shopped on the street and brought in bread and meat and fruit and wine and bottles of cognac. She was not pregnant and she was not nursing, so she could eat and drink what she wanted, she said. They drank wine with breakfast, from the bottles, and it soured Gib's stomach. Melanie laughed and gave him mineral water. She poked slices of apples and pears into his mouth, and she took bites out of peeled oranges, and the juice dribbled off her chin and fell on her breasts and belly. And when they'd eaten breakfast, she'd want to go to sleep again—or to make love.

Monday was the day when Melanie went alone to meet the young woman who finally acknowledged that she might be able to gain them access to agents of the National Alliance of Russian Patriots. After she met Gib in the Tuileries Garden and they had lunch together, they spent the afternoon in the *Jeu de Paume*, appreciating the Impressionists—something Gib had wanted to do. They had a long dinner that evening in a cafe, a tourist trap, on Montmartre. Melanie insisted she loved the wine in the cafe, though there was nothing special about it in Gib's judgment, and they took a bottle of it back to their room.

"That's good! Ahh, God, it's good!"

She had undressed and was sitting propped up in bed, with her legs stretched out before her and the bottle tucked between them. She had drunk from the bottle on the way back, in the taxi. She was drunk.

Gib took the bottle from between her legs. He tipped it and took a swallow of the red wine—so as to have an excuse for having taken it from her. It *was* good, though not as good as she thought, and he too was drunk—half-drunk, anyway.

"C'mon," Melanie said, reaching. She wanted the bottle back.

"No, you'll drink it all," he said.

She shrugged. "There's some other," she said. She leaned over the side of the bed and seized a half-empty bottle from the floor. "Here," she said, offering it to him. "Gimme back that one. It's my favorite."

He handed her the bottle. "Don't you think . . . ?"

". . . I've had enough? Huh-uh. And don't you try to tell me when I've had enough, either, lover. I'll be the judge of that. God, it's good!"

He wanted to say she was apparently not a very good judge, but he didn't say it. He sat down on the foot of the bed and began to undress. He watched her drink some more of the wine and then pour some in the palm of her hand and rub it over her breasts. She stretched luxuriously, yawned, and then leaned back to grin and yawn some more and lower her eyes to stare admiringly at the gleam the wine had put on her nipples.

Gib lay down beside her. He had eaten too much, drunk too much, and come to bed too late. He was sleepy, and she was drunk. Every night since he flew over from New York, they had made love when they went to bed. But maybe they wouldn't tonight.

"You're thinking of the girl, aren't you?" Melanie asked. She made him know he had been silent and she had been watching him lie and blink his eyes and blow long breaths which puffed his cheeks.

"No," he said.

"What's her name? The one in New York."

"Leslie."

Melanie put the mouth of the bottle to his closed lips and tipped it. The wine ran over his chin and cheeks, and she laughed. She raised the bottle and drank.

"Melanie . . ."

"Sticky," she complained, feeling with a fingertip the wine that was drying on her breasts. "Lick it off for me, won't you?" she asked, and she leaned over him and let a breast hang against his mouth.

"Melanie . . ."

"You've been thinking about the girl. You going to marry her?"

"I don't know."

Melanie stared intently at the bottle for a moment. Then she put it aside on the floor by the bed. She sat quiet for a while, in the self-contemplation of intoxication. Then she swung out of bed and opened the tall glass doors to the balcony. She walked out and stood there in the cold air.

"Melanie!"

Gib scrambled out of bed and switched off the light in the room. She was standing out there naked. He pulled on his pants and went out to bring her back.

"I don't give a damn," she said to him as soon as he was beside her, before he said anything. She stood with her hips touching the railing of the balcony, with her back arched and her arms up and her hands clasped behind her head.

"Come in, Melanie."

She turned her head to look directly at him. "I am not coming in," she said.

He glanced around nervously. Some of the shops were still lighted, and there were a few people on the street, four stories down.

She was taking deep breaths. Flexing her shoulders and twisting her body from the waist, she luxuriated and murmured sensually. The air around her was cold. Touching her, Gib felt her tremble as the wind struck her. He put his arms around her.

"God, it's good!" she said.

Later in the night, she went out on the balcony again and threw up over the railing. He did not follow her out that time. Lying beside him in the bed, she reeked of sour wine, so much that he lost all interest in touching her and slept as far away from her as he could. In the morning she was sick and apologetic. But she knew what she needed, and he went out and got it for her: a bottle of dark and brutal bitters, at which she grimaced and drank bravely, while he watched only half sympathetic, the other half of him amused with a satisfied, peculiarly American sense of justice. When about noon she was able to go out, they encountered on the street a grinning young man who saluted her with mock gallantry. Apparently he had seen her on the balcony during the night.

"You two are a pair of children playing games," the Russian said harshly. He said it to both of them, but his gray eyes were on Gib's face, as if to signify that the words were meant especially for him.

This was almost all the Russian had said. They had sat across his tiny desk from him, in his Spartan little office, and had told him why they were in Paris, what they had come to learn. Gib had told him all about the Traver investigation, everything he had discovered and how his apartment had been bugged and how the police had descended on him. The Russian had watched unblinking while they talked, had said nothing, had shown no reaction to anything they told him. He was a hard, thin, gray man, about fifty years old probably. He was the man they had finally been allowed to meet, after ten days in Paris. He had said nothing to them as to who he was, but the people who had arranged for them to meet him said he was an agent of the Alliance.

His name was Aleksandr Leonidovich Shtemenko. He took a package of cigarettes from the pocket of his gray, double-breasted jacket, lighted one, and inhaled deeply. He closed his narrow little eyes—eyes set in the center of a maze of deep wrinkles—and for a moment broke his long silent stare. "Games," he said while his eyes were shut, with a weariness in his voice that betrayed and finally shattered his nurtured image of hostile skepticism.

Melanie was not watching him closely enough, or she was not able to turn off quickly enough the annoyance his comment had aroused in her. "You're not being fair," she said to him. "You judge too quickly. I'm surprised. I thought you would be more clever than that."

Shtemenko shrugged. He turned his face away from them and fixed his stare on the blank gray wall.

"John Steppel," Gib said. "What I want to know is: Who was John Steppel?"

"How should I know?" asked Shtemenko.

"Maybe you don't. Maybe you can't find out. We thought it was worth coming to Paris to find you and ask you."

"Suppose I tell you who he was," Shtemenko said to the wall. "Then what? Do you publish what I tell you in your little newspaper? Do you go looking for this man Steppel? Or what?"

"Maybe we go looking for him," Gib said.

Shtemenko glanced at Gib's face. "He might kill you, if he's what you think he is." The faintest hint of a smile crossed the Russian's face, for the barest instant. "You hadn't thought of that, had you?"

"No," Gib admitted, "I hadn't. But . . ."

"Why do you assume everyone but yourself is a coward?" Melanie asked irritably.

The Russian ignored her. "Don't you want to know why Traver was betrayed?" he asked Gib.

"Yes, if you can tell me."

"I can't tell you. That's the point," said Shtemenko. "It was a matter of internal discipline within the ranks of the Communist Party of the United States, undoubtedly. I would be surprised if anyone still remembers the matter, let alone has kept a record of it. It may have been a Dreyfus affair for American drawing room liberals, but to us it was nothing."

"Nothing is nothing, in your business," Gib said.

Now Shtemenko did smile. "Oh?" he said. "What do you know of our business?"

"If," Gib said, "you can identify John Steppel as a Soviet agent who did in fact carry orders direct from Moscow, then the Traver case was more than you suggest. If you will do that much for me, if you will see if you have any record of the name John Steppel, you will have helped me immensely and you will see that I am really on the track of something."

"It's very unlikely we have any such record."

"Is it a great deal of trouble to check?

The Russian paused thoughtfully, drawing deeply on his cigarette. He shrugged again. "I suppose not," he said.

"We'll be grateful."

Shtemenko said they should not again try to contact him, that he would reach them in a few days, when he had something to tell them. So they spent another weekend in Paris.

It rained on Sunday. Gib had plans for Sunday, but because it rained they stayed in bed until the middle of the afternoon. The day was warm, the warmest since they came to Paris, and Melanie opened the tall doors to their balcony so the fresh damp air off the rain would blow across them as they lay in bed.

"I've been wondering about something," she said to him. She was sitting erect and brushing her hair, and he was lying in the pillows. It was noon, but he was still half sleepy. He did not ask what she was wondering. He only raised his eyes. "I've been wondering," she went on, "if you and I will . . . Well, what I mean is, I wonder if you and I are going to still mean anything to each other, when this is all over."

Melanie looked down at him with that faintly wise and subtly skeptical expression that was most characteristic of her. She waited for him to answer, still slowly brushing the long dark hair that hung as low as her elbows. Her voice had been soft, and the question had seemed casual, but as always there was something intent beneath.

"I'm sure we will, Melanie," he said, conscious that it was a shallow answer and not the one she wanted.

She looked down with the same lofted chin and the same knowing eyes, but with a faintly accusing new small smile. "Does your girl in New York know you sleep with me?" she asked.

"I suppose she does," he said. "She asked me if I would, and I didn't say I wouldn't. She knows we did before."

"Are you in love with her?"

She was watching him closely to see the impact of the question.

"Are you?" she asked again when a moment had passed and he had not answered.

Gib drew a deep breath. "Yes, I guess I am," he said. "I've thought about it this past week. It's easy enough to think you're in love with someone when you're with her and touching her. The question is, how do you feel when you're . . ."

A flicker of something hard passed across Melanie's face in the instant of Gib's abrupt self-conscious pause, and she interrupted him with a crisp voice. "How do you feel when you're sleeping with another girl and making love with *her?* That's the question, huh? I've provided you a nice test."

"Melanie . . ." he said. He reached for her hand, but she pulled it away. She did not jerk it away, she simply pulled it away firmly, and she stood and went to the open doors and tipped her head and looked out, as if she were intent on the slow, steady rain. She stood there with the same disregard she had shown when she was drunk for the chance that someone on the street might glance up and see her. Her back was toward Gib, and he could not tell what was on her face. He could see her shoulders rise and fall with deep, rhythmic breaths. "Melanie, what can I say?" he asked.

He watched her shoulders rise as she filled with a slow breath. "Nothing," she said on the top of her breath. "You don't owe me any words."

He dragged himself up and sat slumped in the middle of the bed. She was a beautiful girl. He stared at the curve of her back and at her smooth, taut bottom.

"Melanie," he said quietly. "I didn't want to hurt your feelings. I . . ."

"I haven't got any feelings."

"Please, Melanie . . ."

"Don't apologize to me," she said quickly, swinging around to face him. "You don't owe me any apology, and besides I couldn't stand to hear. I don't like to see you emasculate yourself."

"All right."

She came toward the bed and tossed aside the hairbrush. "I suppose she's very young and pretty, and very much in love with you."

"I think so."

Melanie sat down on the bed. "Is she going to be enough woman for you? You've developed a healthy appetite, and you've learned to like some pretty sophisticated tricks. Is she going to be able to take care of you? Was she a virgin?"

Gib stiffened with a deep breath. "She was . . . no virgin," he said. "And she . . ."

"She does all right, huh?"

He nodded.

"All right," Melanie said. She leaned over the side of the bed and picked up a nearly empty bottle of wine. "All right, Gib. The reason I asked you the original question, about whether you and I would mean anything to each other later, was because I wanted to tell you something. I wanted to tell you I'm not going back to Amsterdam. My theater group is coming home to Europe in three or four months. They are going to do another tour here, starting in Brussels. I'm going to Brussels to wait for them. I have a job lined up, to tide me over until they come back and I can join them again."

"A job?" he asked. "Doing what?"

She cocked her chin and smiled defiantly. "Stripping. In a club. I did it for a while in Soho, years ago, and I'm not bad. A man I know helped me get this job. I went down to Brussels and showed them what I can do, and they hired me. It's a living until my theater group comes back for me. It's a living, Gib, and I don't want to hear any crap."

"What about little Erich?" he asked.

"That's the rest of the story," she said rigidly. Her face became tight, and her eyes were hard. "Erich is not mine any more. That's why I'm not going back to the boat. He's not there any more. He's with his new parents now. Carole took him to them while I'm away. With Ginny. She gave up Ginny too."

Gib's eyes were closed, and his body had slackened. "Melanie, for God's sake," he whispered resignedly.

"Don't you give me any crap," she said. She strained to keep her voice. "He's a bastard child. He has no father, and most people would say he has no mother. Well, he has parents now, a cute young couple in Amsterdam. His new daddy is an instructor in a technical high school. His new mommy can't have any children of her own. They took him and Ginny both and were overjoyed to have them. I gave him up. It was the right thing to do. I have no doubts about it. It was the right thing."

Gib sought her emotions. Except for a moment at first, when she had seemed to reach into herself for composure, she was strong, almost unemotional. He did not think she could hide anything, if he looked hard enough; and he looked and did not see. She seemed now only to be waiting for him to say something. Her chin was up, and her eyes were calmly on his.

He shook his head. "I don't see how you could do it," he said quietly.

"Oh, you don't, Mister Jesus Christ?" she said evenly, in full control of her voice. "Well, would you like to marry me and be a father to the bastard I begot on the stage of a theater? It probably isn't too late to get him back. I'll be a good wife to you. I won't take off my clothes in public or do anything to embarrass you. I'll still be the daughter of Erich Traver, but you should be able to live with that. I have everything a woman needs to make a man happy. We can go back to Amsterdam and get Erich from his new parents before they get too attached to him to give him up. We can leave tomorrow, tonight even. We can send word to Shtemenko. He'll see us when we come back. Are you interested?"

"Melanie . . ."

"No, you're not interested," she said. She shrugged. She put her hand on his and squeezed. "It's all right. It's okay. But don't give me any crap. If you're not going to be part of my life, then don't try to tell me how to live it."

They sat across the tiny desk from Shtemenko again, there by his summons, and listened to him talk. This time he was not quite so formidable. He was not hostile. He was precise, crisp, hard, and apparently in a hurry.

"Don't you have a saying in the United States?" he asked. "Something to the effect that God loves drunk men, little children, and the United States of America? Well, whether you represent one of the three or not, God seems to love you—the god of luck at least. It seems we do know your John Steppel."

Shtemenko smoked short, fat, strong cigarettes. The close air of the little office was foul with the sour, biting smell of his smoke. Gib, straining for a breath of clean air, nodded his acknowledgment of Shtemenko's unsmiling sally.

"John Steppel," Shtemenko went on, "was an alias used by a Soviet agent. He used it in London in the thirties and during the War, we know, and in the United States from 1946 to 1953. It seems likely the man identified by your informant was in fact this man. If so, you have come across the trail of an important fellow. Do you have any pictures of the man your informant spoke of? Or at least a physical description?"

Gib had to shake his head. He knew he had been stupid not to have asked Levine to describe Steppel.

"Well, get one," Shtemenko said crisply. "Send it here to me."

Gib nodded and glanced at Melanie. He had warned her to keep quiet and not to antagonize Shtemenko, and she was sitting with her hands clasped on her lap and her face set in an unnatural placid mask.

"John Steppel," Shtemenko went on, "was a name used by an NKVD agent—Major Alekseii Parotikin. He was a career intelligence agent—well trained, dedicated, clever, vicious. He was an important man, for a while."

"Franklin Levine thinks he had the authority to order a man's death," said Gib.

Shtemenko nodded. "Likely he did."

"Well then," said Gib. "If Steppel—or Parotikin—gave the Levines and others their orders to testify against Erich Traver, isn't it likely those orders came directly from Moscow?"

"Yes."

"Which makes the Traver case a great deal more significant," Gib suggested.

Shtemenko allowed himself a faint, short smile, and he nodded. (A smile seemed unnatural to that pinched, controlled face, so unnatural it seemed like the drawn smile on the face of an animated cartoon character: a smile that was limited to a brief flexing of the lips and moved nothing else of the face.)

"Where is Parotikin now?" Gib asked.

Shtemenko ignored the question. "He spoke American English," he said. "Even when he was stationed in London, he was identified as an American, not an Englishman. He also spoke German flawlessly, but he was trained to pose as an American. He devoted his whole life to that pose and to the work he did. He never married, had no home, no interests. He was a dangerous man."

"Franklin Levine was afraid of him," Gib said.

"You should look for a woman," Shtemenko went on. "There was a woman who worked with him. Nadya Kharina was her name. When she was in England she used the name Judith Baldwin. She worked closely with Parotikin and probably went to the States with him. She came as close as anyone ever did, we suspect, to distracting him from his work. You might find some trace of her. Remember, she called herself Judith Baldwin."

"Where is Parotikin now?" Gib asked again.

"Dead," said Shtemenko. "That is why I suggest you look for traces of Judith Baldwin-Nadya Kharina. She is still alive. The last we heard of her, she was in East Berlin, still an agent of Soviet intelligence. But Parotikin is dead."

"A natural death?" Gib asked.

Shtemenko shook his head. "He was called back to Moscow shortly after the death of Stalin. He was one of Lavrenti Beria's people, and Beria wanted him at home, where he could use him. They were going to govern Russia, you know —Beria's people. When Beria was killed, many of his people were eliminated also. It was a purge of sorts. Parotikin disappeared. Shot, probably. Maybe poisoned or strangled. Dead, anyway."

Shtemenko busied himself with lighting another cigarette, giving Gib a moment to ponder and to frown toward Melanie. "You asked me a few minutes ago," he said to Shtemenko, "to send you a photograph or at least a description of the man we identify in Washington as Steppel. Does this mean your organization will take an interest in the case?"

Shtemenko shrugged while still fumbling with his cigarette, and after a moment he said, "We are not making you a commitment. What you are doing is interesting. We will receive further information from you, if you care to send it. We may give you additional help, if it is in our interest." He nodded and tapped his chest with one finger. "If it is in *our* interest, you understand. Ours."

Drawing the hot smoke from his cigarette deeply into himself, Shtemenko narrowed his little eyes and gradually withdrew from Gib and Melanie, until his nodding was no longer an affirmation of what he had just said to them but only a weary, faintly comforting gesture to himself.

LONDON

"You're a liar. That's the central fact of your whole history, Mr. Traver. You are a colossal, unembarrassed liar."

Gib was shocked by himself, obviously more than Traver was shocked. Traver only shifted his eyes slightly—the movement blurred and rippling behind the thick, gold-framed lenses of his spectacles—and settled a calmly grim and contemptuous gaze on Gib's flushed and angry face. "Indeed?" he said.

It was Mrs. Traver who stiffened, glared, and spat out her sudden fury. "You're an insolent little *bastard,* Mr. Hubbard," she snapped.

Melanie sighed. "Shut up, mother, for Christ's sake," she said. "He's only saying what we all know is true."

Traver was in his chair, in the dim brown light of his bridge lamp, with his newspaper still on his lap. Although Gib had been there a quarter of an hour—and had come by appointment in the first place—Traver still sat with the posture and air of a man who had been interrupted. His right hand rested on his cane. His left was between the sheets of the newspaper. He had been turning the pages and glancing over the paper all during the conversation.

Mrs. Traver had brought in tea. She had been stiff and

hostile since Gib came to the door, and now she was rigid with an anger that was not going to abate, now or later.

Melanie was slouched in the other overstuffed chair, the one where her mother probably usually sat. Melanie was wearing a half slip and a bra, and she was barefoot. She had been drinking when Gib arrived, and when her mother went out to make the tea, she had gone for a beer. She was marked by the strain of the prolonged angry confrontation she had been having with her parents. Her face was red and puffy. Her hair was uncombed and tangled. Her voice was tired and throaty.

She had insisted on staying with her parents in the house in Bloomsbury. He was the one who had insisted on her coming to London. He could not judge how much she blamed him for the agony of these four days. She had spent one night with him—the night before last—in his room at the Park Lane. She had wept in the night. She told him in the morning it had been over little Erich, but he suspected it had been over more than that.

"I think it might be better, Mr. Hubbard, if you *just left,*" Traver said, quietly but emphatically.

"No, godammit," Melanie interjected. "He knows the truth about you. You're going to hear it from him. Then you're going to tell him the rest of it." She turned her head away from him and away from her mother, and she added, "If you ever expect to see *me* again."

They had travelled by train from Paris to Brussels and then had flown across to London. She'd had to stop in Brussels to obtain permission from her new employers to delay for a week her debut in their club. He had seen the club. They already had posters up—promising MELANIE TRAVER! ARTISTE EXOTIQUE INTERCONTINENTALE! They were reluctant to let her have a week, and they looked on him with an evident suspicion that he, and not the necessity of visiting her family on urgent family business, was the reason. But they obviously valued her, and they agreed.

It had taken him two days in Paris to talk her into going to London. Until they left Brussels, he was not sure she wouldn't change her mind. For the two days after their second meeting with Shtemenko, he had talked to her about it, trying to convince her he needed her there when he again met with her father. It had been a tense two days, during which she had spent much of the time away from him, on secret errands, not telling him where she was going or when she would be back. He sat alone in the hotel and waited for her. He wrote long letters to Senator Jordan and to Frank Kennedy, giving them his report of what he was doing in Europe. His reports were much longer and more detailed for Melanie's long absences. He had to wait for her without really knowing she would return at all. When finally she said she would go to London with him, it was with the comment she was not sure the Traver investigation was worth a confrontation with the Travers.

Carole was in Brussels. Quiet and wistful, she confirmed that little Erich was with his new parents, and so was Ginny. Melanie had gotten Carole a job in the club too, as a hostess. She was already living in Brussels and had found rooms to share with Melanie when Melanie returned from London.

On the plane over the Channel, he had not been able to talk with Melanie much. She was not in a mood to talk, though he was anxious to penetrate her mood and seek understanding with her, to re-enter a personality from which he had been gradually excluded in the past few days. She was not curt with him. But she was introspective, and she looked out the window while they talked and let the conversation trail off and die. He was not sure if she was angry with him, or sad, or disappointed, or disillusioned—or if so, exactly why.

Watching her as she stared out the window at the clouds over the Channel, he tried to reach her by taking her hand. She accepted his touch, turned her fingers around his hand, squeezed reassuringly, and held on; but she did not break her reverie or look at him. So he sat there, holding her hand and watching her, letting his eyes and his thoughts play over her well-formed legs, the full curve of her hips, the free weight in her blouse, the sheen of her hair, the soft, faultless lines of her profile. They had still slept together the last two nights in Paris and the one night in Brussels, as ardent as ever. He recalled and savored the warm length of her body against his back as they slept. She would be with her parents in London and would not sleep with him there. In fact, maybe they would never sleep together again, since he was going home from London and God knew when he would see her again. That tugged at him as he sat looking at her. She was right (and maybe even she didn't know how *much* she was right) when she said she was everything that could make him happy. It was easy to think—it was hard *not* to think just then—of giving up a lot of things for her. It was possible to think just then about trading everything else he wanted in the world for her. He turned as pensive as she seemed to be, sad and regretful.

Their arrangement for London was that she would go home and confront her parents alone. She would have out her personal battle with them, and only when that was over would she call Gib to come for his own confrontation with Erich Traver. Maybe it would be a day or two before she called.

It was two days before she telephoned him, and when she finally did call she asked him not to come yet to the house off Tottenham Court Road but to meet her somewhere for dinner. He suggested The Sovereign, a little Mayfair restaurant a few blocks from the Park Lane Hotel, and she came there, about seven that evening.

"I have to ask you something," he said to her when they had finished their dinner and were sitting over coffee. During two hours she had said nothing significant, nothing he had expected. He could see on her face and hear in her voice the strain of whatever was happening between her and her parents, but she did not choose to talk about it, and he had not chosen to press her. She had talked about London mostly, about places she had lived and worked. It had been forced, nervous talk. Obviously she had been talking around the things that were dominant in her mind. He guessed she did not feel emotionally ready to tell him anything important yet, and he was content to wait a little, confident she would tell him, in good time, anything he needed to know. When he said to her he had to ask her something, it was a different subject he had in mind—one which had troubled him the past few days.

He did not quite know how to ask her his question. It was of the essence of his nature not to know how to ask it. Because, what he wanted to know was if he had hurt her, or knocked down an illusion she had entertained about something between him and her, when he had admitted to her, a few nights ago in Paris, that he was in love with Leslie. In his mind he had reconstructed and relived, a dozen times, the night when he told her. He remembered her every word and gesture. And he knew it was from that night—when he gave it his concentrated thought and analyzed it—that she had begun to withdraw her confidence from him. He had hurt her. It was easy enough to see. Yet, he could not believe it. All his life and experience and all his personality denied it. It was a colossal conceit. She would laugh at him when he asked her.

But he asked her, anyway.

Melanie did not laugh. She smiled softly. "You've gained a little self-confidence since I met you, haven't you?" she asked. "Did I give you that?"

The answer was that she and Leslie had both given it to him, but he did not want to tell her that. He answered her question with a nod.

"Well," she said. "Don't worry about it. You can't hurt me. I love you, yes, but not in a way that forbids you to love anyone else."

He was not sure of her answer, because he couldn't look into her eyes.

When they left the restaurant she did not want to take a cab for Bloomsbury, so they walked down to the Park Lane and sat in the lounge for a few more drinks. She'd had gin before dinner, and she had some more now. She told him about her confrontation with her parents. She did not say much, only that it had been as painful as she expected. "We deserve each other, I suppose," she said. She kept on drinking. The gin didn't loosen her. It hardened her. She said she hated her father and mother. She said if it had not been for their petty hatefulness she might have been . . . oh, lots of things.

"Look, Gib, for Christ's sake!" she complained to him later, a little after midnight. She was in his room in bed. He had not asked her there, and she had not suggested she wanted to come. When the bar closed they had simply left the lounge and come up to bed, as if there were nothing else to do. She was undressed and was lying awake on his bed. He was in the bathroom for a while, and when he came out she was lying there naked on his bed. He was aroused, and he'd had too much to drink to be sensitive to her mood or restrained about moving to take her. "Could you just once, just for one night, be so kind as to keep your hands off me, you horny little bastard?"

He mumbled something confused, something angry and apologetic at the same time.

"Okay, okay. You mean well, but can't you, for the love of God, have vision enough to see I couldn't stand to be mauled and screwed tonight? You've had it every night I've been with you. Can't you let me rest one night?"

He rolled away from her and turned his back. Because of what he'd had to drink, he went to sleep shortly, in spite of the raging dismay she had loosed in him. He went to sleep, but it was not good sleep. He awoke from time to time all during the night. Whenever he awoke enough to listen carefully, he could tell she was awake. Once he heard her crying. His impulse then was to touch her, to try to comfort her, but he was afraid. Besides, he was reluctant, a little unforgiving. He listened to her for a while, and when she stopped crying he went to sleep again.

He woke twice after daylight. The first time, in the gray quiet light of very early morning, he saw Melanie was alseep at last. The second time he woke abruptly to find her on her hands and knees above him, with her head down to kiss his body. He moved to rise, but she murmured no and pushed him down. For most of an hour she made him lie taut and still while she made love to him. He watched her, catching only occasional glimpses of her face through the hair that hung down and hid it. He saw her eyes were swollen from crying and from a night—maybe more than one night—of bad sleep. She made love gently, knowingly, and with self-effacing determination. It was her apology to him. He understood that too late. If he had understood it soon enough he would have stopped her. She made love to him until he was totally depleted.

She lay down beside him when she was finished. He kissed her. He told her, after a few minutes, he had heard her crying in the night. She said it was because she had wakened and listened for little Erich breathing in his crib, had listened hard for him—until she remembered he was not hers any more.

Gib's impulse was to offer sympathy, but an abrupt thought intruded: that he had watched for a long time for some sign of emotion about the child. He had begun to wonder if he would ever see it. And in a moment another thought came: that he could not entirely believe he had seen it yet. He believed something else instead: that Melanie was no longer telling him the truth.

And that being so, there was no point in asking again if he had hurt her when he told her how he felt about Leslie. He was not satisfied with their talk about that, and he wanted to talk about it again. But if it did have anything to do with the diminished confidence between them, the talk would be self-defeating. It would only generate evasions, and maybe lies.

Coming then, the next evening, to the house off Tottenham Court Road to meet Erich Traver once more, Gib approached Melanie with a certain measured apprehension. Finding her as he did, slumped haggard and defeated and half undressed in a sagging chair, pulling beer out of a bottle, avoiding his eyes, he was disheartened even before he was struck by her parents' immediate hostility. During the first few minutes of bristling confrontation and grudging talk, he was not even sure she would take his side.

The Travers kept coals smoldering in the living room grate, and the house was overheated even more than it had been before. Erich Traver, with the lines of his face deepened by tension, held his head tipped to one side, held his jaw so tight that little rippling twitches showed along the sides, and stared at the small blue and orange flames curling around the glowing coals. "I am not accustomed," he said in sullen introspection, "to being called a liar in my own home."

"I don't know why," Melanie said in lowered voice. "I've called you one often enough, right here. And mother has called you that and worse. Don't play the pious martyr. You play it very badly."

"Melanie, please . . ." said Mrs. Traver.

Gib too stared at the coals in the grate. He was embarrassed that he had outright called Traver a liar a few moments ago. It had been a failure of self-control—caused by Melanie.

"Why did you come here again, Mr. Hubbard?" Mrs. Traver asked.

Gib looked up. He looked first at Melanie. "I came," he said, "to find out if Mr. Traver is interested in seeing the truth told about himself, or if he is as much determined to hide it as everyone else is."

"I've told the truth all along," said Traver, shaking his head a little but not looking away from the fireplace. "I've done all I could do, for years, to make the truth known."

Gib shook his head. He looked at Melanie, and this time her eyes met his, giving him what he took to be encouragement. "Since I talked to you before," he said to Traver, "I've had talks with both the Levines, husband and wife. Did Melanie tell you?"

Traver's head swung around, and he glared at Melanie. "She didn't tell us anything," he said.

"I waited for you," Melanie said quietly to Gib.

Traver pulled his cane out of its resting place, brought it around and tucked it between his knees, and with his hands clutching it he leaned forward toward Gib. "So what do you think you know?" he asked Gib scornfully.

"Well, let's start with the fact that you really were a member of the Communist Party," said Gib. "I know that."

Traver smiled. "Whoever told you that told you a lie," he sneered.

Melanie sighed noisily. "For Christ's sake," she complained.

"Erich . . ." Mrs. Traver warned her husband, in a quiet but peremptory tone.

"Who told you I was a Communist?" Traver demanded.

"It doesn't make any difference," Gib said. "It doesn't

matter who told me, because I'm not taking someone's word against yours. There's enough evidence to prove it."

"So," said Traver. "You're going to write a newspaper story, telling that Erich Traver was really a Red. That will make you a very famous journalist, won't it? What will you be? The hundred forty-first or the hundred forty-second to publish this marvellous revelation?"

Gib shook his head. "I'm not going to publish it," he said. "It isn't important enough to publish. Whether or not you were a Communist was only a minor point in what happened in 1953, and you were only a minor character. What I'm interested in is . . ."

"A *minor character*? *I* was a minor character in the Erich Traver affair?"

"You were a sacrificial goat," said Melanie.

"Oh," said Traver. "My ingenious daughter calls me a sacrificial goat. My whorish daughter. My *stripteaser* daughter. She and her dapper little journalist. A fine pair."

"Erich . . ."

"You could have been convicted at your first trial," Gib interjected forcibly. "Because you did just what you were accused of doing. You carried secret information out of your office in the War Department—later the Department of the Army—to Soviet couriers. You were guilty of what you were accused. But even that is still not the important point of the Erich Traver affair."

Traver, still clutching his cane in both hands, eased himself back in his chair, slackened, and regarded Gib with a skeptical, no longer contemptuous, gaze. "The Levines said this?" he asked quietly.

"Yes."

Traver looked at his wife, but she was looking at Gib and did not move her eyes from him.

"Mother," said Melanie. "Tell him to tell the truth."

Traver shifted his eyes to Melanie. "Do you think you'd know the truth if you heard it?" he asked.

"I don't think *you know* the truth," Melanie said. She glanced at her mother. "Neither of you."

Traver's anger rose again. He glared at Melanie for a moment. Then he shrugged. "Are we to hear it from you?" he asked.

"Mr. Traver," said Gib. "I'd like to mention a name to you. Will you tell me if you know it?"

Traver looked at Gib as if he welcomed an interruption to the exchange with his daughter. "What's the name?"

"John Steppel."

A faint, thoughtful frown came to Traver's face, and he exchanged a glance with his wife. "The Levines told you that much, did they?" he said.

"Do you know who John Steppel was?"

"I suppose you're going to tell me."

Gib nodded. "He was an NKVD major named Alekseii Parotikin. He received orders directly from Moscow and passed them on to Communists in the United States. He was a lieutenant of Lavrenti Beria, and he was killed when Beria fell."

"Steppel's dead?" Traver said with a small smile.

"Did you know who he was?" Gib asked.

Traver glanced once more at his wife, who sat high and tense in her chair. She nodded at him, and for a long moment he sat thinking and frowning, nibbling his lip almost imperceptibly. Then he spoke. "I knew he was a Russian," he said.

"Do you know what he did to you?"

Traver smiled a twisted, bitter smile. "What do you have in mind?"

"He gave direct orders to members of your Party cell to testify against you at your perjury trial. Esther Levine and the others were rehearsed in their testimony and sent to court to testify on specific orders from Steppel-Parotikin. Franklin Levine was expelled from the Party and may have risked his life, because he refused to obey those orders."

Mrs. Traver had risen from her chair while Gib was speaking, and now she knelt abruptly before Traver and clasped her hands over his where they still clutched his cane. For an instant, before Traver was distracted by his wife, Gib had seen a hard frown begin to stiffen his face and his jaw drop, his mouth fall open, as if he were about to say something angry; but then his wife captured all his attention, and his whole countenance and body softened with anxiety to reassure her. He pulled a hand from under her hands and reached out to touch her shoulder. He glanced distractedly at Gib but settled his eyes on his wife's face.

Gib looked at Melanie. She had put her beer bottle aside and was staring at her parents. Her swollen eyes had narrowed, and he saw her draw a deep breath.

"Mr. Hubbard," said Traver without taking his eyes off his wife. "Do you have any better evidence of what you say than Frank Levine's word on it?"

"Yes," Gib said. "I don't have much, and it's circumstantial, I suppose. But it's enough to convince me."

"I'm not surprised entirely," Traver said. He lifted his eyes to Gib for a moment. "I suspected it. I thought about it while I was in prison. For some time I didn't think of much else. It disturbs me to hear you say it. But it's no shock."

Traver put his hands under his wife's hands and encouraged her to rise. He smiled at her. "It's no shock," he said again.

"Why did they do it to you?" Gib asked. "Why did the Party betray you?"

Traver shrugged and shook his head. "That's what I thought about in prison, mostly. I suspected they had done it, but I couldn't think of any reason. I still can't. Oh, I suppose I was a bad Communist, not sufficiently disciplined. But I did good work for them. I believed in the Party, and I did good work. I can't think of why they would do that to me."

"They broke up the cell," said Mrs. Traver. "Exposed it. Scattered it."

Traver nodded. "Yes. They wouldn't have done that, just to make an example of me. Would they? Do you know, have you found out, why they did it?"

"No," Gib said. "But it had something to do with Benjamin Slusser. He knew the testimony was rigged by Steppel. He was a part of it, some way."

"An alliance between Steppel and Slusser?" Traver asked. "Between the NKVD and the House Un-American Activities Committee?"

"Apparently," said Gib.

"No wonder you say I was a minor figure."

"I'm looking for the reason," Gib said. "It had to be something bigger than just you. They scuttled you for some bigger reason."

"Which is why I called you the sacrificial goat," said Melanie.

Traver cast Melanie an unfriendly, unforgiving glance and kept his attention with Gib. "Do you have any idea as to what their motive may have been?" he asked.

"Not really," Gib said.

"Well, I have no idea either," Traver said. "I can't help you. The sacrificial goat would be the last one to know."

Traver had said he was not shocked, and probably he wasn't. But Gib, in the past few minutes, had watched him abandon a measure of his pride. It was replaced with bitterness. Traver was a measure weaker, a measure older, than he had been minutes ago. Mrs. Traver could see it. She had returned to her chair, and there she sat stark upright, staring at her husband with fixed, horrified eyes. Melanie did not see it. Either she had drunk too much or she did not care enough to watch, but she sat unchanged, looking at her father with the same casual scorn, tipping her bottle from time to time to pull a swig of beer. Gib hoped she would dress and leave with him when the interview was over.

"I have another question," Gib said. "A less significant one maybe."

Traver shrugged. "Ask it," he said.

"We know that Parotikin worked wtih a young woman. She was a Russian. . . ."

"Nadya Kharina," said Mrs. Traver.

"You knew her by her Russian name?" Gib asked, surprised.

"She was brought to a Party meeting by Steppel shortly after he arrived in Washington," said Mrs. Traver. "She was introduced to us as Mary Anne Waring, a Party comrade from California who would be working with Steppel. We were told she might sometimes carry word from him. She was a pretty young girl, and she spoke English perfectly. It was easy to believe she really was from California. But after only a few weeks she became seriously ill. She had pneumonia. She came to us, to Erich and me, and said she could not go into a hospital and asked us to take her in and care for her. Which we did. We called Steppel, and he consented. He came to see her once. She was very sick, to the point of death. And when she was in a delirium she spoke Russian. We found out who she was. Later she begged us not to tell Steppel. She said he'd kill her."

"Did she tell you she was a trained agent of the NKVD?"

"No, she didn't tell us that much. She only said she was a Russian girl who had been sent to Washington to help Steppel."

"Was she still around in 1953?" Gib asked.

"I don't know," said Mrs. Traver. "Not long after she recovered, we were told in a cell meeting, by Steppel, that

Mary Anne Waring had been given a new assignment and would not be in contact with us any more. We were told to pretend we did not know her, if we saw her. I did see her once or twice later, six months or a year later, and I followed orders. I didn't speak to her, and she didn't speak to me."

"She had a telephone listing," said Traver. "It was in the book. I saw it later—1950 or 1951. She might be in the States yet, for all I know."

"As a matter of fact she's in East Germany," said Gib. "But can you describe her? Can you tell me what she looked like?"

"We can do better than that," said Mrs. Traver. "We have a photograph of her. It must be around somewhere, in some of the old things. I think we can find it."

"Steppel would have shot her for sure if he'd known she let us take her picture," said Traver grimly.

THE WHITE HOUSE

"Gentlemen, the President."

Lattimer Young had spoken, forcibly injecting a low, significant voice into the conversation and abruptly stopping the desultory talk in the Oval Office. He stood, and everyone stood. The President entered the room.

President Warren Bradley had smiled at someone—perhaps a young secretary—outside the door. Between that smile, which he left out there, and the new one with which he approached his visitors, there was an instant when his face settled, apparently with relief, into his natural mask of stern concentration. But it was only for an instant, and after that revealing instant his control reasserted itself, and he smiled and nodded and extended his hand toward Senator Jordan.

"Alan," he said.

"Warren," said the Senator.

"Mr. President," said Lattimer Young, whose face had

perceptibly tightened with disapproval when he heard the Senator address the President by his first name. "May I present . . ."

"May *I* present, Mr. Young?" the Senator interrupted, and without waiting he said to the President, "Warren, this is Steve Novatny, my counsel. I think you've met him. And this is Frank Kennedy, editor-in-chief of *The Spark*. And this is Gilbert Hubbard."

The President shook hands with each of his visitors. His grip, as Gib noted, was strong. But it was short. He nodded to each of them. He looked into their eyes, and he kept his smile. But he did not say anything. He did not even repeat their names. When he had shaken each hand, he nodded toward the couches near the fireplace and asked them to sit down.

"Is that a cold rain?" the President asked, tipping his head toward the window; but before any of them could answer he stepped to his desk and began to frown over a typewritten document that lay neatly centered on his uncluttered blotter. Gib wondered if the President perhaps required a memorandum of who these visitors were and why he was seeing them, but abruptly he snatched a pen out of the holder on the desk and rapidly scrawled something, not apparently his signature, across the paper. His back was toward his visitors, and he glanced over his shoulder at them. Then, finally, he came to the heavy gold wing chair that faced the two parallel couches and the fireplace and sat down.

"You're looking well, Warren," said Senator Jordan. "It still seems to agree with you."

The President, gradually dispelling whatever was on his mind and beginning to concentrate on his visitors, frowned and nodded. "It does agree with me," he said without a smile. "I like it. I can't remember anything I've ever liked as much."

Gib was intent on the President, a little surprised at how

compact and solid and severe he looked. He was fifty-two years old. Everyone said he had not aged in the presidency, and apparently that was right. He had long been bald, with an imposing high dome of forehead standing above his square, stern face; but his baldness did not make him look old, for where the hair grew, around the sides of his head and at the back, it was thick and black, without a strand of gray. His eyebrows, beloved of political caricaturists, were black and arched and forbidding above his cool, gray eyes. When he frowned those eyebrows turned down into fierce, slanting black slashes, like the eyebrows on Samurai warriors in old Japanese prints—as which he had occasionally been pictured by cartoonists. He tended to hold his mouth the way he held it now: rigid, wrinkling his thin white lips, making an indentation between his mouth and chin, giving him, probably without his entirely intending it, a prim and disapproving mien—the reason why he practiced on his smile. Under his chin, Gib noted—more conspicuous in person than it was in his pictures—he showed his one sign of aging and deterioration: a loose fold of flesh like the wattle on a large lizard, sagging into his collar. He was conscious of it, and sometimes he pinched it between his thumb and index finger.

"That's candid," said the Senator, referring to the President's admission that he liked being President. It *was* candid, and it surprised Gib too; it was contrary to his impression of the way this man talked.

The President shrugged. "I hope," he said, "my invitation was not a great inconvenience to any of you."

The Senator smiled broadly. "Not at all," he said with a quick, dismissing gesture of his hand. This also surprised Gib. On the way to the White House in the car the Senator had been nervous and sullen about it. He said he did not like command appearances.

The President smoked. He did not smoke in public and

had made it known he did not like to be photographed smoking, but it was no secret that he did. He had cigarettes and an ashtray on the table by his chair, and he lit a cigarette now, taking the moment while the lighter was before his face to let his eyes pass over Frank Kennedy and Gib in a quick, critical examination. He was not subtle about making and filing away in his thoughts a firm first impression of each of them—particularly of Kennedy, who had come to the White House casually dressed in a well-worn tweed jacket, unpressed slacks, a dark green shirt, and a necktie knit in an Argyle pattern.

"I am not a regular reader of your paper, Mr. Kennedy, Mr. Hubbard," the President said. "I see an issue of it occasionally."

Frank Kennedy who was thoughtfully pinching his chin and had his fingers entangled in his beard, shrugged. "To be altogether frank, Mr. President, *The Spark* is not published for people like you," he said. "Though we'd be pleased of course if you did read it."

The President took a deep drag on his cigarette, and letting the smoke out of his mouth on the same breath with his words, he spoke to Gib while his eyes lingered on Kennedy. "I understand, Mr. Hubbard," he said, "that you represent the latest assault on the Erich Traver conviction."

The statement was not casual. The President was not just making conversation. He turned his eyes coolly on Gib and waited to hear what Gib would say.

Gib was checked for a moment. He felt like a schoolboy haled before the principal to account for some childish misdemeanor. He felt that way, intensely, for one moment, and then in the next he began to understand that likely this was just the way President Warren Bradley wanted him to feel—because maybe this was the assessment President Warren Bradley made of him. He glanced at the others sitting around him. He was not looking for one of them to help him, but he did want an instant's escape from the President's cold, demanding eyes. He was conscious that he was taking too long to speak. They were all looking at him now, waiting, and so he spoke, feeling unready.

"No, Mr. President," he said. "I'm not attacking the conviction. I know Traver was guilty."

The President reached out to his table and tapped the ash off his cigarette, finding the ashtray unerringly without ceasing to stare hard into Gib's face. "You acknowledge his guilt, do you?" he said. "That's something new. I had the opposite impression of your opinion. Your articles last fall implied I had participated in railroading the man."

Gib shook his head. He felt more ready to speak now, and to say something. "When I first researched the question, last fall, I read the 1953 accounts, I read the articles, the books, and so forth, and I got the impression Traver was probably not guilty. His trial was a travesty of justice. But when I began to investigate the case on my own, one of the first things I learned was that Traver was guilty of the charge placed against him. He really was a Communist."

The President's brows rose expressively and his face softened a little as he glanced at his special assistant Lattimer Young, who sat at the far end of one of the couches. Then he looked back to Gib again, with the same stern, schoolmasterish, accusing frown as before. His lips were hard and white and turned down, and he held his cigarette just under his chin in tightly curled fingers. "Well, if that is so," he said. "If Traver really was guilty, really was a Communist, then what is the point in what you're doing? What do you think you're going to prove?"

On the way to the White House in the car, they had all discussed why the President had called for them, and they had anticipated some of the things he might say. They had anticipated these questions he had asked just now, and they had agreed on the answer. The answer—part of the answer, anyway—was that if the President thought what Gib was doing important enough to summon them in to cross-examine them about it, then obviously there was some point in it. It was a temptation simply to answer his questions that way. But Gib didn't. He had another answer ready.

"The point, Mr. President," he said, "is that the trial was a travesty of justice, as I said before. Some of the most important testimony was perjury, rigged and rehearsed. It . . ."

"That's a serious charge," the President cut him off. "You can prove it?"

"I can publish it," said Frank Kennedy.

"I have no doubt you can," the President said coldly, without looking at Kennedy. "It's been published before, that and worse. My question was, can you prove it?"

"*My* question," Senator Jordan interjected, "is, why do you want to know?"

The Senator—tall and thin and tanned and white-haired—sat high and dramatic and even a little triumphant on the edge of the couch, confronting the President with mocking wide eyes. The President, not moved except likely to scorn, looked up at him without a tremor of annoyance.

"I think I have some right to know," the President said. "It's manifestly another attempt to use the old Traver case to embarrass and discredit the people who were involved in it—principally me."

The Senator grinned and shrugged and was ready to say whatever had made him grin, but Gib spoke first. "It's more than that," he said to the President.

When the President's eyes settled on Gib this time, they had changed. They were curious and annoyed, more than accusing and hostile. "Really?" he said. "Do you have a better motive? Are you sure your friends share it?"

Steve Novatny spoke for the first time, cutting off the Senator once more, before he could make whatever brittle comment he had ready. "Would you like a short summary of what Gib has learned about the Traver case, Mr. President?" Novatny asked.

The President crushed out his cigarette in his ashtray. "I suppose so," he said with taut impatience, looking down at what he was doing.

Novatny began to talk, and Senator Jordan, annoyed apparently to have his counsel telling what he himself wanted to tell, settled back disgruntled, glanced away out the tall windows, and finally fixed his eyes on his own clasped hands and seemed to have withdrawn from the conversation. Gib saw. He was increasingly disillusioned with the Senator lately—for his endless political staging, for his obsession with flair, and right now for the way in which he had been enjoying the drama of his confrontation with the President.

Today the President actually came off better in the contrast. He sat there now, solid, grim, intense, and self-contained, a formidable man. He had not used any of the political platitudes that so much characterized his public statements. He was showing none of that awkward, head-on, strained sincerity he showed on television. He was relaxed—in the sense that a man is relaxed in his self-confidence when he is doing what he knows he does well. He was at his best in private, in complete contrast to the Senator, who only seemed to function well, in Gib's newly impatient judgment, in public.

The President listened while Novatny talked, holding his eyes most of the time on Lattimer Young; and Gib thought he saw something significant between them, suggesting they knew, or had guessed, much of what Novatny was telling them. Novatny did not say how Gib had learned what he knew. He only told them what Gib knew and had reported: that Traver was in fact a Communist and that the Communist cell of which he was a member had testified against him on the specific orders of an NKVD officer named John

Steppel. He told the President that Benjamin Slusser, at least, had known how the testimony was inspired and had participated in rehearsing it.

"Your evidence against Ben Slusser had better be more valid than I suspect it is," the President said. "He's in a tough mood. He's in a mood to bring an expensive lawsuit against someone. He's tired of having his name misused."

Senator Jordan revived. He smiled. "Are you suggesting Corny Vanderhoof misused his name?" he asked.

The President shook his head. "No, not Vanderhoof," he said.

(What Cornelius Vanderhoof had reported, in his Washing column, was that Benjamin Slusser was not, perhaps, as completely retired from politics as had been supposed, since he was a frequent, and seemingly confidential, visitor to the White House. A member of the White House Press corps, whose conservative Midwestern paper did not want to publish the information, had told Steve Novatny that Slusser was in and out of Washington once or twice a month, that he always, apparently, came to the White House during these visits, and that his comings and goings seemed to be confidential, since no one was willing even to acknowledge knowing who he was. Novatny had reported this to the Senator, and the Senator had called Vanderhoof. Vanderhoof had checked the story out for himself, found it was true, and had run the mention in his daily column.)

"As a matter of fact," Novatny said, "Gib has just turned up something new about Slusser, something that sheds an entirely new light on two or three things. Are you interested, Mr. President?"

The President tightened his lips. He glanced first at his watch and then at Lattimer Young. "I suppose so," he said again.

They had decided to tell the President the latest they had

learned about Benjamin Slusser. Gib was not enthusiastic about telling, but the others had overruled him.

"You tell it, Gib," Novatny said.

"I can't reveal the source of some of this information, Mr. President," Gib said, putting an emphasis that was a little bolder than necessary on these words. "I have to protect this source. But someone in whom I have complete confidence identified the John Steppel that Steve mentioned as a Major Alekseii Parotikin of the NKVD. Parotikin had a subordinate who worked for him, a woman named Nadya Kharina. When I talked with Erich Traver the second time, I mentioned the name Nadya Kharina, and both Traver and Mrs. Traver immediately admitted they had known a young woman by this name. They . . ."

"Then Traver *admitted* he was a Communist," the President interrupted. A look of triumph had come to his face.

"Yes," Gib said. "He admitted it."

"Good," said the President, and he smiled.

"Don't change the subject," said Senator Jordan curtly.

The President shrugged. "Go on, Mr. Hubbard."

Gib nodded. "The Travers, as it turned out, actually had a photograph of Nadya Kharina. It was a group photograph, and they let me take it to a photographer's shop in London and have it copied. I had the shop also make me enlargements of the girl's face only. This is a copy of that enlargement, Mr. President."

The President took the picture Gib offered him and stared at it with a skeptical frown. The enlargement was fuzzy, but it showed, still quite identifiable, a pretty blonde girl in her early twenties.

"She used the name Mary Anne Waring," Gib said. "She was in the United States six or seven years, living in Washington. At first she attended meetings of the cell of which the Travers were members, which is how the Travers met her; but later she was apparently assigned to more confidential work, and the American Communists were ordered to stay away from her. Anyway, she established an identity as a California girl, and she made a home here and found work. She lived among people in Washington who never had the faintest suspicion she was Russian. Some of those people are still here and remember her."

"And identify her from this picture?" asked Lattimer Young, to whom the President had passed the picture. "I think it would be a little difficult to make a positive identification of anyone from this picture. There must be hundreds of girls in Washington who look like this—attractive young blondes."

"Don't try to cross-examine my witness, counsellor, until *I'm* finished with him," Steve Novatny said with a lazy smile toward Lattimer Young. They had been in law school together and had known each other ever since.

Gib looked at the two of them and waited, and when neither of them seemed about to say anything more, he went on, speaking to the President. "She was listed in the Washington telephone directory for several years. I went to the address listed and found that the house which had stood there was gone, had been torn down for an office building. But I checked property records and found that the house had been owned by a Mrs. Amos Howard. Mrs. Howard still lives in Washington, in an apartment. She is in her seventies now. She remembers Mary Anne Waring, remembers her very well. I showed her the picture and asked her if that was Mary Anne, and she said it definitely was. She had rented Mary Anne a room most of the time Mary Anne was in Washington. She remembered her as a sincere, hard-working girl of regular habits, who gave her no problems. She didn't know much about her associations, except that young men called for her frequently. She told me Mary Anne had worked in a restaurant on F Street. She couldn't remember the name."

"But you found it, I'm sure," the President said dryly.

"I found it," Gib said. "Mary Anne had worked there all right, first as a waitress, then as cashier. The bartender has worked there long enough to remember her. He told me to look for a girl named Rose Pettorini, who was Mary Anne's best friend. Rose was a waitress, and when Mary Anne quit, Rose took her place as cashier. Rose stayed on for a good many years after Mary Anne left, but she finally got married and quit. The bartender had no idea what Rose's married name was. But on a hunch I went back to Mrs. Howard, and Mrs. Howard knew all about it. Rose had been one of Mrs. Howard's roomers too. Rose and Mary Anne had lived together with Mrs. Howard. That's why they were such good friends. So finally I found Rose Pettorini—now Rose Wagner. Rose could talk for hours about Mary Anne Waring. She knew everything there was to know about her—except that she was a Russian really named Nadya Kharina."

"She identified this picture?" Lattimer Young asked.

"Yes," said Gib. "But the most important thing she told me was about Mary Anne's boy friend. Mary Anne was a good-looking girl and dated a lot, but after a while she settled on one young man and went out with him and nobody else. They even told Rose they were thinking about marriage. Rose was real pleased, as she put it, to see Mary Anne getting such a good catch. The young man was just the nicest young fellow you could imagine, a real gentleman. He had a good job. He was some kind of government lawyer. His name was Ben Slusser."

The President had apparently identified Mary Anne Waring's young man about ten seconds before Gib pronounced the name, and his annoyance with the way Gib was spinning out the story—which Gib had noticed and almost relished—had hardened instantly into anger. "I take it those are your facts," he said. "Now what do they imply?"

"There are lots of holes in that story, Mr. Hubbard," said Lattimer Young, speaking Gib's name but looking at Steve Novatny. Young had been a subdued personality in the White House for a year or so. Earlier he had been called the President's bull terrier, because of the way—as they said—he rushed out yapping whenever anyone criticized the President. He was a thin, intense, pipe-smoking, conservatively dressed lawyer.

Gib glanced at Lattimer Young, but substantially he ignored him and spoke to the President. "Mary Anne Waring disappeared not long after the second Traver trial," he said. "She told Rose she had to go home to California because her father was dying. She left, saying she'd be back in a few weeks, but she never came back. Rose called Ben Slusser and asked about her, and he told the same story—that Mary Anne had gone home to nurse her sick father through a terminal illness. Steppel-Parotikin, incidentally, left Washington about the same time. We know where *he* went—back to Russia."

The President had ignored Lattimer Young's comment and Gib's finish to the story. Fixing Gib under a surly stare, he waited for the answer to his own question. He asked it again. "I still want to know," he said, "what you infer from this story. Assuming what you say is true, what is it supposed to mean?"

Senator Jordan had come to life and was grinning. "I'd think that's clear enough," he said.

"I want to hear him tell it," the President said.

Gib looked for a moment at Steve Novatny, then at Frank Kennedy. "All right, Mr. President," he said quietly. He was subdued by a sense that he was moving into something very hazardous now. He had a great deal more confidence in the facts he had learned than in the conclusions to be drawn from them. He spoke with a troubling sense of exposure. "We know," he said, "that John Steppel was a Soviet agent and that he gave the orders to the cell members to testify against Traver. Their testimony was true insofar as it established that Traver was a member of the Communist Party, but it was false in the details and incidents described to give it verisimilitude. It was rehearsed. We know Benjamin Slusser discussed that testimony with Esther Levine before the trial, but he was not one of the trial lawyers. He rehearsed her testimony with her, and so he almost undoubtedly knew that part of it would be perjury. He could hardly help knowing. Besides that, as we now know, Benjamin Slusser was closely involved with the Soviet agent Nadya Kharina. It's a little difficult, I think, to escape the conclusion that Slusser, who was an attorney for the House Un-American Activities Committee, worked hand in hand with the Communists to rig a conviction of Erich Traver. The question is, why? What was important enough to produce an alliance like that? That's what I want to know."

"Do you imply that *I* might know?" the President asked sullenly.

"He didn't imply that," Steve Novatny firmly interjected.

"Well, I'll imply it," said Senator Jordan. "What I'd like to know is, why does Slusser make secret visits to the White House? That's what I'd like to know."

The President scowled wrathfully and raised a finger to add accusing emphasis to something—evidently something furious—he was about to say. He was cut off short by Lattimer Young, who faced the Senator with darkening concentration and, stiff with vexation, swelled and said crisply, "Senator Jordan, may I remind you that you are talking to the President of the United States?"

The Senator shot an unbelieving frown at Young, and then he shook his head and said, quickly and quietly—"Oh, shut up, you insolent little ass." He said it with no anger, for Young's vexed indignation had been so incongruous as to be comic; and Steve Novatny, even before the Senator's words were all out, threw back his head, clapped his hands, and laughed hard and loud.

Gib was watching the President and saw him check his temper. The President looked from Novatny to Young and back, distracted and gradually more quizzical than angry, and visibly he softened and withdrew into an introspective but alert defensiveness. He reached for his cigarettes and lighter. His eyes settled on Lattimer Young, who sat in confused embarrassment, apparently about half aware that his interruption had been fortunate even if it had made him look foolish.

Senator Jordan, for this once anyway, was at least as sensitive as Gib was to what had almost happened. He watched the President for a moment, until the President's eyes finally reached him, and then he shrugged easily and comfortably and without a smile but still with a soft voice, he said, "You asked us to come here, Warren. Did you have anything special in mind?"

The President nodded. He was holding his cigarette in one hand, his lighter in the other. He seemed to have forgotten them. "Yes," he said. "I had something special in mind." He remembered his cigarette then and lit it, fixing his eyes on Gib. "You're coming up with new information on the Traver case," he said. "Maybe your information is accurate. Maybe, because you are talking to some people who did not choose to talk before—or did not choose to tell the truth before—you are coming closer to really knowing what happened than anyone else has done in twenty years. But I'd like to make two suggestions to you. The first is that you do a disservice to your country if your only motive in this is to embarrass the President—and that would be so, no matter who might be the President, whether it be Senator Jordan or me. My second suggestion to you is that the publication of your new information and your speculations about what it means will have exactly the opposite effect from what you expect and intend."

"I'm interested in the second suggestion," said Frank Kennedy.

The President had eased more than a little. Settling back in his chair with his cigarette, he spoke with some confidence, and still he spoke mostly to Gib. "I'll be frank with you," he said. "You think there was some kind of irregularity in Ben Slusser's conduct with respect to the Traver matter. Well, I suspected the same thing twenty years ago. It was never more than a suspicion, and I have no more idea now than I did then if he really did anything wrong. But let me suggest to you what the suspicion is worth."

The door opened, and the President was interrupted for a moment by a young man who entered the Oval Office with a folded note for him to read. The President was quick with it, shook his head, and sent the young man out.

"Let's suppose," he said to Gib—a little less relaxed now after the interruption, sitting more erect and leaning with an elbow against one arm of the chair—"that all your information is good and everything you suspect is true. Let's suppose you can prove that Ben Slusser did somehow conspire with the Communists to get testimony against Traver and that part of the testimony was false. Now, to make that information public, you also have to release the information that Traver actually was a Communist all along. That, in turn, implies that he likely was guilty of the espionage charge brought against him at his first trial. So, what you are going to tell the American public is that Ben Slusser conspired with *some* Communists to get a conviction of *another* Communist —a particularly notorious and brazen and well-detested

Communist. How do you think the American public is going to react to that? Are they going to condemn Ben Slusser? Or congratulate him?"

Now Gib's face was hard. "I don't think," he said, shaking his head and squinting with distaste, "the American people are going to condone rigging a trial with perjury to get the conviction of anyone. I think there's a sense of justice and fairness that overrides . . ."

"Last January," the President said, "the Russians captured our Jupiter satellite and hauled it down out of space into Siberia. They precipitated what everyone now calls the Jupiter crisis. We lived through a tough two weeks, and we're still not sure they won't try to capture the new Jupiter. Whatever their motives may have been, they made a stupid blunder so far as American public opinion was concerned. Our people weren't frightened, and the American public today is in an angrier anti-Communist mood than it's been in any time since the fifties. Sure, you know lots of people who are going to be indignant about any irregularity you can find in the Traver conviction. Those people have always been indignant about it, and the fact that the charge against him was true won't make any difference to them. But what are the majority going to think?"

"That's pretty cynical, Warren," the Senator said coldly.

"It's realistic," the President said. He lowered his head to reach the cigarette in his hand, instead of raising the hand, and he looked up at Senator Jordan from under his brows. "Realism is cynicism when you're on the short end of it."

Gib, sick with his quick and bitter judgment that the President was probably right about the reaction his story would produce in the country, was ready with a tart comment, the boldest words he had dared speak to the President. But the intervention of Frank Kennedy stopped him. Kennedy had something of his own he wanted to say. "If that's the reaction you think the story will produce," he said with the special hauteur of sarcastic skepticism, "then why are you so anxious to have us not publish it?"

The President turned his head and eyes slowly toward Kennedy. "Your paper has said I profited from the Traver conviction. Maybe that's right. Maybe I did. In any case, my name is associated with it, and the more fuss you can raise about it the more you can align and solidify a certain segment of opinion against me. I don't think you can succeed in really embarrassing me or really hurting this administration, but I don't mind telling you I'm not especially enthusiastic about seeing you try. I have a personal motive, of course; but aside from that, I sincerely don't think you serve your country well by reviving old hatreds and stirring up controversy and dissension."

"That's not a very original thought," Senator Jordan remarked dryly.

The President shrugged the shrug of a man who is satisfied he has offered an unanswerable argument. "Most of the truth in the world has come to be expressed in clichés," he said. He shrugged again. "In any case, I can't stop you, or probably even influence you. But I do suggest to you that the most you're likely to accomplish—frankly, the most I hope you accomplish—is to stir up a noisy fuss among professional civil libertarians. I hope you won't think it's worth it."

GREENWICH VILLAGE

Leslie was a fitful sleeper, a quick waker. When at four AM someone rang their bell and pounded on their door, she rolled out, pulled on her shorts and a shirt, and was out of the bedroom before Gib managed to struggle up on his elbows, or clear his eyes, or orient himself in time and place. By the time he was sufficiently conscious to understand that someone was at their door in the middle of the night, Leslie was already talking to someone in the living room. He put his feet on the floor and reached for his shorts. By the time he got his pants on, the conversation outside was at an end and Leslie closed the apartment door. She returned.

"Frank Kennedy sent this," she said. She had a newspaper. "He sent that girl over here to wake us up and . . . give it to us." She was looking at it, quickly scanning something. She was reluctant to hand it over. But she did. "*Chicago Tribune*," she said.

Gib did not have his contact lenses in. He put on a pair of glasses he kept on the night stand. He switched the lamp brighter and frowned grimly over the newspaper.

The story was on the bottom of the front page. It was a by-line story, under the name of a reporter whose name Gib did not know. The headline was:

Truth at Last Told:

TRAVER GUILTY ALL ALONG, DISCLOSURE

The beginning of the story read:

After twenty years, the truth is now known. Erich Traver, charged with espionage and convicted of perjury for his involvement in Communist spying in Washington, was guilty as charged.

Twenty years of controversy, inspired by liberals and civil libertarians who refused to believe the evidence and maintained stubbornly that Traver was a martyr, now ends. Traver, long-time darling of the far left, really was a Communist and a traitor to his country.

Ironically, the perjury conviction which sent Traver to prison after the government failed to prove espionage charges, was the result of connivance between investigators for the House Un-American Activities Committee and representatives of the Communist Party. For reasons of their own, perhaps involving Party discipline, the Communists assisted in the 1953 prosecution by offering members of a Party cell to refute Traver's sworn testimony that he was not a member of the Communist Party.

Ironically too, the recent investigation which produced conclusive evidence of all this has been sponsored by a liberal Democrat senator and conducted by a reporter for a far-out left wing newspaper in New York—in anticipation of entirely different results. Gilbert Hubbard, a cub reporter for . . .

Leslie interrupted Gib's reading. "What's it say? C'mon. I want to know too."

Gib sighed heavily and shook his head. "It's our story," he said. "They've broken our story. Just about everything we know. It's all here." He turned to an inside page, where the story was continued and where pictures of Erich Traver and of Benjamin Slusser appeared. "Everything we know, just about everything," he said. "Except for the editorial viewpoint, I could have written the story myself."

She crawled into the middle of the bed, where she could read over his shoulder. "How could that be?" she asked. "Where could they have gotten it?"

"What's the difference?" he asked. "They got it, and they've published it. So that's that. That's the end. We're out of the Erich Traver business, and I don't know who looks like the greatest ass: Senator Jordan or Frank Kennedy or me. Or Erich Traver. Anyway, it's all over. Our big story is out, and somebody else published it. Nice work. Brilliant journalism. Shit!"

When Steve Novatny called Frank Kennedy and told him he was flying up from Washington and would be in New York a little after noon, Kennedy told him to come to Gib's apartment instead of to *The Spark* office. They'd have privacy there.

"Debacle!" Gib said. He had a Scotch and soda in his hand. The remains of his lunch littered the coffee table. Leslie was in the kitchen, pouring drinks for Kennedy and Novatny, and making a sandwich for Novatny, who hadn't had lunch on the plane. "An absolute goddam debacle. We look like a bunch of idiots."

Novatny had loosened his tie but still wore his jacket, in contrast to the rest of them who were in khakis and sweaters and who'd had a few drinks ahead of him. "Oh, it's not that bad," he said quietly.

"It is for me," Gib said. "It is for us."

Taking it instantly that the comment set him outside the circle, Novatny shrugged and said, "All right. Have it your way. You look like idiots."

"How'd it happen?" Gib asked, subdued a little. "How did it get out? Have we overlooked a bug somewhere in this apartment? I run a nervous search for them about every goddam day."

Novatny shook his head. "No. Nothing like that. The leak was with us. One of our staff people. Anyway, you know, we haven't been all that secretive. Not lately. We talked pretty openly to the President and Lattimer Young. They could have decided it was good tactics to break the story themselves, in a friendly paper. But that wasn't what happened.

One of our staff didn't like what we were doing and told the story."

"How long have you known?" Kennedy asked.

"Since yesterday, when he quit."

Novatny accepted from Leslie his sandwich and a martini. He thanked her and stood up to take off his jacket before he began to eat.

"It's all finished," Gib said mournfully.

"Well now, I don't want to jump to that conclusion," Frank Kennedy interjected quickly. "That's something we have to talk about."

Gib shrugged. "About what?"

"To start with, for one thing," Kennedy said firmly, "you have to do a story telling our version of what you've learned. We can't just ignore the Traver matter, now that the story has broken. Our name is being used, and we have to put out our story. And soon. And that's your job."

"I'll win the Pulitzer Prize for anti-climax."

"Whether you win any prizes or not . . ." Kennedy said.

"He's already won a prize this morning," said Leslie. "For histrionics. All morning."

Gib raised his eyes toward her. "Thanks."

"I don't think you look like an idiot yet," said Novatny. "But you can in the next few days. You're going to be asked a lot of questions. You're a public figure all of a sudden. If you handle yourself badly, you can still be an idiot and have the debacle you're talking about. Or you can save a lot for yourself."

"Save what? That's what I want to know. *Save what?*"

"That's what we're going to find out," said Frank Kennedy. "See what happens. See what the public reaction is. Then we'll decide what to do, whether to drop the whole Traver business or do something more with it."

Kennedy finished his drink quickly. He had to leave, had to go back to the office. Leslie offered Novatny a second sandwich and another martini, which he accepted, and he spread himself out, relaxed, in his chair and openly studied the apartment and the girl. When she was in the kitchen, he bluntly asked Gib if she lived with him. Gib said she did, maybe temporarily. She had moved out of some rooms that were so shabby they were depressing, and she hadn't found anywhere else yet. Novatny smiled knowingly and said he wished her no success in looking.

Novatny got up to take a closer look at a charcoal sketch of Leslie that Gib had recently bought and hung. "Ah, my friend," Novatny said, "I'm afraid I have something more to add to your perfect day."

"I need something more."

"I know you do," Novatny said. He frowned over the picture. "Not bad at all," he said. (Leslie's artist was getting better. He had caught in this sketch the subdued and subtle smile of amusement which lurked almost unseen beneath a characteristic thoughtful solemnity she showed the world. That was why Gib had bought the picture.) "Who's the artist?"

"What else is it you have to tell me?" Gib asked.

Novatny blew a short sigh. "Okay," he said. He picked up his jacket and took from the pocket a folded piece of paper. "This," he said, "is the Senator's statement about *The Tribune* story. It's been released."

Gib read the typewritten statement. It said—"Senator Alan Jordan made the following comment this morning on the Erich Traver revelations. 'Mr. Gilbert Hubbard and the newspaper for which he works are to be congratulated for an effort in the best traditions of American journalism. The Hubbard investigation of the old Erich Traver case has demolished the sham behind the long-time claims of various prominent political figures to have been the ones who ran Traver to ground, since it now appears that the Communist Party itself provided a HUAC investigator the evidence that convicted Traver. Newspaper accounts to the effect that I have been the sponsor of the Hubbard investigation have greatly exaggerated; however, my staff has offered Mr. Hubbard assistance from time to time, in searching congressional committee records etc. at his request. I am pleased that members of my staff were able to give Mr. Hubbard some little help. Since it would be inconsistent, however, with the freedom and integrity of the press for any journalist to work with the sponsorship of a senator or other governmental figure, I want to emphasize that I am not a sponsor of Mr. Hubbard or of his newspaper.' "

Gib nodded and grinned sarcastically as he finished reading. "A real vote of confidence," he said.

"He also told a reporter who called him this morning that your investigation was over and he did not expect any of his staff to give you any more help. You'll probably read that somewhere."

"The cowardly lying son of a bitch can go to hell."

Novatny smiled. "He also sent me up here as a personal messenger from him to you. His message—in *my* words— is, 'Disregard all public statements. I'm still one hundred per cent in your corner.' "

"Oh? Then we are not to believe anything he says in public, huh? Just wait for the private word. Is that it?"

A tolerant smile remained fixed on Novatny's big dark face. "The man is vulnerable, Gib," he said gently. "You don't know what it is to be a politician, how vulnerable it makes you."

"My sympathy."

"They can't get at *you*," Novatny said. "You have an independence the Senator hasn't had since he was your age. You don't know what it is to be vulnerable to what the news media say about you. You don't know what it is to have to read the clippings every morning to see how they're using your name."

"No? Well, maybe I'm going to find out."

Over the next three weeks, every morning the clippings were brought to his desk at *The Spark*—the clippings and a pile of mail. Each night he took them home, and they accumulated. Eventually, Leslie brought home a large cardboard box from the supermarket, and she swept most of them in, leaving out only the important ones, which she sorted carefully and arranged on the coffee table. She knew better than to dump those in the box. He would want them. He kept reading them and reading them, every night.

The Times immediately identified the significance of the new information about the Traver case. It suggested editorially that the FBI reopen the case to see if any evidence could be found which might suggest what larger motives had led the Soviet Union to betray Erich Traver and sacrifice the cell of which he had been a member. ("Our files are closed on that," the FBI Director said bluntly the next day, when the editorial was read to him.)

Some newspapers, the newsmagazines, two or three leading columnists, and one network television commentator were critical of the Warren Bradley of twenty years before for having allowed the Traver case to go to trial without disclosing his suspicion that something was wrong with part of the evidence. If, they said, he actually knew the trial was rigged with perjury, then he was guilty of serious wrongdoing. But they did not regard it as proved that he had known, and in any case they tended to dismiss the whole matter as history.

The more typical reaction around the country was reflected in the syndicated Blair McKinney column, which ran in fifty-five newspapers. "We are well rid of the Travers," he wrote. "Europe is welcome to them. It has been an item of left-wing faith in this country that Erich Traver was a martyr. The left will have to find itself a new martyr. It may well have to find itself a new villain too, since what we now know about Erich Traver makes a young Congressman of twenty years ago, named Warren Bradley, look even better than we thought."

The President, Gib said repeatedly to Leslie, had been not far from right in his cynical appraisal of how the country would react. "What we have to accept," Gib said, "is that whatever *you and I* may think of Bradley, the man did not get to be President and get re-elected for a second term by being a bumbling bourgeois idiot. We talk that way so much we get to believing it. The fact is, he's an astute politician, and he knows exactly what he's doing. He senses the mood of the country and exploits it with complete cynicism. There's not a grain of principle in him. If he thought the popular mood called for a Communist, he'd be a Communist. If he thought it called for a Nazi, he'd be a Nazi. If he thought it called for a vegetarian, that's what he'd be."

"Do you think Senator Jordan is any different?" she asked.

"No. The only difference is, he miscalculated. The only thing that redeems him for me is that he's stuck with a political philosophy a little closer to my own."

In the pile of clippings that Leslie did not dump into the cardboard box were some about Gib himself, personally, and even some about her. These were the ones he read and re-read the most.

Time called him "a slight, pale, intense young man, probably more driven than inspired, and apparently not sure if it is a zeal for truth that drives him—or his utter loathing for Warren Bradley."

Newsweek said he was "at the age of twenty-five, a seasoned professional crusader, a perfect representative of a generation that does not choose to believe anything anyone has ever believed before, unless it can prove it for itself. He is, whatever else one may wish to make of him, an idealist in action."

A Chicago editorial called him "a cub reporter for a scruffy Greenwich Village sheet which deals mostly in socialism and obscenity, a professional scoffer who has used the pages of his paper to belittle and ridicule his country and everything its people cherish."

"He's nothing but a little smart-ass," said Congressman Harold Packard of North Dakota, Republican leader of the House, whose office in a quick press release complained that the Congressman had been misquoted and had really said, "Hubbard is a little smart-*aleck*."

Blair McKinney, in his fifty-five papers, said, "Young Hubbard was sent out to find evidence that Erich Traver was not guilty, that he was in truth the martyr his liberal friends have always proclaimed him. Hubbard went at it with enthusiasm, but when he stumbled on evidence that proved Traver was in fact guilty, his enthusiasm for writing the story collapsed almost as fast as his paper's enthusiasm for publishing it. That is why he did not write it and his paper did not publish it, and the story was finally broken by *The Chicago Tribune*."

And the President, asked at a press conference if it were true that he had met and talked with Gilbert Hubbard, smiled easily, shrugged lightly, and said, "Oh, yes. Frankly, he impresses me as a young man who'd do almost anything to get attention."

Several newspapers took note that Leslie Perruchot—variously identified—lived in Gib's apartment. *Time* called her "a boyish, barefoot, kittenish revolutionary, one of the aimless dissatisfied children who drift from nowhere to nowhere, without ambition, without morals, without purpose, sustained by nothing but an endless supply of misdirected and often undirected indignation." The story was accompanied by her picture, which had been taken by a wire service photographer and distributed to many papers. He had found her lounging on the stone steps outside the building, enjoying the early-spring sunshine and wearing the clothes she had taken to wearing as soon as the weather had turned the least bit warm—a pair of little shorts and a loose, ragged T-shirt. She'd been sitting with her legs stretched out in front of her, and the picture showed the black soles of her bare feet. ("Anyway, he didn't catch me picking my nose," she'd said to Gib when she first saw the picture in *The Daily News.*)

Leslie received more than a hundred letters, about ten per cent of them obscene. Gib received two or three thousand, mostly abusive. He had his telephone number changed and unlisted a few days after the story broke, to cut off the calls.

A fat, fortyish sister of Leslie's came to the apartment to demand that Leslie come home to Long Island. The visit was unannounced, and unfortunately Gib was at home. "Who is this Gilbert Hubbard? The right hand man of God? You know what's wrong with you? You know what I object to? *You have no respect.* You have no respect for Leslie, or you wouldn't have her living here like this. You have no respect for elementary morals. Or for the country we live in, or the government. You don't have respect for anything that anyone else lives by. That's the trouble with people like you, you think you have the right to decide everything all over again—everything that's been decided, all over again, all for yourself."

His mother, on the telephone from Albany, had the bluntness to tell him directly what his father had been trying to say subtly in fifteen minutes of fumbling circumlocution. "Look, Gib, your senseless attack on the President of the United States is humiliating your father and hurting his business."

"Hurting his business?" Gib had asked skeptically. It was an old threat. Ever since he was a child she had been telling him that any non-standard, disapproved conduct would hurt his father's business.

"I wasn't going to tell you, Gib," his father had said then. "But I guess you have to know. In the past week, three big companies we've done business with for years, for generations in fact, have notified me that they've reduced the amount of merchandise they'll carry with us, except on a thirty-day-pay basis. It's what you call *retaliation,* Gib."

"That's exactly what it is. And there's only one way to stop it. I'll write . . ."

"*No.* If you publish an attack on the companies I have to do business with, it'll only solidify the business community against you, and against me. It'll only suggest to others how to apply the same pressure. We're sound and can live with this thing. But if you do anything to make it worse, it could become damaging. I don't ask you to stop doing what you believe you have to do. But I . . ."

His mother interrupted. "It's about time you grew up, Gib, and faced the realities of life. Don't you agree it's about time?"

One day the third week after the story broke, he went uptown to have lunch with an old friend of his, one of his professors from Columbia. In the restaurant he was recognized by a woman, and she came to his table and abused him loudly for being "a tool of the Communists" and "one of the people who's spoiling this country." Her husband was a veteran who'd fought for this country. And so on. When he got home, there was more hostile mail, addressed to him there and not at the office. Included was a copy of a resolution passed by the Marietta, Ohio, Junior Chamber of Commerce, deploring "the spirit of divisiveness" in the country and condemning "all baseless, intemperate, and non-constructive criticism of American traditions and institutions and holders of high offices." He did not go to meet Leslie at work that evening, and when she came home at seven he was asleep on the couch. He'd made himself three martinis and had drunk them with a small sandwich, and he'd gone to sleep without carrying the dishes back to the kitchen.

She changed out of the uniform she knew he hated before she woke him. She fixed him a sandwich and a Coke, and they were ready on the coffee table when he wakened to her touch on his shoulder and pushed himself up, a little headachy and a little dizzy.

Leslie was grinning. While he was waking she had spied the Jaycee resolution and was reading it. She began to chuckle.

"It isn't funny," he said hoarsely.

"Yes, it is. Where's your sense of humor? Send it back to them. Tell them to jam it up the division in their backsides."

"Okay," he said wearily. He sat up, saw the sandwich she'd made, and reached for it. He began to eat appreciatively.

"Bed?" she asked. "When you've finished your sandwich and Coke, I mean."

He nodded.

She offered him more than orgasm and satiation. Lying in bed together, warm in their complete and easy intimacy, they took comfort from each other—and in these weeks especially *he* took comfort from *her*. Many nights they did not reach a climax, didn't try to. Many nights it was enough just to lie together naked in the warmth beneath two blankets, just to hold each other close in the dark, to touch, to fondle gently, to drift slowly to sleep. When he woke in the night, after trouble in his dreams, she would be there close to him, with her back to him, for him to fit his body to, and he would go back to sleep. Some nights she needed him. Most nights those weeks, he needed her. And some nights, when they needed sex, they had it, and it was good. Both of them were fascinated with how easy it was for them, how quickly they aroused each other, and how fully they were satisfied when it was over. This night—the night when she finally made him laugh at the Jaycee resolution—they slept part of the evening and awoke half aroused. They made love for two hours then, and he did not wake from nervous dreams that night.

The telegram from Melanie came on a Sunday.

URGENT REPEAT URGENT YOU RETURN PARIS IMMEDIATELY.

MELANIE

He sent the answer within the hour.

IMPOSSIBLE. BUT WHY?

GIB

Her next wire was delivered in the middle of the night.

SHTEMENKO.

MELANIE

Novatny came to New York and came to Gib's apartment on Tuesday evening. "Frank Kennedy and I think you should go," he said. He paused for a moment, making the motions of savoring the martini Leslie had mixed for him but probably actually taking the moment to decide whether or not to add what he said next—"The Senator thinks so too."

"Why?" Gib demanded. "For a vacation?"

"Your work on the Traver matter isn't finished," Novatny said. "The investigation is not over."

"In spite of what the Senator says?"

"I've come up from Washington twice now to assure you about his support."

"It's hard to believe him. If he's telling me the truth, he's lying to the public. If he's telling the public the truth, he's lying to me."

"Will you come off that horse shit?" Novatny asked in a sarcastic drawl, out of a twisted mouth. "In the first place, does whether you go ahead or not depend on what the

Senator thinks? Or on what I think? Does it depend on what Frank Kennedy thinks, even? I thought you were the independent little bastard that went your own way, no matter what."

"I am," Gib said quickly and crisply. "I make my own judgments, and right now it's my judgment that the Traver investigation—if that's what we should call it—is so screwed up from beginning to end that there's very little point in going on."

Novatny held his martini under his nose and inhaled the smell of the gin. His eyes fastened for a long moment on Leslie's nipples, showing plainly through her thin old T-shirt. He took a sip from his martini. "Okay," he said. "If I have to give you some kind of pep talk, Gib, like the football coach in an old B-movie, you can go to hell. But you're the one who was telling us only a month ago that the real significance of the Traver case remained to be uncovered. This guy Shtemenko. Who knows what he's got? After the way you described him, I'd go anywhere to find out what he's come up with. You want my advice, the Senator's advice, Frank Kennedy's advice, you go to Paris. *This is your deal, by God.* You gonna back out, for Christ's sake?"

When Novatny was gone, Leslie sat in the middle of the coffee table, squatted there in her familiar old posture, and fixed Gib with a scornful eye and lofted chin. "You goyish prick," she said. "There never was a chance you'd back out. What did you want from Novatny? Have you pulled the same line on Frank Kennedy? What are you trying to do, get them to talk you into doing what you know perfectly well you're going to do anyway?"

Gib grinned. "I guess I want a little reinforcement," he said.

"It's a stupid tactic," she said. "You might have wound up having to beg them to let you go."

Something like that happened. He was to fly to Paris on Friday. Thursday afternoon he got a call from Novatny in Washington. Novatny was apologetic, but the Senator, it seemed, had received complaints from big campaign donors about the use of campaign funds to support trips to Europe for the likes of Gilbert Hubbard. To keep things quiet, just for the moment, the Senator was forced to withhold any more money. He was sorry. Novatny was sorry. And Frank Kennedy was sorry, but *The Spark* couldn't finance the trip either. It had other projects that needed money. Gib's angry words about the abrupt switch didn't help him with either man. They stopped saying they were sorry. They began saying flatly that he simply had to understand that circumstances . . .

Gib sold some bonds he had inherited from his maternal grandfather and paid for his ticket with his own money.

He left Leslie at the apartment this time. She could not come to the airport with him. He insisted she could not. He anticipated reporters and cameramen and fuss at the airport, if it got out that he was flying to Paris again. So he left her, sitting on the couch in their living room, not crying, but looking as desolate and abandoned as she'd looked when he left for Europe on the first of these trips, in January.

Her hair was tied back behind her ears. (She'd told him, the first time he saw it that way, that she'd tied it back to please him; but he'd suspected she'd done it because the restaurant where she worked insisted she come to work with it that way.) Her tiny gold earrings showed. (He'd discovered, to his surprise, that her ears were pierced.) She had a strange, thoughtful expression on her face, and she toyed distractedly with the buttons on the little blouse she was wearing that day. She had kissed him in the bedroom when he was closing his suitcase, and after that she sat quietly away from him and ignored the brittle chatter with which he tried to distract both of them from the sadness of another separation. He told her he loved her.

She did not look up. She just sat there with her eyes down, fumbling with the buttons on that little white blouse. It was as if something were very different. It was as if the pressures of the past three weeks had finally reached her. The blouse was much too small (God knew where she'd gotten it), and when her shoulders were high a little brown skin showed between the tail of the blouse and the waistband of her yellow shorts. She rubbed the sole of one foot with the big toe of the other.

Suddenly he was concerned about leaving her alone, and he told her if anything happened to call Frank Kennedy. She smiled faintly. He told her not to worry, nothing would happen, the storm was pretty much over. She nodded. And then he had to go. He kissed her, and they didn't say anything more, and he left her.

On the way to the airport, Gib brooded about Leslie and her strange, desolate mood. And on the way an ugly thought came to him: that someone, in one of the articles about him, had used an alarming phrase—"open and notorious cohabitation." In a telephone booth in the TWA terminal, he called Frank Kennedy and asked him to check with his lawyer and see if it were still some kind of blue-law crime for a couple to live together in the same apartment without being married, and if it was, to get Leslie out of there and find her another place to live. Kennedy scoffed gently but said he'd call the lawyer. Gib laughed weakly and said he supposed the call was silly. But, he reminded Kennedy, the police had invaded his apartment, allegedly to search for marijuana . . .

This was the kind of thing Steve Novatny did not take into account when he minimized your vulnerability. He was too old to know or share the new insecurity. He was too confident and insensitive to understand it. He did not know, and in common with nearly everyone else his age, he chose not to know. He would have laughed at this worried little telephone call. But he would have laughed too at the suggestion that the police might come and ransack your apartment and strip you naked to search for marijuana. His judgment was no good about things like that.

Oh no, they could not get at you if you were not a politically ambitious United States Senator but were just Gib Hubbard, boy reporter. What could they do to you, after all? They could only humiliate you, make you look an ass, deny your integrity. But that was all right. (It really was all right, in a sense that Steve Novatny could not understand, because you could live nicely with all this if you didn't care, and you really didn't have to care.) They couldn't do anything more to you, could they? Or might the police just happen to come again looking for marijuana and this time bring some with them so they could drop it and be sure to find it? Oh no, that couldn't happen. Steve Novatny couldn't believe it could happen and couldn't understand why Gib Hubbard did not have much confidence that it couldn't happen. Steve Novatny did not know. He didn't know, and in his blind, stubborn ignorance he was unafraid. Well, Gib Hubbard wasn't ignorant, and he wasn't unafraid. He was not intimidated. But he was afraid.

And so was Leslie. That was what he had seen in her, that had seemed so strange, when he left her. She was going to be alone while he was gone, and she was afraid. Short of his worst fears—which maybe were a bit far-fetched—there was still enough in their situation to overwhelm her, because in spite of all her brittle, cynical, hard, determined independence, she was still very much a fragile little girl.

He wished, suddenly, he had brought her with him. Maybe from Paris he should send for her. Melanie could help him find a place for her maybe, and he could keep her in Europe while he was there, or until they felt secure again about things at home. Silly maybe. . . . Or maybe not.

NADYA KHARINA

PARIS

"Vous fumez trop, Aleksandr Leonidovich," the Russian woman who apparently did not speak Russian complained to Shtemenko. She blew a noisy breath and fanned her hand back and forth in front of her face to clear the air of the heavy smoke from Shtemenko's thick, dark cigarette.

Shtemenko closed his eyes for a moment and sucked deep on the cigarette. *"Pas possible,"* he said dryly.

The woman turned to the young man who sat beside her. *"De quoi parlent-ils?"* she asked querulously, directing a gesture toward Shtemenko and Gib and Melanie.

The young man shrugged and gave Shtemenko an appealing glance.

Shtemenko sighed. *"L'Américain parle anglais seulement,* Vera Ivanovna," he said with firm, quiet patience. *"Je le regrette."*

"Tell her I'm sorry," Gib said to Melanie.

"Why?" Melanie asked quietly. "She speaks French only, and you speak English only. Big goddam deal." She raised her voice and said to the woman, *"Mon ami le regrette, Madame."*

The Russian woman looked at Gib, half contemptuous, half pitying. "Umhh," she said, and she shrugged.

"Senator Jordan," Shtemenko said to Gib. "I was speaking of Senator Jordan. If he means to impress us with his sincerity, he can come here himself. Will he? Will he come, do you think?"

Gib shook his head. "I'm sorry. I don't think so."

Shtemenko glanced at the Russian woman, who was showing her impatience again. "Translate for her," he said to the young man who sat beside her. "You understand English."

The young man nodded and began to whisper to the woman. His name was Yuri Tyulenev. The woman was Vera Ivanovna Kravchenko. Yuri Tyulenev was chubby and pink-faced, short of breath and nervous. They were meeting in his apartment, and his wife—a fat, placid, pregnant girl—sat just beyond the door in the next room, pretending to read but probably listening. Vera Ivanovna Kravchenko was a flushed and frowzy matron in a flowered pink dress. She wore a straw hat with a veil. Shtemenko was as before: lean and sinewy and gray, grim and calm. The three were a committee—they said—of the governing council of the National Alliance of Russian Patriots. They did not inspire unlimited confidence, and Gib was disappointed.

"Senator Jordan really isn't all that important," Gib said to Shtemenko. "I intend to go on with my work whether Senator Jordan supports it or not."

"I'm afraid I can't agree with you," Shtemenko said. "I'm afraid we think he is important."

"My newspaper will support me and publish whatever I report," Gib said.

Shtemenko shook his head stubbornly. "I am afraid," he said, "that what you report and what your newspaper publishes is not very important. I dislike having to remind you of it, but you and your newspaper are not very influential in the United States. The Senator, however harshly *I* may judge him, is a man who is listened to when he speaks. You are not."

"I could argue with you about that," Gib said.

"And I wish I could accede to your argument," Shtemenko

said with a polite nod. "But I cannot. We are talking now about a hazardous investigation, involving very large issues. We could risk our lives to obtain information for you, only to have you dismissed as a young dreamer or a liar when you reported it in the United States. I am sorry."

Gib raised his chin. "In other words," he said, "I am being dismissed. I am being kicked out."

Shtemenko shook his head quickly. "Oh, no," he said. "We want you to continue to participate. In fact, I think we will insist you do. But we want you to bring in someone besides yourself. What we are talking about is too big for you alone, or for your newspaper alone."

"Aleksandr Leonidovich!" Tyulenev exclaimed. He was protesting that the conversation was going too fast for him to translate.

"A moment please," Shtemenko said to Gib, and then he turned to the Russian woman and began to talk to her in French.

Gib had a glass of chilled white wine on the table before him, which had been poured for him when the meeting began, and he had not until now touched it. He picked it up and sipped. The wine was good, light and fruity. It calmed him a little. Melanie touched his arm and shook her head. They watched Shtemenko and the woman talking.

Maybe the two Russians were arguing, because the woman's voice was querulous. But really you couldn't tell; she had been querulous in everything she said.

Gib put the wine glass down again on the thick white cloth, and he glanced once more around the room—at the French bourgeois furnishings and at the black and white cat which prowled back and forth across the sideboard, stepping delicately on the plates and saucers.

Melanie touched his arm again. "I'm sorry about this, Gib," she said. "This is new. He didn't say anything about it before."

Gib shrugged. It was not a shrug of dismissal but a shrug of sullen acceptance of what he could not control. "I didn't get into this thing for my personal glory," he said.

"You're entitled to some, just the same, if you can get it," she said.

The pregnant girl in the next room kept glancing at Melanie, as did Yuri Tyulenev, while Shtemenko and Vera Ivanovna Kravchenko talked. They were looking at her tight pink and yellow pants and shirt—which even the dour Shtemenko had noticed with a small grin of appreciation when he first saw them. Melanie returned the glances of Tyulenev and his wife, conspicuously conscious that her appearance was defiant of these dark, bourgeois surroundings and these humorless bourgeois people.

"My friends and I agree, of course," Shtemenko said to Gib, turning abruptly away from the Russian woman. "You must convince the Senator. He must come."

"How? How am I to convince him?"

Shtemenko closed his narrow little eyes for an instant. "He must understand, and you must understand, that the larger implications of the Traver affair are beyond considerations of his political ambitions and beyond considerations of your young idealism. We are not certain what we will learn if we take up your investigation in earnest. But I can tell you this: that questions of the gravest international import are involved."

"You want to know what Senator Jordan will say to that?" Melanie interjected aggressively.

Shtemenko cast cold eyes on her. "What?" he asked, manifestly resentful of the challenge.

"Bullshit."

In the abruptly silent moment that followed the word, Yuri Tyulenev did not see Shtemenko's angry scowl, and he grinned and asked, "Aleksandr Leonidovich, *comment dit-on* 'bullshit' *en français?*"

"*Merde,*" Shtemenko said grimly, without looking at the young man.

"I've tried to tell you . . ." Melanie said to Shtemenko with an intense annoyed grimness that entirely matched his own. She stopped, caught up in exasperation over Shtemenko's haughty, unyielding grimace, and she turned to Gib and spoke to him. "I've tried to tell him," she said, "that he cannot persist in this attitude of . . . of melodramatic conspirator. If they are going to work with you and Senator Jordan, they'll have to tell you what they are thinking. They have to trust you that far." She turned on Shtemenko once more. " 'Questions of the gravest international import,' " she said contemptuously. "You've used that phrase with me, too. But it's meaningless."

Shtemenko spoke to Gib. "She is a persistent young woman," he said with bland solemnity.

"Well, it's a good thing I am," Melanie said. "If I hadn't been, you'd have dropped this whole thing a long time ago, and you'd never have found out that 'questions of the gravest international import' are mixed up in the Traver case."

Shtemenko looked at Melanie for a moment, apparently now just conceding his patience and waiting for her to talk herself out before he went on.

"I'm not being unreasonable . . ." Melanie said, and she allowed Gib's frown to stop her.

"I am curious to know," Shtemenko said. He glanced quickly back and forth between Gib and Melanie. "I must know if your Senator Jordan—and for that matter, if you two young people—are ready to share in the risks my friends and I propose to take. I am not convinced that Senator Jordan is. . . . Well, let me put it this way. I have been intrigued by a colorful expression that I am told American gangsters use. I will adopt that expression and hope I use it correctly. What I want to know is, will Senator Jordan put his cock on the anvil?"

"Comment dit-on . . . ?" Yuri Tyulenev asked, but Shtemenko waved him off.

Gib grinned, but in a moment he was serious again. "What risks are you talking about?" he asked.

"Logic might have suggested to you what must be done next," Shtemenko said. "Perhaps it has. The investigation has been carried about as far as it can go on this side of the Iron Curtain. The solution to your problem is on the other side, and we must go there and get it."

Gib's breath was checked by the implication behind what Shtemenko had just said, but his curiosity was momentarily strong enough to impel him to form a question and ask it. "Go where and get what?" he asked.

"You might guess," Shtemenko said. "I told you before that Nadya Kharina, the woman who worked with the late Major Alekseii Parotikin, lives and works in East Germany. We must go there and interview her. It may be the only possible way of learning what motivated the Kremlin in the Erich Traver affair. If Nadya Kharina is not the only living person who knows, certainly she is the only such person we can reach."

Gib was aware that Tyulenev had stopped translating. With the name Nadya Kharina in the conversation, the Russian woman would know what Gib was being told, without translation. She and Tyulenev were staring at him, as was Shtemenko, obviously to see how much courage he had. He did not know how much he was showing. It didn't make any difference how much he was showing. However much it was, it was more than he felt. Risk their lives, Shtemenko had said.

"We make the crossing occasionally, some of us," Shtemenko said quietly. "It's always dangerous."

"What makes you think you can find Nadya Kharina and talk to her?" Gib asked.

"We know," Shtemenko said. "We've checked into that."

"And you expect me to go with you," Gib said.

"Yes. You. And Senator Jordan. That is the risk we have to take, and you must take it with us."

"And me," Melanie said. "I want to go."

"No. Just Mr. Hubbard. And Senator Jordan."

That night Gib walked from his hotel to the club where Melanie was working. It was a long walk, a very long walk, through streets still wet with the afternoon's rain. But it was all right; he did not want to reach the club too early. Melanie did not finish until three in the morning, and Gib did not like to sit there and wait, where he was not particularly welcome anyway.

He'd had dinner at his hotel. Then he'd read and slept fitfully in his room until about eleven, when he called Steve Novatny in Washington. It was six in Washington, and he reached Novatny at home in his apartment.

"I've heard silly, ridiculous propositions in my time, Gib, but this one sets some kind of record."

"Okay. Just tell me, yes or no: is Jordan in this deal or isn't he?"

"On that deal, no. Hell no. He isn't going into East Berlin incognito, hell no. What do you think he'd be risking?"

"I know what he'd be risking. The same as I'll be risking, no more, no less."

"You're going?"

Gib checked himself for an instant. He hadn't really answered that question, even for himself. He hadn't had enough time to think about it. But he had to say yes to Novatny, if he was going to keep alive any argument that the Senator should come with him, so he said yes.

"You're out of your mind. What does Frank Kennedy say to all this?"

"Nothing. He doesn't know about it. I haven't called him."

"You'd better."

"I need Jordan. The Russians here say they won't go on with the deal, won't take the risks, unless the Senator shows his sincerity, comes and shares the danger."

"What the hell kind of logic . . . ?"

"I told you. They want a prominent American, a major public figure with a good reputation, to witness the interview with Nadya Kharina, so that when we come back and tell what she says, it will have some chance of being believed."

"Well, it's not going to be Alan Jordan, Gib. There's no point in talking about it. He's not going to risk his whole career, maybe his life. I won't even make the proposition to him. Besides, you might as well know, he's getting more and more flack about you."

"So he's backing off?"

"Well . . . he's going to be more cautious."

"All right. To hell with him. Listen. Get me somebody else. Get me somebody I can substitute for Jordan, somebody big enough to satisfy my Russians. Come over here yourself and bring the candidate with you, and I'll try to get these people to buy him."

"Gib, you're out of your skull."

"No, I'm not. Look, Steve. These Russians I'm dealing with are tough, serious people. They say we've only just begun to uncover what's involved in the Traver case. They think they have a good chance of finding out why the Kremlin sacrificed Traver, and they think it's a very big deal, not just old history but something that's still going on maybe. They aren't kidding about risking their lives, and if they think it's that important, then somebody from our end should support them all the way."

"They aren't taking any risk at all, Gib. When they made it a condition that Alan Jordan go into East Berlin incognito, they imposed an impossible condition. They must have known that."

"No. No, Steve. Besides, if that's so, we can call their bluff. But I don't think it's a bluff. I think what we've been doing has now gotten big, very big, and I think this is a hell of a time to be backing out."

"Well, you'll never get the Senator to go. I won't even ask him."

"Get me somebody else then. Bring me somebody. Don't let me down, Steve, for God's sake, not now."

"Let me chew it over a little. Call me tomorrow night again. And you better call Frank Kennedy."

An uncomfortable old feeling had returned very strongly—one that had dominated him at times in his life: the feeling that people were tolerating him as a shrill little boy. The Russians seemed to think of him some such way. Shtemenko had all but said so. Maybe Senator Jordan did too, and Steve Novatny, and possibly even Frank Kennedy, while they all smiled at him and encouraged him as they would a child, watching him posture and strut. It was a painful feeling, but it persisted in his mind like an unwanted tune.

He would not be ashamed if he turned out to be too afraid to go, when the time came. There were things in him of which he was capable of being ashamed, but the possibility that he was a coward was not one of them. He did not esteem courage, not the kind he supposed it would take to go on a cloak-and-dagger mission into a dangerous city. He wouldn't be proud of his courage if he turned out to have it, and he wouldn't be ashamed if he didn't.

With him, whether he risked his life was not a question of character—not of courage or loyalty or any other element of what people called character. It was a question of value, calculated value. Was the risk worth taking? That was what he had to decide, weighing the risk against the likelihood or non-likelihood of accomplishing anything by taking it. Maybe this attitude would be called cynicism, or maybe a rationalization for cowardice. He didn't care. It was the only basis on which Gib Hubbard was going to risk his safety, and he was the only one who was going to decide if he would do it. He would make a bad soldier, he had always said.

While he walked the last couple of blocks, when the blue sign on Melanie's club was in sight up the hill a little, it began to rain again, lightly. He pulled on the raincoat he had been carrying, and because his thought had been interrupted he turned it in another direction, toward Melanie.

He remembered now how she had suggested to him that afternoon that he come to the club a little earlier. Instead he was coming later, intentionally. He began to think it had been insensitive of him to linger in his hotel room and then walk all the way here. On this trip he had been in a mood to depreciate Melanie, and now suddenly he began to wonder if she had noticed. She had, last night, detected his troubled distaste for what she was doing with her life now; and her quick, earnest self-justification had been startlingly unlike her.

"I wanted to be in Paris," she had said. "I thought I *should* be here, where I could call Shtemenko every few days and keep him aware of us. So I *am* here, Gib, without any money or any other help from anybody. I . . ."

"I'm here at my own expense too," he had said, entirely missing—as he now decided—the point she was trying to make.

Inside the club, she came to his table only for a moment. She hadn't even enough time to sit down. It was time for her to do her strip. All she said was, "I hoped to see you sooner," and she said that very quietly and a little reproachfully.

This was the fifth or sixth time he had watched her performance. She had talked brightly about her talent, and from that talk and the way she had been billed in Brussels as a featured performer, he had supposed she did something novel, something more than just strip. If he had thought about it realistically he might have known that stripping, after all, is stripping, and basically there was little Melanie or any other girl could do to make it much more. All she would do was come out in the tiny square of vacant floor in the middle of the close-packed tables, in a space where there was not enough room really to dance; and there, with the band pounding out a loud and simple rhythm for her to follow, she would swagger around with bumps and grinds, wearing a forced broad smile, and pull off her costume piece by piece until she was stripped to a tiny black G-string which did not quite cover her pubic hair. It would not take long. The people at the tables would applaud perfunctorily when the band stopped, and Melanie would gather up her costume and carry it off with her as she retreated to the dressing room. It was not much, and even though she wanted him to come to the club and see it, she would be subdued and defensive when she came back to his table.

Before he saw her strip, he'd wondered how he'd react to it. Now that he saw her at it every night, he was a little surprised at his reaction: that she did not arouse him in the slightest. (In the flat, pink light they put on her, her skin looked chalky smooth; and with her fixed smile and exaggerated movements, she looked like some kind of pink rubber caricature made up to mock a man's erotic dream.) He remembered Leslie's utter scorn for this kind of thing, and maybe Melanie . . . well, maybe she shared with him the hurtful feeling that people around him were smiling on him and behind their smiles tolerating him for a shrill little boy—tolerating *her* for a tawdry stripteaser from a second-rate nightclub—someone not to be taken too heavily into account in any calculation. Instead of being aroused by her nakedness, more and more he felt sorry for her. And he was the more surprised because he had not supposed he could feel that way about Melanie.

She never looked at him while she was out there under the pink lights. That was something else. . . .

When she returned to his table he had finished two Scotches, and he asked her if she could leave.

"No, not until the club closes. Did you call Washington?"

"Yes."

"Will Jordan come?"

"No."

Melanie sighed heavily. "Then what happens?"

"I don't know. I asked Novatny to find someone else."

"So your Senator Jordan has abandoned you," she said. "He's another cheap political hack."

Gib shrugged. "Frank Kennedy says I'd be a fool to go into East Berlin with Shtemenko."

"Did he tell you not to go?"

"Yes."

"Do you take orders from him?"

Gib shook his head.

"Congratulations."

The noise of the band introducing another stripper interrupted their conversation; and for the next few minutes, while the girl worked, they had to sit and watch her. Melanie was intent and introspective. Gib guessed her thought: that she herself looked no more real and no less grotesque when she was out there under the pink lights. He had made a judgment that Melanie was probably unique among these girls. He would have liked to know the little blonde who was stripping now, to see if he was right.

"Anyway, you *are* going, aren't you?" Melanie asked as soon as it was quiet enough to talk.

"I won't have to decide unless Novatny can come up with someone who'll satisfy Shtemenko."

"I'd like to meet this Novatny."

"What do you think of our Russians anyway?" he asked. "How much confidence do you have in them?"

"All kinds of confidence," she said, leaning across the table toward him. "Listen, they're tough people. They've been going and coming through the Iron Curtain for decades. They have people working on both sides, all the time."

"Yes, and a lot of them have been killed," Gib said.

Melanie looked hard at him, from under stiffened brows. "You afraid?" she asked.

"You're damn right."

She nodded and sighed. "I don't blame you. I trust Shtemenko, though. There'll be no blundering. Those people are no fools. They aren't interested in playing little tin hero. But the thing that interests me most is their motivation, and that's why I'd like to go if I could. If those people think they're going to get information worth risking their lives for, they must think it's something pretty big. And you can figure also that they're not just going over there to stalk Nadya Kharina. They know where she is and how to get her, or they wouldn't be going. You've *got* to go, Gib. And your friend Novatny has got to come up with somebody. *He's got to.*"

Novatny did, but not for two weeks, and Gib, running short of money, had to move out of his hotel and into Melanie's flat. It was there, in Melanie's tiny sitting room, that he met for the second time with Shtemenko's committee. This time Yuri Tyulenev was not present. The committee consisted only of Shtemenko and Vera Ivanovna Kravchenko.

"No. No, Mr. Hubbard, it is impossible," Shtemenko said immediately when Gib told him who Novatny had recruited. "We would have accepted a substitute for Senator Jordan, but not this man, not another journalist. No. It has to be a public figure, a respected public figure."

Gib was prepared for the objection. "Would you have accepted Walter Lippmann if he had agreed to come?"

Shtemenko's lips hardened and whitened. "Well . . ." he said. "I suppose so. But that is not who you are proposing."

"No, and I don't mean to suggest to you that Cornelius Vanderhoof has the status of Walter Lippmann," Gib said.

"But I do mean to tell you that he's an extremely well-known columnist in the United States, he is a public figure, and he probably has the confidence of the American people more than any politician. You said you wanted someone whose word would be believed. Well, Cornelius Vanderhoof would be believed."

Shtemenko turned to Vera Ivanovna Kravchenko and translated what Gib had said into French. The woman stared at Gib. Her face was flushed and stiff. She shook her head.

Shtemenko blew a short, impatient sigh. "This Vanderhoof," he said. "Is he a man of the right or left, a Republican or Democrat, or what?"

"He has a reputation as a moderate liberal," Gib said. "He writes a Washington column that appears five times a week in maybe a hundred newspapers. He's had this column for years. He knows everyone in Washington, and everyone knows him. I'll be altogether frank with you. I think he's a better choice than Senator Jordan. The Senator, after all, is a politician and a partisan Democrat, and besides that, it's well known that he has ambitions to be President. Those are handicaps when it comes to credibility, and Cornelius Vanderhoof doesn't carry those handicaps."

Shtemenko turned again to the Russian woman and began to speak to her in French. Gib looked around, wondering if he could find wine, or at least tea, to offer them. They had shown up unexpectedly. He knew they were coming this day, but he'd thought they could come after noon. Instead, they had come in the morning. Shtemenko had asked Melanie to leave and let them talk with Gib alone. She had gone out, not just angry but hurt, leaving Gib with that to think about as well as with the confusion of having them come when he was still in bed and of having to bring them into a littered room and clear a space for them to sit. He was unshaven and dressed only in T-shirt and slacks. He hadn't had his breakfast. Melanie had come home after four this morning, drunk. It seemed they'd hardly gone to sleep when the banging on the door announced the arrival of Shtemenko and the haughty, matronly Vera Ivanovna Kravchenko. Melanie had muttered something to him about being bourgeois in his embarrassment, as she stalked out of the flat.

Melanie had gotten testy too because he was getting daily letters from Leslie. "So, okay, she loves you, for Christ's sake, does she have to smother you in sugar and flowers?" she had said when she was drunk. When she was not drunk she didn't say anything. An unopened letter from Leslie was lying on the table. Melanie had tossed it at him as she left. He was tempted to open it and read it while Shtemenko talked to Vera Ivanovna Kravchenko in French.

"Is there to be no one else?" Shtemenko asked. "Is there no *possibility* of anyone else?"

Gib had determined to be aggressive about this. "Why should there be?" he asked. "Why think of anyone else, when we have someone this good?"

Shtemenko turned and translated this immediately. Then he said to Gib, "You have a great deal at stake. Are *you* satisfied?"

Gib nodded. "Yes," he said.

And he *was* satisfied, really satisfied. It was a special, personal satisfaction. He'd had to fight Novatny over the trans-Atlantic telephone, pleading, goading, cursing, and actually one night even weeping. Novatny and Kennedy, and on one call even the Senator, had tried to shout him down. They'd called him a fool, a child, a sucker for a good lay (meaning Melanie) or for a White Russian confidence man (meaning Shtemenko). They'd told him he was obsessed and didn't know when to quit. But, apparently, most of the time they were talking to him this way they were also talking to Vanderhoof. And Vanderhoof had done some checking on his own, to find out who the Alliance of Russian Patriots was and who Shtemenko was. Four nights ago Novatny and

Kennedy had tried on the phone, for one last time, to make Gib admit the adventure was insane; and when he persisted, Novatny had suddenly said, all right, he would fly to Paris in a few days and would bring Cornelius Vanderhoof with him. They wanted to talk with Shtemenko directly and would reserve final judgment until they did. This morning, the morning when Gib was with Shtemenko in Melanie's flat, Novatny and Vanderhoof should be on their way. They were due in Paris during the day.

"Does this man Vanderhoof know the risk he will be taking?" Shtemenko asked.

"Yes. I'm sure he does."

"And you understand yourself," Shtemenko said. "If you are somehow caught by the *Volkspolizei,* you will be a long time in prison—if, indeed, that's the worst that happens to you."

Gib nodded. He'd never really gotten to make his value judgment. The thing was going to happen because he had been so effective an advocate, and in a sense it had sneaked up on him. It was like accounts he had read of men who did brave things in battle: they did them, not because they judged they should, but because the situation developed around them so they had no alternative. People who had judged they should not go were going because he had insisted they should, and in securing their decision he had foreclosed his own option to make one.

"You will go with false documents. . . ."

"There is one more thing," Gib said. "Vanderhoof has imposed a condition. He will not go unless Steve Novatny goes too. He has known Novatny for years and trusts him. He wants a friend with him."

Shtemenko's chin came up in annoyance. "We will interview all of you at length before we finally consent to take any," he said. "If this Novatny is trustworthy, then perhaps . . ."

"And I've been asked to raise once more the question of Miss Traver's going. She feels very strongly about it."

Shtemenko shook his head firmly. "No," he said. "Not Melanie. Very definitely not."

BERLIN

Once you were inside the Checkpoint you were trapped. If they didn't like the looks of you or your passport, you could not back out: you were on their side of the line and inside their walled compound. Passing the Western control station was easy enough. It was nothing but a wooden shack in the middle of the street. You didn't even have to stop. The American sergeant on duty just looked at you lazily and a little scornfully, as if to tell you he thought you were out of your mind. The East German guards raised the barricade readily enough, too; and you drove inside the Checkpoint and found you were going to sit there until your turn came to be examined.

The whole Checkpoint was perhaps a hundred yards long. Vehicles entering from the East had to twist back and forth through a maze to get in. The maze was formed of a strong concrete and steel wall. Nobody was going to rush the Checkpoint, even with an armored vehicle.

Gib was driving their rented Volkswagen. Novatny was in the front seat beside him. Vanderhoof was in the back.

There was plenty to see while they waited. A truckload of sand was going through, and two soldiers were up on the sand with pointed steel rods, pushing them repeatedly down through the sand to the truck bed, to find—or impale—anyone covered by sand. Another guard had a little mirror set on a wheeled cart, which he could push under a vehicle and get himself a view of the undercarriage, to see if anyone was hanging under there. They opened anything large enough to conceal a person, or half a person. They obviously were not much concerned with *what* might be coming through the Wall, only with *who,* and they were busy being efficient and thorough.

Novatny had made some small, weak joke when Gib first stopped, but that was all any of them had said since they entered the Checkpoint. No one knew the guards had directional microphones aimed at waiting cars to pick up people's talk, but no one knew they didn't, either. Novatny was smoking a cigarette and watching the guards with narrow-eyed intensity. Vanderhoof, in the back seat, was breathing heavily and holding his hands tightly clasped in his lap to control them. His silence was unusual. He had been garrulous and had made Gib like him in the few days they had spent together. Gib himself clutched the steering wheel and stared hard at the procedures being carried out with the people in cars ahead of them. If the East German guards searched their persons, they were in trouble. Each of them was carrying two sets of false passports.

"Those are machine guns," Novatny said finally. He was looking up at the square, cream-colored tower in the center of the Checkpoint. The guards in the glass enclosure on top had a view of the whole Checkpoint, and they did have machine guns, inconspicuously mounted but still visible to anyone who looked hard enough.

Gradually Gib moved the Volkswagen forward in line. It would not be long. The passports were perfect, so far as Gib could tell. They had left their real passports in Paris and had been travelling with the false ones. No one had looked at them closely until now, but he was confident of them. The only real risk was that the guard might take a capricious notion to ask them to show what they were carrying in their other pockets.

Their scheme for entering and leaving East Berlin was simple. Shtemenko had assured them it was virtually foolproof. Going in, they would show the first set of forged passports. The guards' procedure was to copy onto a list the names and passport numbers of everyone going in, and anyone coming out later had to be on that list. Waiting in East Berlin were three confederates of Shtemenko's, carrying another set of forged United States passports. This set of passports bore the same names and numbers as the ones the three Americans were carrying, but the photographs in them were of Shtemenko's three men. Gib would turn the car over to them, and they would come back through the Checkpoint. The guards would cross the three names and numbers off the list, and there would be three Americans in East Berlin of which the *Volkspolizei* would have no record. Coming back in a few days, the process would be reversed. Shtemenko's three men would return, showing passports bearing the same names and numbers as those on the second set the Americans were carrying. Gib and Novatny and Vanderhoof could then come out, and Shtemenko's men, who were stationed in East Berlin, would stay there. The greatest and best deceptions are the simplest, Shtemenko had said.

A guard approached their car. Gib opened the door and got out.

"American?" asked the guard, in English only slightly accented.

"Yes."

"Passports, please," said the guard. He was a thick, muscular young man, a German who would have been called a perfect Aryan thirty years before. His cool blue eyes were so bereft of humor that it would have been difficult to imagine him laughing. He had apple cheeks, stern white lips, and a hard jaw. His gray-green uniform fit him badly. The shirt was open, showing his white undershirt, and his cap sat jauntily back on his head. He had a squat little pistol in a squat little holster hung on his belt, and he carried a clipboard with a sheaf of papers clipped on.

Gib handed over his passport, and Novatny and Vanderhoof handed theirs out the windows of the car. The guard opened each passport and studied each photograph solemnly, glancing up two or three times from each to compare the picture with the man. When he was finished examining the passports, he detached three forms from his clipboard and put the three passports under the clip in their place.

"List the amounts of currency you are carrying," the guard said as he handed over the forms. "Of each country." He opened the door of the car and stuck his head in to peer around, looking for anyone who might be crouching on the floor. Then he walked behind and opened the engine compartment. He pointed at the trunk latch, and Gib opened the trunk. "What is the purpose of your visit?" the guard asked.

"Just tourists," Gib said.

The German looked at him skeptically. "What do you expect to visit?" he asked.

"The Pergamon Museum, principally."

"The State Museum. When will you return?"

"In two or three hours."

The guard nodded and seemed satisfied, but he kept on his face a practiced, lofty look of skepticism, suggesting intentionally that he did not believe a word. He stood back and waited while the Americans counted their money and listed it on the forms he had given them. When they handed over the completed forms he walked away, taking forms and passports into the low-lying, cream-colored stucco building nearby.

Gib watched him go. He glanced into the car at Novatny, who was lighting another cigarette, and at Vanderhoof, who was counting his money again. Gib leaned against the fender of the car and forced his hands to hang still at the sides of his legs. He glanced up at the sun, which bore down hard on the hot pavement of the Checkpoint, and he felt the sweat rolling down the curve of his spine. He was scared. He hadn't been scared very many times in his life, not this way, not physically; but he was now, and there was nothing he could do but stand there and wait and savor his fear. He compared it with what he had felt the night the police searched him in his apartment, and he was rational and contemplative enough to decide it was not very much different. He remembered how that fear had stayed with him and hurt for days after the experience; and, knowing that he likely was going to be scared all the time he stayed in East Berlin, he wondered how long it would take him to be over it this time.

The guard was not gone long. He returned and handed over the passports and the currency forms—the latter now bearing a conspicuous official stamp. "You may drive on through," he said, and then, without a sign of a smile on his face and with nothing in his voice, he added, "Welcome to the German Democratic Republic."

Slowly, conscious of the guns in the tower and the eyes that watched, Gib drove out of the Checkpoint and began to negotiate the turns in the maze which led into Friederichstrasse. Only when they were out in the open street did Novatny break the dead silence in the car by saying, "Well, I hope it's that easy going back."

Novatny had a street map. It was not marked, but he had been rehearsed about the route they were to take. What Gib had told the guard was true: they were going to the Pergamon Museum. But, in case any suspicion had been aroused and any notice was to be taken of where they went, they were going to go like tourists, on an indirect route past some of the sights of East Berlin.

So, on Novatny's directions, Gib turned off Friederichstrasse and made a westward swing around the block and up Wilhelmstrasse past the grassy mound that marked the site of Hitler's bunker. Reaching Unter den Linden, they paused to look at the Brandenburger Tor, which they had seen half an hour ago from the West and now saw from the East;

and then they turned into the great boulevard and drove directly into the heart of East Berlin. They drove slowly along Unter den Linden in the bright sunlight, looking at the people and the shops and the traffic, silently comparing the somber austerity here with the garish prosperity of West Berlin.

They were to be at the Pergamon Museum at 3:20. Gib was to meet their contact at 3:40. They were to leave the museum at 4:30. They had time to wander through the rooms and look at the exhibits.

The collection of archeological treasures of the Pergamon Museum, once carried away to Russia but now returned, was outstanding and beautifully arranged. The museum was crowded. Groups of visitors from nearly every Communist nation in the world mingled in the rooms, and more than once the three Americans found themselves brushing shoulders with Russian officers as they stood looking at some Greek or Persian artifact. The Russians easily identified them as Americans, by overhearing their language or eyeing their clothes, and they were curious and stared at them when they thought the Americans would not notice. They were careful about it. They were as anxious to conceal their curiosity as the Americans were to conceal theirs.

"They're no threat," Novatny said when they were out of earshot of a group of Russians but were conscious that the Russians were looking at them. "They're as much foreigners here as we are. We speak more German than they do."

"It's the political police we need to worry about," said Vanderhoof. "And you can damn well bet they're here. You'll have to watch it damn careful, Gib, when you go to meet our man. Quit glancing every ten seconds at that goddam watch."

"All right," Gib said. He managed to smile up into the ruddy face and white mustache of Cornelius Vanderhoof.

"You keep track of the time and tell me when to go to meet my man. I'll rely on you."

"We have plenty of time yet," said Novatny, "but I suggest we locate the men's room. It'd be a hell of a note if you couldn't find it when the time comes."

Trying not to look purposeful, they moved a little more quickly through the rooms, until they found the men's room, and having found it they moved away from it. Gib would return there at 3:40, as scheduled.

He came back at 3:39 and stopped outside the door to read a notice, so he would open the door and step in at precisely 3:40.

He went in. He was to see one man. Three men were in the room.

One was urinating. One was washing his hands. One was looking out the window and smoking a cigarette. None of them met his eyes or took any apparent notice that he had come in. He had to wait until two of them left.

He stood behind the one who was urinating, as if he hadn't noticed there was a second toilet. That would take some time. But the man glanced around and saw him and hurried to make way for him. He had to step up then and use the toilet. For an instant he thought of sitting on the toilet, but if he took his pants down he wouldn't be able to move quickly if two men abruptly left the room. So he took out his penis and urinated a little, letting it clatter noisily into the pool of water in the bottom of the toilet. Then he stopped, and he stood there flexing his shoulders as if it hurt him to urinate.

He heard the man who had just finished, washing his hands. He let some more urine fall. He glanced over his shoulder. He could not see the others, because of the old tin walls of the booth in which the toilet was located. He let some more urine come, and then there wasn't any more. But still he stood and hung his head, as if he were in pain. He heard the door open and close. The man who had finished and washed his hands had gone out. Then at last, thank God, the man with the cigarette stepped up to the other toilet and began to urinate. Gib heard his cigarette hiss as it hit the water.

He had to stand there for a little while yet. The other man seemed to have a gallon to get rid of, but Gib waited him out, and when finally the man stepped out to wash his hands, Gib came out to wash his. The third man—the one who had been washing his hands when Gib first came in—had lifted himself up and was sitting on the window sill, looking down at his stomach and kneading it with both hands, as if he had a belly ache. Gib decided this man was the contact. He was killing time too.

The man who had just finished with the toilet cast Gib a curious glance as they stood side by side at the two wash bowls. Gib bit his lip, to say it had been painful to use the toilet and he still didn't feel good. The man, who was dressed in a suit with a cut that was strange to Gib—he might have been a Hungarian or a Czech—frowned involuntarily and looked embarrassed. He washed his hands more quickly than was natural, dried them hurriedly on the single towel that hung between the two basins, and went out.

Gib looked up at the man on the window sill, now that they were alone. The man had been watching him, but as soon as their eyes met, he looked away. Gib reached into his pocket, took out the keys to the Volkswagen, and balanced them on the curved edge of the wash basin. He reached for the towel, turning his back on the man and the keys. As he dried his hands, the man dropped down from the window sill, passed behind him abruptly, and left the room. Gib looked down at the basin. The keys were gone.

He found Novatny and Vanderhoof five minutes later,

where they said they would meet him, in the room with the wall of glazed blue Assyrian lions. They had forty minutes yet to spend in the museum before they could go out to the car, where they expected to find the man who had taken the keys waiting to drive them to their hiding place. They were to hole up now, to wait for their interview with Nadya Kharina.

"It's encouraging, that he took your keys," Vanderhoof said quietly when they were momentarily apart from anyone else. "I haven't been able to suppress entirely the apprehension that we might come into East Berlin and find no one."

"We've placed a hell of a lot of reliance on Shtemenko," Novatny said. "The secretive bastard."

They wandered through the museum for the rest of their time, distracted from the exhibits by the people around them and again from the people by the exhibits, and still again from both by the tension that dominated them. When finally it was 4:30 and they went out to the car, the man from the men's room was sitting behind the wheel.

The man was smoking a cigarette, which he threw away as he saw them coming. He was thin and sharp-faced, with a dark complexion. He was wearing American clothes and a very American pair of sunglasses. Gib had been careful not to give him more than a couple of quick glances in the men's room and had not noticed that he was dressed to go back across the sector border as one of the three Americans in the Volkswagen.

"You are precise about your time," the man said as they got into the car. "That's good. You've learned one of the first rules of survival."

His English was not bad. An American would not take him for an American, but a German guard at Checkpoint Charlie, unless he was an expert on dialects and accents, would not notice the difference.

"Where are we going?" Novatny said. He sat beside the man in front.

The man shrugged. "What difference? I'll come to drive you back as far as the museum. If I don't, it will be because I've been caught, and in that case you'll never get through the Checkpoint anyway. But follow the streets on the map. You may as well know where you are."

He set out north and east, naming the street he was taking, and Novatny squinted at the map and began to follow.

"What do you mean, if you're caught we'll never get back through the Checkpoint?" Vanderhoof asked from the back seat. Vanderhoof was a diminutive man with conspicuous indignation. He leaned forward and asked his question sharply, his neat little bow tie bobbing under his tanned face and his thick white mustache.

The man shrugged again and glanced back. "If I'm captured, I'll tell everything I know about what we're doing," he said. "And so will you, if you're captured. Don't think you're some kind of hero, and don't think I am. To escape the kind of thing they'll do to make us talk, we'll tell them anything. And you might as well tell them at the beginning, before they start on you."

"A man might show a little courage, for a while anyway, to give his comrades a chance," Vanderhoof argued.

"You're Mr. Vanderhoof, aren't you?" the man said. "Don't be an ass."

Vanderhoof started to say something more, but the man cut him off with an impatient gesture and then stabbed his finger at the map on Novatny's lap, to show him the turn they were taking. The streets were drab and of a sameness. Away from Unter den Linden and the city center, East Berlin was even more austere. It was actually chilling, Gib thought.

They hadn't very far to go. Following a brick street with a trolley track in the middle, they made a sudden turn and stopped in front of a building two doors away from the intersection.

"You have an apartment here," the man said. "It's not luxurious, but it's adequate, and it is very well suited for our purposes."

Vanderhoof spent most of his time at the window, standing with one foot on the sill, then with the other, then straightening his back and wandering away, only to come back after a few minutes to take up his station once more and stare down at the street. Novatny sat at the table. A deck of cards had been provided for them, and he spread out before him a game of solitaire which became increasingly elaborate and incomprehensible as he improvised variations and variations on variations, all his own. He smoked all the cigarettes in the flat, both his own and the German ones left there for them, by the middle of the second day. After that he grumbled and kept talking about going out, but he didn't speak German; and Vanderhoof, who was the only one who did, even a little, would not violate their explicit instructions not even to open the door. Gib kept to the couch much of the time. Novatny and Vanderhoof shared the one bed, in the bedroom, and Gib slept on the couch.

They were not to go out. They had food to last them four or five days, beer and wine and brandy, the cards and cigarettes, a few books (all in German, however), and a couple of sealed boxes under the bed, which they'd been told not to open. It was an old building, put up solidly of brick in the nineteenth century, so solidly that they heard hardly a sound of the neighbors they knew they must have above and below and all around them. Children lived in the building—Vanderhoof saw them going in and out at the door below the window.

They must have shouted and cried, people must have

played radios, people must have walked about in their flats and sometimes knocked and banged things. They must have. But the only sound that proved anyone else lived in the building was an occasional muffled thump from above and frequently a gurgling in the pipes that were exposed and ran down through one corner of the living room.

"They flush their pots, anyway," Novatny said.

They had a drab living room, furnished with the couch, a table, one overstuffed chair, and three heavy straight chairs. There was no carpet or rug. In the tiny kitchen there was a sink and a cabinet for their food, no refrigerator. In the bedroom, the bed took up all the space. The bathroom had a toilet and a tub. Light at night came from bare bulbs—clear ones, with the glowing filaments exposed—hanging at the ends of wires from the ceiling, one in each room. They kept the windows open all day, and it was hot anyway. At night, even with the windows closed, the flat got cold.

Besides smoking while the cigarettes lasted and playing solitaire, Novatny drank more than his share of the beer and brandy. He kept a bottle among his cards, and he hunched silently over the table with a scowl, introspective and quiet to a degree Gib had never seen before. It was unlike Novatny. He was afraid, and that was how he showed it.

Vanderhoof talked. "I was over here during the late unpleasantness," he said, staring out the window. He was talking to Gib, and Gib had to strain to hear him. "During the winter there, '44 and '45 you know, I . . . uh . . . wandered into an old French farmhouse, up on a little hill, and there was an old *gran'pere* there, name was Coulondre, and he had a pretty young girl living with him. He had some wine. I had some rations. I ate with them. The girl had been a collaborationist, had a German boyfriend and had a child by him. When the village was liberated, they'd shaved her head, stripped her naked, and run her out of town. They'd set her right out on the road and threw rocks at her until she ran. The old man had taken her in. Her parents in the village had the baby. The old man, old Coulondre, had—believe it or not—a great big view camera, used 8 by 10 film or some such size in centimeters, and he had a collection of photographs of this girl, the most beautiful pictures you could ever see. You could look at those portraits he'd done of that girl, and you could read what had happened to her, her whole life story, just in those pictures. She looked like nothing but a coarse little peasant girl, with nothing much of a face, but he saw, and got on that film, the real character and beauty of that girl. I'll never forget those pictures as long as I live. I figured you'd be some kind of arrogant little horse's behind, Gib. If somebody'd told me a month ago I'd be sitting here in this goddam hole in this goddam city, risking my ass like this on your say-so, I'd have called him a raving maniac. It turns out I'm the idiot. I never got to Berlin. Too damn bad, too. I'd have been safer here during the shelling than I am now. It's curious about that Traver girl, though, isn't it? What is it about her and her old man, do you suppose? Think they really hate each other, or just talk that way? What ever happened to that baby she had?"

This was how he talked—compulsively and very quietly, making you strain to hear, rambling on to no purpose for a while and then suddenly interjecting a string of questions. Gib answered the questions as shortly as he could, consistent with being courteous. He realized he was being cross-examined. The questions were perceptive, most of them, and Gib understood that while none of the chatter conveyed any information, the questions demanded a great deal of it. Little by little Vanderhoof was learning all he wanted to know about the Traver case. And he was making judgments—of Gib himself in particular, as Gib readily saw.

But he liked Vanderhoof. He'd known his name for years, as the name of an honest, moderate, and careful journalist.

Gib knew also that it took courage for Vanderhoof to come here. It also took a judgment of Gib and his work that Gib found very flattering. He had been amazed when Novatny called and said Cornelius Vanderhoof would come to Paris and was willing to go to East Berlin. It was a sort of professional endorsement that Gib valued very highly.

"It's hard to believe," Vanderhoof said, "that there are that many policemen on every street in this city." He frowned at what he saw from his window. "They give me chills. I have a feeling this building is surrounded."

Gib had plenty of time to be afraid and to savor what fear was like. Tuesday had been the day when they came through the Checkpoint and holed up in the flat. Nothing happened on Wednesday or Thursday. The building was quiet, and after a while it was easy to imagine it was ominously quiet. Vanderhoof kept talking about the policemen he saw from his window, and in fact, nearly every time Gib went to the window to have his own look, there was a man in uniform on the street. It was easy to imagine a watch had been set over the building. The policemen who stood on the corners of the intersection below all yawned and lounged on one foot and then the other, and were obviously bored; and yet it was easy, when one of them glanced past the window from which Vanderhoof stared, to imagine a purpose in each casual glance. A frightened imagination was even more active than an erotic one, Gib discovered. He was glad for distractions, but Vanderhoof's talk and penetrating questions were about all the distraction he had, and they were not enough.

It was bad at night especially, when the other two were asleep behind the closed bedroom door and he was alone in the dim living room. He could not sleep. Maybe Novatny and Vanderhoof couldn't either, but they did not come out of the bedroom from the time they went in, about midnight each night, until morning. Supposing they were sleeping when he could not, made Gib all the more uncomfortable. He would lie as long as he could on the couch, and then he would get up and prowl around the flat and stand at Vanderhoof's window and stare down at the faintly lighted street. He thought of Leslie, and he was sorry he had come here and put his life in the hands of strangers who might return and might not.

Thursday night—or Friday morning actually, since it was well after midnight—he was on his couch, uncomfortable, dozing a little, when someone tried the door.

He stiffened. He was not sure what he'd heard, or if he'd only dreamed it in his half-sleep. But he had come instantly alert, and he lay with his breath suspended, listening.

He could see the door. The light from the street was sufficient to lend the room a dim, gray definition. He could see, and he had a feeling his fear had given his ears a special sensitivity which magnified the silence and lent it a totality in which the slightest sound would explode and roar.

A sound did. He heard a key being pushed into the old lock. He heard the grating of the levers. He was half erect, on his elbows, when the door abruptly swung out, and there, in the yellow light of the hallway, stood two Russian soldiers.

EAST BERLIN

The first Russian stepped through the doorway and stood just inside, peering into the gray shadows with calm and open curiosity and no caution. His face was too much in the dark for Gib to read his expression, but he seemed to see Gib on the couch, and he showed no sign of alarm. He just stood there. The other Russian, still outside in the hall, did not even look into the room. His attention was on something down the hall. He stood with his hands on his hips, breathing heavily as if the climb on the stairs had winded him. Someone Gib couldn't see said something, and the soldier nodded. So there was a third one, and maybe more.

"*Kto tam?*" the soldier outside the door asked the one inside.

"*Odin Amerikanyetz,*" said the one who was looking at Gib.

Immobilized except for his thoughts, Gib's head was filled with a furious, flashing kaleidoscope of ideas and images, each one vivid for an instant but too quickly gone to define itself. In the same short moment he saw a thousand reasons why these Russians were here and a thousand ways to act with them. He got enough control of himself to push his body erect and lower his feet to the floor. And that was as far as he moved before the third man came in.

"*Kotorii Amerikanyetz?*" the third man muttered distractedly as he came through the door and squinted into the dimness with obvious impatience. Short and heavy and wearing ill-fitting civilian clothes, he was puffing, and he ran the back of his arm across his forehead as he squinted at Gib. "*Gde svet?*" he asked the soldier.

The soldier, apparently familiar with the room, reached for the switch and turned on the light. Then Gib saw who the third man was—: Yuri Tyulenev, the apple-cheeked young Russian in whose Paris flat Gib had first met with Shtemenko's committee. "Mr. Hubbard," said Tyulenev. "Are the others in the bedroom?"

Gib had slackened, and he began to tremble. He nodded.

"Let them sleep," said Tyulenev quietly. He glanced around the room, as if to satisfy himself that everything in it was ready for what he planned to do next. He went to the window and pulled down the blind. He made an abrupt gesture toward the soldier, and the man went out.

Gib glanced toward the bedroom door, wondering for an instant how Novatny and Vanderhoof could still be asleep. He controlled his trembling, but he wondered if Tyulenev had not seen it while it lasted. He was conscious, painfully conscious, that he had dissolved into ineffectualness, and now he took his breath and tried to seem in command of himself. "Is Shtemenko with you?" he asked.

Tyulenev frowned and smiled. "Not he, not Shtemenko," he said. "That man couldn't take a risk like this."

Gib nodded and suppressed a troubling thought. He put his feet in his shoes, thinking that might make him seem a little more controlled. "Is everything all right?" he asked.

"Everything is all right, just as planned," Tyulenev said, and as he said it he nodded toward the door.

The two soldiers pushed through, supporting between them the limp body of a woman.

She hung loosely between the two men, but she struggled spasmodically to lift herself. She tried to make her feet move and support her, but they only flopped uselessly behind her as the two men dragged her into the room. In the center of the floor they let her gently down, and she sat there for a moment, a handsome, middle-aged woman, well coiffed, wearing an expensive-looking colorful silk dress with a necklace of some kind of glittering stones. She tried to focus her eyes on the men around her, but she couldn't. She tried to talk, but her urgent, pleading words came out only as gurgling sounds. She sat weaving for a moment, and then she toppled over and lay helpless on her back.

Tyulenev grinned at Gib. "Nadya Kharina," he said.

Gib had guessed that. He stared. The picture the Travers had given him was more than twenty years old, but it was easy to see that this woman, now more than forty-five, was the girl in the photograph. She was Mary Anne Waring with twenty years' maturity.

"Would you recognize her?" Tyulenev asked Gib.

Gib glanced at one of the soldiers, who was locking the door again. He looked again then at Nadya Kharina, and he nodded at Tyulenev. She was not wearing her hair long any more. Her skin was no longer the smooth, faultless, youthful skin her photograph had suggested; it was a little looser and a little darker and maybe a little less alive. She had tiny explosions of lines at the corners of her eyes. (And her eyes were a fascinating gleaming pale blue the picture had not suggested.) The skin under her chin had loosened a bit and was drawn down in faint lines along her throat. But she had not thickened. She was a thin, handsome woman with a strong, memorable face.

"I suppose I shouldn't ask you how . . . ?" Gib said, shrugging away the end of his question.

Tyulenev shook his head. "No. It doesn't make any difference." His eyes narrowed, and he smiled slyly. "You didn't suppose she'd come voluntarily?"

"No."

"No," said Tyulenev quietly and without expression. His attention had shifted to the other two men, who now knelt over Nadya Kharina, seized her, and turned her on her stomach. She made a shrill, garbled protest as they pulled her arms behind her back and held them there. They ripped the sleeves of her dress and used copper wire and a pair of pliers to bind her wrists together. She gasped—and Gib winced—as they twisted the wire so tight that it pinched deep into her flesh. When they had bound her wrists rigidly together behind her back, they moved down and wired her ankles together the same way. She began to weep and groan.

Tyulenev, who was watching Gib's face, touched him on the arm and said, "Don't feel sorry for Nadya Fedorovna. Just remember, she's been a counter-intelligence agent for years, and what we're going to do to her is nothing more than she's done to hundreds of people."

Gib closed his eyes and nodded, but his throat and stomach hardened just the same. When the two men were finished, they turned the woman up on her side and left her lying there near the couch, facing Gib and blinking and trying to focus her eyes on him. She sobbed and she tried to talk. He could not have understood her words, probably, even if she had spoken English; but he didn't have to understand words to know what she was trying to say. She was sick from whatever they had used to drug her. She was terrified. The wire cut her, and she was in pain. She was begging for mercy. Gib turned to Tyulenev and began to shake his head.

"Don't even say it," Tyulenev said sharply. "We know what we're doing, and we have too much at stake to be hindered by a queasy stomach."

Gib frowned deeply but conceded his silence. They would not be moved by anything he could say. He looked again at Nadya Kharina, who was whimpering tearfully to herself. The skin at her ankles was deeply scored by the wire and had turned angry red and white. He knew it had to be worse at her wrists, on which there would be some tension from her shoulders.

"It will be morning before she can talk with us," said Tyulenev. "Maybe we can sleep a little."

Gib glanced at him, showing surprise and disbelief, and began to shake his head.

"Why not?" asked Tyulenev. "You'll have a hard day tomorrow."

"I haven't slept much since I've been here," Gib said. He glanced at the bedroom door. "My friends seem to manage it. We don't seem to have disturbed them, either."

Tyulenev raised the blind, and one of the others switched off the light. "The walls in this old building are thick," he said. "The doors are heavy and fit tight. That's one reason we chose this place. Your friends haven't heard anything. Anyway, we can rest at least, even if you can't sleep. It will be two or three hours before she can talk."

The two uniformed Russians took off their tunics and boots, rolled the tunics around the boots to make rests for their heads, and stretched out comfortably on the floor. Before long they fell asleep. Tyulenev sat on one of the hard straight chairs and rested his elbows—and later his head—on the table. He never entirely went to sleep, but he slipped fitfully toward it and back, and time must have passed faster for him, without his losing all his awareness. Nadya Kharina quieted for a while. Gib was left alone, sitting awake on the couch, and finally, reluctantly, he kicked off his shoes, put up his feet, and leaned back into a corner of the couch to wait for morning.

It was too shadowy dark to study any of the others very closely, but he watched Tyulenev for a long time, and wondered. In his flat in Paris, in the shadow of Shtemenko, in the midst of his bourgeois traps, and under the steady eye of his pregnant wife, Tyulenev had seemed only fat and pink-cheeked and shallow. He had seemed even less likely than Gib himself to come here where he was tonight and do what he was doing. Tonight he did not look any different, really. He still had apple cheeks and seemed boyish. But his voice was harder. Here he was in charge, and he knew he was, and he was confident. He was a deceptive man, and Gib hoped his new judgment of him was better than his first judgment.

He could not watch Tyulenev long, though. Nothing could distract him very long from the bound and straining figure of Nadya Kharina. Even while she was quiet, during the first hour after they turned off the light, she did not sleep. Gib could see her open eyes. She breathed heavily. For a while at first she would try to move, almost as if she could not remember how tightly she was bound, and each time she made an abrupt movement she gasped as the wires cut her. As time passed and the drug wore off she became lucid enough to know she must not jerk against her bonds, and then she began a long and restless, very slow and cautious twisting and turning, seeking some little relief of the strain on her wrists or the ache in her shoulders. Gib watched her, in an anguish of pity.

After two hours she was lucid enough to talk. She spoke urgently in Russian to Tyulenev, pleading tearfully at first and then angrily and finally quietly and rationally. Tyulenev would open his eyes from time to time and look down languidly at her. He never spoke a word. After a while she despaired of him and began talking to Gib, first in Russian and then in German. Gib could only shake his head. He shook his head and indicated with a gesture that Tyulenev was the man in charge. So she spoke to Tyulenev again but finally gave up, and after that she only lay silent and worked her arms and shoulders against the wire, trying to find relief from the pain which obviously worsened as time passed.

She said nothing more to Gib, but she still faced him, and most of the time her eyes were on him. Down there in the shadows on the floor he could see her eyes. The faint light from the street lamp shone weakly through the window and seemed attracted to the woman's staring eyes, so he could always see them. They were blue, but in this light they looked gray, and the pupils were hard black. He could not face them. He kept looking away, then looking back, then looking away. When the dawn light entered the room, he could see the bright blue again, and in her stare he could see glittering furious hate. He turned his face rigidly away.

When the room was fully light, Gib finally fell asleep. Exhausted by his own wretched self-reproach and all the rest of it, he slept deeply. But only for twenty minutes or so. When he woke, Novatny and Vanderhoof were sitting at the table and Nadya Kharina had been lifted onto one of the heavy wooden chairs and stiffly bound to the rungs and seat and back with more tightly twisted wire.

"Well, Sleeping Beauty returns," said Novatny scornfully as soon as he saw Gib's eyes open.

"It will do no good to talk to him," said Nadya Kharina. She and the two Americans had apparently been carrying on a conversation while Gib slept and while the three Russian men were in the bedroom.

"Did you know how this was going to be?" Novatny asked Gib. He and Vanderhoof were in their trousers and undershirts. Apparently Tyulenev had rousted them out of the bedroom without much ceremony.

"How what was going to be?" Gib asked, pressing down a yawn.

"That she was to be forced to talk," Novatny said. "Did you know that was what they planned?"

Gib shook his head, noticing how hard the woman's eyes were on him. "I didn't know," he said.

"I won't believe a word that's extracted from her by force," said Vanderhoof sullenly.

Gib was troubled by their speaking this way while the woman sat there listening with a scornful, calculating lift in her eyes. He wondered what she'd said to them just before he awoke, to have made of them her allies, almost, against him and Tyulenev. He was about to say something cautioning to them, but Tyulenev came out of the bedroom lugging one of the boxes that had been under the bed, and he was followed by the other two Russians, now dressed in heavy blue coveralls—the contents apparently of the second box.

"Gentlemen," said Tyulenev with a grunt as he let down the box he was carrying.

"Did you hear what I said?" Vanderhoof asked him.

"I heard you, Mr. Vanderhoof," Tyulenev said, with breath shortened either by the work of carrying out the box or by impatience. "But what you choose to believe is not my problem. We have come here to get certain information. We are risking our lives to get it. So, *I* am going to get it, whether you like it or believe it, or not."

"Who decides what we do?" Novatny demanded. "Who's in charge?"

"*I* am, Mr. Novatny," said Tyulenev. "And don't you doubt it for a moment."

"This is all so very foolish," said Nadya Kharina. Her English was American-accented and flawless. She lifted her chin and her shoulders to give some emphasis and dignity to what she wanted to say, and she winced, because even this small abrupt movement had made the wires bite her. "It's foolish," she said again. "You'll all be killed. Your only chance of survival is to release me."

Novatny rose, shaking his head, and went to the window. "No good, lady," he said. He stood looking down at the street. "We know what'll happen if we let you go. Do you think we're fools?"

"That's exactly what she thinks," Gib said, and the woman glared at him.

Vanderhoof was slumped heavily on his chair, looking old this morning, with the flabby white flesh of his shoulders—which were exposed by his vest undershirt—making a contrast with his ruddy face. "I'm supposed to go home and publish what she tells us," he said quietly. "How can I believe anything she says, or publish it, if it's extracted from her by mistreating her?"

Tyulenev, by now irritable and impatient, stamped his foot petulantly. "Your sympathy for this woman is a misplaced sentiment," he said to Vanderhoof. "Over the years she has presided at the . . . at what you'd call the mistreatment of . . . of hundreds of men and women. She'll preside over yours if she gets the chance."

"It's a lie," said Nadya Kharina.

Vanderhoof shrugged. "It's not sympathy that troubles

me," he said. "It's credibility. Even now, when she's tied up here and under *threat* of torture, how could I believe anything she says? She'll say anything you suggest to her, once she's in enough pain or enough fear."

Novatny came to Vanderhoof's side. "Let's you and me go in the bedroom and get our shirts on, Corny," he said. "And talk a little. Hmhh?"

Vanderhoof nodded and followed Novatny into the bedroom. They closed the door.

Gib studied Nadya Kharina's eyes as she watched the two men leave. He thought he saw calculation and contempt. But then when the door closed, he saw her eyes soften and turn apprehensively toward Tyulenev, as if she had been counting, desperately, on the restraint she thought Vanderhoof and Novatny imposed. He also saw her turning slightly inside the wires that bound her, moved probably by an irrational but persistent instinct never to stop testing her bonds.

"Tell us about the United States, Nadya Fedorovna," Tyulenev said to her. He dragged a chair close to her and sat down facing her closely. "That's what we want to talk with you about: the years you spent in the United States."

She looked past Tyulenev, into Gib's face. "You're an American, aren't you?" she asked. When he nodded, she said, "I've never been in the United States."

Tyulenev glanced at Gib. Then he said to the woman, "You were in England."

"Yes, but never in the United States."

"You lie, Nadya Fedorovna."

She shook her head. "I don't lie," she said.

"You lie," he said again.

She hardened. "What you should be asking me," she said to him in a rigid whisper, "is what agreement we can come to for you and your friends to live. I know what you intend, but you'll never live long enough to finish it. What's more, your old friend in the other room is right: no matter what you do to me, I can still lie to you. What you're doing, you're doing for nothing."

Tyulenev pushed back his chair and turned to Gib. "Why don't you go in the bedroom and talk to the old man?" he said. "It would be better, you know, if he would come out and listen to the interrogation. Maybe you can convince him he should. Keep him in there until I call you out. I'll knock on the door when I'm ready for you."

In the bedroom Vanderhoof was sitting on the rumpled bed, and Novatny was leaning in the corner. They had taken time out from their earnest conversation to put on their shirts, but Vanderhoof was gesticulating with both hands and saying, "I have to acknowledge it. In all honesty, I have to acknowledge it."

"Acknowledge what?" Gib asked as he closed the door.

"That I knew all along what they'd likely do to that woman," Vanderhoof said. "I never assumed she'd meet with us and talk voluntarily. My indignation now must look a little foolish, coming as late as it does. When I agreed to come here, understanding what I did, I became a party to whatever they do."

Gib rested both hands on the foot of the bed and stood there looking at Vanderhoof for a moment. Finally he said, "I guess that's right."

"Well, what about *you?*" Novatny demanded of Gib. "Does it bother you?"

Gib nodded. "It makes me sick."

"You're the only one here who could have stopped it," Novatny said. "Back when they first proposed this idea, you could have said no."

"Did you understand," Vanderhoof asked Gib, "that they planned to kidnap and mistreat her?"

"They didn't tell me," Gib said. "But I suspected." He looked up at Novatny and nodded. "Yes, I could have refused to come here, or to ask you to come."

"Well, why didn't you then? I thought you were the idealist. Doesn't torturing a woman offend your ideals?"

"Sure it does."

"Well, then?"

Gib's eyes narrowed, and he lifted his chin defiantly. "Do you really want to hear a whole philosophy?" he asked. "I don't think you do, but I'll say this: an idealist is a highly vulnerable thing to be in this world."

"It *is here,* where we are *now,*" Vanderhoof suggested.

"It is where we come from," Gib said grimly. "People get their heads bloodied for very little in our country too." He stopped, took a long breath, and added quietly, "But I don't think you want to talk about that now."

Novatny shook his head. "That's right, we don't." He shrugged and lowered his voice. "Anyway, I suppose it makes no difference what we think. We have no control over the situation."

"That's right," Gib said shortly, still defensive.

Vanderhoof sighed deeply and rose from the bed. He stepped toward the door as if he meant to go out, and Gib backed up and leaned against it, trying to make his move look fortuitous so they would not guess he was intentionally blocking the exit. But Vanderhoof had no intention of leaving the room. He hunched and flexed his shoulders slowly and elaborately, apparently to relieve the morning stiffness, and then he sat down again. "It doesn't solve *my* problem, anyway," he said almost inaudibly, under his breath.

"What?"

"I still don't see how we can believe anything the woman tells us," Vanderhoof said. "If they hurt her, she'll say anything they suggest."

"I've thought about that problem," Gib said. "The answer

is that *we* must conduct the questioning. We already know a lot of the facts. She doesn't know how much we know. If we're careful of how we question her, I think we can tell when she's lying."

"Elementary exercise in cross-examination," Novatny said dryly.

Vanderhoof sighed heavily once more. "I suppose so," he conceded reluctantly. "I'll reserve judgment."

Their discussion having reached that conclusion—which each of them understood *was* a conclusion—they fell silent for a long moment. Their thoughts were the same, Gib understood: they were suddenly conscious, acutely, that what they'd been talking about was really going on outside the door. Gib moved away from the door because the other two were staring at it and at him, and in an instant he was staring at it himself. Vanderhoof whispered a question. He wondered how long it would take. Novatny grumbled quietly that he wished to hell he had some goddam cigarettes. Gib felt tight and hard all over, and it got worse, and he kept quiet.

Maybe because they were silent themselves, they began to hear sounds through the door. The old wood was heavy, as Tyulenev had said, but they could hear his voice and could tell he was angry and speaking Russian. He stopped. Then they heard a faint voiced gasp. He said something more, and they heard another gasp. The woman's voice was strangely muffled, and they could guess that she was gagged with something jammed deep into her mouth. Tyulenev's voice was low after that, and in the bedroom they could barely tell that he was talking. But again they heard Nadya Kharina's sudden sucked gasps.

"I don't buy it, Gib," Novatny said accusingly. "I don't buy it at all."

"Do you think *I do?*" Gib asked sharply.

Vanderhoof began to shake his head and started to say

something. But he was stopped short by the woman's scream. Even through the gag she screamed in agony, not once but on every breath for a quarter of a minute, sucking in the scream as she drew breath and then coughing it out.

"My God," Vanderhoof whispered. Gib and Novatny had closed their eyes, and their fists were clenched. "My God, that's enough, surely it's enough," Vanderhoof said.

And apparently it was, for in another moment someone knocked softly on the door.

One of the Russians was removing the gag from Nadya Kharina's mouth as the three Americans emerged and saw her. She was moaning and whimpering and turning her head from side to side, making it difficult for the man to untwist the wire which was tied around her neck and between her jaws, like a horse bit. The wire had been so tight it had cut the corners of her mouth. Two short little cuts were bleeding. She was bleeding too on the arms and at the wrists, where she had strained against the wires. The man gave up trying to untwist the wire which held her gag. He cut it and jerked the rag out of her mouth. She began to cry. It was shrill and hysterical.

The three Americans stood aghast and yet morbidly curious, because it was not at all apparent what they had done to her. They had partly stripped her and then had tried to cover her again before they opened the bedroom door. Her bright silk dress and the lace-trimmed slip under it had been slit down the front and then carelessly pulled together again to cover her breasts. Her skirt had been pushed up under her bottom, and her pants were below her knees. One stocking had been torn off, and the straps from a garter belt hung loose on one side. But no marks were to be seen. If any had been made, the Russians had covered them before they let the Americans out.

"What'd you do to her?" Novatny asked.

Tyulenev, now grim and subdued, only shook his head.

Gib did not ask. He figured it out. On the leg from which they had torn her stocking, there was a thick braided copper wire. It ran to the box Tyulenev had lugged out from the bedroom, and another wire ran from the box to the socket on the wall. The handle of a long probe stuck out of the box. They had been burning her with high-voltage shocks. God knew where. Gib didn't want to know.

Tyulenev went to the kitchen. Nadya Kharina, though she was letting her head loll, turned up her eyes to see where he went, and through her low moaning and shrill sobs she tried to say something to him, something in Russian, a plea, the same words over and over. She was begging for something, probably not the glass of water he brought. But she drank it. He held the glass to her lips, and she held in her sobs and took the water, all of it.

Tyulenev sat down on one of the straight chairs which faced Nadya Kharina. He reached out with his toe and dragged the other vacant straight chair up closer, and he looked up at Gib and nodded to the chair. "Do you want to talk to her?" he asked.

Gib, though a twisting at the bottom of his guts resisted his coming any closer to the woman, nodded and approached the chair. He glanced over his shoulder and saw that Vanderhoof and Novatny were taking places on the couch. All of them were close to her, and she looked up at each of them, showing each of them her tear-softened, frightened, defeated eyes.

"Nadya Fedorovna," Tyulenev said firmly to her. "You will talk with them now. You will answer their questions and tell them the truth."

She cut off her last sob and said something in Russian to Tyulenev, asked him apparently some question.

"No," he said. "And you will speak English so they can understand everything you say."

She looked at Gib. "All I asked him," she whispered, "was to loosen some of the wires a little."

Gib frowned at Tyulenev. "Can't we?"

Tyulenev shook his head in little jerks. "Are you crazy?" he asked. "She hasn't answered a single question yet."

Nadya Kharina began to sob, and again Gib glanced over his shoulder, toward Vanderhoof and Novatny. Their faces were hard and grim, but they said nothing, and their eyes shifted and would not meet his. He looked back to the woman. Her cheeks were wet with tears. She was sweating. He could see it glistening on her bare leg and on her chest. He could smell it, in fact. Her eyes were closed, but two or three times she opened them for an instant and squinted dully at him through the tears. He turned to Tyulenev.

"Nadya Fedorovna," said Tyulenev. He spoke gently but purposefully, and she raised her face and looked at him. "You will talk now. Control yourself and listen to what the man asks you. And answer his questions. Now." Tyulenev looked past Gib to Vanderhoof and Novatny, and he said, "She told us repeatedly we would not live to finish questioning her. She will delay us any way she can."

She was facing Gib, and though she was still sobbing softly and squirming against the wires that bound her to the chair, she was attentive. So Gib said to her, "We want to talk to you about the time you spent in the United States."

She nodded.

EAST BERLIN

The interrogation of Nadya Kharina took more than an hour. She remained tightly wired to her chair, occasionally begging for a little relief. Tyulenev would not hear of it, not until she had answered every question. Gib asked the questions. Tyulenev sat threateningly to one side. The other two

Russians waited in the kitchen. They could not understand the interrogation, so they drank the rest of the beer. Vanderhoof, increasingly tense, took up his station at the window once again and stood with one foot and then the other on the windowsill while he listened and frowned. One of the Russians had some cigarettes on him, and Novatny took two or three from him. He sat on the couch and smoked.

"Who did you work for? Who was your superior while you were in the United States?"

She licked her lips. "His name was Parotikin."

"Who was he?"

"He was an intelligence agent."

"A spy, in other words."

"Yes."

"What was the rest of his name?"

"Alekseii. His name was Alekseii Parotikin."

"Why were you sent to the United States? What was your assignment?"

"I was to do whatever Parotikin told me to do. I had been taught English, in a very intensive course. First I was sent to England and assigned to Major Parotikin. I was only eighteen years old then. Parotikin knew he was going to the United States later, and he was learning American accent and American customs. He had two American expatriates to teach him. He had me join in the study. Eventually we went to America."

"What did you do there? What did Parotikin have you do?"

"I worked for Parotikin. I did whatever he told me. We worked with American Communists, in Washington."

"You worked with Party cells."

"Yes."

Gib glanced at Vanderhoof. "Tell us the names of some of the American Communists you worked with," he said to the woman.

She shook her head. "There were many. It's difficult to recall specific names."

"Do you remember Erich Traver?"

"Traver?"

"Yes, Erich Traver—the one who went to prison eventually. Did you know him?"

She shook her head slowly. "I don't think so," she said.

Gib pushed his chair back a little. He looked at Tyulenev. "She's lying."

Gib didn't watch what they did to her. He couldn't. Tyulenev summoned his two men, and the three of them hovered over her, pushing roughly in between him and her so Gib could not have seen all of what happened if he had wanted to look. He saw Tyulenev reach for the electric probe. He heard Nadya Kharina gasp and shudder and scream—through a gag. He jumped up from his chair and joined Vanderhoof at the window, leaning on the sill and hanging his head.

"I'm not sure I can go on with this," he whispered to Vanderhoof.

Vanderhoof glanced at him. His eyes were narrowed. "You have to now," he said in a dull, low voice.

When he looked again at Nadya Kharina, her head was tipped far back. Her face was fiery red. Her mouth was wide open, and one of the Russians was holding the gag in it with his hand. She was moaning and sobbing. Her split dress had fallen open, exposing her breasts. Tyulenev was kneeling before her. He and the other Russian were wiring her legs together at the knees. The insulated wire from the probe lay between her legs. The probe itself was thrust back under her skirt. Whether it was lying in contact with the tender skin between her thighs—or had been pushed up into her sex—you couldn't tell. Anyway, they were wiring her legs together to hold it in place.

Novatny got up from the couch and came to Gib at the

window. "Don't lead her so much with your questions," he said quietly. "Make her tell the story."

Gib whispered. "Do you want to take over?"

Novatny shook his head and went back to the couch.

"Tell us about Erich Traver, all about Erich Traver."

Nadya Kharina took longer to recover this time. Tyulenev gave her water, and she drank it thirstily. But she sobbed deeply for a long time, and no threat would frighten her into stopping. She hung her head and cried. Her face remained flushed. Her eyes were swollen and wet. And she trembled. Tyulenev kept prodding her, until finally she looked up at Gib and seemed as if she could comprehend. He told her to talk about Erich Traver.

She nodded. "I knew him," she whispered. "He was a Communist. He worked for the War Department, later the Department of Defense. He was a minor functionary, but he had access to some information we could use. From time to time he brought out data that was worthwhile." She whispered, but she tried to regain a voice, and a few of her words were voiced.

"Did you know Mrs. Traver?"

"Yes. When I was first in Washington I was ill. The Travers took me in and nursed me."

"Nadya Fedorovna," said Tyulenev. She jerked her head around toward him, terrified by now even of his voice. "You see, you did know this man Traver very well. You lied to us before. You had better not lie to us any more."

She looked back at Gib and fixed her eyes on him, as if there were refuge in him. Her lips were swollen too, and unnaturally red. Maybe she had bitten them. She was drenched with sweat. There was a definite sharp and musty odor of it. The beads and streams of it glistened on her exposed chest and on her small bare breasts. Her glittering jewelled necklace lay on wet skin.

"Go on. Tell us about Traver," Gib said gently.

She nodded. "He was a petty spy," she said. "A petty traitor. He was nothing in himself, but he was involved in something more important."

"Tell us about that."

"Well . . ." She swallowed dryly. "I had not been in Washington long before an opportunity came for me to do something more important than follow the doings of men like Traver. I was working in a restaurant and living in a boarding house. I was supposed to be a girl from California. Parotikin encouraged me to have as much social life as possible, to meet young men who worked in the government, to see if we might find one who could be used. I was taken to parties and moving pictures and to bars for drinks by a whole succession of them—civil servants, military officers, even a member of Congress. But the one Parotikin chose for me to cultivate was a young lawyer from the South, by the name of Benjamin Slusser. He worked for the House Un-American Activities Committee, and Parotikin thought it would be a delicious irony if we could recruit to *our* cause a member of the staff of the House Un-American Activities Committee."

She stopped and hung her head for a moment, and Gib said, "Benjamin Slusser."

"Yes," she said. She had found voice now and spoke softly, in a tone more high and fluid than had been her natural voice. "Slusser. He was . . . I suppose I should say he was a fool. Yet he was not. He was a very clever young man. He was an able young man. But I managed to do what Parotikin wanted. I was only nineteen or twenty years old at the time, and I was pretty. Benjamin Slusser fell in love with me. He became devoted. He wanted to marry me.

"Parotikin gave me a story to use on Slusser. I told Ben that I was living in Washington under an assumed name. I told him my father in California had been involved in the

Longshoreman's Union and was a member of the Communist Party. I told him I was afraid the files of the Un-American Activities Committee might contain something about my father and possibly even about me. I said my father was an old man, and sick, and it would kill him to be exposed to public rage and maybe even to prosecution. I asked Ben to find out for me what the Committee files contained about my father.

"He agreed to do it. Parotikin had given me the name of a real California Communist to use, so the files did contain something. Ben Slusser came back to me very upset. He said someone had talked to a Committee investigator about my father, so there was a report on him in the files. It wasn't very important, but it was damaging information."

She stopped and said something in Russian to Tyulenev. He sent one of his men to bring her another glass of water.

"I cried," she said to Gib. "I told Ben it would kill my father. I said I wanted to find myself a better job than what I was doing—waiting on tables in a restaurant—and what was in that file would prevent my ever getting a better job in Washington. So . . . Well, the man loved me. He was honest about that. He offered to remove the report from the files. And he did. He brought it to me, and I gave it to Parotikin.

"After that the thing progressed. I can give you the details if you want. We made Benjamin Slusser an agent for us. He was much more important than Erich Traver ever was. Parotikin used a combination of techniques on him. He gave him money. He blackmailed him. The more Slusser did for us, the more Parotikin had against him, to use to blackmail him. In the end we even told him I was a Russian. I think that was what he feared most: having it revealed that his fiancée, whom he had introduced to everyone, was a Russian agent. He'd have been scorned and laughed at, driven out of Washington."

Tyulenev put the glass of water to her lips. "Were you Parotikin's lover?" he asked her.

She frowned. "No." She tipped back her head as she swallowed some of the water, and she drew a deep breath. "If you had known Alekseii Parotikin . . ." she whispered hoarsely. "He loved no one, not even himself. He had no emotions. He was a perfect intelligence agent, totally devoted. He lived in a bare room, ate little, never saw a show or read a book. I used to say to myself that he probably didn't even use the toilet." She looked down at the glass and put her chin out toward it. Tyulenev let her drink some more water.

"So what about Traver?" Gib asked.

She closed her eyes. "Traver," she whispered. She sighed and let her head fall forward, and with her chin down on her chest she breathed audibly and seemed to be seeking will and strength. Then she looked up at Gib. "Please," she said. "Ask him to loosen the wires a little. They hurt me." She looked down at the insulated wire that lay between her legs and went to the probe. "And ask him to take that thing . . ."

"Nadya Fedorovna," said Tyulenev firmly. "Tell us about Erich Traver."

She tipped back her head and flexed her aching shoulders. "Please . . ." she whispered.

"Tell us about Erich Traver, Nadya Fedorovna."

She opened her eyes and fixed them on Gib. "Traver," she said softly.

Gib jabbed an angry finger toward Tyulenev. "Look . . ." he said.

Tyulenev stopped him sharply. "Ask your questions. Do you want to get out of here today? Today we have a good chance of escaping alive, tomorrow much less. She knows that. Go on with your interrogation."

Gib surrendered. "Tell us about Traver," he said softly to the woman.

"Traver," she said again. "He was insignificant. He was a fool, an undisciplined intellectual playing at being a Communist. Parotikin looked around for a man we could use, could sacrifice, and Traver was perfect."

"For what?" Gib asked. "Why did you want to sacrifice him?"

Nadya Kharina kept her eyes down, as if she had to strain her memory to recall long-forgotten facts. "It had to do with Ben Slusser," she said. "Parotikin decided to do something for Slusser, to promote his career and make him more valuable to us. He was, after all, still only a civil servant, even if it was on the staff of the Un-American Activities Committee. Suppose we could make him a Congressman, a *member* of the Committee instead of just an employee? That was what Parotikin wanted. Do you understand?"

Gib nodded. "Yes, the whole thing. But go on and tell it."

She hung her head for a moment again. Suddenly her face jerked up angry. "You can at least cover me," she said to Gib. "Do I have to be naked too?"

Gib did not wait for permission from Tyulenev. He reached out and pulled her torn dress across her breasts. By now he had noticed small red swellings in her wrinkled brown nipples. That was one place where Tyulenev had touched her with the probe.

"Thank you," she said. She still had enough will left to make her voice sarcastic. She glanced at Tyulenev and saw his warning frown. "Traver," she said quickly. She glanced past Gib at Novatny and Vanderhoof. "Some of you know how it was in the United States in the early fifties," she said. "What was the best way to promote Benjamin Slusser to something important, like a Congressman? The answer was to give him the reputation of a great anti-Communist. A lot of cheap political careers were built that way. Isn't it true?" she asked, looking up at Vanderhoof.

Gib looked around. Vanderhoof's jaw was set grimly, but he was nodding.

"All right," she went on. "Traver was a petty traitor. We

were contemptuous of him and could live very well without anything he did for us. If Ben Slusser exposed Erich Traver as a Communist spy, it would make Slusser a hero to the hysterical American public. That was what Parotikin wanted. He arranged everything. Traver was ordered to steal some documents from his departmental files. An embassy staff courier with diplomatic immunity was sent to New York to have a secret rendezvous with Traver. Slusser was to arrange for the rendezvous to be exposed and Traver arrested. That was what was done. And that's the story of Erich Traver."

Gib glanced around at Novatny and Vanderhoof. "All right," he said to her. "But something went wrong, didn't it?"

Her chin rose. "What do you mean?"

"Traver was not convicted," said Gib.

She nodded. "Oh, yes. Slusser failed. Parotikin was furious. He wouldn't speak to Slusser after that and forbade me to speak to him. I was assigned to other work."

Gib sighed and shook his head. "Don't lie," he said very softly. "I don't want to see you hurt any more."

Tyulenev swung out of his chair, crossed behind the woman, and knelt beside the box which controlled the electric current to the probe. He looked up at Gib.

She, intent on Gib, did not notice Tyulenev. "If you know everything already," she said captiously to Gib, "why do you ask me to talk? I've told you about Traver. That's what you want to know." She lowered her voice. "I know who you are," she said. "I remember reading about how you have re-opened the Traver case." She nodded. "Well, now you know all about it."

Tyulenev spoke to her quietly. "Nadya Fedorovna . . ."

She snapped her head around and saw him kneeling over the box, with his hand on the switch inside. "*NO!*" she cried. "Don't do it! No! Please! Please!" She jerked her face around to Gib. "Tell him no! Please!" Then she began to beg Tyulenev in Russian.

Tyulenev's hand flicked back and forth inside the box. She took only an instant's jolt of the current, but she gasped loudly and stiffened painfully against the wires. He did it to her again. "That was your final warning, Nadya Fedorovna," he said.

Gib had never seen anything like it—: The sweat came out all over the woman, in only a moment, and suddenly she gleamed and stank. Jerking convulsively, she had pulled her dress apart again, and he could see the sweat appear on the blotched skin of her chest. In another moment the beads were running down between her breasts, making long glittering streaks.

He was sweating himself. He felt it going down his back.

She sucked in breath and cut off a sob. "I understand what you want to know," she whispered quickly before the sob broke loose and shook her whole body. She cried for another moment, and then she said hoarsely, "I'll tell you." She turned to Tyulenev. "I'll tell him," she promised.

"Go on," said Tyulenev. He had settled on his chair again, looking tired and apprehensive.

She pulled a noisy breath through her teeth. "You want to know about the President of the United States, don't you?" she said. "Isn't that what you want to know?"

Gib glanced quickly at Novatny and Vanderhoof. He nodded at her. "Yes."

"Slusser," she whispered, "was very anxious to have Parotikin's scheme work, and he did everything he could to cooperate. He . . ." She swallowed and wet her throat to make a little voice. "He set to work to build a case against Traver. He used the Committee's investigators, and with Parotikin's help he put together a dossier against Traver. He did not actually discover the Party cell of which Traver was a member. Parotikin saw to that. But he found that Traver was a member of some front organizations. He found some writings of Traver's—speeches and articles—that parroted the Party line. He identified two or three close friends of Traver's as men who had been involved in the Popular Front. Oh, Slusser's job was easy. Once Parotikin had put him on the track, Slusser had no trouble putting together the kind of case, half fact and half innuendo, that would satisfy the House Un-American Activities Committee. Traver had kept his actual membership in a Party cell a secret, but he had been a dilettante Communist, without the discipline to work quietly and keep his indignation under cover. He . . ." She coughed and shook her head.

"And Traver actually was stealing Defense Department secrets," Gib said.

"Yes," she agreed. "Everyone carried out Parotikin's little charade. Never suspecting, Traver lifted some papers from his office files and carried them to New York for his rendezvous with the Soviet courier. Slusser followed him, just as Parotikin arranged for him to do. Slusser saw him pass the papers to the courier. After that, Slusser prepared the open hearing before the Committee, at which Traver would be exposed in a great public spectacle."

Nadya Kharina raised her shoulder and pushed her head down against it, trying to brush the tears and an eyelash out of one corner of her eye. She couldn't. She sighed heavily, and she kept blinking and twisting her eye, and the tears kept running.

"Parotikin," she went on, "had misjudged the way the House Un-American Activities Committee worked, and the hearing was not what he expected. Ben Slusser, after all, was still only an employee of the Committee. He might build a case against Traver and prepare for a spectacular public hearing, but at that hearing it was going to be a *member* of the Committee, a Congressman and not just an employee, who would make the show and get the glory. After all, that was what the Un-American Activities Committee was for: to promote the political careers of its members." She looked past Gib to Novatny and Vanderhoof. "Am I not right?" she asked.

Vanderhoof was still standing with one foot on the windowsill. "Many people have always thought so," he said.

"At the hearing," she said, "it was Representative Warren Bradley who accused Traver. It was he who asked the questions of the witnesses. Ben Slusser only sat behind him, out of the light, and prompted him with material from the file. The only time when Slusser was in the light was when he himself testified. It was Bradley who got the attention which Parotikin had expected Slusser to get. Parotikin was furious, but he was at the same time impressed."

"Impressed with what? With Bradley?" Novatny asked.

"Yes. Warren Bradley was a young man then. He was a Navy veteran. He was in his second or third term in Congress—from a district in Michigan, I think it was. He performed well. He was an actor. The Traver hearings made him a national figure. Or to say it more accurately, Parotikin made Bradley a national figure."

Nadya Kharina stopped. Her face was red and wet, and she was breathing in spasms. Gib had seen her showing more signs of exhaustion, and he wondered if Tyulenev saw and was judging. Tyulenev might have to loosen the wires that bound her, whether he wanted to or not. She never stopped twisting her shoulders, searching for some little relief for her wrists and arms. Now she squirmed on the seat of the chair, trying to push her hips forward or to shift them from side to side. Gib guessed what she was struggling to do: she was trying to move the probe. But she could not move her hips. The wires were too tight. She gave up. She slackened. She looked at Gib for a moment, closed her eyes and sighed, and dropped her head heavily.

Gib allowed her a minute, and then, seeing Tyulenev's nervous impatience, he said to her gently, "Traver was not convicted."

"No, he wasn't," she mumbled without lifting her chin from the slippery wet skin of her chest. "The Justice Department prosecuted him after the Committee hearings. They had no choice but to prosecute, even if they didn't think the case against him was very strong. Ben Slusser was the only witness who had seen Traver pass the information to the courier, and he was not witness enough. Some of the jury were not convinced. The jury did not convict. Slusser looked like a fool. Parotikin's scheme had failed. And that would have been the end of it probably, if Bradley had not revived it."

She stopped again, and Gib prompted her. "Go on. What did Bradley do?"

"Bradley publicly demanded that the Department of Justice prosecute Traver for perjury, for having denied he was a Communist when he testified before the Un-American Activities Committee."

Nadya Kharina suddenly lifted her face, glistening with tears and sweat, and for an instant showed an expression almost of triumph; she almost smiled. "Here," she whispered with pride and defiance, "was where Parotikin showed what a genius he was. Bradley was a man with too much ambition for his ability. He was not stupid, but he was always too grasping and impatient to be clever. He was shallow. He was venal. And Parotikin, who was a great master, toyed with him. Parotikin manipulated him with delicate finesse and subtlety. Parotikin . . ."

"Nadya Fedorovna," said Tyulenev wearily. "Don't rhapsodize. Just tell us what Parotikin did."

She caught herself up tensely and glanced fearfully at Tyulenev. "To convict Traver of perjury," she said through her labored breath, "they needed real evidence that he was a member of the Communist Party. They needed better evidence than Slusser had given the Committee. The Justice Department told Bradley they could not prosecute Traver on the basis of the evidence in the file. Bradley was desperate. His bright new political reputation was the result of the Traver hearings. He had piously accused Traver of being a Communist, and now Traver—instead of being convicted and sent to prison—was threatening to sue Bradley and Slusser. Some of the newspapers were already saying that Traver had been *recklessly* accused. He . . ."

She had lost control of her voice. She hung her head and sobbed and gasped.

"You're going to have to do something for her," Gib said to Tyulenev.

Tyulenev frowned and nodded. "Let her go on a little," he whispered. He slapped her arm. "Talk, woman," he said sharply.

"Bradley was desperate to find evidence," she said in a hoarse, strained whisper. "But he put *Slusser* in charge of the search for it. Slusser still worked for Parotikin, and Parotikin played a game with Slusser and Bradley. The Committee investigators did turn up some leads which might have led them to Traver's Party cell; but Slusser, doing as Parotikin told him, put them off every time. Parotikin was laughing."

"What about the FBI?" Vanderhoof asked.

"Everyone still trusted Slusser," she said. "He had worked on the case longest and was presumed to know the most about it, so every investigator started with him."

"And no one found anything," Gib said.

She shook her head. "Not until Parotikin was ready for them to find it. He was a master, playing a game with fools."

"How did he play Bradley?" Vanderhoof asked. Vanderhoof had moved away from his window at last and was standing behind Gib.

"He waited until Bradley was desperate. Traver was talking to the newspapers, threatening to sue Bradley for libel unless Bradley admitted the accusations had been false. Bradley had some speaking engagements coming up, and he was going to have to say something about the Traver case. That was what he had been invited for: to talk about the Traver case. He had to do something, either put out his chin and insist that Traver actually was a Communist, or admit that he might not be, or keep quiet about it, which would have been an admission too. That was when Parotikin sent me to see Bradley."

"Sent *you?*" Vanderhoof asked skeptically.

"Yes, me. I knew Bradley, and I knew his wife. Bradley and Slusser were good friends, and I was still officially Slusser's fiancee."

"You lied about that a while ago," Tyulenev said. "You said you were ordered to break off with Slusser after he failed to get Traver convicted of espionage."

Nadya Kharina turned a frightened face toward Tyulenev and began to cry. "I'm not lying now," she whispered shrilly. "I'm not. . . ." Her head fell, and she began to sob violently.

"For God's sake, man!" Vanderhoof snapped at Tyulenev.

Tyulenev frowned at the weeping woman. He reached in his pocket and pulled out a small pair of wire cutters. Leaning forward, he snapped the wire which bound her legs together at the knees, and he seized the rubber-insulated wire and pulled out the probe. (This was Gib's first close look at the probe. It was like a small version of a cattle prod: a tube of bakelite or some such material with the wire going in one end and a metal tip on the other, crudely stuck together with friction tape.) Tyulenev then reached behind Nadya Kharina and cut the wires which bound her wrists.

She could not raise her arms. Her freed hands hung limply at her sides, and she made feeble, twitching efforts to raise them. Her wrists were deeply scored, darkly bruised, and cut by the wire. Her hands were discolored. They had turned a morbid bluish-gray, and they were stained with dried blood which had run down from her wrists. Her knees had not been as long or as tightly bound, but they were marked by the wire. She had let her legs fall apart as soon as the wire was cut, and Gib, sitting directly in front of her, could see bright red burns on the insides of her thighs. Her legs and hips and crotch were drenched with pungent sweat. Even the seat of the chair was wet.

"All right, Nadya Fedorovna," Tyulenev said with a slow, tired impatience. Her head was still down and she was still sobbing, but her eyes were open and she was looking at her wrists and at the burn marks on her thighs. "All right, Nadya Fedorovna."

She lifted her head. "A drink of water," she whispered.

"*Voda!*" Tyulenev snapped at the two men in the kitchen. "Now go on and talk, Nadya Fedorovna."

She nodded, and Gib prompted her. "You went to see Bradley," he said.

"Yes. Ben Slusser had introduced me to Bradley and had even taken me to a reception where Bradley and Mrs. Bradley were honored—this, though I was only a waitress in a restaurant. Bradley received me when I called on him at his apartment. I told him I knew a woman who would testify that she knew Traver as a member of a Communist cell. It was a bad hour for Bradley, and this sounded like his salvation. He was almost naïve about what I said. He was joyful in his enthusiasm even before he thought to ask me such an obvious question as how *I* should have happened to find this witness."

Her voice was low and broken by shuddering. She was staring at her hands, which she could not raise. She jerked her arms from the shoulders, but her hands only hung and trembled.

"Go on," said Tyulenev.

"Parotikin had rehearsed me in exactly what I was to tell Bradley," she said. "I told him the woman ate regularly at the restaurant where I worked and had become acquainted with me there. I said she had approached me because she knew I was the fiancée of Ben Slusser, who was well known as a lawyer for the Un-American Activities Committee. I told him the woman was an old Communist who had quit the Party when Soviet Russia signed the pact with Nazi Germany in 1939. I said she was willing to testify that she had known Erich Traver in the late '30's as a fellow member of the Party and had seen him at cell meetings. Then I told Bradley—as Parotikin had ordered—that I doubted the woman was telling the truth. I said I thought she had motives of her own for wanting to become a witness against Traver."

Nadya Kharina raised her eyes and focused on Gib's face. A little expression had returned to her face: a hint of curiosity as to whether the Americans understood what she was telling. She licked her lips and looked at Tyulenev. He let her have a sip of water.

"What we wanted to know," she said, "was how Bradley would react to a witness who might be willing to lie against Traver."

She stopped for another sip of water, and Vanderhoof squatted down beside Gib so he could look directly up into her face. "Well," he said. "What did Bradley say?"

She lifted her chin scornfully. "He asked me," she said, "if I thought the woman would be convincing."

Nadya Kharina went on to tell how she and Slusser and Parotikin gradually involved Congressman Warren Bradley in building a structure of perjured testimony against Erich Traver. At first Slusser told Bradley that the woman who had come to the restaurant was a break in the case but had a sketchy memory for details and would have to be coached thoroughly to make her a believable witness. Bradley did not object to coaching the witness. Then Slusser told him that the woman had given them leads to other witnesses but that one of those witnesses would not testify unless he was coerced with a threat of prosecution. Bradley did not object to the coercion. Then Parotikin had Slusser tell Bradley that another witness demanded five hundred dollars for his testimony. Bradley provided the money out of his campaign funds. Finally, Parotikin sent the members of Traver's Party cell—chief among them Esther Levine—to be the principal witnesses. Slusser turned the case over to the Justice Department, and Traver was indicted. Only then, with the trial just weeks away, did Parotikin order Slusser to tell Bradley that some of the witnesses would be flatly lying when they testified against Traver.

"How did Bradley react to that?" Vanderhoof asked. He had taken Tyluenev's chair, was sitting beside Gib and facing Nadya Kharina, and was asking most of the questions.

As much as she could she was sucking and licking her wrists and trying to rub life back into her black hands. She had no control over her fingers but had managed clumsily to push down her skirt and push her dress across her breasts. She was still completely immobile, bound tightly to the chair by wires around her ankles and hips and body, but with her hands movable she was pushing the wires out of her cuts and relieving some of the most painful pressures. She had drunk two glasses of water and had regained some of her voice, but she was so intent on being able to move a little and ease some of the worst pain that she seemed not to hear some of their questions.

"Talk, woman," said Tyulenev sharply.

Her chin jerked up. She was terrified of Tyulenev. "Bradley," she said. She went on to talk with her hands awkwardly clasped before her face. "He was upset, very upset. He asked Slusser how Slusser could have done that to him, how he could have put him in a position like that. (I was there. I had been present at several of the conversations, and by this time I think Bradley suspected I was something besides a waitress.) Slusser asked him what he wanted. Did he want to convict Traver or didn't he? He said they could still call off the prosecution. They could call the Justice Department lawyers in and tell them they suspected some of the witnesses were lying. Bradley nearly broke down and wept. He said no, it was too late. Slusser said it would not be too late until the case actually went to trial. Bradley said no, it was already too late. He went out that very night and made a big speech—to an American Legion meeting I think it was—saying how the nation must be always vigilant against people like Erich Traver."

"I remember the very speech," said Vanderhoof grimly. "I was there."

"The second day of the trial, after Esther Levine had testified, we told Bradley everything," she went on. "We even told him I was a Soviet agent. And, of course, we told him that Slusser had been working for the Soviet Union for almost a year. It was a risk. Bradley might have informed on both of us. But he didn't. Parotikin had judged him correctly."

"What if Parotikin had been wrong?" Gib asked. "What would have happened to you?"

"Parotikin had promised Ben Slusser and me that we could flee the country, that it was all arranged for us to go that same night if Bradley had. . . . But I don't think it was true. I think Parotikin was prepared to sacrifice Slusser and me. He had big things in mind. If Bradley had broken and had informed on us, it would have meant a scandal in Congress that would have shaken confidence in the entire government. As it turned out, Bradley did not inform, and Parotikin got what he really wanted; which was Bradley himself."

Vanderhoof let out all his breath, so much he seemed to shrink. He closed his eyes and shook his head. "Now you are going to tell us," he said slowly, "that Warren Bradley . . ." And he stopped and did not finish.

She pressed her injured wrist against her lips, but she nodded. "He was compromised," she said. "I took over from the point where I was identified to him. I told him we could, any time we wanted, take Ben Slusser out of the country and let him tell what had happened. Bradley blustered and said he'd see me hanged as a spy. Then he broke down. He wept like a child. He got drunk. He got sick, and I had to take care of him. Oh, he did it all, went through all the stages. Finally, the next day, when he'd settled down and become rational again, I told him it wouldn't be too hard. We wouldn't ask much of him. And we didn't. Parotikin was very careful with him. Bradley was too valuable to risk on anything petty."

"You used Warren Bradley . . . ?"

"He was elected to the Senate that fall," she said. "He owed his election to the reputation he won in securing the imprisonment of Erich Traver. Parotikin wanted him on the Armed Services Committee, and that was where he got himself. When the Senate Armed Services Committee met in secret session, to hear secret testimony from the generals and admirals, Bradley would tell me or Slusser what was said. We never asked him to steal documents or anything like that. We never even tried to control his vote. We just used him to find out what was said in secret sessions of the Armed Services Committee."

"How long did this go on?"

She shook her head. "I don't know. After the death of Stalin, Parotikin was called home to Moscow. Not long after that, I was called home and reassigned. We had only a few months to make good use of what Parotikin had so carefully built, but I can't believe our successors let such valuable properties as Benjamin Slusser and Warren Bradley go to waste."

They asked her more questions, but she had nothing more to tell them. She had been assigned to other work, she said, and had not kept in touch with what happened in the United States.

The three Russians prepared to leave. Tyulenev told the Americans they would be picked up early in the afternoon and taken back to the Pergamon Museum, from where they would return to the Checkpoint.

Tyulenev took another glass of water to Nadya Kharina, and he offered her a large yellow capsule. She shook her head at the capsule, but he told her he would force it down her throat if she didn't take it. Her fingers would not close on it, so she took it from him on the tip of her tongue and swallowed it. She drank the water.

"You all realize," she said through clenched teeth, "that none of you will ever leave the German Democratic Republic alive. It makes no difference what I've told you. You'll never get out with it. You will all die right here in Berlin."

The capsule took effect shortly. She struggled against it, but it overcame her, and she fell unconscious, still bound to the chair and hanging in the wires.

Tyulenev said something to his men in Russian. Abruptly the two of them drew knives out of their coveralls, and they faced the Americans with the points thrust toward them. Then, with the horrified Gib and Vanderhoof and Novatny held at bay, Tyulenev looped a cord around the throat of the unconscious Nadya Kharina, and strangled her. He tore a sheet off the bed and threw it over the body, and the body sat there, bound to the chair, until the three Americans at last could get away, shortly after noon.

THE JUPITER CRISIS

PARIS

The crowded Caravelle which brought the three Americans back to Paris circled Orly Field for most of an hour. French air traffic controllers were disputing with the government again. The traffic pattern carried the Caravelle in a long southwestward loop out over Versailles; and Gib, sitting at the window, watched the Palace slide under the airplane wing half a dozen times. Versailles didn't look like much from the air, and the sight of it did not raise his spirits or engage his thoughts. It did not distract him from the affected solemnity and silence of the two men who sat with him—Vanderhoof and Novatny.

"It wasn't worth it, Gib," Vanderhoof had said, and that was about all he had said since they returned through the Checkpoint and hurried to Tempelhof to catch the first plane they could for Frankfurt and then this one for Paris. He meant that what they had learned from Nadya Kharina was not worth murdering her at the end of her ordeal. Novatny agreed, emphatically.

Gib agreed too. Nothing could justify killing the woman. But after you said that, then what? The woman was dead, but what she had told them was important beyond their remotest hopes, and Gib was resentful that these two chose to sit in the silence of affected mourning—with an implication loud in their silence that he, Gib, bore a greater share of responsibility than they did. He had been shocked. He was sick with regret. It was very heavy in him. But he was filled with excitement too, over what Nadya Kharina had told them, and he wanted to talk about it.

The Caravelle was filled: one cramped passenger for every seat; and Novatny, who'd had to make a stop on their way between the Checkpoint and Tempelhof so he could buy cigarettes, had smoked all during the flight as if he had to make up for the couple of days when he'd had no smokes. Gib was irritated with Air France and with Novatny. His back hurt, and his eyes burned. With his elbow on the armrest and his chin in his hand, he watched the outskirts of Paris slip below and wondered if they ever would land.

"Do you think you can write any of it?"

Vanderhoof's question half startled Gib. He swung around and confronted the thoughtful, frowning face and the thick white mustache.

"I mean," Vanderhoof said, "that the woman, after all, accused the President of the United States of treason. And all we have on it is her word."

Gib tugged himself around in his seat. Vanderhoof was leaning toward him. Novatny was ignoring them. Novatny seemed completely preoccupied in relieving whatever symptoms remained of his two days' nicotine deprivation, tugging on his cigarette as if he were eating the smoke.

"It's not much to go on, to accuse the President," Vanderhoof said.

"We have more than that," Gib said. "Everything she said fit into something else we already knew."

"I noticed that," Vanderhoof said. "And she couldn't have faked everything, not in the circumstances. I think she knew from the beginning that they'd kill her when they were finished with her."

Gib nodded. He was glad that Vanderhoof had at last decided to talk, but he tried not to show his enthusiasm too openly, not in the face of Vanderhoof's still excessively solemn mood. "I suppose likely she did," he said quietly.

Vanderhoof frowned more deeply. "I've been thinking of some of the implications of what she told us," he said. "We'll be thinking of them for months, I imagine, and new ones will occur to us every day. Right now, one in particular is sticking in my mind."

"What's that?" Gib asked.

Vanderhoof leaned toward Gib a little more and lowered his voice. "Let's suppose," he said, "that what Nadya Kharina told us is true, and let's suppose also that Warren Bradley never got off the hook and is still a dupe and a traitor. That's almost impossible to believe, even with what that poor tortured woman told us, but let's suppose it's true. If it is, Bradley must be an extremely valuable man. They would use him only rarely, I would think, only on the most important matters, and only very cautiously and subtly. But he would be extremely valuable. If he is that valuable, then we have to anticipate that they will protect him. We have to anticipate they will do whatever they think they have to do to protect him. Do you follow me?"

"Including killing us, you mean?" Gib said.

"Yes. If what Nadya Kharina told us is true, then our lives are in danger, and they will be until . . . Well, until what? Until Bradley is exposed, or . . . I don't know what."

Gib nodded. "When they called Parotikin home, they must have sent someone to replace him, and probably there is still someone in the States just like him."

"He was a killer, wasn't he?"

"That's what I was told."

Shtemenko met them at the airport and drove them into town in his own car. "I have unhappy news," he said as soon as they were inside the car. "Yuri Tyulenev did not return."

"What do you mean?" Novatny asked.

Shtemenko glanced irritably over his shoulder at Novatny, as if he could not believe that anyone could miss his meaning. "He was not to come back through Checkpoint Charlie, as you did. He was to have come across at Helmstedt. He failed to appear. He is more than a day late now, and we think he will not come."

"You think he's dead?"

"Let us hope so."

Gib, sitting beside Shtemenko in the front seat of the Citroën, spoke quietly with him as he drove toward the Champs Élysées and the Étoile, to drop Novatny and Vanderhoof at the Royal Monceau. Gib told him what had happened in Berlin and a little of what Nadya Kharina had said.

"You will have to tell it all to Melanie," Shtemenko said. "She is waiting. Also, I want my colleague Vera Kravchenko to hear your report. She is not just a fat old lady, you know."

"I'm sorry if I've given the impression I thought so."

"She is not Yuri's mother," Shtemenko said. "But she was very close to him, and she is upset that we have lost him."

"You think there's no chance?"

Shtemenko shook his head. "No. We probably lost the two who worked on the other side, as well."

"What about the three who were in West Berlin while we were in the East?"

"We've heard from them."

"I'm sorry about Tyulenev," Gib said.

Shtemenko seemed to ignore that. "We all must meet somewhere," he said. "I think perhaps my flat . . . I have a little protection around it."

"You think we need protection now?"

Shtemenko shrugged.

They met the next morning in Shtemenko's apartment, in

a building which surprised Gib for its location on a tree-shaded avenue of quiet old Second Empire homes. The flat surprised him too, for its elegance. It was tastefully and expensively furnished. Everything, the flat itself and everything in it, was archetypically French. Shtemenko, the brusque, scowling, chain-smoking Russian, seemed out of place in it.

Melanie was already there when Gib arrived with Vanderhoof and Novatny. He had tried to call her, to meet her in the evening, but he had not been able to reach her. She was not working at the club any more, and though she still had her rooms with Carole Levine, neither of them was at home when he stopped there. She had not called him. Still, Shtemenko had said she was anxious to hear from him.

"I'm going to translate into French for Vera Ivanovna," she told Gib as soon as she had greeted him. "So don't talk too fast. Remember the trouble Yuri had."

Melanie seemed to have conceded something to the occasion or her surroundings. She was wearing a dress, a black dress with a loose sort of peasant-blouse top, pinched at the waist with a knotted cord, and a long, full skirt. And stockings. She sat beside Gib, facing the tall eastward windows which let fresh, white, morning light into the room and made everything airy and cheerful, with some of the light in her complexion and some in her hair, so she shared the bright innocence of the morning. She said she was relieved that Gib had returned.

"So am I," he said. "I learned something about being afraid."

"Have you talked to Leslie? Does she know you're back?"

"She doesn't know I went. But yes, I called her last night. She hadn't heard from me in ten days and was very upset. I think she guessed that . . . something was going on."

Vera Ivanovna Kravchenko had not arrived, and Shtemenko offered coffee to his guests while they waited. He asked Melanie to help him prepare and serve it. It turned out that Melanie made the coffee and served it without much help from him.

When she had returned and the coffee was served and she was stting beside Gib again, he said to her, "I gather you've been here before. You seem to know where the kitchen is, and the coffee and all."

Melanie smiled and turned her eyes toward him without turning her head. "Yes," she said. "I've been here before."

"More than once," he said.

She looked at him, and her smile was gone. "Yes, Gib, more than once."

Vera Ivanovna Kravchenko arrived, flushed, puffing, and apologetic. She was the same as before—fat, dressed in gray crepe, her face veiled with a veil of netting that hung from the brim of her straw hat. She settled in a chair, accepted a cup of coffee from Melanie, and regarded the three Americans with the same querulous, half hostile eye with which she had regarded Gib when they met before. Shtemenko had said she was upset over the loss of Yuri Tyulenev. If she was, she didn't show it.

Gib told everything that had happened, in detail, speaking slowly so that Melanie could translate into French. Shtemenko asked a few questions. The woman asked two or three—about Tyulenev, how he had conducted himself. Gib said competently and bravely. Novatny tried to add something to that, something about brutality, but Gib cut him off with a curt comment that surprised himself as much as Novatny.

"So," said Shtemenko when Gib had finished. He had risen and circled the room uneasily while Gib talked, and now he was at the windows, opening them outward a little so that a fresh air, smelling of green leaves, could fill the sheer curtains and escape past them into the room. He said, "So," again, and he looked down at Vera Ivanovna Kravchenko and said something to her in Russian.

The woman gave a Gallic shrug. "*Quoi ensuite?*" she said.

"Yes," said Shtemenko. "Precisely. What now?"

"We've spoken of that a little," said Vanderhoof.

"I should imagine," said Shtemenko.

"It's difficult," said Vanderhoof quickly, "to accuse the President of the United States of treason."

Shtemenko had sat down again and was toying with a delicate, translucent, bone china cup, swirling the dregs of coffee in the bottom of it and scowling over it. "Anyway, it's *old* treason," he said. "It's old history. Who cares about it now?"

"I think many Americans will care very much about it," Gib said.

Shtemenko shook his head and turned down the corners of his mouth in a strong, scornful grimace. "I didn't sacrifice Yuri Tyulenev," he said, "to find out that your President was a weakling and an ass twenty years ago, nor to bring him down politically either. We have more at stake than that, I hope."

"Then you suspect they are still using him, even today," said Vanderhoof.

"I don't know," said Shtemenko. "But if they are not, if he somehow escaped them and is free of them today, then we have lost a good man's life for very little."

Novatny had been showing more and more skepticism as they talked, and now he asked, "How do you propose to find out?" His question was a challenge.

"That is where your friend Senator Jordan could be helpful," said Shtemenko coldly.

"If he can find the courage to be helpful," Melanie interjected. She looked away for a moment from her hurried translation for Vera Ivanovna Kravchenko, who looked instantly dismayed to hear Melanie joining into the conversation in English. "Your friend the Senator is a little overdue, isn't he?" Melanie asked.

Everyone ignored what she said, but she had ruptured the conversation, had broken its logic, so that for a moment it stopped, and everyone took the silent moment to ponder self-consciously. Finally Gib said quietly, "My whole purpose was to learn the truth about the Erich Traver case. Well, I guess I know it now."

Melanie supplied what he had left unsaid. "It doesn't make so much difference really, does it?"

Novatny shook his head. "It's a whole new mystery," he said. "The other one, the Traver affair, had some limits, and you had some hope of finding the answer. You *did* find it, in fact. But this . . . I mean, to look at the whole presidency of Warren Bradley and try to find some evidence that he has betrayed the country. . . . Well, there's no place to begin to look. The mystery is too much for us. It's unmanageable. It's beyond us."

"*Not so,*" said Vanderhoof, with a finger jabbed hard toward Novatny. "Not so, by God. We *do* know where to look. Down in Georgia, that's where. I even wrote a column about it, based on your tip, Steve. Remember?"

"What . . . ?"

"*Slusser,*" said Vanderhoof. "Don't you remember the suggestion you gave me about Benjamin Slusser? You told me to check with the White House correspondent for the Cincinnati . . . Which was it, *Enquirer?* Anyway, whichever paper it was, I talked to the fellow as you suggested, and he told me that *Benjamin Slusser is a regular visitor at the White House.* What's more, he's a secret visitor. No one seems to want to acknowledge knowing him. Remember? I wrote the column, speculating on why Benjamin Slusser should see the President so often and why no one at the White House wants to talk about it. Remember?"

Novatny nodded.

"The day when we talked to the President in the Oval

Office," Gib said, "that column of yours was mentioned. The President didn't like it. Remember, Steve?"

"I remember."

"And something else," Gib said. "When I met with Slusser in Georgia, he denied he went to Washington very often, or ever talked to the President. He lied about it."

Vanderhoof was nodding, holding a loosely clenched fist to his mouth, pushing his mustache up against his nose. "The possibilities. . . ." he mused. "The goddam possibilities." He turned to Gib. "One more fact yet," he said. "The fellow from Cincinnati told me that one of Slusser's clandestine little visits to the White House was on the night of January . . . well, January something or other—I forget now the date. But it was right in the middle of the business about the satellite—the Jupiter crisis. Ben Slusser paid a visit to the President, in other words, at the very most difficult hour of Bradley's presidency, at the very hour when you'd think the President had no time for any socializing with an old buddy. What the hell do you suppose Slusser was doing there then? The possibilities are absolutely staggering."

"Let's don't be staggered too quickly," said Novatny. "It's a temptation."

Vanderhoof turned to talk to Shtemenko. "Before I let them talk me into coming here and going with them to Berlin," he said, "I was spending most of my time trying to unravel the mystery of the Jupiter crisis. And believe me, it *is* a mystery. It's filled with contradictions and illogic, and I've been able to find no rational explanation for it. It's possible, just possible, that what we learned from Nadya Kharina suggests the explanation." He nodded at Shtemenko. "As I said before, the possibilities are staggering. And I'm not talking about old history, my friend. I'm not talking about old treason."

They left Shtemenko's apartment in mid-morning. The talk

had gone on for a little while, but it had turned desultory. Everyone had more or less withdrawn from it, had turned inward to think on what Vanderhoof had suggested.

All of them left together, and Shtemenko followed them down the broad, carpeted stairway toward the foyer and the glass double doors to the street. Melanie led the way with Vera Ivanovna Kravchenko, holding the fat old lady's arm and speaking French to her. Gib and Novatny followed, and Vanderhoof and Shtemenko hung back a little, talking quietly and privately. Gib would remember later that he had smiled for an instant, because he noticed the concierge peek out to see who was coming down the stairs. It was just as the wizened old woman pulled her head back and closed the door that Gib heard the two shots outside the glass doors.

Then the glass doors swept up the stairs toward them, in a roaring violent wave of smoke and fire and shards of glass and flying wood and stone. He saw Melanie swept backward off her feet by the impact of the wave, saw her tossed back with her arms flung high above her head. Then it all hit him, and he saw nothing more. Trying later to describe it, he said it was like being a pedestrian struck by a red-hot car. It hurt terribly, but only for a moment, because he lost consciousness.

PARIS

Vera Ivanovna Kravchenko died in the hospital two days after the bomb blast. Melanie lost the sight of her right eye, and her right leg would never again support her weight unassisted by a crutch or cane. Steve Novatny would require a long course of plastic surgery to repair his face. Vanderhoof and Shtemenko, who had been farther up the stairs, were treated for cuts and released from the hospital within hours.

As for Gib, he would always believe—though he had to

acknowledge it probably was a fanciful belief—that he could detect on his own body a sort of crude outline of Melanie's body, since she had been in front of him and had caught the storm of flying glass that would have hit him. Both his arms were badly torn. The right was only scarred, and though it was stiff he could use it readily enough. The muscles and tendons of the left were damaged deeply, so that he would need therapy to learn to use it again, and it never would be strong. Shards of glass had torn across his scalp, ripping away hair and flesh. It looked deathly, but the doctors said his hair would cover the permanent scars. He wasn't sure about his hearing. He kept listening for small sounds.

One of Shtemenko's security guards had shot the bomb-thrower just outside the door, and the bomb had gone off there. If the bomb had exploded inside the foyer, as had been intended, likely they all would have died. The wounded bomb-thrower had escaped in the confusion, and the police had no clues as to who he was.

Gib's father and mother arrived in Paris two days after the bombing, bringing Leslie with them. They came to see him every day, and they said they would stay in Paris until he could fly home with them. Erich Traver and Mrs. Traver came to see Melanie and stopped to speak for a moment with Gib. They were quiet and polite and said nothing. Vanderhoof, who might have gone home, stayed in Paris and spent most of his time with Shtemenko, discussing the Jupiter crisis and searching in the records of the Alliance for anything that might support the theory that was growing in his mind. He came to the hospital daily to talk to Gib and Novatny. Gib was anxious to leave, and the doctors said he could after a week.

It was painful to see Melanie. Her right eye was covered with a huge gauze patch, and the left eye didn't seem to see.

She was pale. Her mouth was set stiff and pinched, as if she blamed the whole world for what had happened to her.

"Lex will help me," she said without expression to Gib, who had asked her if she would go back to England with her father and mother, or if not, how he could help her.

"Lex?"

"Alexandr Leonidovich Shtemenko."

"You and . . . *Shtemenko?*"

She nodded. "Sure. Sometimes. We needed his help, didn't we? He and I became . . . very close friends."

Gib frowned. "I don't understand," he said.

Melanie smiled faintly. "I know you don't," she said. "Lex and I talk tough to each other. He's made you think he doesn't like me and doesn't trust me. But he's asked me to marry him, and I've accepted."

"I can't believe it."

"Why not?" she asked. "Can you think of a better man, a stronger man?"

"It's sudden."

"Not so sudden. I've been in Paris a long time."

Gib encountered Shtemenko in the hallway between Melanie's room and his own. He looked hard at the self-possessed, icy Russian, trying to see what Melanie perhaps saw. He didn't see it. Shtemenko was a dour, forbidding man. Nevertheless Gib offered him his congratulations.

"Ah. She told you," Shtemenko said.

"Yes. I'm afraid I can't conceal my surprise."

"My first wife died six years ago," Shtemenko said. "Melanie and I think we have a great deal to offer each other." He glanced toward her door. "The precise nature of what we will give each other may have been altered somewhat . . . now. Still, I am happy, and she is." The Russian's sharp, cold eyes settled on Gib's eyes with a firm, steady, enigmatic gaze. "She will be a good wife to me," he said. "I will be a good husband to her."

It was difficult to see Leslie alone. She came with his parents, and though they hurried away self-consciously toward the end of their visits to let Leslie talk to him without them, Novatny was in the other bed and Gib was not alone with her. He arranged as soon as he could get up to sit with her on a little stone balcony overlooking a bleak paved courtyard, but even there they had the company of other patients the first two times they went out. They kissed and talked, but she was restrained because they were not alone. On the third day, they sat down on chairs in the sunshine, and luckily no one else was about.

"Something new?" he asked, nodding toward a bright yellow pants suit she was wearing. It was linen, he guessed, and looked expensive, and he knew perfectly well it was new and where she had gotten it.

"Your mother bought it for me," Leslie said. She looked down self-consciously, and her dark hair swung forward and hid her face from him. "Do you like it?"

"It looks good on you."

"Your mother . . ."

"Has a sense of style and the fitness of things," he said. He grinned at his own clothes. He was wearing a maroon robe and gray pajamas his mother had sent immediately to the hospital, after her first visit when she saw him propped up in bed in a hospital gown.

"She sure has," Leslie said. "A sense of style and the fitness of things. She doesn't like my pierced ears. I think she has an idea I could have the holes patched somehow. But she's been very kind to me. So has your father."

"Don't let my mother try to make you over in her own image, Les."

"She's a handsome woman."

"Yes, but I remembered you sitting in your skimpy shorts and an old T-shirt, on the steps of our building, showing the world the dirty black bottoms of a pair of very pretty bare feet."

She glanced away from him. "When are you going to tell us where you've been and why someone wanted to kill you?" she asked. "Your father and mother want to know. So do I."

"I'll tell you, Les. I won't tell them. They'll find out sooner or later, probably. The French newspapers are full of speculation about who tried to kill us and why, and I can tell you that some of the speculation is exactly correct. But we'll talk about it later. It's too long a story for now."

Two white-clad young doctors hurried across the brick-paved courtyard below, their heels and soles reverberating off the stone walls around the courtyard. The soft but over-hurried sound of their French conversation drifted up to the balcony, incomprehensible. Gib saw Leslie watching them and was glad she was distracted.

But she was not distracted, really. She was still intently thoughtful, and she looked at him for a moment and then spoke. "We'll be flying back together," she said. "I don't know when we'll be alone again. I have to tell you something."

He nodded, moved to sympathy by her quiet solemnity, and he looked hard at her, seeing she was troubled and anxious to know why.

"You have enough to think about," she said, "but you have to know this. I'm pregnant. You made me pregnant some time before you left."

She looked up at him, with a wistful appeal in her deep brown eyes, and he said, "It's all right. It's all right, Les."

"I feel like a fool," she said.

He shook his head. "No . . ."

"Yes." Again she looked away and lowered her head, and her hair partly obscured her face. "I feel like a child who ignored every warning, played with matches, and now has to admit she burned herself."

"No, Les, it's not like that."

She looked up again, so he could see her face. He had noticed how much the sun had darkened her skin. In only a few days in Paris, walking in the gardens with his father and mother, the olive sheen of her face had been replaced by a glowing tan that looked bright and vital.

"I guess I wasn't careful enough about the pills," she said. "Anyway, I'm going to have an abortion. I have an appointment for it in two weeks."

Gib frowned hard. "I don't think I want you to do that," he said. He drew a breath. "No, I don't want you to. I want you to have the baby. We'll be married as soon as we get home."

Leslie smiled but shook her head. "I've made up my mind," she said. "I knew what you'd say. You've said exactly what I expected. But I've made up my mind. I want to marry you sometime. I want to marry you soon, in fact. But I don't want a baby right away. I don't want it just yet. You'll know I'm right when you quit being emotional."

"I'll never quit being emotional, Les."

She shrugged. "Will you be at home, so you can go to the hospital with me?"

"Yes."

"All right. Don't worry about it. It's no big deal. I'm not very far along, and the doctor says it will be easy."

Gib sighed. He was conscious, suddenly, of just how much the shock and loss of blood had weakened him. He was tired suddenly, too tired to do anything more than frown and shake his head and say quietly to her, "I don't like it, Les. I really don't like it."

"Don't try to talk me out of it, Gib."

They would be able to fly to New York on Monday. Gib's father, who brightened and strengthened conspicuously when he could be in charge of doing something, made the arrangements. After he and Gib's mother and Leslie had left the hospital Sunday afternoon, Vanderhoof came to the hospital with Shtemenko. Shtemenko had gotten a private room for Melanie, and they met in her room—Melanie and Shtemenko, Vanderhoof and Novatny, and Gib.

Melanie was still in bed. She would remain in the hospital for another month at least. Novatny's face was covered with bandages. Gib's head was bandaged, and he carried his arm in a sling. Vanderhoof leaned against the windowsill, and the rest of the men had wooden straight chairs and sat stiffly around the bed, oppressed by the sight of Melanie and by the antiseptic white cubicle which was her room. (A crucifix hung on the wall above the foot of her bed. She had asked to have it taken down, but it was too tightly fastened.)

"I want to talk to you," Vanderhoof said. "I want to talk to all of you. I don't know what chance we might have but this."

Melanie had to turn her head to see past the thick pad of gauze on her right eye, to see Vanderhoof. Turning her head stretched the bandages around her throat, and she winced. "So talk," she said hoarsely. "I want to know everything that happens, everything any of you learns, every idea you have. I think you owe me that much."

Vanderhoof nodded. "We owe you more than that. I wanted you to hear. I want you to know everything. Right now, I want you to hear me talk about the Jupiter crisis."

Novatny snorted. "Corny has Jupiter on the brain."

Vanderhoof ignored Novatny. "I've told you all before," he said, "that I've worked and pondered on the Jupiter crisis for weeks. The things that happened make no sense. They don't, that is, unless you suppose for a little that maybe the President of the United States was working hand in hand with the leaders in the Kremlin, on a very subtly contrived project in support of a basic tenet of Soviet foreign policy.

If you suppose that for a moment, you can see a pattern of logic in the Jupiter crisis."

"If you are ready to assume," said Novatny, "that the President of the United States is a traitor."

"Well," said Vanderhoof. "Unless Nadya Kharina put together a clever and elaborate pack of lies, while she was under extreme torture, we know Warren Bradley was a traitor once. Maybe he is yet. That he should have taken time in the midst of the Jupiter crisis to have a private conference with Benjamin Slusser is more than suggestive, in my judgment. Bear with me, Steve. Let me tell you what I think."

Novatny shrugged. "Okay. Go ahead."

"The Russians captured the Jupiter Twelve," said Vanderhoof. "Note that: They *captured* it. They didn't just destroy it in space, which they could have done easily. They captured it, at the cost of what must have been a difficult and expensive operation. Either way, whether they captured or destroyed it, they risked war with the United States. They had to know, from the beginning, that the President couldn't simply let them get away with it. No President of the United States could do that, in the face of American public opinion. So they mounted a very costly operation, they risked something very serious, maybe even war, and they made a big show in the United Nations—for what? The United States always had the ability to launch another Jupiter, and when we did the Soviets simply lay down and played dead. Why? Why, if Jupiter Twelve was so important to them, wasn't Jupiter Fourteen just as important?"

Gib nodded. "I asked the same question in *The Spark* six months ago," he said.

"I know you did," said Vanderhoof. "I read it."

"Wasn't it important," Shtemenko asked, "for them to

capture the pictures, so they could display them? Doesn't that explain why they captured the satellite, instead of destroying it in space?"

"Yes, the pictures are the key to the whole thing," Vanderhoof agreed. "The pictures the Jupiter was carrying when the Russians captured it were maybe the most important ones it ever took. I mean, didn't it ever occur to anyone that it was an amazing coincidence that when the Jupiter was captured it was carrying pictures which caught the Chinese in the act of building launch silos aimed at Japan?"

"There were other pictures," Novatny said.

"Yes." said Vanderhoof. "Besides the pictures of the Chinese silos, there were detailed pictures of a Soviet ground-to-air missile station and a power plant. It was almost as if the Russians captured the Jupiter carrying a catalog of its most interesting shots. It must have just completed a very productive orbit. I've often wondered if it ever did as well before, or if Jupiter Fourteen has ever done as well since."

"Anyway, what do you suggest happened?" Melanie asked.

"Well, you have to look at the results of the Jupiter crisis," Vanderhoof said. "Look at the long-term major results. It didn't change things much between the United States and the Soviet Union. We put up Jupiter Fourteen to replace Jupiter Twelve. The Russians grumble about it, but they haven't done anything. We're back to status quo, so far as space reconnaissance is concerned. We're back to status quo so far as United States–Russian relations are concerned. But something else has changed. Something else has changed significantly.

"You remember how the Jupiter crisis interrupted the closing rigamarole of the Western Pacific Trade Conference?" Vanderhoof went on. "And do you remember what the Conference was really about? It was an effort to normalize trade and diplomatic relations between Red China and some of the other nations of the world. And do you remember what happened to that effort after the Japanese saw the pictures of the silos being built to aim nuclear rockets at Japan? The effort came to an abrupt end. No Japanese government could possibly take further steps toward a Japan-China *rapprochement,* in the face of the public hysteria produced by those pictures. Without Japanese leadership, the small nations of the Western Pacific abandoned the idea too. And the United States, which had been heading toward full diplomatic recognition of Red China, quietly cut off all talks, in the midst of the excitement produced by the Jupiter crisis. In thirty days the diplomatic postures of two major nations and a flock of small ones, toward China, were radically changed—from cautious friendship to suspicious hostility. If that wasn't a triumph for Soviet foreign policy, suggest me a better one."

Shtemenko was nodding vigorously. "Yes," he said. "Absolutely. It was a triumph for the Kremlin. China is as isolated now as it was ten years ago."

"But what about the silos in Manchuria?" Novatny asked. "I think I know what you're about to say."

"Probably you do," said Vanderhoof. "The Chinese screamed that the pictures were faked. They denied they were building any such silos. They . . ."

"But the Jupiter Fourteen pictures confirmed that they had been," said Novatny.

Vanderhoof shook his head. "The Jupiter Fourteen pictures, taken you remember almost a month after the Jupiter Twelve took its pictures of the Manchurian site, showed some massive bulldozing and signs of heavy equipment being moved in and out. Our interpretation of those pictures was that they showed the Chinese dismantling the silos that had been discovered by Jupiter Twelve. But suppose they were not that? Suppose they were pictures of some other kind of construction job the Chinese had going on?"

"Coincidence. . . ."

"No," said Vanderhoof. "Suppose the Soviets, through their own reconnaissance, knew the Chinese were tearing up the earth on that particular site in Manchuria, building something or other but not missile silos. Suppose the Soviets fed the CIA—very subtly, through some double agent maybe —a tip that the Chinese were building something suspicious in Manchuria, anticipating that the CIA would then ask for Jupiter photographs of the area. The President is kept advised daily about the orbits of the Jupiter satellites. He knows where the Jupiter is going and what it expects to photograph, each day. Suppose he gave that information to the Soviet Union, so that the Jupiter could be captured just after it had flown a mission over the Chinese construction site in Manchuria. And suppose finally, that the Russians substituted their own faked pictures for the ones the Jupiter actually took of the site—to make the Japanese think the Chinese were aiming nuclear rockets directly at them. Suppose all that, and the Jupiter crisis begins to make some sense. It could have manufactured a major triumph for Soviet foreign policy."

Novatny was nodding. "Yes," he said. "Or a major disaster for everyone who took part in it. The Chinese could prove the pictures were faked—if they were. Suppose they had called for an impartial investigation on the site, by a committee of neutral representatives?"

"No," said Vanderhoof. "The Chinese Reds are too intransigent to submit to anything like that. They did let a French jouralist travel to the site. I talked to him yesterday. He said he was convinced the Chinese were telling the truth. He published his account of what he saw, but no one paid him any attention. He's a left-wing writer, already known to be sympathetic to Peking. That's the only kind of investigator the Chinese would let into the country, and he's the very kind no one will believe."

Melanie had been thinking of something else. "No wonder they tried to kill us," she said. "And maybe it wasn't the Bolsheviks. Maybe it was the CIA."

Gib shook his head. "No. If the President . . . Well, he wouldn't dare involve many people, not an agency like the CIA. If he is what we think he is, he'd have the help only of a very few."

"Yes, but who?" Novatny asked.

"You're all in mortal peril until you find out," said Shtemenko.

"Anyway," Vanderhoof said. "I don't, of course, know I'm right, but if any real part of what I've guessed is correct, Warren Bradley betrayed the United States in the Jupiter crisis. He acted as an agent of Soviet foreign policy."

"Some of the papers have called the Jupiter crisis the finest hour of his presidency," Gib said wryly.

"It will be something else if we expose him," said Vanderhoof.

THE WHITE HOUSE

They reached the White House during a violent, early-evening summer storm, and in the Oval Office they found the President standing moodily at one of the windows behind his desk, watching the torrent of rain and how it glistened with the stabs and flashes of blue-white lightning. He was alone when they came in the office—Gib and Vanderhoof and Novatny—standing there with his hands behind his back, his neck buried in his shoulders, brooding on the storm and likely on his anger and resentment. When they were announced to him by a discreet and retreating secretary, he turned reluctantly away from the window and dropped heavily into his chair, without offering to shake their hands, with no word by way of greeting. They sat down uninvited, as he scowled across his desk and let his cheeks puff out and his shoulders fall as he exhaled and settled.

"I hope this is not too inconvenient for you," he said. "But I've had an urgent message about you three."

"Inconvenient!" snapped Vanderhoof in shrill anger. "It is very inconvenient, sir. It is damned inconvenient. But I wasn't aware that our convenience was considered. I had the distinct impression that if we had declined to be inconvenienced, we'd have been *forced* to come here."

The President frowned darkly, his heavy black eyebrows turning down and in. "I'm sure you didn't really believe that," he said coldly.

"No?" said Vanderhoof curtly. "Well, it's not very often that a man is snatched off an airplane at Kennedy Airport by the Secret Service and flown to Washington in the Vice President's plane, without so much as a chance to make a telephone call to explain to people where he's going."

"You could have made any calls you wanted," said the President. "Including calls from the plane itself. Or"—he shrugged—"you could have declined to come this evening, if it was all that inconvenient. I simply sent word that I wanted urgently to see you, and I sent transportation for you."

The President of the United States was lying—facing them across his desk in the White House and lying. That was Gib's judgment, and as much as he knew about Warren Bradley, as much scorn as he felt for him, he still was shocked. The man was, after all, the President.

It was inconceivable he did not know how they had been confronted at the passport station at Kennedy Airport by three scowling, muscular men, who identified themselves as of the Secret Service and demanded—did not invite, *demanded*—that he and Vanderhoof and Novatny come with them. The immigration officers and New York police standing around had obviously been alerted to what was going to happen, and they too scowled, giving a distinct impression that they would intervene with force if the demand to go were refused. Gib had hardly had time to say a word to Leslie and his parents. He sat now in the Oval Office of the White House, still dressed in the light blue knit shirt and khaki chinos in which he had flown from Paris. His arm hung in a black sling, and his clothes were faintly damp from the dash from the helicopter in the rain.

The President said all he had sent was a request and transportation. The President had to know better. It was chilling to face a man with his power and hear him talk like this.

"That's what you're going to tell the press conference when you are asked about what I'm going to write of this incident," said Vanderhoof.

The President seemed willing to let that close the subject. He turned over some papers that were stacked in a tight pile on his rigidly neat desk. "We've received," he said, in a vaguely recitative tone that suggested he had thought carefully about how he was going to say this, "a formal protest. We've received a formal protest from the government of the Soviet Union. It recites that three American citizens: Cornelius Vanderhoof, Stephen Novatny, and Gilbert Hubbard, illegally entered East Berlin, with forged documents, and there conspired in the murder of a Soviet citizen, one Nadya Kharina. It . . ."

"One Mary Anne Waring," Gib interjected.

"According to *you,*" said the President with a condescending glance at Gib. "According to the Russians the victim Nadya Kharina was an expert in certain cost accounting techniques and was on loan from a Soviet industrial agency to the East German tool and die industry. According to the protest, the body of this woman was found in a flat littered with empty liquor and beer bottles, and she had been savagely tortured and sexually abused before she died of strangulation. The police have arrested three men who have confessed to the crime and implicated the three of you. The Russians suggest that you should be returned to East Berlin to stand trial."

"You'll play hell trying to send us back," Novatny growled furiously. Novatny's face was still heavily bandaged. The flight across the Atlantic had tired him, and he had been uncharacteristically subdued until now. "You son of a bitch," he muttered wearily.

The President had drawn a breath and was holding it impatiently until the end of the interruption. "I have already refused to do anything toward having you returned," he said. "Aside from the tough legal questions involved, it would be politically impossible. Since you three were nearly killed in Paris, you are some kind of momentary heroes. Since no one seems to know who tried to kill you, or why, it is being assumed generally that the Communists did it. And that, by some strange logic, makes heroes of you."

"It shouldn't seem a strange logic to you," Gib said. "Logic like that made you President of the United States."

The President shrugged and let the challenge go by. "I don't believe very much of what the Russians say. I don't believe all they say about you. But I do believe a woman is dead, and I do believe that somehow you three are responsible." He stopped and rested his eyes on Gib. "I'll tell you why I believe it, Mr. Hubbard. Because I suspect the woman they called Nadya Kharina really was the one who lived here as Mary Anne Waring, just as you say. That would make it plausible."

Vanderhoof's chin had come up, and he was staring obliquely at the President. "Are you interested in hearing what Nadya Kharina told us?" he asked.

The President seemed surprised by the question, and he put his clenched fist to his chin and pondered for a moment. "All right," he said. "I'm curious."

Vanderhoof glanced at Gib and Novatny. They had not

yet agreed to reveal what Nadya Kharina had told them, and Vanderhoof likely would have stopped if either of the others had raised an objection. But neither of them did. "She told us," he said slowly, quietly, cautiously, "that she worked for a Major Alekseii Parotikin of the NKVD. Under Parotikin's orders she became the fiancée of Benjamin Slusser, and by bribery and blackmail they made Slusser a traitor. They rigged the prosecution of Erich Traver to enhance Slusser's prestige and usefulness. That didn't work out very well, but they found themselves another man. The three of them—Parotikin and Kharina and Slusser—gradually entrapped a young Congressman from Michigan. They helped him build a reputation as a fierce Red-baiter. They helped him win election to the Senate. And they used him. They made him pay for everything they did for him. They made a traitor of him too." Vanderhoof began to nod, and he kept nodding. "Does the story sound familiar?"

The President nodded. "Very familiar," he said. "It was a lie twenty years ago when I first heard it, and it's a lie now. I was threatened with it then. I've been threatened with it since. Now, apparently, I'm to be threatened with it again. It's like the old story that Roosevelt died of syphilis. It isn't true, but it won't go away, and it's too fantastic to deny."

"It's supported by a great deal of evidence," Gib said.

"What evidence?" the President asked loftily. "The testimony of an admitted Communist spy? Testimony taken from her by torturing her? The Russians say you were all drunk and that she was sexually abused."

"I resent . . ." Vanderhoof said angrily, but he was interrupted by a flash of lightning and a clap of thunder that rattled the room.

"Do you deny the woman is dead?" the President asked, interjecting his question into the instant of silence that followed the thunder. "Do you deny you had some part in killing her? Do you deny she was tortured to get the story you just told me?" He shook his head. "No, I don't hear you denying any of it. Have you told Alan Jordan what you had to do to that woman to get what he wanted from her?"

"What does Alan Jordan have to do with it?" Novatny asked.

"You work for him," said the President. "So does Hubbard, one way or another." He looked at Vanderhoof and shook his head. "I can't imagine how they sucked *you* in. But they did somehow, and they made you a part of Jordan's perpetual political vendetta against me."

"Just let me remind you of something, Mr. President," said Vanderhoof. He was suppressing his fury, and his voice was hollow with forced calm. "If you think Alan Jordan can use me, just let me remind you that *you've* never been able to do it, and you've tried more than once."

"It doesn't make any difference," the President said. "I know why Novatny went to East Berlin and did whatever he did. I know why Hubbard did. Whatever *your* motives may have been, they were tainted by *their* motives, which were political. They went to Berlin to resurrect this old story against me, to give it some new credence by forcing a one-time Communist spy to confess to it. You found the woman. You tortured her, and you killed her. I wonder if Alan Jordan knew what you were going to do. I wonder if you've told him what you did. I'd like to know if his hatred for me and his political ambition go so far as to countenance murder. I'd like to know if he has any conscience."

"A nice speech," said Novatny scornfully. "A nice, pious speech. And a nice ploy, if you can get away with it: to turn attention away from yourself and what you've done, to make someone else seem to be the villain of the piece. Nice. But you won't get away with it."

The President was angry. His anger, fed by the frustration of having to maintain the self-control he imposed on himself as much, almost, as by the talk, had deepened all through the conversation. Now he chewed for a moment on his lower lip, before he began to speak through his teeth. "I wish I could send you three back to East Berlin," he said. "Together with Alan Jordan, who is a co-conspirator in the murder you shrug off so lightly. Well, maybe I can't do that, but don't you think I'm defenseless. All you have is a fantastic story you extracted by torture from a Communist spy—before you murdered her. With that and no more you plan to go to the American people and tell them their President is a traitor. Well. You just try it. You just see what happens. I warn you. I warn you, goddam you."

GREENWICH VILLAGE

Gib walked between the bus stop and his apartment, in a thick and acid heat. The sun was a hot white blur in a heavy gray-white sky, half obscured by a blanket of wet fumes that hung over the city and let the heat come down and then held it down. Heat radiated from the pavements and from the walls of buildings, spread in waves from the hot steel bodies and fiery engines of trucks and buses, and lay like greasy smoke in the still, weighted air. Gib's clothes were wet with pungent sweat. His throat and lungs burned with another heat that he sucked in with every breath. He walked wearily, with the sweat and fumes smarting in his eyes.

He was tired, prematurely tired, not yet wholly recovered from his injuries. His left arm hung down and swung as he walked, and he clenched and unclenched his fist; but he wished he'd worn the sling another day, because the arm ached. He was wearing sunglasses, but they kept slipping down his sweaty nose. He wore a hat, a straw hat, to cover the angry red marks on his scalp, which the hair had not yet grown to cover. He was tense with impatience, with irritation. He was annoyed at having to walk around the people lounging on the sidewalk in escape from the hot wet heat inside their apartments. Some of them knew him and spoke to him, and he was short with them. He made his way, measuring with every step the remaining distance to his apartment, his refuge; and his irritation turned to exasperation and then to anger. Seeing a small crowd collected on the sidewalk ahead—as he had expected—he swung off the curb, kicking the litter under his feet, and crossed the street.

The crowd he had crossed the street to avoid was congregated—still angry, after two days—around the wreckage of a storefront theater which had been torn apart night before last by a crewcut mob that had come to close a play called "Henry". The windows were shattered, and the glass still littered the sidewalk. The chairs and some of the stage settings and props had been thrown out onto the street, and most of the wreckage still lay. Half a dozen small American flags had been planted in the debris, together with some hand-lettered placards on sticks. The placards said—DECENCY! Some of the people standing around the wreckage saw Gib across the street and recognized him. Some of them called to him and raised their hands in the clenched-fist salute. Someone had climbed up and smeared a sign in white paint across the red-brick facade of the building, above the windows. Those crude white letters said—FUCK DECENCY!

Gib turned the corner into his own street. He'd had no lunch, but the mixed odors of frying fish and barbecuing spiced chicken, hanging on the air in his street and mixed with the diesel smoke and gasoline fumes, did not whet his appetite. It was too hot to eat, and in his frame of mind his guts were too tight for eating anyway. Even a Scotch and soda he had drunk last night in his living room had lain all night on his stomach like a lump of jelled acid. He reached the door of his apartment, which had been his goal as a refuge all the way downtown on a crowded bus and all the way along the hot streets, with the thought, abruptly, that he really had no purpose in coming here and could not stay.

It was hot inside, and dark. You couldn't run air conditioners because of the power shortage, and he had pulled all the blinds to keep out the sunlight which would strike the windows. He did not switch on the lights. He just pulled off the sunglasses and tossed them on his couch, relieved to have them off his nose. He stood for a moment in the hot dim silence of his living room, undecided whether to throw himself down for a half hour's rest or to hurry on out and to the office. He went into the bedroom, kicked off his shoes, and settled down for a little rest on the bed.

He lay among Leslie's clothes, scattered on the bed. He had slept among them last night, without moving them. Two pairs of shorts—one the yellow ones—and two T-shirts, a pair of panties, a bra. The yellow pants suit his mother had bought her in Paris was lovingly hung in the closet, together with a couple of her dresses. Her casual clothes were scattered around everywhere, not just on the bed. They made the place seem vacant and gloomy, because she was not there. She was in the hospital.

He had taken her uptown yesterday afternoon. They had gone on the bus. This morning, very early, her pregnancy had been terminated. He had gone to the hospital early, so as to be waiting when she came back to her bed. They had let him talk with her for a while and had told him he could come back and take her home late this afternoon. She had laughed about that and said she wanted to stay in the hospital, where they had air conditioning, power shortage or no, and she asked the nurse what kind of pain she should fake to make them let her stay a few days. The nurse, who was gray and fat and jovial, had taken her cue from Leslie's mood and said she couldn't expect to occupy a nice cool hospital bed very long when all she'd had was a vacuum cleaning. Then Leslie had looked into Gib's eyes and said, "Yes, that's all it amounts to—a vacuuming. Slurp! and it's gone—up the tube and down the drain, the short, uncomplicated life of little Gilbert Hubbard, Junior."

It was not restful to lie in the oppressive heat and gloom, in the wet and stink of sweat, and think about what she'd said. He couldn't reach any conclusion anyway. He had known that the abortion stood between them and something remained unspoken about it, but whether or not the unspoken had now been said, he was not sure.

He got up, took an apple from the refrigerator, and went out.

He walked along the streets again, with his arm back in the sling and the sunglasses back on his wet, slippery nose. He still thought of Leslie: of what a tough, resilient little girl she was. The streets were sullen. People stood about or sat on the steps and curbs, drinking beer, some of them, or nibbling listlessly at food. Driven into the streets by the heat, they were angry: some of them generally, at the way it had been for a week, and some of them specifically, at the crewcuts who had come running down the streets bawling decency.

It was unbelievably hot at *The Spark*. Fans had been brought in from people's apartments, and papers everywhere fluttered and settled, fluttered and settled, as the fans oscillated. They stirred the dust and the heat. People worked in as little clothing as possible, and they littered the offices with cups and bottles as they drank cold drinks and sweated and drank some more. But they all moved. *The Spark* had a lot to say that week. ("The Stars and Stripes have been put to some strange uses in the life of this nation. Our flag has been used to sanctify some odd causes, but none stranger, none odder, none more vicious and none more contrary to the spirit of the 'Republic for which it stands' than to carry it at the head of an irrational mob of—of what? enraged bank clerks? hopped-up Jaycees?—which came to the Village Monday night to destroy a theater where a play was being played that offended their sense of 'decency.' ") All the staff worked hard, harder even than when the air conditioners ran, putting out an angry paper every day.

Someone said to Gib that Frank Kennedy wanted to see him in the one-time living room that was Kennedy's office, and when Gib got up there he found Kennedy sitting with Cornelius Vanderhoof. The two of them were drinking cans of beer out of a bucket of ice and nibbling at some cheese and crackers.

"How's the girl?" Kennedy asked.

Gib nodded. "Coming along nicely. She said there was nothing to it, and I guess she's right."

Kennedy popped a can of beer and pushed it across the table toward Gib. "You've got a kick in the ass coming, you and Leslie," he said. "There's a story on the wires about how Les was pregnant by you and had an abortion. It'll be everywhere by tonight."

"God, her mother and father don't even know it," Gib said.

"Could be part of the President's counterattack," said Vanderhoof. "You know?"

Gib shook his head. "I didn't know you were in town," he said.

"Gib," said Kennedy. "Would you like to move Les into my apartment for a few days? It's cooler there, and people won't know where to find you to bug you."

"I appreciate it," Gib said. "I'm going up to the hospital to bring her home tonight."

Kennedy tossed a key across the table.

"I brought you something," Vanderhoof said. He reached to his jacket, which with his necktie was hanging over an extra chair, and he took out of the inside pocket a sheaf of folded papers. "Your copy," he said, handing the papers to Gib.

Gib glanced at the sheets. He did not take time to read them through, but he knew what they were: the typescript of a newspaper article—

NADYA KHARINA'S WASHINGTON

First of a Series of Articles
by
Cornelius Vanderhoof
and
Gilbert Hubbard

In a drab working-class flat in East Berlin last month, we listened while a woman talked. She was a handsome woman in her forties. Twenty years ago she was a beautiful girl. She was a Russian, a trained intelligence agent, attached to the agency the Russians used to call the NKVD. Twenty years ago she was a Soviet spy. Her assignment was Washington, D.C. . . .

Gib smiled wanly. "Looks good," he said.

"Not so good," said Vanderhoof. "That's why I'm here. It seems my syndicate is not willing to distribute our articles. What's more, my papers won't publish them."

Gib sighed heavily and shook his head. "Figures," he whispered.

Vanderhoof nodded resignedly. "Well, it's like Warren Bradley told us," he said. "We're accusing the President of the United States of treason, on the word of a woman who was an admitted Communist spy. Not only that, but we have to admit she was brutally tortured before she talked. And what's more, she's dead, so no one can talk to her any more, to check on what we report. It's not enough evidence,

Gib. It's not enough to accuse the President of treason. I can understand the attitude of my editors. They have some sense of journalistic responsibility, and they have to keep the laws of libel in mind. I think any newspaper would be reluctant to take a risk like this, even if it hadn't been warned by the White House."

Gib rose out of his resignation for an instant. "They were warned?" he asked. "Threatened?"

Vanderhoof shrugged. "Well, I don't *know* they were."

Gib twisted inside his damp clothes and settled back wearily in his chair. He took a swig of his beer. It at least was cool. The fan lifted the papers he had put down on the table, and they glided on the breath of hot air and scattered on the floor around and behind him. He made no effort to stop them. "So now what do we do?" he asked.

"I don't know," said Vanderhoof. "I came up to New York to talk to Frank here about publishing the series in *The Spark*. He and I have agreed, though: it might not be a good idea."

"So what do we do now, forget the whole thing?" Gib asked.

Vanderhoof shook his head. "Keep working," he said. "Until we prove our case."

Gib sighed and closed his eyes. "What about the Senator?" he asked. "Has he done anything about what we told him, I mean about the Jupiter crisis?"

"A little. He was very impressed, Gib. He's convinced that the President conspired with the Kremlin and that the Jupiter crisis was a rigged show, just as we theorized. But it will be difficult to put together the information to prove it, and in the meantime he wouldn't dare make a reckless public statement on it."

"I wouldn't want him to do anything reckless," Gib said sarcastically.

"Senator Jordan is relying on Steve Novatny to work on

this for him," said Vanderhoof. "Steve's in the hospital again. The doctors are doing the first work on his face this week."

"There's only one way we can prove the Jupiter pictures the Russians showed the United Nations Security Council were faked," Gib said. "Go to Manchuria and see the site, if it's not too late."

Frank Kennedy smiled. "I think you *would* go, if you got the chance," he said to Gib.

"You wouldn't dare try it unless the Chinese were willing to let you in," said Vanderhoof. "And if the Chinese let you in, then no one in this country would believe anything you reported. You can't win with that idea."

"Someone at NASA must have been suspicious of the pictures the Russians showed the Security Council," said Gib. "Someone in the CIA. . . ."

"That's what Steve Novatny is supposed to find out," said Vanderhoof. "It'll be tough. Everyone in the government is afraid to talk to him, or to me or you. The word's around on us. We're poison."

"I've been poison for a long time."

"This paper is poison," said Frank Kennedy. "We're used to it."

Gib snatched up from the table the last sheet of the typescript Vanderhoof had given him, the only sheet the fan had not blown on the floor, and he wadded it into a ball and hurled it across the room. "We're in worse shape than if we'd never started this business," he complained angrily. "We've learned the truth, and we can't do anything with it."

" 'And ye shall know the truth, and the truth shall make you free,' " said Leslie. "Isn't that what the goys say?"

"One of the chief goys, Saint John," Gib agreed.

"Hmhh," she nodded. She was lying on the couch in Frank Kennedy's living room. Gib had brought her down from the hospital only about an hour ago. She was dressed in the yellow shorts and a T-shirt, the things he had brought her from his apartment. She was a little weak, and she was drinking a chocolate milk shake he had brought up from the delicatessen. "Mmhh, Saint John. John, the saintly John. The truth will make us free, will it? I somehow doubt it."

Gib had thrown off his shirt and was pacing the living room of the apartment barefoot. Kennedy's place was on the fifth floor of his building and had cross-ventilation, so that a little air was moving. The air was not cool, and it carried the smells of the street, but at least it moved a little, and with a determined imagination one could make himself suppose it had come from the ocean. Opposing it was the hot decor of the apartment—a professional decorator's work in oranges and reds and browns, with bursts of hot color assaulting the eyes from a dozen unframed paintings fastened to the walls, and with hot, red-shaded lamps casting a homely warmth over everything. It would be a great place for a frigid winter evening, Leslie said. Gib paced and sweated, and she watched him and complained that he made her hotter.

He sat down and lowered his eyes and chin to watch a bead of sweat running down the middle of his hairless chest.

"Either put on your shirt or take off your pants," Leslie said. "I don't like the look of a man half dressed like that."

He grabbed his shirt from the table before the couch and pulled it over his head. "Are you sure you're all right?" he asked.

"I'm okay."

"Let's get married and go somewhere, Les. Let's don't live here. Let's go to England. I'm sick of living where the cards are stacked against me and I'm playing against a crooked dealer. You can't win, and you can't change anything."

Leslie let out a short, shrill breath. "Okay," she said. "If you're going to quit, quit. If you're not, stop whining."

"You're a tough little bitch."

"You're supposed to be tough yourself. You have a reputation for it."

"You know better, Les."

She shrugged. "You've functioned."

"For what?"

"What'd you expect?"

He vented his discouragement. Slumping in the chair facing the couch and sipping with grimaces from a strong Scotch and soda he'd mixed for himself a little earlier, he said what he'd said in the office, and more: that all he'd risked and done seemed wasted, that the truth had no impact. He said it had not been worth it.

"That depends on what's in *you,* baby," she said. "That's what it's been for, so far as I'm concerned, and whether it's worth it or not depends entirely on you."

That struck him dumb for a long solemn moment, and he was thinking about what to say to answer her when the telephone rang.

It was Frank Kennedy. He said he'd had a report that the crewcut mob was in the Village somewhere, so he was going to stay at the office for a while. They had surmised that the people who hated "Henry" enough to attack its theater probably hated *The Spark* too. Frank told Gib to stay in the apartment with Leslie and not come out on the street, no matter what happened.

Gib went to the window. *The Spark* offices were only half a block away and on the opposite side of the street. He could see the lights burning in the building. He could see people moving around in the offices. But the street was quiet. Between the brick buildings it was a valley of thick heat.

He said he was hungry and suggested he might go down to the delicatessen and bring them up something, but she ignored the suggestion and said she still did not understand why the Russians would have faked the Jupiter crisis. He explained to her once more—this time with more patience than when he had been rushed with enthusiasm—that the Russians feared China above all, so it was a basic tenet of Soviet foreign policy to prevent China from establishing normal relations, particularly trade relations, with the rest of the world. With a little relaxation of the tensions along its eastern and southern frontiers, China would turn more of its attention to its northwestern border—the border with Siberia. During the year preceding the Jupiter crisis, China and its Pacific neighbors, and the United States, had been making significant moves toward the relaxation of tensions and the establishment of normal relations. By displaying the faked Jupiter photographs to the United Nations Security Council, Russia had made it appear that China had been building aggressive nuclear missile launching silos at the very moment when its diplomats were talking peace with the diplomats of the nations at which the missiles were aimed. The plot was fantastic, but it had worked.

"Well," said Leslie. "It looks as if old Mao Tse-tung was right."

"He was?"

"Yes. He always said the Russian revisionists and the American imperialists would be drawn together in a conspiracy against China."

"He was wrong," Gib said. "The American imperialists didn't conspire against China. Only President Bradley himself. That is, if our theory is right. It's still only a theory, you remember."

"It's more than that," she said. "It makes such perfect sense, I'm convinced."

He nodded. "Unlike most of the people of this country, you *want* to be convinced. They don't. Basically, deep in their guts, they don't want to believe that their President—any President, not just Bradley—could betray them."

He was hungry, so he went down to the street to the delicatessen. It was still muggy and quiet, but he met people on the street who insisted the crewcuts were coming. He was stopped by a young man and a girl, who asked him if it were true, and while he was telling them he didn't know, another couple overheard and came up and said it was true. And they said this time the crewcuts were going to be sorry. We're not going to stand by this time, they said, and let them destroy anything they want.

Back upstairs, Leslie said she did not see how anything as large and complex as faking the Jupiter crisis could be long concealed. "A lot of people had to know," she said. "It must have taken the cooperation of . . . what? . . . how many?"

"You don't need many people if one of the people you have is President of the United States," Gib said. "All Bradley had to do was communicate to the Kremlin the time of the orbit in which the Jupiter was scheduled to make that pass over Manchuria. If the Russians fed the CIA a tip that the Chinese were building missile silos in Manchuria, sooner or later that tip was going to be checked out by Jupiter reconnaissance. The President is kept advised of the Jupiter's schedule. All he had to do was tell the Russians when it was supposed to take pictures of the alleged Chinese construction site in Manchuria. The Russians had the faked pictures ready, and they captured the Jupiter immediately after it flew over Manchuria. Simple, if our theory is right. And it wouldn't require the cooperation of more than a very few people in this country. Conceivably it could have been done by the President and no more than one or two others."

"Well, there's nothing anybody can do to make Bradley talk," said Leslie. "What you have to do is get to one of the others."

Gib blew a sigh through pursed lips, closed his eyes, and nodded. "That brings us back to ol' Ben Slusser, down in Georgia."

"Is he important?" Leslie asked. "I mean, is he *still* important, *now?*"

"We know he was at the White House at least once at the very height of the Jupiter crisis. Apparently he had access to the President in the midst of what was supposed to be a critical hour in the nation's history, when the whole government was mobilized on an emergency basis. We can only guess what that means, but it's possible Slusser was the courier, bringing Bradley the word from Moscow, or taking Bradley's word back. He worked for the Kremlin once. He could be working for it now. It's hard to think of ol' Cornpone Ben as a Soviet agent, but that's what he was twenty years ago, so he could be yet."

Leslie smiled, with an ironic lift of her brows. "What you need," she said, "is that sour-faced Russian, Shtemenko. If he were here, he'd go down to Georgia and kidnap Slusser and beat the truth out of him."

Gib frowned and nodded soberly. "It may be the only way we'll *get* the truth out of him," he said. "And it's as good as any other suggestion I've heard today."

"Oh, really?"

"Yes. I was told this afternoon that I'm too young and impatient. So, while Frank Kennedy and Vanderhoof sit around admiring their maturity and patience, Bradley and Slusser laugh at us and destroy the evidence we should be out digging for."

He got up abruptly and went to the kitchen to make a snack for them out of what he'd brought from the delicatessen. He poured himself another Scotch, too.

Back in the living room, as he spread the food on the coffee table and sat down beside her to eat, Leslie asked him if he realized she might never be able to go home again, now that her family had seen the news stories and knew she'd had the abortion. He said they would marry now and make their own home. But she said she wouldn't even be able to *visit* her home, maybe. His thought shifted, from an image of her fat, shrill sister, whom they both might never see again without ever missing her, to the image of her father, that grand, patriarchical old man he'd met and talked to last winter. He'd heard Leslie say scornful things about the old man and had never really thought about how much she must love him. He realized you could love an old man like that even if you couldn't love much that he did or said—like, if you loved God, you loved Him in spite of the state of the world, for which He was responsible. Gib was trying to make words to say to Leslie when he heard the first shouts of the crewcut mob coming up the street.

They scrambled up from the couch and rushed to the window. Leslie ran around the room switching off lights, so they could watch from the darkness and not be seen from the street.

The crowd marched up the middle of the street, carrying flags and posters lettered DECENCY. One of their leaders ran out in front of the advancing crowd and shouted and waved his arms, and the crowd began to sing, raggedly at first and then strongly and together—"God Bless America." They marched with a conspicuous swagger, and they did not wave their flags but jogged them up and down rapidly, without rhythm and not in unison. Perhaps two hundred of them gathered before *The Spark* and stood there menacing it, singing and shouting and jogging their flags and signs. They sang "God Bless America" twice more, hoarsely, while the stragglers caught up and increased their number to maybe three hundred. Then they sang "America the Beautiful" and "Onward Christian Soldiers."

"Who are they?" Leslie asked Gib. From the window she could not make out much about them. They were all men. There were no women in the crowd. Most of them were young, and they were uniformly ordinary in appearance.

Their slacks and shirts were stained with sweat, in the close, oppressive heat. It was an exaggeration of their barbering to call them crewcuts, but none of them had long hair, and none of them had beards. The postures in which some of them held themselves, together with their exuberance in singing and jogging their flags up and down, suggested that many of them had been drinking—though from the distance of the window that could only be a guess. "Who are they, Gib?" she asked again.

"Nobody," he said. "And that's just the point, isn't it?"

They finished singing down on the street. For a brief moment they were silent, and then abruptly they began to throw stones and brickbats they had brought with them. In the course of a minute or so they broke out every window in the front of *The Spark* building.

"The police, for God's sake!" Leslie shouted at Gib over the crash of glass.

Police cars sat in the intersections at both ends of the block. But the officers stayed in the cars.

The front rank of the crowd rushed up the steps and began to assault the doors of the building. The booming and cracking echoed ominously along the street. The doorframe splintered, and the doors sagged backward. But abruptly the invasion ended, before the first man broke through. A shower of small plastic bags came down suddenly from the roof, breaking on the heads and shoulders of the crewcuts and splattering them with the fluid the bags contained. The ones wet with the liquid staggered back down the steps, shaking their heads and frantically wiping their heads and faces with their shirts.

Gib laughed thinly. "Urine," he said to Leslie. "We've been pissing into plastic bags for two days."

The crewcuts ran. The crowd broke, and some ran out of the block one way, some the other. One group, on the way, stopped to shatter the windows of a small art shop which was displaying an assortment of revolutionary posters. Someone on the roof there threw down bricks and chunks of paving stone. Two of the crewcuts were felled and left lying bloody on the street. Their companions ran on and abandoned them.

When the block was deserted, the police moved in. They hurried to give first aid to the men lying on their backs in the street. Shortly, an ambulance came, and more cars. Some of the police went inside *The Spark* building, and soon they came out again with Frank Kennedy and took him away in a car. Gib, watching from the window, could not tell if Kennedy was under arrest.

Leslie left the window before Gib did. She sat down again on the couch, in the darkened room, and began to nibble spiritlessly at the food spread out on the coffee table. Gib switched on a lamp when he came away from the window and silently sat down beside her. The telephone rang, and a caller from the office told him Frank Kennedy had in fact been arrested—for admittedly having organized the barrage of urine-filled plastic bags.

"Sure," Gib said to Leslie when he'd put down the phone. "Not one single goddam crewcut arrested. Just Frank Kennedy. That's all. Just Frank. We're *outcasts* in this society, Les. That was *America* out there on the street, waving flags and throwing stones. Those are the God-fearing, right-thinking people who are the backbone of this country. That's where the power is. They're the people who elect the likes of Warren Bradley. They're . . ." He stopped, choked on his frustration.

Leslie pushed his Scotch and soda toward him, and he took a heavy swallow of it.

"The Russians in Paris were fools to try to kill us," he said. "They were afraid of us, afraid of what we knew and what we could do with it when we got home. They don't understand America, or they'd know you can't do anything with the truth nobody wants to hear and everybody is afraid to publish."

"Maybe when Frank gets out of jail he'll have some new guts," she suggested. "Born of indignation."

"I don't know," said Gib. "Maybe Frank's getting old. He's getting timid. He's built something, his own newspaper, and he's afraid to risk it. That's the trouble with a newspaper eventually, isn't it? It becomes a big capital asset, and you have to protect it like any other piece of property."

Gib got up and paced for a long moment. Leslie watched him, nibbling with a little more interest at her food. Her head was cocked to one side, and she looked at him with steady, upward eyes—an expression that communicated, not quite contempt, but certainly skepticism.

"All right," he said abruptly. "Are you with me if I get in big trouble?"

She nodded, without much changing her expression.

"It may be big trouble, Les. I mean big trouble, big personal trouble."

Leslie shrugged.

Gib went across the street and told the assistant editor of *The Spark* that Frank, in the conference that afternoon with Vanderhoof, had decided to publish the Vanderhoof-Hubbard articles on Nadya Kharina. The first of the series was to run on the front page in the morning. It was plausible, and in the confusion the assistant editor believed it. By the time Frank Kennedy returned and stopped the press run, more than thirty thousand copies of *The Spark* had been printed and put in circulation, with the Vanderhoof-Hubbard article on the front page.

Gib had left the office before Frank returned. He had stayed only long enough to see the first copies come in and to mail one special delivery to Benjamin Slusser in Canton, Georgia.

Gib took Leslie home to their own apartment. That was

where Frank Kennedy reached him on the telephone and fired him.

Gib took Leslie to Albany for a couple of days. They visited with his parents, and Gib cashed the last of the bonds he had inherited from his grandfather. That provided him the money he would need to take Leslie back to Europe. His parents objected violently, but that was what he and Leslie decided to do. They might stay somewhere in Europe and never come back–if Gib could find some way to make a living there.

They returned to Greenwich Village and set to work closing the apartment, packing things in boxes.

GREENWICH VILLAGE

When Frank Kennedy banged on the door, Gib was in bed asleep, and Leslie lay propped up with two crumpled pillows, reading by the dim yellow light of a small lamp on the bedstand. It was not late, not yet midnight. Though the summer heat had tempered and the power shortage had ended so they could run the air conditioner in the window, the apartment was still hot, and Gib was sprawled broadly over the bed, face down, with his bottom up. She had pushed him over several times when he first went to sleep, but now she was lying near the edge of the bed, curled awkwardly to accommodate him. When she heard the knocking on the door, she looked up from her book for a moment, looked down at Gib to see he had not awakened, and then lowered her eyes to her book once more and went on reading.

Frank Kennedy was persistent. His knocking turned to banging, and he called Gib's name. Gib woke.

Leslie swung her feet over the edge of the bed then, picked up a T-shirt from the floor and pulled it over her head, and went out into the living room. Gib watched her sleepily as she switched on a light and made her way among the cardboard cartons stacked on the living room floor. She asked at the door who was there. Frank Kennedy identified himself, and she looked around for a pair of shorts, found a pair on the couch, pulled those on, and opened the door.

"I've got to talk to you," Kennedy said. "Got to talk to Gib. What'd you do, anyway? Disconnect the phone?"

Leslie nodded. "We're moving out."

"That's what I heard."

Kennedy glanced around the room, at the packed boxes, at the telephone with its wire hanging loose, at the walls starkly bare, at the empty bookcases. He sat down on the couch. His bearded face was flushed, and he frowned and puffed out his cheeks and blew a sigh.

"Sleeping Beauty will be out in a minute, I suppose," Leslie said. "Like a beer?"

Kennedy shook his head. "Where you going?" he asked. "Where you been?"

"We're going to Europe," she said. "Back to Paris first, to see Shtemenko and Melanie. Then probably to London. We're going to see if Gib can find work in Europe, so we can live there. We've been to Albany to explain to Gib's parents —and to say good-bye."

"Forgive my asking," Kennedy said, "but do you two have enough money for this?"

She shrugged. "We have enough to go, and enough to live a few weeks, until we find something."

Kennedy nodded, frowning at her with intent curiosity. "Whose idea is this?" he asked.

"Gib's."

Gib, in the bedroom, overheard all this conversation, and so he forced himself to come awake, to sit up and yawn widely and stretch. He pulled on a pair of pants and a shirt and came to the door and stood there looking at Kennedy. He was glad to see him, but he was apprehensive, remembering the angry words shouted into the telephone the last time they talked. He stood and waited for Kennedy to speak.

Kennedy did. "I didn't come here to make peace with you," he said. "I came to tell you something."

Gib sat down, attentive but still heavy-lidded.

Kennedy glanced at Leslie and asked her, "You haven't had your television on, I suppose? Haven't seen the news?"

Leslie shrugged. "What for? To hear a few more quotations about what a vicious little bastard Gib is? No, thanks."

"Well, if you haven't had your radio or TV on tonight," Kennedy said, "then I suppose you haven't heard that Benjamin Slusser is dead."

Gib's head jerked up. "How? What happened to him?"

"No one seems to know. He died at the Atlanta airport, in one of the concourses, on his way out to a plane. It's a busy public place, and he couldn't have been alone more than a minute; but no one saw what happened. He was found lying on the floor just outside a telephone booth. Apparently it was a heart attack."

"Oh, fine," said Gib bitterly. "They can say I killed him. They can say the shock of reading the lies I published about him caused his heart attack. Fine. Just fine."

Frank Kennedy nodded, and his lips curled in a sarcastic grin. "It's already been suggested. And it's no fanciful suggestion, either. When the police searched his body for identification, they found he was carrying fifty thousand dollars in cash. They opened a case that was lying beside him and found a hundred and seventy thousand more. Besides that, he had a plane ticket for San Diego, and the ticket was not in his own name."

"What was he doing, taking off for Mexico?"

"It looks that way."

"Are you sure it was a heart attack?" Leslie asked.

"No," said Kennedy. "But it looked like one. There will be an autopsy."

Gib sighed and for a moment sat looking down at his bare feet. Then he looked up at Kennedy. "Have you been sued?" he asked.

"No. Now, of course, the man who was most likely to have sued us is dead."

"No one would have sued you," Gib said. "They couldn't afford a public trial on the questions raised in our article."

"That was my decision to make—whether we could be sued, whether we should run the article," Kennedy said firmly and grimly.

Gib shrugged.

Leslie asked a question. "Did he leave a family? Slusser, I mean."

"No, he never married," Kennedy said. "He is survived by a brother. The brother, incidentally, *demanded* the autopsy. He is quoted as saying he thinks Slusser was murdered."

"I've been here all evening," Gib said.

"The brother thinks the Communists murdered Slusser."

"That might not be such a bad guess."

Kennedy almost ignored the comment. He was looking around at the packed boxes. "What I came here for," he said, "was to suggest you don't leave yet. God knows what's going to happen now."

"Well, you haven't been sued, and I haven't been arrested," Gib said.

"I want to know something, Frank," Leslie interjected. "Are you going to publish the rest of the series of articles that Gib and Vanderhoof wrote?"

"I don't know for sure," said Kennedy. "I've thought about it. I called Corny in Washington tonight, to ask him what he thought. He doesn't know what to do, either."

"I could tell him what to do," Gib sneered.

"Maybe you could at that," Kennedy said sharply, settling on Gib a hard frown of disgust. "Maybe you could, if you'd come down off whatever it is you're on and start thinking.

What's the matter with you, Gib? Don't you wonder where Slusser got all that cash? And where he was going with it? And why he picked *today* to take off? And whether he died a natural death? Those are the questions Vanderhoof was asking, and they're the ones you should be asking."

"Sure," Gib said, holding his chin contemptuously high, with his eyes wide and bright. "Sure, he asks questions like that on the telephone, in private. Is he ready to ask them in public? In print? Now that Slusser's dead, is he ready to press the question of what Slusser was doing at the White House during the Jupiter crisis?"

Kennedy shook his head. "I don't know," he admitted. "He was busy. He was writing something. He didn't tell me what he's going to say in tomorrow's column."

"Well, how about you, Frank? Are you ready to ask the questions? In print?"

Kennedy nodded. "Sure. Damn right. What'd you suppose? I'm going to ask them, front page. Do you want to work on it with me?"

Gib pressed his fist to his mouth. "You fired me," he said quietly.

Kennedy nodded. "For damn good reasons. And I'm not hiring you back or recommending you to any other newspaper, until you learn who owns the paper and who runs it. But I'll take you on to work on this story. I'll pay you for what you do."

Gib shrugged. "It's my story," he said.

"I acknowledge that. I wouldn't make the offer otherwise."

"All right. I'll put my shoes on."

The next afternoon Gib was in *The Spark* office when the report of the Benjamin Slusser autopsy came in on the wire. A faint trace of cyanide had been found in the brain. Slusser had committed suicide—or had been murdered.

They reached Vanderhoof on the telephone. He had sent

an assistant of his to Atlanta last night, and the man had called him three times, to give him more information than was on the wire. Vanderhoof told Gib and Kennedy that the cyanide had been found only in Slusser's blood and brain, not in his mouth, throat, or stomach. No capsule had been found, or any fragments of one, either in or on the body or on the floor around where he had been found. How the cyanide had reached his brain was a mystery, but it was the cause of death.

Gib put in a call to Shtemenko in Paris, and in the middle of the evening he reached him. After a quarter of an hour's conversation, Gib sat down at the typewriter in his office and wrote a story for the Friday morning edition of *The Spark*—:

In October of 1957, in Munich, an anti-Soviet Ukrainian leader by the name of Stepan Bandera was murdered by an agent of the KGB—the Soviet Committee of State Security. Bandera's body was not marked by violence, and he seemed to have died of natural causes, a heart attack perhaps. An autopsy, however, disclosed traces of cyanide in his brain. As in the case of Benjamin Slusser, who died Wednesday evening in Atlanta, no glass splinters were found in the mouth or stomach, no traces of the capsule in which the victim might have taken the cyanide.

The man who killed Stepan Bandera defected to the West eventually, and confessed. He confessed that he had killed Bandera and another man as well, with a pistol, which fired at close range, explodes a cloud of deadly cyanide gas in the victim's face. The victim dies almost instantly, with the appearance of having succumbed to a sudden heart attack. The pistol makes little noise. The man who fires it takes an antidote and can escape quietly. It is a favorite murder weapon of the KGB.

On the same Friday morning when this story of Gib's ran in *The Spark*, fifty-five newspapers carried Cornelius Vanderhoof's Washington column, asking why Benjamin Slusser, who had been accused by Nadya Kharina of being a traitor and a Soviet agent and who now had died in most mysterious circumstances, had been a visitor to the White House during the most crucial hours of the Jupiter crisis.

On Saturday morning *The Spark* published the second of the series of articles Vanderhoof and Gib had written together. It was run with Gib's name only. The first article had told Nadya Kharina's story of how she arrived in Washington and helped Parotikin make a traitor of Benjamin Slusser. It was in the second article that the name Warren Bradley was first mentioned. Sunday papers all across the nation reported that Gilbert Hubbard and *The Spark* were accusing the President of the United States of treason.

Gib and Leslie moved out of his apartment on Saturday morning and took rooms in a hotel, registering under false names. Sunday morning they received a call from the police, who had learned their whereabouts from Frank Kennedy. With a detective they returned to the apartment. During the night it had been broken into, and everything they had left there had been ripped, smashed, smeared with paint, and thrown into piles of wreckage. Everything was ruined—the furniture, their clothes, all Gib's books, all the personal things they had packed in boxes to be moved out later—everything.

The heavy double locks on the door were intact, and when the detective saw Gib looking at them, fingering them, he said, "They were opened by a skilled professional pick man."

"Why?"

The detective shook his head. "I think it's a good thing you weren't here, fella," he said.

Sunday afternoon both Vanderhoof and Novatny called and insisted Gib must come to Washington. He would not go without Leslie, so they arranged to fly down on Monday.

WASHINGTON

Somehow they had managed, by dint of good luck mostly, to get out of New York, through LaGuardia, without being mobbed. But their luck did not hold at National Airport in Washington. They were caught at the gate by a crush of shoving, shouting people—reporters, cameramen, well-wishers, ill-wishers, and gawking, open-mouthed curious, all pushing and yelling at once. Pressed back against the wall, half blinded by bursts of blue-white flash and the hot glare of TV camera lights, Gib and Leslie cowered in confusion, blinking and shaking their heads, barely able to understand and wholly unable to answer the questions shouted at them from all sides.

Gib held a protective arm around Leslie, and he kept looking for Vanderhoof or Novatny or anyone who might have come to meet them. A woman reporter grabbed Leslie by the sleeve (Leslie was wearing the yellow linen pants suit), and Leslie furiously slapped away the hand and called her a bitch. The cameras flashed. Gib began to shout back at the reporters, trying to tell them he couldn't hear one question over another. He was wearing glasses (one of his contact lenses had begun to irritate his eye during the flight, and he had popped out the lenses and put on glasses), and the glasses were full of reflections, so he pushed them up over his head. He heard one of the reporters closest to him yell at him that he looked comfortable—a reference to his green knit golf shirt, his olive slacks, and his white sneakers—and for the first time he could smile, even grin. The cameras flashed again, but he could not grin long. They were pressing him too hard, and there was no way out.

"Did you come to Washington to accuse the President of the United States of treason?"

He heard that, and so did most of the crowd, which lowered its din to hear his answer.

Gib shook his head. "We came here to do some more work toward our goal of getting the truth before the American people."

"Is it the truth, in your opinion, that President Bradley is a traitor?"

"I don't . . ." He had to stop to let the clamor subside. "I don't attach the labels. I'll give you the facts, and you decide what that makes the President."

"Who killed Benjamin Slusser?"

"I don't know."

"Have you heard the charge that Congressman Morris made this morning: that the people who killed the Kharina woman may have killed Slusser? Do you have any comment on that?"

"None, except that it's ridiculous."

"It's being suggested that you yourself are a Communist. Do you deny it? If you deny that, how do you label yourself politically?"

"I deny it, and I don't label myself at all."

"You *are* a registered Democrat."

"That's right."

"Do you have any explanation as to why Benjamin Slusser was at the White House during the Jupiter crisis?"

"I have a firm idea, but I'm not ready to say what it is."

"Have you received a subpoena from the Senate Internal Security Subcommittee?"

"No."

"Are you two married now?"

"No."

"Will you be talking to Senator Jordan during your stay in Washington?"

"I don't know."

Gib was able to begin sliding along the wall, making a little progress toward breaking away. The just-curious bulk of the crowd was drifting off, leaving him and Leslie with the press and TV people only. He began to nod and wave, pretend he did not hear their questions, to say thank you, thank you, and to move. Gradually he led Leslie out of the crush. A few reporters followed them and kept up their questions until he had picked up their luggage and caught a cab.

At least Novatny had taken the trouble to reserve hotel rooms for them, and at the hotel they found they had privacy. No one knew they were there, except Novatny and Vanderhoof, both of whom called during the afternoon. Gib and Leslie were summoned to Novatny's apartment for dinner.

In the apartment when he and Leslie arrived, Gib found not only Vanderhoof and Novatny but also Pamela Pitt, the blonde English girl he had met there when he first visited Novatny last winter. She was the same as he remembered: sleek and poised and almost too smooth to be real.

"We're pleased you could come," Pamela Pitt said, and the suggestion in these words that she was the hostess for this dinner made Gib glance conspicuously at Novatny, so that when he looked back at her, Pamela's lips were faintly pursed in an amused, knowing little smile.

Novatny was enigmatic. His face was half hidden by bandages, and he had drunk a good deal, in Gib's judgment, and lolled in a pair of slacks and a gray sweatshirt on his couch. "You two were on television this evening," he said.

"You're a hero, Leslie, to some people at least," Vanderhoof said. He too had been drinking some, but it had only made his ruddy face a little more ruddy and his smile more fluid. "Or, *heroine*, I suppose I should say."

"I can just imagine," Gib said grimly.

"What'd I do?" Leslie asked ingenuously.

Vanderhoof laughed. "At the airport. The camera and mike caught you telling Helen Wagnall, one of this town's most prominent and most thoroughly obnoxious newshens—telling her, I quote, 'Get away from me, you bitch.' Bravo! Bravo!"

"It was beautiful," said Pamela, speaking in her soft, precise Oxonian English.

Leslie shrugged. Unconcerned, she sat down on the couch beside Novatny.

"Scotch?" asked Pamela.

Gib settled into a reclining chair facing the couch, and Novatny said to him, "If you'd watched the TV news, you'd know that Bradley has called a press conference for Tuesday night, all networks."

"What for?"

"The announcement from the White House said he would refute the charges made against him by . . . by, quote, 'one or two irresponsible or misinformed political writers.' I trust that you are the irresponsible one and Corny is the misinformed one. He's beginning to hurt. He didn't think anyone would have the guts to publish the Nadya Kharina story."

"No one did," said Gib.

"Ah," said Vanderhoof. "You'll be pleased to know that eighteen of my newspapers are going to start running our series, beginning tomorrow morning, Monday."

"Why the change of heart?"

"The death of Slusser, to start with. Plus the stories coming up from Georgia that no one can explain where Slusser got the two hundred twenty thousand dollars. Circumstances keep giving new plausibility to what Nadya Kharina told us. As a matter of fact, Bradley has fallen into our hands by calling a press conference to refute us. Papers that wouldn't have carried us before will carry us now. Otherwise their readers won't know what it is the President is denying."

"Sounds like he's getting nervous," Gib said.

"He has reason," said Vanderhoof. "Look at some of today's papers—Baltimore, Los Angeles, Milwaukee. Their White House correspondents have all sent back stories saying they too noticed Benjamin Slusser at the White House and wondered what he was doing there."

"Hindsight," said Gib.

"Good enough," said Vanderhoof. "Christy, from Baltimore, writes that he actually went to Lattimer Young and asked him what Slusser was doing in the Executive Wing late at night during the most critical hours of the Jupiter crisis. He writes that Young told him he hadn't seen Slusser and was not aware that Slusser ever visited the White House."

"We've seen editorials in half a dozen prominent newspapers," Novatny said, "all calling on the President to explain why Benjamin Slusser was there during the crisis."

"That's what he's going to explain at the press conference, I suppose," Gib said. "You can bet he'll have some slick story."

Novatny shook his head. "It won't make much diffierence what he says about Slusser. He'll have a hell of a lot more than that to explain by Tuesday night."

"He'll explain away Nadya Kharina easily enough," said Gib. "Just like he warned us."

"Not so easily any more," said Novatny. "The chickens are beginning to come home to roost."

"What chickens?"

You'll hear about some of them Tuesday afternoon," said Vanderhoof. "I've gotten you two tickets to the Senate gallery. Our friend Senator Jordan is going to deliver himself of a blast."

"Oh, he found his courage?"

"He found it," said Vanderhoof. "You helped him. And so have Steve and I."

"Well, congratulations to us all," said Gib.

"The situation has changed, Gib," said Novatny. Conquering for a moment the effects of what he'd been drinking, Novatny sharpened his voice and words, and twisting his body and pushing down on his elbows, he lifted himself erect on the couch. "The political realities have changed. When you forced the publication of that first article, you blew the whole deal open. It was a stupid, irresponsible thing to do, but it worked. That, plus the murder of Slusser, changed everything. Suddenly Bradley is not so formidable. Suddenly he's vulnerable."

"Oh," Leslie interjected softly. "Suddenly the President is so vulnerable that even a hack politician like Jordan can find the guts to attack him."

Novatny glanced at her with a surprised, then irritated, frown; and he lowered his eyes and tightened his lips and reached for his glass.

"Gib," said Vanderhoof firmly, signalling that he was taking command of the conversation. "Suppose you were a man in some government agency—NASA, let us say—that had some part in controlling Jupiter Twelve. And suppose you've been a little puzzled, a little troubled, ever since the Jupiter crisis, because you noticed some small irregularity in the control procedures, just before the Jupiter was captured. What do you think you'd do?"

Gib shrugged. "You're telling the story."

"All right. You're a space scientist. You've made a career

with NASA. You've developed skills that are in no particular demand anywhere else. A frown from someone high up in the Administration can destroy your career. The irregularity you thought you noticed was nothing very big in itself. It might not mean anything. It . . ."

"Hey," Gib interrupted. "You're not talking about a hypothetical man, and I'm not interested in hearing about a hypothetical man."

Vanderhoof nodded solemnly, and then he smiled. "All right," he conceded briskly. "The Jupiters are launched and controlled by NASA, but since their primary mission is military reconnaissance, where they go and what they photograph is ordered by the Department of Defense. There is a joint liaison committee between NASA and the Department, but it rarely meets. In everyday practice, both Jupiters—Twelve and Fourteen—have received their mission orders through the office of Assistant Secretary of Defense Fred Schellenberg. Any agency that wants Jupiter surveillance of any particular target, puts in a request to Schellenberg's office. Schellenberg's staff reviews those requests and coordinates them and prepares a tentative flying and picture-taking schedule for Jupiter each week. Schellenberg reviews those plans, goes over them with the generals, the admirals, the CIA, and whoever. Then, once a week, he sits down with a representative from NASA and tells NASA what the Jupiter is to do the following week. The NASA man tells him if what he wants is technically feasible, suggests alternatives and changes if necessary, and finally takes the orders back to NASA."

"Who *is* the NASA man?" Gib asked.

"Ah. That's the point," said Vanderhoof. "Ordinarily it's Dr. Jonas Black."

"And Black is your hypothetical career man who saw something irregular?"

Vanderhoof nodded. "Because Jupiter can photograph a

target from various angles and altitudes, Black is always told, not only *what* is to be photographed but *why* it's to be photographed—that is, what the pictures are to be used for."

"This Dr. Black," Gib suggested, "must be privy to more classified information than most anybody else in the government."

Vanderhoof shrugged. "I suppose so. During these conversations about the Jupiter targets, Dr. Black is usually told who has ordered the photographs. A great variety of departments ask for them, but most of the requests come from the generals and admirals or from the CIA. *But not the request to photograph the alleged Chinese missile silos in Manchuria.* That came directly from the White House. It was the only request that ever came from that source, so far as Black knows. In other words, the President himself sent Jupiter Twelve on its fatal orbit."

"Not necessarily," Gib said. "A tip on the silos could have come through diplomatic channels, and the White House could have sent it directly to Schellenberg's office, without going through any other agency."

"Never did before," said Novatny. "Never has since."

"Dr. Black," said Vanderhoof, "thought it was strange at the time. When it was the orbit ordered by the President himself which resulted in the capture of Jupiter Twelve, he thought it was more than strange. But there could have been lots of explanations for it. And, for him to suggest out loud that it was strange would have amounted to some kind of accusation by him against the President. Besides, so far as he could see, the Jupiter crisis came out all right in the end, from the point of view of the United States anyway. So he just kept his mouth shut."

"Until now," said Gib.

"Until now. Now he reads in the papers about Nadya Kharina and about Benjamin Slusser and about how Slusser was at the White House during the Jupiter crisis. He reads and hears that the President's conduct in the Jupiter crisis has become suspect, a subject of controversy. Now he's ready to tell someone what he knows."

"Lucky to find him," Gib said.

"No luck at all," said Vanderhoof, shaking his head. "I've known for months that Dr. Black was the NASA liaison man to Schellenberg's office, and I also figured that being a non-political sort of fellow he was the one most likely to tell us something if there was anything to tell. I've talked with him several times—took him to lunch. When the fury broke this week, I called him again, and he told me the story."

"Which you then told Jordan."

"Which I then told Jordan."

Gib nodded thoughtfully. "So what's Jordan going to do?"

Novatny answered. "In his speech on the Senate floor, he's going to call the Jupiter crisis a great unresolved mystery. He'll review the Nadya Kharina accusations. He'll talk about the Slusser murder and ask why Slusser was at the White House during the crisis. He'll tell—without naming Dr. Black—that the fatal orbit over Manchuria was ordered directly from the White House. And then he's going to review the recent history of U.S.–China relations and the abrupt termination of the talks that were going on at Honolulu. Finally, he'll demand a full Senate investigation of it all."

WASHINGTON

"Mr. President."

Senator Alan Jordan had risen, and he addressed the Vice President of the United States, who presided over the Senate from the marble-framed dais. Senator Jordan was tall and tanned and handsome, and he was conspicuously confident in the drama of the moment and in his personal flair for his role. He stood with his shoulders high, glancing sharply and yet amiably around the chamber and up at the galleries.

Vice President James Hennessy looked down on him with unconcealed reluctance to recognize him. He too glanced around the chamber, nervously. Eighty-one senators were on the floor. Most of them lounged in their seats, pallid and lumpy and sleepy and inattentive. Few of them turned their heads to look at Senator Jordan when he rose and asked for recognition. But eighty-one of them were there, and the galleries were filled.

Vice President Hennessy was a young, red-headed, pink-faced, vigorously partisan Irishman, the former mayor of Los Angeles. He had been Vice President only eight months, and he had not learned to enjoy presiding over the Senate or to keep his equanimity while doing it. His frown pinched his brows as he nodded and said grudgingly, "The Senior Senator from Connecticut, Senator Jordan."

"I rise, *Mr. President,*" said Senator Jordan with a faint, genuinely amused smile, a curt nod at the dais, and a careful measure of scorn in the thinness of his voice, "to discuss before the Senate a matter of significance to the history of this decade, indeed Mr. President, perhaps to the history of the Republic. I rise to propound certain questions, here, before the Senate and before the nation. If the answers to those questions are what the evidence I have at hand suggests the answers are, then, Mr. President, this nation faces a governmental crisis, a crisis of a nature which has occurred only once before in the history of the Republic, if indeed it ever has occurred before."

Senator Jordan stopped. He looked around. It was a pause for emphasis, and it won the attention of two or three more senators. "I am reluctant, Mr. President," he said in a rising voice, with a single chopping gesture of his hand. "I am reluctant to be the one who rises to report to the Senate the information I have to report today. I am reluctant to be the one who propounds the questions I will propound. I should have preferred that one of my colleagues on the other side of the aisle should have been the one to rise for these purposes, so that any implication of partisanship might have been avoided."

He paused again. "But it is not so," he said with a deep nod. "The information has come to *my* hands, and I would be derelict in my duty if I did not report it to the Senate and ask the questions it implies."

The Vice President toyed with the gavel and kept his eyes fixed on Senator Arthur Hadley, the Minority Leader, as if he appealed to the old and experienced Senate war-horse to stop this thing before Jordan went on and did it. Old Senator Hadley, heavy-lidded and gently nodding, might have been asleep, for all the attention he appeared to be giving either Senator Jordan *or* the Vice President.

Senator Jordan bore down on his words. "The issue which I am duty-bound to bring before the Senate and before the nation, Mr. President, is no less an issue, *no less an issue,* than *the integrity and the loyalty of the President of the United States.*"

The Senate stirred and stiffened. Senators looked up. Some filled visibly with breath. Some shifted in their chairs, or frowned, and three or four shook their heads. That they had known in advance what Jordan was going to say had not robbed it of its impact. The impact was a shock. And Senator Jordan paused, with his breath stopped, flushed slightly, him-self conscious of what he had done, himself struck by the same impact.

In the gallery, Gib sat with Leslie at his one side, Novatny at the other, and—probably unconsciously—Leslie squeezed his arm. Gib was intensely nervous, apprehensive, unhappy with Jordan's florid senatorial style of oratory, filled with dread that he was about to witness an historical debacle. But gradually his judgment of Senator Jordan was changing, and he gained a measure of confidence—just enough to let him loosen a little and let down his shoulders. He decided that whatever you might call Alan Jordan, political hack or whatever else, and however little Jordan had contributed to the work up till now, this was his hour, when he was doing what he could do better than anyone else, at a point in the battle where his unique talent was the best you could have on your side.

"The questions to be raised this afternoon, Mr. President, have their origins in events almost forgotten. The evidence, some of it, relates to things that happened twenty-five years ago. Other parts of it relate to things that happened this year, this month in fact, and actually to things that are happening right now."

At this point the Senator consciously lowered the pitch of the drama. He began to talk about the history of the Erich Traver case, and he took the time to discuss it in some detail. He raised the names of Major Alekseii Parotikin, Nadya Kharina, and Benjamin Slusser. He had not yet mentioned the name of Warren Bradley, but the course of the narrative clearly suggested he was about to mention it, when he was for the first time interrupted.

"Mr. President, will the Senator yield for a question?"

Senator Arthur Hadley, the old Republican from Indiana—they said he'd been in Congress since the Administration of William McKinley—had spoken. He was shrunken and spare and slouched in a chair that seemed too big for him. His pink little old face was benign, even cherubic, and his few wisps of white hair were combed very carefully across a pink, liver-spotted bald head. Sitting on the aisle with his legs crossed, he thrust his feet out into the aisle, and his highly-polished, pointed black shoes were conspicuous to the galleries.

Vice President Hennessy said Senator Jordan would yield, before Senator Jordan gave any indication he would, and

Senator Hadley turned around to receive Senator Jordan's nod before he asked his question. But having turned that once, he asked it facing the dais, with his back to Senator Jordan.

"Mr. President," said Senator Hadley in a voice that was thin with age but firm and distinct and expressive. "My friend the Senior Senator from Connecticut seems to be discussing matters that have been of rumor, most of them, around here for a very long time. These matters have been exhaustively considered in the courts, in lengthy trials, as well as having been the subject of investigations by committees of the Congress, where the evidence was carefully considered many years ago. Now, the Senator has mentioned the names of several people who supposedly could tell us something new about these ancient matters. But I am curious, Mr. President. This Russian major with the unpronounceable name, who was supposed to be the master spy, he is *dead.* Then that Russian woman, also supposed to be a spy, she is dead too. And Mr. Benjamin Slusser, who might be able to shed some light on these matters, well, he also is dead. So, Mr. President, my question is this: Does the Senator have any evidence of these charges he is making, in view of the fact that his witnesses all seem to be deceased people? Or does he base what he is telling us and expect us to judge the President of the United States on the basis of old rumors, plus some new ones which have been circulating of late?"

Senator Jordan leaned on his desk, smiling, and waited for Senator Hadley to finish. "Mr. President," he said when Senator Hadley did finish and turned and looked up at him. "I am pleased that my good friend and distinguished colleague, the senior senator from Indiana, has asked this appropriate and very fair question. Certainly there is new evidence. It is my intention to call for a full senatorial investigation of everything I say here today, and during that investigation there will be evidence to support every statement I make this afternoon."

Senator Hadley raised his eyebrows, pursed his lips, and nodded.

"I hold in my hand at this moment, Mr. President," said Senator Jordan, "a piece of new evidence of some of the facts I have just been discussing. It is a letter, and I will read it to the Senate."

He held a small, pale blue envelope above his head for a moment. Then he lowered it, opened it, and took out the letter.

"I received this letter only a few days ago," he said, taking out of his coat pocket a pair of reading glasses. He adjusted the glasses on his nose and then glanced over the several typewritten blue sheets. "Very frankly, Mr. President, I spoke on the telephone to the man who wrote this letter, and I asked him for it. I asked him for a letter, and he wrote it. It is a rather important letter, I think.

" 'Dear Senator Jordan,' it reads.

" 'I am sure you will understand my hesitance about communicating with you, or with anyone in any official capacity in Washington, on the subject you and I discussed on the telephone yesterday evening. I feel certain this letter, which you have asked me to write, will have most painful consequences for me. I am impelled, however, by a thirst for justice; and in all honesty I suppose I must acknowledge that I feel a sense of inevitability in the whole situation—a sense that all the things I dread are going to happen anyway, no matter what I do—and that therefore I may as well do what is truthful and right.

" 'To communicate the truth to you, as you have asked, requires of me nothing less than a confession of a guilt I have spent one-third of a lifetime denying. My wife assures me that I will be relieved of a burden by so confessing and will be enabled to live out more happily for having done so, the few remaining years allotted to me. I am skeptical that this is so, but I am acceding to her judgment and your importunity.

"'I know Mr. Gilbert Hubbard. I have had several intimate interviews with him. I have read the newspaper articles written by him and Mr. Cornelius Vanderhoof, which you say are currently being published in the United States. Copies of these articles, in typescript form, were provided by Mr. Hubbard to my daughter, Mrs. Alexandr Shtemenko, and she in turn forwarded copies to me. In those articles there is contained much information which has never come to my attention before. I am able to tell you, however, that everything reported in the Hubbard-Vanderhoof articles which is within my personal knowledge, is accurately reported.

"'From 1937 until 1953, when I went to prison for perjury, I was an active member of the Communist Party of the United States. I personally knew Major Alekseii Parotikin as a Soviet agent sent from Moscow to direct Soviet espionage activities in Washington. He personally identified himself to me as such, on more than one occasion and in the presence of other persons who can testify to this fact. Major Parotikin brought to Washington a young Russian girl named Nadya Kharina, to work under his command. She lived in Washington under the name Mary Anne Waring and was identified to Party members there as an American-born Communist. She stayed in my home during a serious illness, however, and during the weakness of that illness she identified herself to me and my wife as a Russian and told us her true name.

"'I have no personal knowledge of the relationship between these two Russian agents and Mr. Benjamin Slusser or Congressman (as he then was) Warren Bradley. Insofar, however, as the Hubbard-Vanderhoof writings relate to the matters I have mentioned above, I can testify that they are accurate, within my personal knowledge.

" 'I will, upon request and without subpoena, and upon the advancement of necessary expenses, return to the United States to testify to matters within my knowledge. The issues now raised substantially transcend the personal loss I shall undoubtedly suffer from returning and being a witness. I trust, however, that the United States will do me the justice of granting me immunity from further prosecution, and I should appreciate your advising me specifically on that point.

" 'I should add that I do have a few items of documentary evidence, including a photograph of Nadya Kharina and including also specimens of her handwriting and that of Major Parotikin, which I can transmit or bring to the United States.

" 'Very sincerely and respectfully yours,

" 'Erich Traver.' "

In the midst of a silence and under the stares of most of the senators on the floor, Senator Jordan laid the letter on his desk and removed his reading glasses.

He picked up where he had stopped when Senator Hadley had interrupted him. Referring to notes and speaking quietly, he related the motives which had caused Parotikin to conspire in the prosecution of Erich Traver. He called Benjamin Slusser a traitor. He went on to tell how Slusser, Kharina, and Parotikin had recruited witnesses out of Traver's Party cell and how, gradually, they had involved Congressman Warren Bradley in their scheme.

Gib, sitting between Leslie and Novatny, felt exposed in the Senate gallery—exposed and self-conscious. Before the session opened, when the senators were coming into the chamber, Senator Jordan had pointed Gib out to a few senators. Others, who had seemed to know he would be there, had identified him for themselves—some of them with manifest suspicion or scorn or even hostility. Just now, when the Traver letter repeatedly mentioned his name, some of them looked up at him, and the galleries had identified him too. He was not sure he had any friends anywhere in the chamber. And it troubled him, as he sat there listening to Jordan talk of a full congressional investigation, that he would be a witness, subject to long and hostile cross-examination by men who would loathe him.

Senator Jordan began to talk about the kidnapping and confession of Nadya Kharina. "It is true, Mr. President, as my friend the senior senator from Indiana has mentioned, that Nadya Kharina is dead. We have, however, three reliable witnesses to what she said that day in East Berlin." He pointed to the press gallery. "Cornelius Vanderhoof, a journalist with an old and distinguished reputation in this city, a reputation for scrupulous accuracy and fairness, was present and heard her confession." He pointed to the gallery. "Gilbert Hubbard, a young man who is winning himself a nationwide reputation as a courageous reporter, was present. And finally, my own aide, my counsel, Steve Novatny was there."

The Senator went on, but many eyes remained fixed on the gallery. Novatny's face was still bandaged. He was conspicuous. Gib was glad he had bought himself a suit—and bought Leslie a dress. The suit, of necessity picked up quickly, with time for no tailoring but to make the pants the right length, looked drab, in Gib's estimation—brown and dull and determinedly modest—and he was glad that was the way he looked.

The Senator was scrupulous about what he called his report to the Senate. He was indicting the President of the United States, and he was careful to put in the record every fact he had.

He talked about the murder of Benjamin Slusser. The identity of the killer remained a complete mystery. Senator Jordan was more interested—as in fact the newspapers had been for the past several days—in the mystery of the two hundred twenty thousand dollars in cash Slusser was carrying when he died. Georgia investigators could find no hint of the source of the money. An examination of Slusser's business and personal records showed nothing of this money. In fact, departing suddenly with that cash on his person, Slusser had left his bank accounts intact. He had made no recent significant withdrawals—from accounts which, in any case, had never totalled the tenth part of two hundred twenty thousand dollars. He had sold no property. Some seventy thousand dollars' worth of stock certificates remained in his office safe.

"A number of witnesses, Mr. President, have reported and are ready to testify that this man Slusser was a frequent visitor to the White House over the years. He had private, personal conferences with President Bradley. And yet, his name has never appeared on the presidential appointments schedule. If I go to the White House to confer with the President, my name is on the list, and anyone can know I met with the President. Benjamin Slusser conferred with the President often, and his name was never on the list. President Bradley cannot explain, probably, why his friend was murdered while apparently fleeing the country with a large amount of unexplained cash, but maybe he can explain why Slusser visited him so often and why the visits were secret."

Senator Jordan stopped, ostensibly to look closely at a note he had picked up from his desk, but actually, to everyone's certain knowledge, as a piece of drama to introduce something for which he wanted particular attention.

"Three witnesses, Mr. President—three White House correspondents—saw Benjamin Slusser in the Executive Wing of the White House on the evening of last January third. I would remind the Senate that at that hour the crisis subcommittee of the National Security Council was in emergency session in the Executive Wing. It was one of the most critical, one of the most crucial, hours of the Jupiter crisis. I call upon President Bradley, most respectfully but most urgently, to tell the Congress and the nation what Benjamin Slusser was doing there at that hour."

Senator Jordan, flushed and risen to the full height of challenge, cast a sharp, even baneful, look around the senate chamber.

"This man Slusser," he went on, "has been accused of treason, on reliable evidence. He has been mysteriously murdered. When he was murdered, he was apparently trying to flee the country, carrying with him a very large amount of cash, for which there is no explanation. He has often been a clandestine visitor to the White House. *And,* President Bradley apparently took the time to see him during the worst hours of the Jupiter crisis. *I think the Congress and the nation are entitled to an explanation!*"

Lowering the pitch of the drama once more, following his own finely tuned sense, Senator Jordan opened his discussion of the Jupiter crisis. He knew he had the attention of the Senate and could hold it now for as long as he wanted. Not a senator of the eighty-one had left the floor. To the contrary, three more had quietly slipped in and taken their seats.

He reviewed the events of the Jupiter crisis, emphasizing the way it had suddenly burst on the world, illogically and without reason, and then had just as suddenly faded away, again illogically and without resolving any question that seemed to have been raised. He reminded the Senate then, that in the history of Soviet foreign policy it was often necessary to look behind and beyond the noisy clamor of threats and confrontations. Soviet Russia, he said, had often precipitated apparent crises, only to divert the attention of the world from something the Kremlin wanted to do quietly on the side, while all the world's governments were braced to meet the crisis and could think of nothing else.

He suggested to the Senate that the Jupiter crisis in actual fact had nothing to do with the right to fly reconnaissance satellites in orbit around the earth. The capture of Jupiter Twelve and the threat to destroy any similar satellite put in space by the United States—which threat was never carried out—was only a cover, he suggested, to divert the attention of the American people, and perhaps the attention of world governments, from something else.

"From what?" he asked. Now, Senator Jordan no longer spoke in the florid style of Senate oratory. He had ceased to speak to the chair. He was talking to the Senate. "I will suggest that the Jupiter crisis," he said in precise words but in a voice so soft that senators had to look at him and listen to understand, "distracted our attention, all too effectively, from a major triumph of Soviet foreign policy. And I must suggest also—sorrowfully and with reluctance—that it seems, upon the evidence, to have been a triumph engineered with the connivance of the President of the United States. It . . ."

"*This is outrageous!* Mr. President, I rise to a point of order!" It was the Republican Senator from Texas who had risen—Senator Holt, a large, muscular, though bespectacled and white-haired, man serving his second term. "We have sat here and listened, Mr. President, to this recital of long-refuted radical accusations against President Bradley, this long-winded, pious repetition of old charges that Communists and their like have long thrown around, and apparently we are now going to hear the Senator say that President Bradley . . ."

Vice President Hennessy, after a hesitation punctuated only by his receiving a fierce glare from Senator Hadley, began to bang the gavel. He banged it three times, stopped Senator Holt, and said, "State your point of order, Senator."

Senator Holt stood swollen for a moment, confused by his rage. "It is outrageous, it is entirely out of order," he said, his voice falling a bit, "for the Senator from Connecticut to stand here and use the Senate floor, to use the shield of senatorial immunity, to make political charges against a man who is not here to defend himself. This is no proper use of the privileges of the United States Senate."

Vice President Hennessy shook his head. "The point of order is . . . is not well taken," he said nervously.

"I appeal from that, Mr. President!" cried Senator Holt in sudden new anger.

"*Mr. President.*" This voice, small and yet icy and heavy, was that of Senator Hadley. "Will the Senator from Connecticut yield for a moment?"

Senator Jordan had stood while Senator Holt interrupted, ignoring the interruption, ostentatiously studying his notes with the attitude of a man patiently waiting for a nuisance to go away. He looked up now, at Senator Hadley, and betrayed some surprise. He nodded. "I yield," he said.

"Mr. President," said Senator Hadley. He stood behind his desk, leaned on it with both hands flat on the top, and spoke over his shoulder to Senator Holt. "I too am pained to hear the accusations being made by the Senator from Connecticut. I am skeptical—I might say, skeptical in the extreme—that the facts, the evidence of facts, will bear out these accusations. But there can be no question whatever, Mr. President, of the right of the Senator from Connecticut to say what he is saying on the floor of the Senate. He is entirely within his rights. Freedom to say whatever one's sense of duty commands one to say is our most cherished tradition here."

Senater Hadley turned his head and looked over his other

shoulder, at Senator Jordan. "The Senator from Connecticut is putting a great deal at risk this afternoon," he said with a severe frown. "He will be called on to prove that what he is saying is true. If he can't prove it, the Senate will know how to deal with him. If he can, we will deal with the consequences of that as well."

For a long moment there was silence, as Vice President Hennessy pondered what he should do. Finally he nodded at Senator Jordan and said, "The Senator from Connecticut, Senator Jordan."

"I have some additional factual information to report to the Senate," said Senator Jordan quietly. "When I have presented that information, I will suggest to the Senate what all the facts imply. All the facts can be proved. There is evidence for all of them. When I finish telling the facts and begin talking of the implications to be drawn from them . . . well . . . others may draw conclusions different from those I draw. I will invite the Senate to draw its own conclusions. I will call on President Bradley to offer his own explanations."

He began to tell how the Jupiter satellites were controlled, by NASA on orders from the Department of Defense. He did not mention the name of Dr. Jonas Black, but he told how the fatal mission, when Jupiter Twelve was captured, was specially ordered, directly from the White House. He emphasized that never before and never since had the White House ordered a Jupiter mission, directly and without the intervention of some other department. He emphasized that the command coordinating procedures which sent the Jupiter to its capture were distinctly at variance from the procedures normally followed.

Then he turned to the foreign policy results of the Jupiter crisis. "Years of careful and patient diplomatic effort, devoted to drawing Communist China gradually into the community of responsible and law-abiding nations, were suddenly scuttled by the United States. Suddenly our hand of friendship, which we had cautiously, almost timidly, extended, was abruptly pulled back. Japan was frightened and dropped its trade negotiations. Other Pacific nations followed the United States and Japan. China, humiliated and confused, withdrew once more into arrogant, egomaniacal isolation. Suddenly China was once more shut off from the majority of the nations of the world, excluded from world councils, shut out of trade, blackballed and damned. *And this represented a triumph for Soviet foreign policy, for Soviet ambitions.*

"*Because* . . ."—and here the Senator stopped to glance around the chamber—". . . Soviet Russia has learned to regard Red China, instead of the United States, as its greatest rival, the greatest threat to its ambition, Lenin's ambition, to dominate a Communist world from the Kremlin. We here in the United States congratulated ourselves on our apparent victory in the Jupiter confrontation. But it was Russia which was the victor. The Soviet leaders contrived the Jupiter crisis to gain for themselves a signal victory in their bitter rivalry with Red China, and we fell for their contrivance and helped them do it.

"*We helped them do it. And I am compelled to charge, Mr. President and members of the Senate, that it could not have been done without the connivance of the President of the United States, who betrayed the interests of the United States and cooperated with the Kremlin to* . . ."

WASHINGTON

Two days later—on Thursday evening—Warren Bradley resigned as President of the United States.

The presidential press conference which had been scheduled for Tuesday evening was cancelled two hours before it was to go on the air. The announcement said that Senator Jordan, in his speech to the Senate that afternoon, had raised so many new charges that the President needed additional time to prepare for his press conference.

Wednesday and Thursday the President kept out of sight in the White House, receiving members of his Administration and members of Congress, but issuing no statements. The limousines drove in and out of the closed White House grounds, bearing grim men to and from their conferences with Bradley, in an atmosphere of crisis almost as deep as the one in January. As always, television cameras watched these comings and goings, interrupting programming to show nothing more than the arrival or departure of another black Cadillac, and the network news personalities stood before their own cameras, with the facade of the White House as background for their talk, and speculated on what was going on.

Wednesday and Thursday were also bitter days, days of furious denunciation, directed mostly at Senator Jordan and his friends. In the House of Representatives, twenty-eight members—nineteen Democrats and nine Republicans—announced they were sponsoring a resolution to impeach Warren Bradley, saying that the only fair and proper way to resolve the serious charges against the President was by a formal impeachment and trial. But at the same time, eight senators not only announced but introduced a resolution to expel Alan Jordan from the Senate.

Most editorials were unfriendly to Jordan, Vanderhoof, and Gilbert Hubbard, calling them irresponsible, egotistical, vicious, vindictive—and characterizing the charges they had made against the President as compounded mostly of rumor, which could not be substantiated. At the same time the newspapers, even the most skeptical of them, called on President Bradley to answer the questions raised. Some of the editorials expressed confidence that he could and would answer the charges, and refute them, but they did say, uniformly, that he would have to do it. They called for specific answers to Senator Jordan's specific charges.

The crewcuts marched once again in Greenwich Village. They came to storm *The Spark* offices, but this time they were turned back by the police.

One editorial writer, later, said the mood of the nation at large those two days was one of disgust and resentment—principally that such a wild political furor should have been loosed in the vacation season, when people did not want to have to worry about such things. The nation's attention was not quite focused on Washington, in spite of tensions raised for politically conscious people, and when on Thursday evening the President suddenly resigned, it came as a heavy shock. The nation, figuratively, blinked its eyes, let its mouth fall open, and shook its head in amazement.

Gib and Leslie were in Novatny's apartment when the announcement was made. They had taken refuge there. The hotel where they had been staying had asked them to leave—out of fear of damage to the premises, since it had become known where they were.

The apartment was littered with dozens of newspapers, which Novatny had ordered and seemed to have read to the very last one. He was drinking but little. They had eaten dinner and had left the television set on, with the sound turned off, to see if any bulletins came on. That the President would appear was announced only half an hour before he did.

Gib was discouraged and full of pessimism. He did not like the names he had been called. Novatny told him he was oversensitive—if you can't stand the heat, etc.—and told him he couldn't play Jack the Giant Killer and expect the Giant not to defend himself. But Gib brooded anyway, and in a moment apart with Leslie said to her they might have been happier if he'd had the good sense to keep a little more quiet and a little more modest. And he returned to the theme that he feared he'd been used as a tool by Senator Jordan. Her response was that, having watched the Senate in session, she couldn't see it would make much difference, wouldn't be much improvement, if Alan Jordan or anyone else were President in place of Bradley. She shrugged contemptuously and said they all looked about equally bad to her.

President Bradley appeared on all networks at nine o'clock. He did not look harried or hurt. He spoke with perfect command of himself.

"I do not for a moment acknowledge any truth whatever in the charges made against me by Senator Alan Jordan or by those members of the House of Representatives who propose to sponsor a resolution of impeachment," he said with the same cold eyes and firm, intense frown that had always characterized his presidential statements.

"The accusations which have been made, though they are false, are very serious indeed. They are apparently supported by a very large quantity of what Senator Jordan and those who work for him characterize as evidence. To refute these charges will require the sifting of all this purported evidence and a detailed review of many events, occurring over a long period of time. It will have to be done in a time-consuming, meticulous way, and by a formal process of investigation, perhaps even by the impeachment proceedings which some members of Congress believe to be the only fair way to hold a trial on these charges.

"In short, my fellow Americans, it appears that for a long time to come I am going to be on trial, before some body which will investigate these charges of course, but in a larger sense before you, the American people. To defend myself, I will find it necessary to devote much of my time and attention to this long trial. We live in difficult times, demanding of the President of the United States every ounce of his energy and concentration. Faced with the necessity of defending my loyalty, my integrity, and my conduct of the public offices which have been entrusted to me, I feel I cannot effectively continue to serve as your President. I cannot divide myself between my duty to this office and the burden and trial which has now been imposed upon me.

"Accordingly, I have this evening communicated to the Congress my resignation as President of the United States.

"I now turn my full attention to the vindication of all I have done in your service. As God is my strength and my witness, I will be vindicated."

The camera continued to stare at him for a long time after he finished speaking. Bradley sat there, waiting for the camera to be turned off, his frown deepening. Suddenly he pushed back his chair, stood up, and walked off.

Gib and Novatny were as amazed as anyone else. They stared at the television tube in silence, until, after a very long moment, they turned away from it almost simultaneously and looked at each other.

Novatny came to Gib and took his hand and shook it. "I really don't know," he said hesitantly, "if we should congratulate each other."

"I don't know why you should," Leslie said sharply. "You've just got yourself James Hennessy as your new President."

Gib was still stunned and almost without thought, but as his mind began to work again, he frowned and began to shake his head at the idea of President James Hennessy.